Heal the Hood

To Uncle Richard
& Aunty Ngozi
With Best Wishes

Odaeze Nwosu

Heal The HOOD

Adaeze Nkechi Nwosu

origami

Parrésia Publishers Ltd.
82, Allen Avenue, Ikeja, Lagos, Nigeria.
+2348154582178, +2348062392145
origami@parresia.com.ng
www.origami.com.ng

Copyright © 2020 Adaeze Nwosu

The right of Adaeze Nwosu to be identified as the author of this work has been asserted by her in accordance with the copyright law of the Federal Republic of Nigeria.

All rights reserved. Other than brief excerpts for reviews and commentaries, no part of this publication may be reproduced, stored in a retrieval system or transmitted in any form or by any means, electronic, mechanical, photocopying, recording or otherwise, without the prior permission of the publisher.

ISBN: 978-978-97857-2-8

Printed in Nigeria by Parrésia Press

This novel is dedicated to my parents, Chioma and Zubbi Nwosu and my sister Ikunna Nwosu.

This novel is also dedicated to my favorite urban fiction writers:
Coe Booth
Travis Hunter
Jason Reynolds
Sister Souljah
Angie Thomas
Renée Watson

This novel is also dedicated to John Green and Nicola Yoon, two YA writers who have shown that love can be found in the most unlikely places and in the most unlikely people.

Lastly, this novel is dedicated to every victim of police brutality and racist attacks.

Chapter One

"Hatima! Hurry up, baby girl, or we'll be late for church!"

I replied, "I'm coming, I just need to zipper up my dress!"

For the record, I hate wearing dresses. The only time I wear them is when I go to church and formal occasions, like weddings. Once I asked Mama why I can't wear a suit like Daddy does and some other women do.

Mama stated, "I'm raising a young lady, not a young man. When you go to church, you'll wear a dress. You can wear pants, shirts, sneakers, and caps at non-formal occasions."

I left the house wearing a purple dress and white shoes. Mama wore an African tie-dyed dress with a matching headdress; Daddy wore a black suit, with a white shirt, a red tie, and black loafers; and Grandma wore an old-fashioned muumuu. She was born and raised in Mississippi; but Mama, Daddy, and I were all born and raised here in Los Angeles.

I entered our Ford – Daddy's pride and joy. Daddy bought the used 1980 Ford Fairmont from a salesman who was planning to take it to the junkyard. He claimed his friends at Oscar's Garage could fix the car and make it brand-new, and he was able to negotiate the salesman down from his original price because he's great at haggling and bargaining. I think the main reason the salesman sold the car to Daddy at a low price was because he believed no one could fix the car and he wanted to get rid of it since no one else wanted it. Daddy had the car towed to Oscar's Garage. He bought some new parts, and Mr. Oscar Brown and the other mechanics were able to get the car running again.

When people see Daddy's new car, they usually say stuff like, "Whoa, Mister Parker! You selling the rock now?"

And Daddy would reply, "No, I'm still lugging heavy suitcases at the airport, and my wife is still serving those rich folks at the Beverly Hills Hotel. But we only have one child to feed and clothe, and we save any cash we can."

Daddy is six feet tall, he wears his dreadlocks in a ponytail, and he's muscular. His arms are the size of baseball bats because of all the luggage he carries and the weights he lifts at home. Mama is five foot eight, slim, and has a beautiful face and a beautiful smile. I am an inch shorter than Mama, which makes Grandma the shortest member of our family. She's a bit chunky and only five foot five, but she can make herself seem taller when she's lecturing someone or beating someone. She's almost sixty, and she has some gray hairs. She keeps her hair in a bun for church and work. I sport braids that I usually hang loose. This Sunday I decided to put some colorful beads on my braids. I have rich brown skin, high cheekbones, medium-sized breasts, and a squeezable butt. I'm a beautiful girl, but I don't try to show that off a lot. When I have a boyfriend, I want one who will like me for my brain and personality, not my external beauty.

Our Crenshaw house is white with a gray-tiled roof and a blue door. It's only one-story like the other houses on West Boulevard. There are bigger houses in South Central Los Angeles, but the people who live in those houses make more money than Mama and Daddy. Our house doesn't look like the LA houses people see in brochures, magazines, television, and movies. We neither have huge houses on West Boulevard nor pools in our backyards. Our lawns and backyards are small, but the grass is usually cut, and some folks grow flowers in their front and backyards. Celebrities aren't our neighbors, and I'm sure they would consider themselves fools if they ever ventured to Crenshaw or certain other places in South Central – their bougie butts might not get out alive.

The drive from our Crenshaw house at 3767 West Boulevard to First African Methodist Episcopal Church is only about ten minutes. FAME Church is the oldest Black church in the City of Angels. I'm obsessed with history, especially Black history. So, whenever anyone has a fascinating story to tell about Black history, I'm all ears. I do most of my research at my high school's library and the Baldwin Hills Branch Library. Since Dorsey High doesn't have all the books I need, the public library is the next best place to go.

The African Methodist Episcopal Church is the oldest Black Christian denomination in the USA and the world. Bishop Richard Allen founded Mother Bethel, a Black Methodist Church, in 1794 in Philadelphia. Twenty-two years later, in 1816, all the Black Methodist churches decided to form a new congregation: the African Methodist Episcopal Church. Richard Allen was its first bishop and Mother Bethel is considered the first AME church.

Now, almost two hundred years later, there are hundreds of AME churches in the USA and other countries. FAME was built way back in 1872 by Bridget "Biddy" Mason. Biddy Mason arrived in California with her master, Robert Marion Smith, in 1851, and five years later, Biddy Mason and her master arrived in Los Angeles. Biddy Mason sued in court with help from White and Black abolitionists in order to win her freedom, and she won. She organized the first FAME meeting in her home and the first permanent church building was established in 1903 on Eighth and Tome. By the 1960s, the area around the church was industrialized and commercialized, and in 1969 the church was moved to its current location at 2270 South Harvard Boulevard.

Dr. Cecil L. Murray, who is popularly called Chip by his friends, is our head pastor. Even though FAME was founded by a Black woman, the number of Black female clergy is incredibly low. But I'm not dissing Dr. Murray; he's a great pastor who has brought a lot of positive change to South Central LA through his community programs.

Whenever we go to church, Grandma sits in the second pew on the right side. She claims that she can see and hear Dr. Murray properly in that spot, but I figure that Grandma thinks the closer a person is to God, the more blessings they'll receive. I want to become an Africanist, not a preacher, but I'm pretty sure God's powers don't work like that.

When we got to church, Daddy parked the car, and we all got out and headed to the sanctuary. Grandma is more than happy to stop and gossip with the church sisters, but Mama and Daddy dislike gossip so we headed to our spot. We sat in our usual place and waited for the service to start.

A lot of Black celebrities also come to FAME, like Arsenio Hall. I've managed to get autographs from some of them over the years, but it is *very* hard to get their attention when *everyone* is mobbing them.

Dr. Murray climbed onto his pulpit. He always looks impressive with his church robes. His strong voice said, "Peace be with you."

The entire congregation replied, "And also with you."

"Unfortunately, I have to start off our service with some bad news. Hours ago, shortly after midnight, the California Highway

Patrol team attempted to pull over a Black man named Rodney King because he was speeding. Mister King led the California Highway Patrol team and the LA police on a long car chase. When Mister King was pulled over, the cops decided to deal with him in a brutal manner. They kicked him and beat him with their batons before they handcuffed him. Mister King was taken to Pacifica Hospital, but thank God that there was a Good Samaritan awake at that early hour in the morning. He does not want his identity revealed to the public yet, but he videotaped the entire attack. Thank God for modern technology. He asked for my help in getting the tape to the media. He knows how effective we preachers are in spreading word about our communities and getting help. I told him we should take the videotape to KTLA, the LA station on which many of us watch the local news. Perhaps, this videotape will show the world what Black people have been suffering at the hands of law enforcement officials since the era of slavery. Let us pray for Mister King and the Good Samaritan."

We all bowed our heads and listened to Dr. Murray's prayer. When I think of police brutality, several names pop up; but one name that really sticks is Bobby Hutton. My parents and grandmother admire several Black activists and other famous Black people like the Black Panther Party. The Black Panther Party created a Ten-Point Platform that is structured similarly to the US Bill of Rights and is seen as the Black Bill of Rights.

In my book about the history of the BPP, I bookmarked the chapter that has the Ten-Point Platform. Point number seven of "What We Want Now" states, "We want an end to police brutality and the murder of Black people." "What We Want Now" describes what the BPP wants from the American government; while "What We Believe" expands on "What We Want Now" by further describing and outlining what rights Black people should have but are consistently denied.

"What We Believe" explains,

> "We believe we can end police brutality in our Black community by organizing Black self-defense groups that are dedicated to defending our Black community from racist police oppression and brutality. The Second Amendment of the Constitution of the United States gives us the right to bear arms. We therefore believe that all Black people should arm themselves for self-defense."

Bobby Hutton was only sixteen when he joined the Black Panthers and was their first recruit. On April 6, 1968, Eldridge Cleaver and other Panthers shot at the Oakland Police in response to Dr. King's assassination, two days earlier. Then, they fled to an apartment building and engaged in a gun battle with the Oakland Police Department for an hour and a half until Hutton took off all his clothes – except his underwear – and walked out with his arms raised in the air to show the cops he had surrendered. But the cops shot him more than twelve times! Since he was a member of the BPP, a group infamous for wanting to wage war against the cops, he was painted as the villain instead of the cops who shot him, and the cops who killed him walked away free. Mama and Daddy explained that even though the cops killed Bobby's body, they couldn't kill his spirit. Bobby Hutton will always be remembered because no one can make us forget him.

Two other Black Panthers who were killed by the police were Fred Hampton, the chairman of the BPP's Chicago chapter, and

Mark Clark. The Chicago Police Department stormed into their apartment early on the morning of December 4, 1969. Clark was on security and had a shotgun; and if a Black person has a gun, then cops can justify murdering the person. Fred Hampton was asleep on a bed with his fiancée, but the cops shot him in the head, dragged his body to the doorway, and left him lying in a pool of his blood. Mark Clark was shot in the heart while other Black Panthers were wounded and arrested on charges of aggravated assault and attempted murder of the officers. The Chicago Police Department, like most police departments, is full of cowards who fancy themselves warriors and protectors. Fred Hampton was twenty-one years old and Mark Clark was twenty-two years old when they died. This is even more tragic because the twenties are when most people have just figured out what they wanna do with their lives, and they pursue their interests with a strong passion. The BPP was considered a dangerous organization because they uplifted Blacks by making them believe that a war is the only way to rise above our oppressors. So, Hampton and Clark's deaths were viewed as justifiable homicides. I'm sure Rodney King's beating will be seen as a justifiable assault due to the fear of Black people that all cops seem to have.

Another name that popped into my head was Eula Mae Love. I learned about her during Black History Month in the eighth grade – thanks to my social studies teacher, Mrs. Smith. Eula Mae Love lived in the West Athens hood of South Central. Her husband died of sickle cell anemia; so, paying the bills and raising her three daughters rested entirely on her shoulders. On January 3, 1979, a utility worker went to shut off her gas, and she attacked him with a shovel. Afterwards, she left to take out some money orders from nearby stores so that she could pay the bills. Again, two more utility workers went to her house, but she attacked them with an 11" boning knife. Then, two cops, one White and one Black, arrived and ordered her to drop the knife, but she refused – maybe she'd never heard the talk about what to do when you confront the po-po. She threw the knife at the cops; and they fired twelve bullets. She died – obviously. These two cops were exonerated a few months later, but the Black community and the LA Commission were unhappy about them getting off scot-free. The Commission concluded that the shooting didn't meet departmental standards because the cops were guilty of displaying poor judgment and reported to the Shooting Review Board that the cops were exonerated based on faulty and incomplete evidence. Mrs. Smith told us in class that the exoneration stood since the Commission wasn't backed by any legal evidence. Mrs. Smith claimed that Mrs. Love wasn't the first Black person to be a victim of police brutality, and she wouldn't be the last. We all know that's true because the Los Angeles Police Department (LAPD) has been beating up Blacks ever since we settled in the City of Angels. She also stated that Mrs. Love's death at the hands of the police finally pushed police officials to further investigate excessive force and police brutality within the LAPD. Obviously, nothing has changed.

I pray that Rodney King survives his beating and the Good Samaritan who got it all on tape won't be harassed by the cops for having proof of what they're really like. I also pray that *real* change happens instead of the false promises we've been told for centuries.

Chapter Two

After church, Daddy drove us back to Crenshaw. I always sit in the back behind Daddy, and Grandma always sits in the back behind Mama.

Daddy said, "It's such a shame what happened to Rodney King. I'm glad whoever that Good Samaritan is, he got it on tape. Maybe the LAPD will finally reap what they sow."

Grandma said, "They have ways to undermine what we do. The police will say something, like Mister King made a threatening movement and that they were scared for their lives in order to justify what they did to him."

I asked, "If it turns out Rodney King has a criminal record, will the cops be able to get away with it?"

Mama said, "Most likely, yes. But we have to put our faith in the justice system and in the Lord."

Grandma said, "The justice system wasn't written with our needs in mind. When the constitution was written, Blacks only counted for three-fifths of a person. We weren't considered humans because Whites spread lies that we were a subspecies of humanity, little more than animals that White people could whip, beat, and mistreat any way they wished."

I figured Grandma might start talking about her childhood in Mississippi and, sure enough, she did.

Grandma said, "Everyone knows Mississippi has the highest number of lynchings compared to others states in the US and Leflore County has the highest number in Mississippi. At least forty-eight are documented. That's why I decided to leave Mississippi when I was pregnant with Suzy Jane. By that time, lots of Blacks had already left the state for the North and the West. I decided to travel to the West Coast since California has warm weather, like Mississippi, and is considered Heaven on Earth. Besides, Suzy Jane's dirty dog of a daddy left me before she was born, and wouldn't own up to getting me pregnant. He knew that once word spread that he got me pregnant, he'd have to marry me. It turns out he was courting another girl from another county, and they both moved North to Chicago. My best friend had just moved to Los Angeles, and she invited me to join her. I was anxious to get away from the cotton fields, Jim Crow, and the Ku Klux Klan; but when I moved here, I discovered there was plenty Jim Crow in this city. There were jobs that had salaries as low as sharecroppers' wages. So, supporting our loved ones was always a struggle. And there's plenty of Klan in Los Angeles. Some are White, some are cops, and some are Asian. But they all have one goal: to bring us down."

Soon, Daddy drove to our house. People on West Boulevard have driveways but no garages. Daddy parked the car in the driveway, next to the house; and we got out and went inside the house. Our home has three bedrooms; my parents' room, my room, and Grandma's room though Grandma only stays here on the weekends so that she can go to church with us and cook us a Sunday soul food dinner. There are also two bathrooms; Mama and Daddy share the first one, and I have the other one all to myself until Grandma stays with us. The only problem I have with Grandma staying with us is the amount of perfume she sprays on herself on Sundays. I always use *a lot* of air freshener to get the scent out.

This house was originally Grandpa Gabriel Parker's. He was born in Florida; his parents were from Jamaica, and I'm sure they moved to the USA for the same reason Grandma moved to LA – for a better life. Grandpa Gabriel fought in World War II with the Montford Point Marines, the first Black Marines in the US Armed Forces. After WWII ended, he moved to LA and got a job as a steelworker. Then, he married Grandma Juliet, who had immigrated to the USA from Haiti. She and Grandpa Gabriel had twin boys, Daddy and Uncle Alonzo. Grandma Juliet died from post-polio syndrome when Daddy and Uncle Alonzo were still kids, and Grandpa Gabriel died from cancer when Mama was pregnant with me. So, Daddy inherited the house. One of my names is after Grandpa Gabriel. My full name is Hatima Gabriella Parker – Gabriella is the female version of Gabriel. Mama and Daddy thought naming me after Grandma might not be great because of the fate of Shakespeare's Juliet.

Daddy was named after a city in Florida because the Parkers wanted to always remember their Florida roots. Uncle Alonzo is named after Alonzo Herndon, the founder of Atlanta Life Insurance and one of the country's first Black millionaires. Mama is named after Grandma's mama, Suzanne Ellen Drake, who was shot by a White storeowner because he thought she was one of a trio of robbers who burgled his store. Mama Suzy Ellen was cleaning a White lady's house at the time of the theft; so, she couldn't have done it, but the White storeowner was never arrested for killing Mama Suzy Ellen because it's considered normal to shoot any "suspicious" Black in the South. Mama is also named after Grandma's childhood best friend, Jane, who died from scarlet fever.

Grandma's full name is Flora May Drake. Flora means "plants" or "plant life" and Grandma's parents had a beautiful flower garden in Mississippi. I guess those flowers reminded them that despite the bigotry that plagued their lives, the world was still a beautiful place.

Since their names have such strong meanings, Mama and Daddy also wanted to give me a name with a strong meaning – thanks to the Civil Rights and Black Power Movements, African names have grown in popularity. Daddy said that when *Roots* was released as a book in 1976 and the television miniseries aired a year after, many Black parents across America named their boys Kunta and their girls Kizzy. Kunta and Kizzy are Mandinka names, but the most popular African names are Arabic and Swahili names. Mama didn't want me to have an Arabic name because she believes the Nation of Islam's strict rules about female behavior are oppressive to women. Malcolm X's wife, Dr. Betty Shabazz, is a Sunni Muslim, and she's one of the proudest Black women I have ever seen. She managed to raise six girls, get her doctorate in education, and is still fighting for civil rights; but Mama was adamant so my parents decided to give me a Swahili name even though most African American ancestors are from West Africa. Swahili is an East African language, but Black Power advocates believe that Black people in America need a common language besides English, and Swahili is the most popular.

My name, Hatima, is the Swahili word for "fate."

Daddy explained, "Everyone has their own fate that makes them unique, but sometimes we need help figuring out our path in life."

Mama added, "Your name will be a reminder that only you and God Almighty can truly determine what kind of person you wanna be."

I went to my room to change into a pair of jeans and a purple t-shirt. My room has posters of Michael Jackson, Janet Jackson, Whitney Houston, Mr. T, Boyz II Men, Hi-Five, Bobby Brown, MC Hammer, the Huxtable family, and the Fresh Prince with the Banks family. I also have maps of the Land of Oz, the continent of Nonestica, and the Narnian universe. My room is my own world. My bookshelf has three shelves, and I own a variety of books. The non-fiction books I have include *The Autobiography of Malcolm X As Told To Alex Haley*, *Soul on Ice*, *Die Nigger Die!*, *Roots*, *Up from Slavery*, *The Souls of Black Folks*, *The Life of Olaudah Equiano*, *The History of Mary Prince*, *Incidents in the Life of a Slave Girl*, *Narrative of the Life of Frederick Douglass*, *The Narratives of Fugitive Slaves in Canada*, *Stride Towards Freedom*, *Strength to Love*, *Why We Can't Wait*, *Conscience for Change*, and *Where Do We Go From Here: Chaos or Community?*

I also have fiction books too like the Oz books; The Chronicles of Narnia; the Redwall books; *Alice's Adventures in Wonderland* and *Through the Looking Glass*; *Watership Down*; *The Adventures of Sherlock Holmes*; *Oliver Twist*; *To Kill A Mockingbird*; *The Color Purple*; and *Lord of the Flies*.

I put on a pair of my Reebok Pumps. I have three pairs of Reeboks but my favorite pair is my Pumps. They're white, orange, and blue, and they always look brand-new. That's 'cause in the hood everybody cleans their sneakers to ensure that they always look new. You're not really down for the hood unless you have dope sneakers.

I started to head out; but Grandma sat on the couch, looking at the pictures of all the famous Black people on our walls. On one wall are pictures of Dr. King, Malcolm X, Medgar Evers, Jesse Jackson, Rosa Parks, Fannie Lou Hamer, Stokely Carmichael, Huey Newton and Bobby Seale, Eldridge and Kathleen Cleaver, Angela Davis, and Shirley Chisholm. On another wall are pictures of Booker T. Washington and W. E. B. Du Bois, two famous Black educators from before the civil rights era. Below them are pictures of abolitionists, people who worked hard to give liberty to victims of slavery and to outlaw the inhumane practice: Frederick Douglass, Josiah Henson, Sojourner Truth, and Harriet Tubman. On another wall are pictures of famous Afro-Caribbeans: Toussaint Louverture, Marcus Garvey, Harry Belafonte, and Bob Marley. Below them are famous Africans: Kwame Nkrumah, Patrice Lumumba, Julius Nyerere, Jomo Kenyatta, and Nelson Mandela.

We also have tables in the living room that have our family pictures. The framed pictures feature Grandpa Gabriel and Grandma Juliet at their wedding, Mama when she was a kid, Daddy and Uncle Alonzo when they were kids, Mama in her wedding dress and Daddy in his tuxedo, baby pictures of me, and my class pictures.

We also have a shelf where we keep our record player and stereo. On the top is our record player, which we use to play vinyl records. But since record labels now release music on cassette tapes and CDs, a lot of folks in the hood have bought stereos. Daddy bought our Sony stereo system, two years ago, so that we can listen to tapes and CDs whenever we want. I also have a Sony Walkman, which I received on my thirteenth birthday. I haven't used it in a while, since Ralph Evans was shot by some cops while he was listening to his Walkman. He didn't hear them tell him to halt; so, they assumed he was resisting them. Thankfully, they only shot him in his right leg. The Evanses filed a complaint and tried to take the case to court, but the cops weren't even indicted. There's a good chance the cops who beat Rodney King won't be indicted either if the grand jury is unimpressed by the videotape.

I sat down with Grandma, looked at the pictures of our Black leaders, and asked, "Are you wondering what they all would say if they were here right now?" Grandma nodded and I replied, "Doctor King would say, 'Our lives begin to end when we become silent about the things that matter.' Malcolm X would say, 'We need more light about each other. Light creates understanding, understanding creates love, love creates patience, and patience creates unity.' Frederick Douglass would say, 'If there is no struggle, there is no progress.'

That means the person who taped what the cops did to Rodney King won't stay silent about police brutality. We need to spread more light in Crenshaw and the rest of South Central in order to unite the communities against injustice. We have to struggle and fight against racism, but it's the only way we can change our world for the better."

Grandma hugged me and asked, "How'd you get to be so smart?"

I replied, "Because you, Mama, and Daddy are among the smartest people I know."

Grandma laughed and said, "If we were so smart, we wouldn't have dropped out of school."

I stated, "You had to drop out of school to help your daddy sharecrop. Mama also dropped out to help you with the bills. Daddy and Uncle Alonzo dropped out of school because Grandpa Gabriel was injured at Reliance Steel and couldn't work for a while."

Grandma said, "We seem to be trapped in a system that's designed to make sure we fail."

I said, "I won't fail. I'll graduate from Dorsey High and go to college. And it won't cost you a dime because the school will cover all my fees."

Grandma stated, "I still don't like this idea of you joining the Marines and fighting nonsense wars."

I told Grandma, "World War One and World War Two weren't nonsense. The Nazis are just as bad as the Klan. Daddy's daddy did his part by shooting at the Japanese in the Pacific. Daddy did his part in Vietnam. I just want to carry on the tradition."

Grandma sighed but didn't say anything else.

I headed out to the recreation center to shoot some hoops. Basketball isn't my favorite sport, but I still like to play. I knew I'd get hungry and thirsty, so I stopped at the convenience store on Martin Luther King Jr. Boulevard. South Central LA is not as bad as most people think. When people think of South Central, they automatically visualize gangsters, drug dealers, junkies, winos, thieves, pimps, and prostitutes; but people also run legit businesses; kids go to school; parents go to work; and people walk, play, and socialize together. Crenshaw is a pretty good place to grow up in as long as a person doesn't become prey to the predators of the street. There are plenty of businesses on MLK Boulevard, including Mr. Peterson's Barber Shop, Pizza Hut, and Lee's Gas Station and Convenience Store. I walked to the gas station and entered the convenience store. As I walked into the store, Mr. Lee watched me closely from his counter. A lot of Koreans own stores in South Central, and they believe that all Blacks are murderers and thieves, but I've never let Mr. Lee's prejudices wind me up. I got a box of Twinkies, a bag of Cheetos, and a bottle of Sprite. Then, I walked to the counter and placed the goods on it.

Mr. Lee rang up the junk food and the drink and said, "Five dollars."

I handed him a five-dollar bill and asked, "Can I have a receipt?" I wouldn't give him any excuse to frame me for stealing.

He typed up a receipt, ripped the paper out of the machine, shoved it and the junk food and soda into a plastic bag, and said, "Now get out of my store."

I said, "You're welcome."

He replied, "I didn't say thank you."

I retorted, "You should have. Without my business or that of my peers, your store would be out of business and you'd be broke."

I walked out, feeling a bit proud that I took a stand for my race.

When I got to the center, I shot hoops at the basketball court with some of the guys, but I didn't sink in as many points as I usually do. The reason wasn't because my best skill ain't basketball but because Mr. Lee was still on my mind. I wondered what Mr. Lee would be like if he were a member of the LAPD. Would he have beaten Rodney King? Would he have a look of disgust on his face like the one he always has when he sees me? Would he always have a look of pleasure because he had a way to beat up the race he hates so much and not get punished for it? As far as I know, a police badge is like a protective shield. If a person has one, then they can mistreat anyone they want and call it justice. When they have that badge, they believe they can beat up anybody with their batons or shoot them with their guns.

Bigots hide behind symbols. The KKK have their white sheets and the badge that consists of a white cross in a red circle, and the Nazis have their swastikas and their "Hail Hitler" hand salute. When the KKK wear their white sheets and bloody crosses, they hang whoever they like from peach trees; and when Germans wore the swastika, they massacred six million Jews and other "inferior" races. As long as neo-Nazis still sport those swastikas, they can keep hatred alive.

I finally realized my heart wasn't in the game, so I called it a day. I ate a Twinkie and drank some Sprite, but I knew I shouldn't fill up on junk food since it was almost lunchtime. I walked back home and when I went inside, I saw Grandma watching soap operas on the Betamax. I went to the kitchen and warmed up two slices of Pizza Hut's pepperoni pizza in the microwave. Then, I ate two more Twinkies for dessert.

Grandma told me, "That junk food is the reason why obesity rates among Black people are higher than they are among other races."

I explained, "I don't eat junk food all the time. On weekends, I indulge myself with junk food as a way to relax from the week's work.

Besides, some of the soul food you serve is considered extremely fattening. That's why Mama and Daddy only let you cook for us on the weekends."

Grandma said, "I prefer to spend my days off with my daughter, son-in-law, and grandbaby. In Mississippi, a good soul food meal was a temporary reprieve from the long days in the field. It gave nourishment to Black folks and helped spread happiness in a dark and lawless state."

I said, "I understand, Grandma. Soul food is part of the African American tradition. We'd be disrespecting our forefathers without it."

For dinner, Grandma made fried chicken, collard greens, mac and cheese, cornbread, and a peach cobbler for dessert. In my opinion, Kentucky Fried Chicken tastes *way* better than Grandma's, but the KFC recipe is top secret just like the Coca-Cola formula. All anyone knows about KFC is that they use eleven herbs and spices in their Original Recipe Seasoned Chicken. But nobody, and I mean *nobody*, has been able to crack the KFC formula.

I took a bite of the drumstick and said, "Just as good as KFC."

Grandma said, "Colonel Sanders must have stolen that recipe from Black folks because the few White-owned restaurants in Mississippi that served Black customers couldn't make fried chicken as good as my mama's."

Daddy ate the collard greens and said, "*This* is how vegetables are supposed to taste. White folks got no imagination when it comes to food. They need to learn to add spice and flavor to food."

Grandma's collard greens are always prepared with a ham hock, diced onions, vinegar, salt, and red pepper. If a person hates eating vegetables, then they should try collard greens. Her mac and cheese always have the right amount of cheese. Cafeteria mac and cheese never has enough cheese; so, it tastes like a person is eating bland pasta. I absolutely *love* cornbread, it's crunchy and sweet and savory all at once; and Grandma's cobblers, pies, and cakes are also excellent. Her peach cobbler has sugared pecans decorated on the crust, and the taste of sugared pecans with sugared peaches always makes my taste buds dance with happiness.

We all went to bed with satisfied stomachs.

School was closed on Monday due to a gas leak. Mama, Daddy, and I heard about it on the radio and called our neighbors to make sure they knew. I spent the extra day off reading and working on my assigned essays. At night, Daddy shook me awake, and I got up and exclaimed, "What's wrong? Is the house burning down? Have the police locked down the neighborhood?"

Daddy explained, "No, they're gonna show the Rodney King videotape on KTLA."

I wanted and didn't want to see it. I had seen Daddy, my friends, and plenty of other people in the hood get harassed by the cops. The cops made them put their hands out where they could see them and patted them down at least three times. I had been stopped by cops plenty of times simply because they thought my skin color and hip-hop clothes meant I was a troublemaker. People have filed complaints, but it hasn't changed anything.

Daddy, Mama, and I sat on the living room couch. The television was turned on, and we got to watch what the cops did to Rodney King. The tape was over a minute long, and it showed the cops beating Rodney King with their batons; they even kicked him! Every time they struck him, I felt like they were striking my heart and soul. That could easily be my daddy being beat down by the cops!

Mama said, "Lord have mercy."

I said, "That's not right."

Daddy said, "You're right, baby girl. That ain't right at all."

I looked up at the picture of Dr. King. He was harassed by cops many times in the 1950s and 1960s and imprisoned many times; he also wrote "Letter From a Birmingham Jail" while he was locked up, showing that the cops could neither break his spirit nor his belief in non-violence. Then, I looked at the picture of Malcolm X. Brother Malcolm always distrusted the police. The cops locked him up when he lived in Boston, but Malcolm kinda deserved it because he was a criminal at the time. Then, the feds kept a close eye on the Nation of Islam, tapping wires and planting outrageous stories to undermine support for the Black Muslims. I looked at the pictures of Huey Newton and Bobby Seale. The Black Panthers called the cops "pigs", and I understand why they believed that. The cops neither protect us nor stand up for us. They use Blacks as little more than scapegoats for their bigotry, hatred, and aggression.

The reporter announced that the investigators were still trying to identify the officers who beat Rodney King.

On Tuesday morning, Daddy dropped me and my best friend, Wanda Brooks, off at school. School is about a twelve-minute walk for me and Wanda, but we don't mind taking a break from walking. Wanda's skin is blacker than mine, and she sports curly hair. She always wears Reeboks, just like me – it's the brand of shoes that most girls in the hood wear. She's two inches shorter than me, making her the same height as Grandma, but she's not intimidated by my height like other girls are. She lives two houses down and across the street from me; and her mom owns the Creole & Cajun Kitchen. Mrs. Reynolds opened the restaurant but when she died, she left the restaurant to Mrs. Brooks in her will. That was good since Mrs. Reynolds' daughters went to college, and they wouldn't want to run the Creole & Cajun Kitchen. Mrs. Brooks and the chefs at the Creole & Cajun Kitchen serve Louisiana cuisine. Wanda's family roots are in Louisiana – the Brookses moved to LA in the 1950s just like how Grandma Flora May and Grandpa Gabriel migrated from Mississippi and Florida. The Creole & Cajun Kitchen is open for lunch and dinner, but Mrs. Brooks leaves her house early in the morning so that she can focus on bills, taxes, supply deliveries, et cetera, before lunch starts; and she doesn't get back to her house until late at night. Wanda's older brother, Andre, also leaves early because he has basketball practice. So, Wanda gets a ride to school from my daddy when he doesn't have a morning shift at the airport.

Mama works an eight-hour shift at the Beverly Hills Hotel's Polo Lounge. She uses a carpool to get to work, every day. Her shift starts at seven o'clock in the morning and ends at five o'clock in the evening. She serves breakfast, brunch, and lunch.

Only rich people have brunch. Folks in the hood call a meal that is not breakfast, lunch, or dinner, snack time. Some folks think most people like to eat at restaurants at night and that Mama is missing out on big money; but Mama has told me that lots of people eat meals that aren't dinner at the Polo Lounge. Some of the customers aren't all hotel guests, but they're all rich, which means they give Mama plenty of tips. Without tips, we would probably be using food stamps and washing our clothes in the kitchen sink. Mama and Daddy are always working hard to make it, but there are times when we don't break even. Sometimes, we cut down the light bill by not watching television and me doing my homework by lantern light; but Mama and Daddy have said that if them going hungry means I'll have more, they'll do it without question.

Daddy is not a gangster, but he has tattoos on his arms. On his right arm, he has a tattoo of a crown with the letters MLK inside it, another tattoo of an X with *Allah-u Akbar* in Arabic underneath it, the AME Church logo, and the Pan-African flag. These tattoos are meant to honor Dr. King, Malcolm X, the AME Church, and the Pan-African Movement. On Daddy's left arm are tattoos of the African National Congress flag, the Jamaican flag, the Haitian flag, and a black panther. The ANC flag honors South Africans who are fighting against apartheid, the Jamaican and Haitian flags honor our Caribbean ancestors, and the black panther honors the BPP.

Daddy and Mama honor all methods that Black people across the world have used to achieve freedom like non-violent resistance, Black Nationalism, Black Power, Black Christian denominations, and the Rastafarian movement. This is because they've all done their part in the worldwide Black struggle.

I was in the passenger seat and Wanda was sitting behind me.

Daddy asked Wanda, "Your brother figured out which school he's going to in the fall?"

Andre is a senior, while Wanda and I still are juniors.

Wanda said, "Andre is still weighing his options. He has his heart set on an HBCU, that much I know."

Blacks usually prefer studying in a HCBU, which is short for Historically Black Colleges and Universities.

When we got to school, Principal Edwards walked up to the Ford and asked, "Orlando Parker, how are you?"

Daddy replied, "All's well and good, except for what happened to Rodney King."

Principal Edwards said, "Yes, I'm praying for him. Hope this means the LAPD will change the way they do things in our community."

Daddy said, "I hope so."

Principal Edwards saw me and Wanda and said, "Young ladies, how are you?"

I said, "Fine, Principal Edwards."

Wanda said, "We a'ight, Principal Edwards."

Principal Edwards said, "You ladies are so beautiful. I'm sure you have plenty of male admirers."

Daddy laughed and said, "I'm not sure about Wanda, but my baby girl ain't allowed to date until she's thirty."

I replied, "Daddy, I told you not to call me 'baby girl' in public."

Daddy said, "Sorry, Hatima, but I can't imagine you loving any man except your daddy."

There are some boys in my hood who are interested in me, but I'm not interested in them. Some don't do well in school, so they're not the sharpest quills on the porcupine. Others are gangsters and drug dealers, and I'm not going to let them ruin my chances for a better future. Daddy's twin brother, Uncle Alonzo, is a member of the Bloods. When Daddy dropped out of school, he joined the Marines and fought in Vietnam, and when he was discharged, he got his job as a baggage handler at the LA International Airport. Then, he met Mama at a nightclub. They fell in love: got married a year later; and, nine months later, I was born.

The Marines weren't appealing to Uncle Alonzo and no jobs were available to high school dropouts; so, Uncle Alonzo started to participate in armed robberies with some Crenshaw gangsters and fenced the stolen goods on the street. The first time Uncle Alonzo was arrested, it was for charges of grand theft auto and assault with a deadly weapon. He stole a 1968 Mustang from a White guy, pistol-whipped the White guy, and knocked him out. Somebody must have called 911 because the cops started chasing him and told him to pull over because the Mustang was a stolen vehicle. Uncle Alonzo was sent to Central Juvenile Hall and set free, a year later.

Since nobody wanted to hire an ex-con, he went right back to stealing anything he could get his hands on; cars, purses, television sets, record players, et cetera. Around that time, the Bloods were formed to compete against the Crips and Alonzo was offered membership into the gang. The second time Uncle Alonzo went to jail was when I was ten. He was arrested for stealing from an electronics store with his fellow gangsters, and all the Bloods were sent to San Quentin State Prison, a maximum-security prison near San Francisco.

One interesting fact is that Stanley "Tookie" Williams III, one of the co-founders and leaders of the Crips gang, is also incarcerated at San Quentin. Uncle Alonzo wrote Daddy letters about life in prison and stated that there were always fights between the Bloods and the Crips. Prison is just like the hood, except the prisoners aren't free to go anywhere and the COs are used in place of the cops.

Uncle Alonzo was set free after three years, but he's still with the Bloods. He lives in Inglewood with Auntie Kalisha and my cousin, Malik. Uncle Alonzo is a member of the Crenshaw Mafia set of Bloods; their territory is mostly in Inglewood because that's where the Crenshaw Mafia were founded but they have some clout here in Crenshaw since this is their namesake. Uncle Alonzo helped form alliances between the Crenshaw Mafia Gangster Bloods and the Inglewood Family Gangster Bloods, the Denver Lane Bloods, and the Weirdo Gangster Bloods in order to increase their influence and profits. There are different sets of Bloods and Crips in South Central and LA County. The Bloods' sets seldom have much allegiance with each other, and the same is true about the Crips' sets. Different Blood sets are more likely to fight each other as much as they fight

HEAL THE HOOD

with the Crips and other gangs; the Crips sets also suffer from the same kinds of conflicts. I know that's complete bullshit.

Uncle Alonzo drives a red 1969 Pontiac GTO. He always wears red clothing: red caps, red bandannas, an LA Clippers jersey, a San Francisco 49ers jersey, and a Chicago Bulls jersey.

Daddy has forbidden Uncle Alonzo, Aunt Kalisha, and Malik from having contact with me. I'm not sure what to think of Uncle Alonzo. I know I'm supposed to love him because we're related, but it's the Bloods and the Crips and other gangs that cause folks outside the hood to think that all Blacks are criminals. It's because of gangbangers and drug dealers that those cops beat Rodney King, almost to death. They probably thought he was speeding away from a crime scene when they pulled him over and beat him.

Thanks to the movies *Lean On Me* and *The George McKenna Story*, which stars one of the hottest Black actors on the planet, Denzel Washington, most people think that ghetto schools are nothing more than training grounds for juvenile delinquents and future convicts. But Principal Edwards is as cool as Principal Clark and Principal McKenna. He's worked hard to make Susan Miller Dorsey High School an institution where kids can not only get a high school diploma but can see college as a real possibility.

Most of the teachers at Dorsey High are Black, but we have a few White teachers. The last principal was White, but he was able to convince the school board to reassign him to another school. I heard that he didn't want to spend another minute with "these ghetto boys and girls who aren't going to amount to anything." Principal Edwards was born and raised here in Crenshaw and managed to get a B.A. and M.A. in education when he went to college. He decided to come back to Dorsey High to become "the man in the mirror." Since he's a respected member of the community, we listen to him and the lessons he teaches are essential to our well-being.

Sadly, Dorsey High's graduation rate is not as high as other schools in LA, and the number of kids who get accepted into colleges is also not as high though it has been rising. The school accepts students from other hoods besides Crenshaw. Students at Dorsey High also live in West Adams, Leimert Park, Jefferson Park, Baldwin Hills, and Baldwin Village. Some even come from bougie parts of the hood, like some streets in Leimert Park. Some classes in Dorsey High can be very boring, but that's just my point of view. I'm not a huge fan of mathematics and science because there's not much imagination in those subjects. In those subjects, there's only one right answer, and in my opinion, life is not like that. In English and humanities subjects, there are multiple answers to our questions. Even though I have only gotten As in every subject I've taken since I started here in the tenth grade, I prefer English, history, civics, and other subjects in the field of humanities. The only math class I'm taking is pre-calculus and the only science class I'm taking is biology, but English, French, and other courses I'm taking are all AP because those prepare students for college-level courses.

In AP English, Mrs. Watkins assigned us a book titled *Animal Farm* in which a bunch of British farm animals get rid of their human masters and attempt to run the farm themselves. Things go downhill because the pigs become even bigger tyrants than the humans, and the other animals are too stupid to see it.

Most of my classmates don't see what this has to do with real life; the only other stories where talking animals are featured in are fantasy novels. I believe fantasy novels have a lot to teach us and even though *Animal Farm* is not a fantasy novel, it still has a lot to teach people. I did some research at the libraries and discovered that

Animal Farm is an allegory of the Russian Revolution. The book can also be an allegory for political systems and societies today.

In *Animal Farm*, Napoleon has brutish dogs that patrol the other animals and kill any dissidents. He also pins all blame on another pig called Snowball when things go bad on the farm. Napoleon's dogs are an allegory for the secret police. The only other books I have read that feature secret police forces are *Watership Down* and *The Lion, the Witch and the Wardrobe*.

When the White Witch ruled over Narnia, she had a secret police force comprised of wolves patrol the country and bring troublemakers to her castle. Then, she used her wand to turn them to stone. The LAPD are like a secret police force; they patrol and control people in the hood instead of protect and serve us. Plus, they like to pin all blame on Blacks when the crime rate rises. If the LAPD were doing a good job, would gangs still cause trouble in our hoods? Aslan was able to save Narnia with help from the Pevensie kids. Since The Chronicles of Narnia is an allegory of Christianity, it means Jesus can save us when we're in trouble. But where was Jesus when Rodney King was being beaten? Where was Jesus when Bobby Hutton was killed? Where was Jesus when Fred Hampton and Mark Clark were killed? Where was Jesus when the Chicago BPP were brutalized and lied about by the Chicago PD? Where was Jesus when Eula Mae Love had to take care of her family by her own broke self? Where was Jesus when the KKK terrorized the Blacks of Mississippi? Where was Jesus when Grandma's mama was killed by that White storeowner? Where is Jesus when the Bloods and the Crips sell drugs, rob stores and houses, and kill people? I find myself wondering why He doesn't appear to do anything when bad things happen to good people.

Dorsey High has Black history classes and my AP African American History teacher is Mr. Ngozi. On the first day of school, he explained that his name is pronounced In-guh-zee. I asked him what kind of name that was.

Mr. Ngozi explained, "I'm from the Igbo tribe in Nigeria." He pronounced it "E-boe." Apparently, the "g" is silent.

I asked, "Does that mean you're a pure-blooded African?"

Mr. Ngozi laughed and said, "I'm not sure about being pure-blooded, but I was born in Nigeria, which is in West Africa."

Wanda asked, "Did you go to an HBCU here in the States?"

Mr. Ngozi said, "No, I studied at the University of Nigeria, Nsukka, and then at University College London, where I got my master's degree in education."

A guy named Devin, who is still sporting the Gumby haircut, asked, "London? Did you have tea with the Queen and watch soccer games instead of basketball?"

Mr. Ngozi laughed and said, "Beware of those British stereotypes. Brits love many sports not just soccer, which they call football. Not everyone in the UK knows the Queen and most Brits aren't big fans of the Royal Family. They believe they're lazy, spoiled, and can do thoughtless things."

I said, "Reminds me of American politicians. Presidents like Andrew Jackson, Rutherford B. Hayes, and Ronald Reagan weren't fit to lead. Besides, the British Prime Minister gets a lot more done than Queen Elizabeth."

In class that day, Mr. Ngozi asked, "Have you all heard about what happened to Rodney King?"

We all said, "Yeah!"

Mr. Ngozi asked, "Can anyone explain to me how historical racism led to Rodney King's beatings at the hands of the LAPD?"

I raised my hand.

Mr. Ngozi called on me, and I said, "The cops have always tried to control people in Black communities because they think there's danger in all aspects of Black life due to the influence of gangs and drugs. The Black Panther Party stated in their Ten-Point Platform that they wanted an end to police brutality. Bobby Hutton's murder was because of police brutality, and the BPP open-firing on the cops should have warned the Oakland PD and all other police departments that Black people were fed up with being oppressed."

Mr. Ngozi said, "Eloquently put, Hatima."

Wanda raised her hand and said, "We should be thankful for modern technology. That videotape has all the proof needed to convict those cops."

Everyone cheered, but Mr. Ngozi interrupted our cheering and stated, "We don't know for sure whether or not Rodney King is an angel. He may become an icon, but he is not completely innocent."

I asked Mr. Ngozi, "What do you mean?"

Mr. Ngozi said, "The police claim that Mister King was intoxicated and drunk while speeding. Driving under the influence is against the law. The cops may be acquitted if they can justify that Mister King was committing criminal acts."

Devin said, "The cops can't beat someone up for driving drunk. If it was a White kid from Beverly Hills driving drunk, the cops would let him off with a warning."

Mr. Ngozi said, "You don't know that."

I stated, "The lives of White people and rich people are considered more important than the lives of Black people and poor people."

Point number five of the Black Panther Platform states,

"We want education for our people that exposes the true nature of this decadent American society. We want education that teaches us our true history and our role in the present-day society."

I believe it's important that we learn not just African American history but the history of other Black people across the African diaspora. The only Black people kids at Dorsey High are interested in learning about are African-Americans, Africans from the Mother continent, and Caribbeans. Mr. Ngozi told us that there are Black people in many other countries such as Brazil, Canada, the UK, Germany, and even Japan. He promised us that if we stuck with his history classes, we would learn their stories.

Marcus Garvey founded the Pan-African Movement. He believed that Black people across the globe have a common history and a common struggle. I know about Afro-Caribbean history because Daddy has told me about it several times. I also know about Southern history because Grandma talks about it in detail. Mr. Ngozi tells us many stories about Nigerians, Black Britons, and other members of the Black diaspora. You can always feel the sadness and joy, and trials and victory in their voices as they tell these stories. I'm glad that they tell me these stories so I can better understand how I fit into the world.

On Wednesday after school, I walked back home to do my homework. Then, I went to catch the bus to Master Shin's Dojang.

As I left home, Mama told me, "Hatima, if teaching at that martial arts school is going to affect your studies, you know that you'll have to give it up."

I said, "Yes, Mama. But I need it to spice up my application. Plus,

HEAL THE HOOD

I'm sure you want me to be able to defend myself without a gun."

The bus from Crenshaw to Koreatown takes about half an hour to forty minutes, depending on traffic. Whenever I go there, my sixth sense always goes off because whenever non-Koreans step foot in this neighborhood, the residents watch them like hawks. Black people in South Central also do the same thing whenever non-Blacks show up. Blacks don't want to mix with other races and neither do the Koreans, and I always wonder if there's really a need to mix races.

Master Shin runs a dojang in Koreatown. Dojang is what Koreans call a martial arts school. He teaches hapkido, a Korean martial art that draws inspiration from other Asian martial arts. Master Shin teaches us striking attacks, including punches and kicks, and grappling techniques, including joint locks, holds, and throws. He also teaches us how to fight with weapons, including knives, swords, ropes, nunchaku, canes, sticks, and staffs. I started coming to his dojang when I was ten, after I saw an ad at the rec center and decided it would be a good idea to learn self-defense. Once I reached my teenage years, some guys would want me to give it to them even if I didn't want to – girls in the hood get sexually assaulted, molested, and raped a lot. Since Mama and Daddy can't keep me in the house all the time when I don't have school, they agreed that learning martial arts would be a good idea. They just don't want me to seek out fights and get arrested on assault and battery charges or earn extra cash in street fights. The gangs sometimes host street fights where teens and adults fight each other until one person is left standing. People from across LA come to Master Shin's Dojang to learn martial arts. Ever since Bruce Lee kicked butts on the small and silver screens, a *lotta* people have been obsessed with Asian culture, specifically Asian martial arts.

Master Shin has explained that there is more to martial arts than just fighting. He also teaches his students the mental and spiritual side of martial arts. Master Shin is like Mr. Miyagi, Master Yoda, and Master Splinter combined into one. He has graying and balding hair and a short graying beard. He's also shorter than me by two inches, but *never* underestimate his height. He can take down opponents over six feet tall! Master Shin gives anecdotes of wisdom now and again, but he's not a walking, talking fortune cookie.

After I received my black belt when I was fifteen, Master Shin let me help him teach new students. So, I teach at the dojang three nights a week; Mondays, Wednesdays, and Fridays. Mama and Daddy think it's a good idea for me to have a job and "learn the value of a dollar." I went to the girls' locker room to change into my uniform, white shirt and pants with a black belt; and as soon as I walked out of the locker room, I saw him. He had been standing outside the locker room; he had most likely seen me walk in and wanted to take me by surprise.

Joshua Yang smiled and asked, "Are you available now?"

Joshua is cute, has his black hair cut short, and has these dimples that appear when he smiles. But it's gonna take more than that for a guy to get on my good side.

I replied, "No, and don't bother asking again."

I walked over to a group of eleven-and-twelve-year-olds, but Joshua persisted.

He asked, "Why won't you go out on a date with me? Am I a lousy fighter?"

I said, "No. I've kicked your butt several times, but that's not why I keep rejecting you."

He laughed and asked, "Do I smell bad? Is it my breath? Do I look ugly? Do you hate my hair?"

I said, "No, it's none of those things."

Joshua asked, "Then, why won't you go out with me?"

I stated, "Because I'm Black, and you're Korean."

Joshua asked, "You really pulled the race card?"

I said, "Of course I did. Whether you like it or not, race is still an important part of American society."

Joshua said, "I still like you and your black skin doesn't scare me off. I think that's very non-racist. I didn't want to pull this card, but I want to ask you this: what would Doctor Martin Luther King do if he saw this?"

I said, "I don't know."

Joshua repeated, "You don't know? The girl who wants to be the world's greatest Africanist doesn't know what Doctor King would say?"

I exclaimed, "Fine! I know Doctor King wouldn't have a problem with interracial relationships; neither would his wife or Rosa Parks, but Malcolm X, the Black Panthers, Marcus Garvey, and Toussaint Louverture would have a problem with it."

Joshua said, "Okay. So, which philosophy do you lean toward; non-violence or Black Power?"

I said, "That's an unfair question. My parents and my grandmother said that was the most asked question during the fifties and sixties. Are you with Doctor King or Malcolm X? Are you an integrationist or a separatist?"

Joshua said, "You're a mix of several of these ideologies. But I know deep down that you like me. Maybe you need more time to figure it out."

I told Joshua, "I have a class to teach."

He walked away to his own group, and my students kept staring at me.

I said, "Why are you all standing like statues? Get into your positions."

On Thursday, ABC News showed the videotape of Rodney King.

The reporter said, "And now the story that may never have surfaced if someone hadn't picked up his home video camera. We've all seen the pictures of Los Angeles police officers beating a man they just pulled over. The city's police chief says he will support criminal charges against some of the men. Here's ABC's Gary Shepherd."

Then, they re-showed the video of Rodney King's beating; and Gary Shepherd said, "The three police officers facing felony criminal charges were among a group of fifteen who stopped a twenty-five-year-old Black man last Saturday night. They beat him, kicked him, and clubbed him, unaware that an amateur photographer was recording the incident on videotape. Los Angeles Police Chief, Darryl Gates, looked at the tape and said he thinks assault with a deadly weapon will be one of the charges."

Then, Darryl Gates said, "When we reviewed, we found that the officers struck him with batons between fifty-three and fifty-six times. One officer rendered six kicks and one officer one kick."

Then, Gary Shepherd said, "Civil rights organizations say the Los Angeles Police Department has a history of brutality and misconduct that goes back a quarter of a century, including one incident that sparked the Watts Riots. So far this year, there have been more than one hundred and twenty-five complaints of police misconduct filed with watchdog organizations."

A Black man with the NAACP whose name was shown to be Jose De Sosa said, "We no longer want to have to wake up each morning not knowing what fear to expect next. Today, we are not sure that the police are there to protect us."

Then, Gary Shepherd was shown on the screen and he said, "But Chief Gates today called the LAPD a 'model department' and said he has no plans to resign. Gary Shepherd, ABC News, Los Angeles."

HEAL THE HOOD

Daddy was working a late shift at the airport, so it was just me and Mama.

Mama said, "It takes fifteen officers to take down one Black man? What is this world coming to?"

I said, "They didn't need to beat Rodney King. There were other ways they could have restrained him and then handcuffed him. Master Shin taught us many ways to defeat an opponent without causing too much harm; attack the weak spots, such as the pelvis and knees; and use joint locks, such as armlocks, wristlocks, and leg locks. Pins and throws also work. Master Shin said that just because an opponent is bigger than us doesn't mean he or she can't be defeated. A martial art hapkido draws inspiration from is jujitsu. The key to jujitsu is using an opponent's strength against them; but I don't think the LAPD know any martial arts, and I doubt any Asian master would teach a bunch of arrogant fools. Master Shin said that if he found out any of us were using his teachings to cause unnecessary harm to others, we would no longer be welcome as his students."

Mama said, "Mister De Sosa got the gist of it. The police aren't here to protect us, but to terrorize us."

I said, "They're like the secret police forces in totalitarian governments across the world. In fact, the LAPD *are* a secret police force. Chief Gates must be a fool if he thinks the LAPD is a 'model department.' The LAPD haven't done nothin' to decrease crime in the ghetto, that's for damn sure."

Mama said, "Every Black child is taught what to do when the police stop you. Not *if* they stop you, *when* they stop you. I pray that someday we'll live in a world where that lecture isn't necessary."

Chapter Three

Five days after ABC showed the clip again, the American Civil Liberties Union ran a full-page ad in the *Los Angeles Times* that asked, "Who do you call when the gang wears blue uniforms?"

When folks in South Central refer to the Blues, they're talking about the Crips or the cops; but now I'm sure the Blues will most likely refer to the LAPD in future discussions. Folks in the hood are being attacked by gangsters *and* cops, which means we can't catch a break from danger. The ACLU also launched a campaign to fire Chief Gates since a lotta people can see that he ain't doing a good job leading the LAPD. A week after ABC showed the clip again, a grand jury returned indictments against Officers Stacey Koon, Laurence Powell, Timothy Wind, and Theodore Briseno for beating Rodney King. Timothy Wind was dismissed from the LAPD, but the three other cops were suspended from the force. They also weren't gonna be paid during their downtime. A lotta folks in the hood get laid off from their jobs, and they also don't get paid during that unfortunate downtime. Nice to know those racist cops will know what that feels like! But some folks, including myself, think that all four of the cops should have been fired and arrested. We also believe that the eleven other cops who watched Rodney King get beaten and did nothing should be charged for aiding and abetting. This is a sign that Rodney King's beating might not be that serious to the LAPD. The world is rigged!

HEAL THE HOOD

According to the news, Deputy District Attorney Terry White, a Black man, asked George Holliday, the White man who taped the beating, "Why didn't you call the police while you were viewing this?"

Mr. Holliday replied, "They were there."

Who is gonna call the cops to arrest the cops? Now that I think about it, that question sounds ridiculous. If Mr. Holliday had called the cops that night, I'm sure they would have told him that the cops are just doing their job and that the description Mr. Holliday gave them of the beating was most likely an exaggeration.

I read in the *Los Angeles Sentinel* that District Attorney Ira Reiner said that it was a most terrible moment when officers sworn to uphold the law were charged with taking it into their own hands. Everyone in South Central knows the cops take the law into their own hands *all the damn time*; but no one takes our complaints seriously because we're poor folks from the hood who apparently, "don't contribute to American society." The LAPD is full of sworn officers of the law, so people believe that automatically makes them the good guys; but just because someone carries a badge doesn't mean they stand for law and order.

Almost two weeks had passed after Rodney King's beating; and everyone in my hood and the other hoods of South Central were howling for blood. But peoples' hatred of the cops who beat Rodney King paled in comparison to what happened on Saturday.

On Saturday mornings, I usually watch cartoons. Even though I'm a teenager, I still love cartoons like *The New Adventures of Winnie the Pooh*, *Darkwing Duck*, *Tiny Toon Adventures*, and *Teenage Mutant Ninja Turtles*. As I was watching cartoons, my phone rang, and I picked it up.

Wanda said, "Girl, turn to the news channel!"

I quickly changed the station.

A female reporter said, "South Central Los Angeles has always been infamous for its violence, but the violence is usually Blacks against Blacks. This morning, a Korean shopkeeper shot a Black teenage girl because she was shoplifting. More on this story as it continues to develop."

I was speechless. First, the cops beat up an unarmed Black man; now, a Korean shoots a Black girl? The world has gone crazy. Correction. The world has always been crazy. It's not just White people and cops who hate Black people. As I mentioned before, a lot of stores in South Central are owned by Koreans. In fact, Koreans own more than half of all stores in South Central. Grandma explained that after the change in national immigration laws in 1965, a large number of Korean immigrants moved to LA. South Central suffered from the 1965 Watts Riots and the 1968 MLK riots; so, Koreans began buying businesses because they were cheap, and there wasn't much competition. Blacks were hoping Koreans would be easier to deal with than White shopkeepers, but they're just as bad. They follow Black people around their stores to make sure we don't steal anything, and they don't hire Black employees. The Koreans claim that the high crime rate makes them afraid of being robbed or shot. For crying out loud, we don't all steal and kill! There is so much more to Black people than meets the eye.

As an up-and-coming Africanist, this reminds me of another devastating event of the 1960s. On September 15, 1963, a bomb exploded at the Sixteenth Street Baptist Church in Birmingham, Alabama. Four girls, Addie Mae Collins, Denise McNair, Carole Robertson, and Cynthia Wesley, were all killed. Addie Mae, Carole, and Cynthia were fourteen years old when they were killed, and Denise was eleven.

Two other Black kids also died on that day.

Sixteen-year-old Johnny Robinson was shot in the back by a cop named Jack Parker – I wouldn't be surprised if Officer Jack Parker's ancestors owned my ancestors during the slavery era. Johnny Robinson was at a gas station not far from Sixteenth Street Baptist. Some White teens drove by in cars, called Johnny and his friends "niggers" and "pickaninnies," waved Confederate flags, and threw bottles at the Black kids. Johnny and his friends retaliated by throwing rocks at the cars, and a police car arrived on the scene. Johnny and his friends ran, but Jack Parker, who was in the backseat of the police car, pointed a shotgun out of the window, shot Johnny in the back and wrists, and killed him before he reached a hospital. Jack Parker gave two different accounts of the shooting. In the first account, he claimed he gave a warning shot; and in the second account, he stated that the shotgun went off accidentally.

The other Black kid who died on September 15, 1963 was thirteen-year-old Virgil Ware. He was riding on the handlebars of his brother's bike, ready to finish their newspaper route. Sixteen-year-old White boy Larry Joe Sims came from a family that didn't support segregation, but he gave into peer pressure and had just attended a segregationist rally with his friends. Larry's classmate, Michael Lee Farley, gave him a revolver as they rode home on Mike's motorbike. When they passed Virgil and his brother, Mike told Larry to fire the gun and scare them. Larry closed his eyes and pulled the trigger, and two bullets hit Virgil in the chest and cheek. Virgil died, and Larry and Mike were charged with first-degree murder, which was surprising to me given the era. But an all-White jury convicted Larry on a lesser charge of second-degree manslaughter, and Mike pleaded guilty to that. A White judge named Wallace Gibson suspended their sentences and gave them two years of probation.

Judge Gibson scolded them for their "lapse", meaning he was upset that Larry shot Virgil with his eyes closed and that Mike gave a gun to a guy who didn't want to use it. He also believed that Larry and Mike were justified in shooting Virgil and, in a way, was rewarding them for doing it. I know, that's sick! Mrs. Lorene Ware broke down in the courtroom and cried over the fact that the state of Alabama didn't give a damn about her boy's death; and James, Virgil's brother, said about the bogus sentencing, "You could get more time than that for killing a dog."

Larry's and Mike's punishments were obvious cases of obstruction of justice.

It's not surprising there was so much injustice in Alabama in the 1960s since it was the second-worst state for Blacks to live in, Mississippi being the absolute worst; but it's easy for certain people to believe that this kind of injustice only happened in the 1950s and 1960s. Some folks – I'm thinking about people who don't live in the hood – seriously believe that Black people have fewer problems in the 1990s than they did in the past.

I thought about Mark Watson from *Soul Man*, who dressed himself in Blackface in order to get an African American scholarship to Harvard Law School; and once he became Black, people saw him differently and treated him differently. He was finally able to see how racism is still a serious issue and how affirmative action is not as wacky as a lotta White people think. I wondered how many would be willing to do a "Blackface experiment" to really see how bad racism is.

In the evening, my other best friend, Imani Fitzpatrick, walked to my house. Imani has rich brown skin like me. She sports a simple ponytail, she's an inch shorter than me, and she wears a pair of worn-out Chuck Taylor All-Stars. Chuck Taylors ain't cool anymore, but some people don't give her a hard time about it because her mom is always working hard to break even. Imani asked, "Hey, Hatima, wanna go to the Creole & Cajun Kitchen for dinner?"

I replied, "Sure."

I left a note for my parents and Grandma in case they came home early, and we walked to the restaurant on West Jefferson Boulevard. The walk usually takes about twenty minutes. Other businesses on the street are Oscar's Garage, Ms. Esther's Hair Salon, and Mr. Hwang's Liquor Cabinet. Ms. Esther is one of the nicest ladies you will ever meet, and she makes sure us girls rock the coolest hairstyles. Mr. Hwang is like most Koreans, distrusting of Blacks and refuses to mingle with the rest of the Black community. But Mr. Hwang's Liquor Cabinet is one of Crenshaw's most profitable businesses, and the winos that can be found lounging around the hood are a testament to that.

There were plenty of people in the Creole & Cajun Kitchen getting their grub on, but we found an empty booth.

Wanda walked to our booth and asked, "Can I get you two ladies anything to drink?"

When Wanda works at the Creole & Cajun Kitchen, she wears black pants and a white shirt that has "CCK" sewn in blue on the right front pocket.

I said, "A glass of Sprite, no ice."

Imani said, "I'll have an orange pop."

Wanda wrote that down on her notepad and asked, "Do you know what you wanna eat?"

I said, "Yes, shrimp gumbo with red beans, please."

Imani said, "I'll have jambalaya with potato salad, please"

Wanda wrote that down and went into the kitchen. She soon

came out with our orders; and Imani and I started stuffing our faces. The food tasted wonderful, as always.

I told Wanda, "Your mom should be opening a chain of restaurants across the USA, like McDonald's and Burger King."

Wanda smiled and said, "My mom doesn't care about feeding the world, just the hood."

Just then, the television positioned high in the corner at the back of the restaurant showed captions that said "BREAKING NEWS", and a Black male reporter with a shaved head said, "A Korean-American woman named Soon Ja Du has been arrested for killing a Black teenage girl. Rachel Woods is at the hospital with the full story."

The scene changed to a White woman with brown hair, holding a microphone. She said, "This morning, Latasha Harlins entered Empire Liquor, which is owned by a Korean family, and picked up a bottle of orange juice. As Latasha approached the counter, a Korean woman named Soon Ja Du accused her of stealing when Latasha put the bottle of orange juice in her backpack. Then, Latasha struck Missus Du thrice with her fist, and Missus Du pulled a thirty-eight-caliber handgun from under the counter and shot Latasha in the head. Missus Du's husband, Billy Heung Ki Du, heard the shot, ran into the store, and called nine-one-one. The LAPD stated that Missus Du claimed she was in danger, and she thought Latasha was a thief. But Latasha had two dollars in her left hand, and that should have been enough to pay the dollar-seventy-nine bottle of orange juice. She also did not have any weapons on her person or anything that could be used as a weapon. There were also two witnesses present at the store. Plus, the store has a video camera that should help the police piece together what really happened. Soon Ja Du is at the hospital being treated for facial injuries and being examined for brain damage. The police have arrested and charged her with first-degree murder. She is then going to be moved to the Sybil Brand Institute for Women."

I yelled, "That's what I call justice!"

One of the men in the restaurant who was eating a bowl of crawfish étouffée exclaimed, "That's right, my sister!"

I hope that the testimonies of the witnesses and the security camera footage ensures that Mrs. Du goes to jail for life.

When Imani and I left the Creole & Cajun Kitchen, we were approached by a red Pontiac after we had walked a few blocks. The driver's side of the Pontiac rolled down, and I was looking into the brown eyes of Uncle Alonzo. He was dressed in a Chicago Bulls jersey, and he had on a red cap and a solid gold Rolex. He also had tattoos of five-pointed stars, red snakes wrapped around red roses with sharp thorns, and the names of his fellow Bloods who had been killed in the line of duty on his left arm.

He asked, "How's my beautiful niece doin'?"

I snapped, "Just fine without you or your gang."

Uncle Alonzo said, "Oh, that's cold. My bro just doesn't understand that family has to stick together."

I asked, "Stick together so that we can do what? Sell drugs? Extort from good, hardworking citizens? Sell women's bodies? Rob people? Kill people?"

Uncle Alonzo said, "You and your friends are in school studying to be doctors, lawyers, engineers, and shit like that. Look at me. I'm making more money than all those college fools will ever make in their lifetimes."

I retorted, "That's dirty money. Madam C. J. Walker, John H. Johnson, Reginald Lewis, and your namesake Alonzo Herndon didn't get rich by terrorizing people. I'm gonna make it to the top the right way."

Uncle Alonzo's wife, Auntie Kalisha, was sitting in the passenger seat.

She said, "The right way is learning how never to be broke another day in your life. Look at my man. He knows how to treat his woman right."

Auntie Kalisha was wearing a red velvet dress with very low cleavage; so, most of her breasts were exposed. Her red fingernails matched her dress, and she wore diamond bracelets. Her earrings were in the shape of Arabic letters, probably to honor the Nation of Islam. I'm pretty sure that Malcolm X and Muhammad Ali wouldn't approve of Auntie Kalisha's dress choice since Muslim women always cover their bodies. It's torture in hot weather, but it keeps the boys off their backs. Auntie Kalisha curls her hair, and she uses hair extensions so that her 'do stretches down to the middle of her back.

Auntie Kalisha met Uncle Alonzo at a nightclub. The Bloods had established themselves as a lethal hood enterprise, and Auntie Kalisha was drawn to the obvious power and money the Bloods' aura exhibited. She had danced with Uncle Alonzo and, just like that, they were hooked to each other. Mama hates Auntie Kalisha because, and I quote, "That bitch dresses like a ho and is a bad example to all the young girls in this neighborhood. You shouldn't marry a man just because he has money. You should marry a man because he's hardworking, loves his family, and worships the Lord."

Grandma almost didn't approve of Mama dating Daddy because of Uncle Alonzo, until Daddy convinced her that he wasn't a gangster like his twin. Uncle Alonzo was invited to my parents' wedding, but he wasn't Daddy's best man.

I said, "Look, Uncle Alonzo, I ain't supposed to talk to you. If

Mama and Daddy find out we're having this conversation, I'll be grounded until summertime."

Uncle Alonzo said, "Listen, Hatima. All this fuss over Rodney King and Latasha Harlins may hurt my business. Folks are calling for better policing, which means the po-po will be keeping an even closer eye on me and my boys. I'm just wondering if you'll tell the fuzz anything if they knock on your door."

I could sense the threat in Uncle Alonzo's statement. One of the reasons why my parents dislike him is because he values money over family.

I told him, "The number one rule in the hood is 'Don't snitch.' I've never squealed to the cops, and I'm not planning on starting now."

Uncle Alonzo smiled and said, "Good. Ya know I spent time in juvie and three years in San Quentin. I don't want the cops to take me away from my hood and my family. A fine-ass woman like Kalisha shouldn't be left alone. And what about my son? Who's gonna teach Malik how to be a man?"

Evidently, Uncle Alonzo and Daddy have different opinions about what a real man is. Plus, Uncle Alonzo definitely doesn't want to leave Auntie Kalisha alone in the hood. Word in the hood spreads fast, like a forest fire, and the word was that Auntie Kalisha was sleeping around while Uncle Alonzo was incarcerated at San Quentin. At first, Uncle Alonzo kicked Auntie Kalisha out but, believe it or not, Uncle Alonzo let her back in. He said that if the Bloods' lawyers had done a better job, then he wouldn't have been tossed in jail and he could have maintained a close eye on Auntie Kalisha. He also said that Malik still needed his mom and he wasn't about to cook and clean his crib himself. He could have hired someone, but I guess he wanted to save money. Plus, he probably has no time to date other women because of all the work he does as a Blood. So, even though other dudes made moves on her, Uncle Alonzo and Auntie Kalisha are still LA County's rowdiest couple.

Aunt Kalisha kissed Uncle Alonzo's cheek and slipped her hand inside his jersey so that she could stroke his chest; and Uncle Alonzo said, "I got other business to take care of so I'm out."

As he drove away, Imani said, "I can't believe you two are related."

I said, "Now you can understand why Daddy and Uncle Alonzo rarely talk. He drops by my dad's favorite hangouts to say, 'Hey', but Daddy claims they have nothing to talk about. He's offered to help pay our bills and my college tuition, but Daddy's turned him down plenty of times."

Imani said, "Good. You don't need that dirty gangster money to go to college."

On Sunday, Dr. Murray led us all in prayer for Latasha Harlins' spirit and for her family. He said, "Jesus, please welcome Latasha Harlins into Your Kingdom with open arms. Please, stretch out Your arms and comfort her family here on Earth. Please, ensure that justice prevails. Please, let the justice system listen to the witnesses and view the videotape with clear eyes. Please, ensure that Latasha's killer does not go unpunished."

The whole congregation said, "Amen."

Latasha was only a year and two months younger than me. She was five-foot-six and weighed one hundred and fifty pounds, which means she's an inch shorter than me and the same height as Imani. If she could get shot for shopping, so can I, Imani, Wanda, and my fellow classmates. If Mr. Lee kept a gun, he probably woulda shot me by now. That's why when I enter Korean stores, I make sure I'm not carrying a purse or wearing a jacket. That way the Koreans can't accuse me of trying to steal anything. Plenty of other Black teens have died in South Central, thanks to the gangsters, the drug dealers, and the cops, but you rarely see them on the news. Because of the senseless war between the Bloods and the Crips, Black kids OD-ing, and cops getting rid of threats to society aren't exactly newsworthy. They're seen as just day-to-day life.

When I got to Master Shin's on Monday, Joshua could immediately tell I was upset.

He asked me, "Yo, Hatima, you alright?"

I snapped back, "That ain't your business!"

Then, he asked, "Are you upset about that shoplifter getting killed on Saturday morning?"

I exclaimed, "What?"

He explained, "I saw on the news that a Black girl in South Central was killed for trying to rob a store. I know what she did wasn't cool and that was no reason for Missus Du to kill her—"

I yelled at him, "Joshua, she wasn't trying to rob the store! She had two dollars to pay for her orange juice! That Missus Du thinks all Blacks are thugs so her fear caused her to see Latasha as a threat even though she wasn't!"

Joshua put his hands on my shoulders and said, "Whoa, whoa, whoa. I'm sorry for jumping to the worst conclusion. Did you know Latasha?"

I said, "No. Contrary to popular belief, not all Black people know each other."

Then, tears started running down my face, and Joshua immediately took me into a storage room stocked with wooden swords, wooden knives, and other weapons. No one could see us in there; and I cried a waterfall of tears, while Joshua held me and let me cry into his shirt.

Ten days after Latasha Harlins was killed, Soon Ja Du was released from prison on a $250,000 bail.

Wanda and I were chilling outside her house after church.

I told her, "They set a murderess free! That's bullshit!"

Wanda said, "I know, sister. Missus Du claimed she was assaulted while in jail, and her family worked hard to get her out because they fear for her safety. A lot of Black people have to deal with fights when they're in jail. You'd think Asians with all that knowledge of kung fu would be able to deal with that."

I told Wanda, "Kung fu is Chinese. I doubt a lot of Koreans know it. Second, hapkido and taekwondo are Korean martial arts. Third, not all Asians know martial arts, just like not all Black people can breakdance and shoot hoops."

Wanda asked, "If Missus Du knew martial arts, do you think her confrontation with Latasha would have gone differently?"

I said, "Yeah. With a roundhouse kick to the neck, Missus Du still could have killed her."

Wanda asked, "Can you do that?"

I said, "Yeah but I won't. My martial arts training is for self-defense only. I seek only to injure not kill."

Wanda said, "But, Hatima, when you become a Marine, you'll have to kill people. How is what the Marines do different from what the Bloods and the Crips do?"

I explained, "The Marines fight to make this country and other countries safe. The Bloods and Crips fight to increase their criminal empires. They fight over parks, buildings, and other shit they don't even own."

HEAL THE HOOD

Wanda laughed and said, "The LAPD fights to keep this city safe, and all police departments across the nation fight to keep all cities safe. But is life any better in Crenshaw or any other ghetto? Do you think life was better for the Koreans and the Vietnamese after the US fought for them? There's a reason why there were so many protests against the Vietnam War."

I explained, "Daddy said the most important thing to remember about serving in the Marines is not to become a robot. You don't have to listen to every order your commanding officer dictates. If your instincts tell you your unit is being forced to carry out foul play, don't do it. You may get a dishonorable discharge, but you'll still be true to yourself."

Wanda asked, "Are you as eager to kill as the Bloods and the Crips?"

I explained, "I'm not interested in killing. It's taking down bullies and tyrants that pique my interest."

Wanda asked, "After you're finished with the Marines, will you become a cop?"

I said, "No way. The LAPD has done too much damage to our neighborhood for me to have any faith in them. They can terrorize people without my help."

Chapter Four

Soon, basketball season ended, and baseball and softball season started. Since Dorsey High doesn't have separate softball teams for boys and girls, our softball team is co-ed. Some parents have a problem with that, but mine don't. We have different changing rooms, and we don't physically touch each other like the guys on the wrestling team do. I tried out for the softball team again, and I got the same position I received last year – shortstop.

Softball is played at a faster pace than baseball, which means my position is more demanding. I'm between second and third base; this means that most balls hit by the batter come to me. My martial arts training has made me very agile, and this is a skill all shortstops need. When the ball comes to me, my job is to throw it quickly to the basemen or the catcher to throw-out the batter. With help from my skills, Dorsey High can give the opposing team three outs in no time and end the inning.

We started reading another book for English class titled, *Lord of the Flies*. I already have my own copy, and I've read it several times. It's about a group of British schoolboys who end up stranded on a deserted island. They try to create their own society until they're rescued, but without any grown-ups to discipline them, they soon start killing each other. They're finally rescued at the end of the book, but the damage is done, and the moral is very clear. If you take away the laws of society, it will reveal that humans are just a bunch of savages.

I thought about the lynchings in the South, the assassinations of the twentieth century, the beating of Rodney King, and the murder of Latasha Harlins. Even when there are laws in place, humans act more savage than animals. The Fourteenth Amendment was supposed to give citizenship and equal rights to Black people, and the Fifteenth Amendment was supposed to give Blacks the right to vote. The Fourteenth and Fifteenth Amendments were the second and third Reconstruction Amendments; but the former Confederacy chose not to enforce the Amendments, which meant over a century of more torture for Black people. Then, the Fourteenth and Fifteenth Amendments became null and void when Jim Crow was legalized by the Supreme Court case, *Plessy v. Ferguson*; and Blacks had to take difficult literacy tests in order to vote.

New laws were passed in the 1960s; the Civil Rights Act of 1964, the Voting Rights Act of 1965, and the Fair Housing Act of 1968. But since Rodney King got beaten, Latasha Harlins got killed, a lot of folks in Crenshaw live in substandard housing, and the schools barely have enough money for new books and equipment, it's obvious the Civil Rights Acts ain't doing shit for Black folks today just like how the Reconstruction Amendments didn't do shit for Black folks between 1865 and the 1960s.

In *Lord of the Flies*, the British boys believe that there is a beast on the island, and they have to kill it, but the true beast is inside of them. There are beasts in every human being fighting for control of our nature. Eleanor Roosevelt said, "In each of us there is the ability to be a beast but also an ability to reach for the stars."

The cops who beat Rodney King and Mrs. Du obviously gave into their inner beasts.

Dr. Murray said that the Devil is always trying to turn people away from God. Lucifer tried to overthrow God in Heaven, but he was stopped. He was kicked out of Heaven and banished to Earth. Then, he attempted to corrupt God's creation by tempting Eve to eat the forbidden fruit. Many people believe that the consumption of the forbidden fruit tainted Adam, Eve, and all their descendants, but Adam and Eve were already tainted before they ate the fruit. They willingly chose to disobey God even though He had already done many great things for them, including giving them life and authority over the animals. Dr. Murray said God knew that His creation may be tainted. So, he set up a Plan B, a Plan C, et cetera. God made sure a Holy Book dedicated to His teachings and the history of the Israelites was written. He also sent His only beloved Son to Earth as a human so He could show us the Way. Jesus died on the Cross to save us from sin and to clear our debt with God. Dr. Murray assured us that God is the Master Planner, and humanity is part of His Master Plan. Since God hasn't given up on us, I shouldn't give up on us, either.

On April 4, 1991, I took the SAT test. It's divided into two sections: verbal and math. Since the verbal section covers reading and writing, I knew I would do well on that part. I'm not as good at math as I am in reading and writing, but I got a good score in the PSAT tests the school gave us last year and this year. I also took SAT prep, which is pricey; but my education is the most important thing to my parents. My parents told me to get at least eight hours of sleep the night before, eat a well-balanced breakfast, and – most importantly – to relax.

Daddy said, "The only thing you can do is your best."

Mama said, "We'll always be proud of you, no matter what."

The verbal section was easy for me, and I liked writing the essay because I always have something to say and write about after I finish reading an article or a book. Some of the math was hard, but I believe I did my best.

A few weeks later, I did the ACT. I also did ACT prep this year, which also costs as much as SAT prep. Most kids only take one of the two tests, but the most studious kids, like me and Imani, take both tests. People usually choose one of two higher scores to send to colleges. Some people score higher on the ACT than the SAT and vice versa. The English, reading, and writing sections were easy. The math and science sections were harder, but I did my best.

Over two weeks later, Soon Ja Du sat before a grand jury that would decide whether or not she should be charged with murder. Deputy District Attorney Roxanne Carvajal addressed the grand jury. Ms. Carvajal explained that the current extreme racial tensions between African Americans and Korean Americans led Mrs. Du to murder Latasha. Ms. Carvajal called four witnesses and played the videotape as part of the prosecution's case. Lakeshia Rashion Combs and her little bro, Ismail Ali, both told the grand jury what happened in the store; and Denise Harlins, Latasha's aunt, also testified and identified her niece on the tape. Gerry Johnson, a police detective, also testified. He described the weapon that was used to kill Latasha and explained that she was shot while walking away. After two hours and forty minutes of deliberation, the grand jury indicted Soon Ja Du for murdering Latasha Harlins.

I was mad that it took them so damn long to come to the decision. It was obvious to me, my parents, my grandmother, and my friends – and even Joshua – that Mrs. Du committed murder. Latasha was a Black girl from the ghetto, so they probably assumed that she *had* to be at fault. Grandma said that if this trial had happened in Mississippi before the Civil Rights Movement, there would be no need for a grand jury. White people could kill Blacks and walk away scot-free, and even if the case made it to court, there would still be no justice. A miscarriage of justice in the courtroom is just as bad as a lynching. We call this country the land of the free and the home of the brave, but that is a lie. This land is still full of inequality and cowardly murderers.

I turned seventeen on April 29, 1991. Most guys and girls on my block ask for clothes, CDs, and other expensive stuff, but I asked my family for books, mostly books about Black history. Grandma stayed at our house on Sunday night so she could celebrate my birthday with us. Mama cooked me blueberry pancakes and crispy bacon. Then, Daddy presented two birthday presents to me that both looked like books. I unwrapped the first present; it was a copy of *Coming of Age in Mississippi* by Anne Moody. Then, I unwrapped my second present; it was a copy of *Pauli Murray: The Autobiography of a Black Activist, Feminist, Lawyer, Priest and Poet*.

I exclaimed, "Thank you! These books look great!"

When I walked out of my house, Wanda came from across the street.

She exclaimed, "Happy birthday, girl! You're seventeen and fine as the summertime!"

I laughed and said, "Thanks, Wanda."

Daddy drove us to school, and when he left, Devin came up and said, "Word through the grapevine is that you're seventeen today."

I said, "Yeah, Devin. What's it to you?"

Devin asked, "You got a boyfriend yet?"

I thought about Joshua. I had warmed up to him ever since I

cried in his arms. I had also apologized for ruining his shirt, but he said he didn't mind. After that, we talked before and after class about whatever was on our minds: school, college, music, television shows, movies, et cetera. I still didn't tell him how Koreans treat Black customers in the hood because he might have friends or family who own stores in the hood. Since Joshua is cute, I'm surprised he doesn't already have a girlfriend. Why in the world is he interested in me? I'm a girl from the hood who wants to be an Africanist and a Marine. Maybe he's not interested in my brain, just my body.

I told Devin, "No, I don't have a boyfriend yet."

Devin asked, "Then, am I allowed to give you your birthday kiss?"

He puckered up his lips, and I mashed Anne Moody's autobiography on his lips.

I said, "Until I get a boyfriend, the only man allowed to kiss me is my daddy."

Devin asked, "If you get a boyfriend, will your daddy kill him?"

I laughed and said, "He may put the fear of God in him, but he won't kill him. In my daddy's eyes, no man is good enough for me, but maybe I can make him change his mind."

When we walked to our lockers, Wanda asked, "So, do you have any serious considerations in the boyfriend department?"

I said, "Yes, but I would be considered a traitor to the hood."

Wanda asked, "Why? Is he White?"

I explained, "No, he ain't White, but he ain't Black either."

Wanda said, "Then he must be either Asian or Latino."

I said, "He's Asian."

Wanda said, "Asian guys are supposed to be smart, so that's a good trait."

I said, "Not *all* Asian guys are smart, but this guy has brains. I'll give him that."

Wanda asked, "Is he brave enough to come to Crenshaw?"

I said, "Yeah. He has a Black belt in hapkido like me, and he knows how to fight."

Wanda asked, "Can he beat you in a fight?"

I replied, "Hell no, girl! I'm still the best fighter in that dojang!"

During lunchtime, I read Anne Moody's story. I kept reading it in my spare time and by the next day I got to "Part Two: High School." When Anne Moody was in high school, she heard through the grapevine that Emmett Till was killed in Greenwood, Mississippi. According to the textbooks I've read, Emmett Till was killed in Money, Mississippi, which is near Greenwood in Leflore County. Since Grandma is from Greenwood, I once asked her how she felt when she heard about his death.

Grandma said, "When I heard what happened to poor Emmett, I was mighty glad that I had moved to Los Angeles. Your mama was a year old, and I knew the chances of her being killed before her twenty-first birthday would be higher if we stayed in Greenwood. I cried when I saw Emmett's body in *Jet*. He was unrecognizable. Mamie Till insisted on an open casket so the world could see what they did to her baby boy. Emmett's death raised awareness about lynchings, the Klan, and what a living Hell Mississippi is."

In her autobiography, Anne Moody's employer, Mrs. Burke, told her why Emmett was killed.

> He was killed because he got out of his place with a White woman. A boy from Mississippi would have known better than that. This boy was from Chicago.

HEAL THE HOOD

> Negroes up North have no respect for people. They think they can get away with anything. He just came to Mississippi and put a whole lot of notions in the boys' heads here and stirred up a lot of trouble.

Anne Moody stated,

> Before Emmett Till's murder, I had known the fear of hunger, Hell, and the Devil. But now there was a new fear known to me – the fear of being killed just because I was Black. This was the worst of my fears. I knew once I got food, the fear of starving to death would leave. I was also told that if I were a good girl, I wouldn't have to fear the Devil or Hell. But I didn't know what one had to do or not to do as a Negro not to be killed. Probably just being a Negro period was enough, I thought.

I know that fear. Every person in the hood knows Anne Moody's fear. The KKK, the gangs, the cops, the entire system tries to kill us just for living our lives. Our parents tell us to speak politely to cops, to do what they say, and to show the cops our hands when they stop us. They tell us not to walk into stores owned by Asians, Whites, and other non-Blacks unless we're gonna buy something.

"Don't walk into stores with big purses or jackets with big pockets so that the storeowners don't think you're gonna steal anything."

Some parents also tell their kids to dress like they have some sense. That means no baggy pants, backward caps, or graffiti shirts. I wear baggy overalls, backward caps, and graffiti-print shirts all the time because I want to, but freedom of expression doesn't always apply to Black folks.

Since things were so bad in Mississippi, Grandma left; since things are so bad in the ghetto, a lot of students work hard at school and in sports to get outta here. I work hard at school and martial arts so I can get into the US Naval Academy (USNA). History is a major at the Naval Academy; so, I'm sure Afro-American history is also being studied there. This way I can follow my passion. Plus, all graduates are commissioned as ensigns in the Navy or second lieutenants in the Marines. After graduation I can either start fighting for my country or go to graduate school at another college.

To get into USNA, a candidate must be an American citizen, be between seventeen and twenty-three years of age, not be married, not have any kids, and have a Social Security Number. Since I just turned seventeen, I'm eligible for a spot at USNA. I was born in LA so I'm an American citizen. I asked my parents to help me apply for a card, and now I have a Social Security Number. Unlike a lot of girls and guys in Crenshaw and other hoods, I don't have kids. Not that many teens get married because marriage seems like too big a commitment, especially for boys. I'm still a virgin and planning to stay one. But is Joshua interested in hitting third base with me?

My grades also have to be great. I always get As and A-pluses in English, history, and other humanities subjects. I get A-minuses in math and science, but I'm hoping my A-minuses won't scare away the USNA. My SAT results were mailed to our house a few weeks after I did both tests. When I got my SAT results, I couldn't believe my eyes; I got a perfect score on the verbal part of the SAT! That's right, I got an 800! My math score was 720 which means my combined score is 1520 out of 1600! Mama and Daddy screamed with delight when they saw my score.

Daddy said, "I only got a ten fifty on my SAT."

Mama said, "I never got to take the real SAT, just the practice test. But I managed to score a twelve eighty-five."

I said, "Scores in the fifteen hundreds range are enough to impress the Ivy League so it should be enough to impress the Naval Academy. A perfect score on the verbal section is also a major bonus."

My ACT results were mailed, a few weeks later, to Dorsey High. I got a score of thirty-five on the English section, a score of thirty-three on the math section, a score of thirty-six on the reading section, a score of thirty-two on the science section, and a score of thirty-five on the optional writing test. That means my total score on my ACT is thirty-four out of thirty-six! I screamed with delight!

Since I scored so well on the SAT and ACT, Mama and Daddy wanted me to apply to other colleges besides the USNA.

Mama explained, "You need a back-up plan just in case the Naval Academy doesn't accept you. Now, your father and I have a lot of faith in you so we're rooting for your dream school, but you need a Plan B, a Plan C, a Plan D, et cetera."

Daddy said, "You know, you could always go to school at UCLA or USC. That way your daddy can keep an eye on you."

I laughed and said, "Daddy, the best part of college is gaining independence. The best way to do that is to go to a school far from Los Angeles or, even better, far from the state of California."

So, I went to the guidance counselor's office to look up Africana programs at other colleges. I'll be a senior next year; so, I have a lot of thinking to do. There are plenty of my classmates who won't have to do much thinking since their grades, SAT scores, and ACT scores are abysmal.

After school, Devin told me, "I don't need this shit. There are plenty of other ways for a Black man to make money without going to school."

I asked, "What are you gonna do? Sell drugs? Sing and dance?"

Devin said, "Your cousin said he could hook me up with the Bloods. Your uncle is always riding that fine Pontiac. Me, I wanna a Mustang."

I told him, "Getting work with my uncle is only going to lead to two outcomes: a jail cell or a casket. Which do you prefer?"

Devin said, "Your uncle was sent to jail and he came home just fine, a few years later."

I said, "Those three years he spent in San Quentin caused him to miss out on what was going on in the real world. He missed three years of Malik's life, and his wife cheated on him with other men. How many years of your life do you wanna lose?"

Devin said, "That was your uncle. I'm gonna be slicker."

I just shook my head. One of the reasons Blacks in the hood are fucked-up is because people keep doing the same shit, hoping it will give them better results than the others who tried it before them. Blacks join gangs, thinking they'll have better luck hustling people and be able to reap the best out of life; but gangbanging only leads to disappointment, no matter how much money you make. Girls let their boyfriends fuck them, figuring that condoms or pills will stop them from getting pregnant; but even with birth control, girls still end up having babies. Then, the girls hope the baby daddies won't abandon them, get arrested, or get killed; but, one of these three things usually happens.

Mrs. Brooks' boyfriend, Tyrell Brooks, got her pregnant when she was sixteen. When her mama found out she was pregnant, she kicked her out. Mrs. Brooks lived with Tyrell at his apartment, and he was able to provide for her because he was a Blood. When Andre was born, his daddy helped take care of him until he got arrested and sent to jail. Then, when he was released, he got Mrs. Brooks pregnant again, and Wanda was born. Mrs. Brooks was able to secure a job at the Creole & Cajun Kitchen and provide for herself and her kids when her man got arrested. Tyrell kept getting into and out of trouble, and Mrs. Brooks kept telling him to leave the Bloods and get a real job, but the money he made gangbanging was too good to pass up. His luck ran out when some cops shot and killed him. Tyrell Brooks believed being a gangster was the only viable lifestyle for him 'cause he believed he was a Black guy from the hood who was destined to become nothing more than a hood rat. But Mrs. Brooks told her kids that she wasn't gonna let them travel down the same dead-end road as their daddy. She told Andre and Wanda that if they even thought about dropping out of school, she would kick them out of her house.

Mama and Daddy have never directly said they will kick me out if I drop out of school. They both work hard to make sure I don't have to drop out to help support the family, but I know me getting my high school diploma will be a victory for Mama, Daddy, and Grandma, not just me.

Frederick Douglass said, "Some know the value of education by having it. I know it's value by not having it."

During the era of slavery, it was against the law for a slave to read and write. Kunta Kinte knew White masters wanted their slaves to remain ignorant. The less a slave knew, the less trouble they made. An uneducated slave couldn't read signs or a map nor could they carry out plans to overthrow their masters. The same thing applies to the present day. Uneducated Blacks can't leave the ghetto because they don't have the skills to get better-paying jobs and, therefore, don't have enough money to buy houses in rich neighborhoods. The authorities want us to stay in this fucked-up state. If we make it out of the ghetto, it would be proof that that we aren't just African monkeys, but human beings with true potential.

Mr. Ngozi said that when the British colonized Nigeria, they set up schools to educate the Nigerians. I asked why the Brits would do that since they just wanted Nigerians to gather palm oil, coal, gold, tin, cocoa, groundnuts, and rubber for them, just like how White Americans just wanted African Americans to pick cotton, chop sugarcane, harvest rice, and grow other cash crops for them. Mr. Ngozi explained that not all Brits saw the Nigerians as brainless monkeys. Some Brits saw their true potential and decided to let them learn, and the Nigerians who did well enough at the colonial schools could study in the UK. Apparently, this practice continues to this day.

When slaves made it to freedom in the North and Canada, friendly Whites helped them build schools and educated them because they knew education is something that belongs to all races. During Reconstruction, kind Whites, along with free Blacks, helped build schools, churches, and other places so that the emancipated slaves could enjoy their newfound freedom.

There are some Blacks who believe that school is a trick, something they don't need to succeed. Another way to become successful is start your own business. Madam C.J. Walker and Alonzo Herndon were uneducated, but they created multi-million-dollar businesses during the Jim Crow era. Charles Clinton Spaulding was also a successful businessman and he even managed to get a high school diploma when he was twenty-three. But a lot of Blacks in the hood aren't interested in legit businesses. I think impatience is their reason. They see thieves, drug dealers, and pimps make lots of money, really fast, and get swept into the criminal lifestyle. Most people wanna become rich overnight but the only way that can happen is if they play the lottery. A *lotta* people in the hood play the lottery, but they never win.

I don't hold a lotta importance on money because I believe it makes people selfish and shallow.

Bob Marley said, "The greatness of a man is not in how much wealth he acquires, but in his integrity and his ability to affect those positively around him."

That means people like Bob Marley, Dr. King, Malcolm X, Frederick Douglass, Harriet Tubman, Nelson Mandela, et cetera, are among the wealthiest people in human history because of the countless people they have influenced and continue to influence.

Chapter Five

The most exciting event in the month of May was Whitney Houston's concert at the Forum. The Forum is an indoor arena located in Uncle Alonzo's, Auntie Kalisha's, and Malik's hood, Inglewood. A lotta concerts are held at the Forum, so I've been there plenty of times. Tickets went on sale a week before the scheduled show. Wanda and I camped out at the Forum overnight because we know that tickets for a Whitney Houston concert sell out faster than ice cream cones during a heat wave. We also bought a ticket for Imani; we knew she would be self-conscious about not being able to afford a ticket.

When Wanda and I presented the ticket to Imani, she said, "This is *sooooo* wonderful! But I can't accept this, I'm sure it cost too much money."

I said, "Girl, there ain't no such thing as too much money when you're spending it on people you love."

Wanda said, "The last show Whitney did at the Forum was back in '87. Do you wanna wait another four years before you can hear the Voice live in concert?"

I said, "There isn't a lot of magic in this world, but a concert by a gifted singer is always able to generate it. Life on these mean streets is tough, and a little magic helps us get by."

Imani smiled and said, "I better say yes before you nag me even more!"

When we heard Whitney sing live that May, it gave us chills! Her vocal range is incredible! She started the concert with "I Wanna Dance With Somebody (Who Loves Me)," one of my favorite songs of all time!

> *Clock strikes upon the hour*
> *And the sun begins to fade*
> *Still enough time to figure out*
> *How to chase my blues away*
> *I've done alright up to now*
> *It's the light of day that shows me how*
> *And when the night falls, loneliness calls*
>
> *Oh, I wanna dance with somebody*
> *I wanna feel the heat with somebody*
> *Yeah, I wanna dance with somebody*
> *With somebody who loves me*
> *Oh, I wanna dance with somebody*
> *I wanna feel the heat with somebody*
> *Yeah, I wanna dance with somebody*
> *With somebody who loves me*

She sang her other hits as well: "So Emotional", "I'm Saving All My Love For You", et cetera. But when she sang her latest hit "I'm Your Baby Tonight", I was sure the endless screaming would bring the roof down!

> *From the moment I saw you, I went outta my mind*
> *I never believed in love at first sight*
> *But you got a magic, boy, that I just can't explain*

Well, you got a, you got a way that you make me feel
I can do, I can do anything for you, baby

I'll be down for you, baby
Lay all my cards out tonight
Just call on me, baby
I'll be there in a hurry
It's your move, so baby, baby decide

Whatever you want from me
I'm givin' you everything
I'm your baby tonight
You've given me ecstasy
You are my fantasy
I'm your baby tonight

The way guys were screaming, you knew they wanted to *marry* Whitney! The way the girls were screaming, you knew we wanted to *be* Whitney! She has an angelic voice and the face and body of a model. But Mama, Daddy, and Grandma all told me to be happy with the way I look and to not be obsessed with changing my body. Like I said before, I'm a good-looking girl; so, I don't have low self-esteem about my appearance.

Soon, June came, and it was the end of the school year. Everyone starts acting crazy when the school year ends, especially the seniors. They pull pranks on teachers, spray paint peoples' cars, initiate final fights, et cetera. Some seniors talk about the colleges they'll be going to in the fall, and other seniors talk about the kinds of jobs they can get in LA – most will become janitors, postmen, waiters, mechanics, bus drivers, or baggage handlers. For seniors who will join the blue-collar class, senior year is the highlight of their lives.

Some seniors have decided to join the US Armed Forces, so their biggest decision is whether to join the Army, the Navy, the Air Force, the Coast Guard, or the Marine Corps. The Army and the Navy are the most popular branches of the Armed Forces. I read in a book in the school library that the US Marine Corps is the smallest US military service, but I think the Marines have a bum rap. They can fight in the sea, on land, or the sky, and they have special units, such as the Force Reconnaissance. Daddy and Grandpa Gabriel didn't make it into the special units, but I'm hoping I'll be the first Parker to become a Force Recon Marine.

Andre has also decided what college he wants to go to. Several colleges offered him scholarships, but he decided to go to Texas Southern University, an HBCU in Houston. Andre, lots of other folks, and myself, watch *A Different World* almost religiously. Life at Hillman looks so cool on the show that Andre figured that life at an HBCU would be the best college experience. I figured out that with all the racial tension gripping LA, the best way for Blacks to survive is to stick together. An old cliché states, "There's safety in numbers."

At HBCUs, Black people can be themselves and not be punished for it. At HBCUs, serious issues, such as racism, urban blight, and incompetent law enforcement can be discussed in the presence of other people who understand the struggle.

I helped Mr. Ngozi clean up some classrooms. We stacked chairs and pushed the desks to one side so that the school janitors could properly clean the floors, windows, and chalkboards.

Mr. Ngozi took some books off the shelves and said, "Principal Edwards has tried to convince the district superintendent and the

Los Angeles Unified School District to give us more money to buy new supplies. But our graduation rate is still lower than some other schools in the LAUSD, and they all don't think it's right to 'reward students and staff for mediocre work.'" Mr. Ngozi made air quotes when he said that, showing that he thinks it's a ridiculous and insulting statement.

I replied, "I suppose that means there aren't any summer bonuses for the staff?"

Mr. Ngozi said, "No. But, thank God my relatives all chip in when we decide to travel somewhere. There are plenty of teachers here who have never traveled outside the USA. I feel fortunate but also guilty because I have easy access to something few other people do."

I asked Mr. Ngozi, "Are your relatives visiting LA again or are you visiting them?"

Last year, Mr. Ngozi's brothers, sisters-in-law, nieces, nephews, and cousins visited him in LA. They all stayed at hotels even though Mr. Ngozi told them there was room at his house. I'm sure they were afraid they may get shot or robbed if they stayed in South Central.

Mr. Ngozi replied, "I'll be visiting my cousins in Toronto."

I said, "Okay. Is there cool stuff in Toronto besides the CN Tower?"

Mr. Ngozi said, "Of course there is. There's the Toronto Zoo, the Hockey Hall of Fame, the Royal Ontario Museum. There are also other attractions outside of Toronto like Niagara Falls, Marineland, African Lion Safari, and Wonderland. There are also national parks across Canada. Yes, Canada is a beautiful country."

I asked, "Is it always cold in Canada?"

Mr. Ngozi said, "Of course not. In the southern parts of the country, it gets very warm in the spring and summer. The province of

Ontario gets very hot between the months of May and September."

I asked, "Do all Canadians love hockey and maple syrup?"

Mr. Ngozi said, "Not all Canadians. My brother prefers soccer to hockey, but his kids watch the NHL religiously. They also prefer Aunt Jemima to maple syrup, but you'll find plenty of maple syrup products in Canadian stores. They sell maple candy, maple cookies, and even maple doughnuts."

I asked, "Any other interesting things about Canada?"

He said, "Yes. It's more progressive than the USA. Toronto is a very multicultural city, and Canada has a diverse population."

I said, "So does the USA."

Mr. Ngozi explained, "Americans believe in assimilation not diversity. When I first came here, people had a problem with my Igbo language and my Igbo clothing. Now, I mostly wear Western clothes and only speak Igbo when I'm among my fellow tribesmen. Other immigrant groups are also forced not to practice their traditions in public because the American way is considered superior. But in Toronto, a person has the feeling they're visiting many countries instead of just one. My brother's kids go to school with Blacks, Whites, Asians, and Latinos. Can you imagine going to school with other students who aren't Black?"

I said, "If I didn't live in the hood, yeah. But in a rich neighborhood I would still stick out since there are only a handful of rich Blacks in rich White neighborhoods."

Mr. Ngozi said, "Some Blacks do stick out in some parts of Canada, and they can be harassed by White Canadians."

I asked, "What else makes Canada more progressive than the USA?"

Mr. Ngozi replied, "I believe the Canadian healthcare system is better than the American healthcare system."

I said, "I've heard that Canada's healthcare system is free. That makes *no* sense. How would doctors make a living?"

Mr. Ngozi explained, "Healthcare in Canada is mostly paid for by taxation. That means medical bills are lower there than in the US, but the people are required to pay for dental care, eye care, and prescription medication by themselves. There are also many free clinics in Canada."

The Crenshaw Community Health Center is where most people in the hood go if they're sick, injured, need shots, or have a toothache. The health bills there ain't bad, but the Health Center can't deal with real emergencies, such as heart attacks and drug overdoses. The closest hospital is Dignity Health – California Hospital Medical Center – and the bills there are no joke. People in the hood have to choose between dying from a disease or becoming bankrupt. Since my dad is a veteran, the US Department of Veterans Affairs (VA) help cover his medical bills, but the VA cover only his medical bills, not my mom's or mine. My parents also have health insurance, but it's not enough to cover Dignity Health's bills. That's why my family and I work hard to keep in good health. We're not gonna let doctors milk us for every penny we have.

When you're a kid, adults are always asking what you'll be when you grow up. Some kids say doctor, teacher, firefighter, and other predictable stuff. Imani wants to be a pediatrician because if kids in the ghetto die from diseases and injuries, there would be no hope for the future, but the one thing I have never wanted to be is a doctor. I'm not afraid of blood or internal organs; if I'm gonna be a Marine, then I'll be seeing plenty of blood and organs when I shoot people. I don't wanna be a doctor because I think it's insane to charge sick and injured people money. Why do so many people like to torture the poor?

Mr. Ngozi continued, "Canada also has strict gun control laws. Mostly cops, soldiers, and other people whose professions require it are permitted to own guns. You also need to acquire a firearms acquisition certificate or FAC for short. Background checks are also run to see if a person has a criminal record. If a Canadian has been incarcerated for severe crimes, then they aren't allowed to own a gun as that would just cause more senseless violence."

I said, "That sounds great. The problem with the hood is so many people are packing heat. The Bloods and the Crips don't deserve guns 'cause they're psychos."

Mr. Ngozi said, "Exactly. Thanks to the gun control laws, Canada is very peaceful. The murder rates and crime rates are lower than the USA's, but it still has crime."

I asked him, "Are all cops Mounties?"

He said, "No, the police dress similarly to American cops."

I asked, "Are they better than the LAPD?"

He asked, "What do you mean?"

I asked, "Does the Toronto Police Department stop folks for being Black and shoot people for being Black?"

Mr. Ngozi sighed, ran his right hand through his hair, and explained, "Police corruption and police brutality are problems in many countries, not just the US. In 1988, the Toronto Police Service gained scrutiny for the death of a forty-four-year-old Black schizophrenic named Lester Donaldson. He was armed with a small paring knife when five Toronto police officers confronted him at his rooming house on August ninth, nineteen-eighty-eight. Lester was shot by one of the officers and died at Toronto Western Hospital. Three days after his death, the Black Action Defense Committee was formed. They insisted that race played an important part in Lester Donaldson's death. Last year, Toronto police officer David Deviney was charged with manslaughter in connection with the killing, but he was acquitted."

I said, "Figures."

Mr. Ngozi said, "Other African Canadians have suffered the same or similar fates. Michael Wade Lawson, a seventeen-year-old Black boy, was shot and killed by Peel Regional Police officers in Mississauga, a few months after Lester Donaldson was killed. Andrew Evans a.k.a. Buddy was killed by a Toronto police officer at a nightclub on King Street West in nineteen-seventy-eight, but the cop wasn't found guilty of any wrongdoing. Albert Johnson was shot and killed by two Toronto police officers in his own apartment, a year later, but the officers who killed him were also acquitted. Sixteen-year-old Marlon Neal was shot and critically injured by a Toronto police officer last year because the emergency brake he was holding was mistaken for a gun.

Lester Donaldson's death helped raise awareness about racism in Canada. The Canadians want us to believe that they're more progressive than the USA, but they still suffer from many of the same sins."

I asked, "What about England? How's life for Black folks there?"

Mr. Ngozi said, "In nineteen-eighty-one and nineteen-eighty-five, a London neighborhood called Brixton suffered from riots. The nineteen-eighty-one riots occurred because Brixton residents thought the Metropolitan Police Service brutalized a Black youth named Michael Bailey. On Friday April tenth, a police constable was trying to get Michael medical help because he had a stab wound, but Brixton residents thought the cop was harassing and arresting Michael. Large groups of Black youths surrounded the cops and threw bottles, rocks, and other junk at the cops. This led to the Met increasing police patrols in the neighborhood. The next day, on

HEAL THE HOOD

Saturday, April eleventh, the Met arrested a Black taxi driver and that resulted in the worst day of the rioting. The rioters were mostly young Black men, but some young Whites joined them. There were lootings, fires, and destruction of cars and property. Sunday, April twelfth, was the last day of the rioting and attacks on the Met were less intense. During the Brixton Riots, over seven thousand cops had to quell the violence and two hundred and eighty-two people were arrested, mostly Black people.

In nineteen-eighty-five, a Black woman named Dorothy Groce a.k.a. Cherry was shot by the MPS because they were seeking her son, Michael Groce, in relation to a crime. Word of the shooting spread throughout Brixton and a group gathered outside the Groce home. They chanted that the cops were murderers and demanded disciplinary action against the police officers involved. The hostility between the Black crowd and the White police force led to street battles and the skirmishes escalated into a riot that lasted two days. During those two days, photojournalist David Hodge died, while forty-three civilians and ten police officers were hurt. One building was destroyed, fifty-five cars were burned out, and fifty-eight burglaries were committed, but the Met say the total number of crimes committed was one hundred and thirty-seven."

I said, "Shit."

Mr. Ngozi said, "Language, Hatima."

I said, "Sorry, Mister Ngozi. Did Missus Groce die?"

Mr. Ngozi explained, "No, but she's paralyzed from the chest down. She was in the hospital for two years and gets around in a wheelchair. The Met officer who shot her, Inspector Douglas Lovelock, was cleared of all criminal charges in January nineteen-eighty-seven and was reinstated into the Met."

I yelled in frustration, "It's messed-up that what happened to

Rodney King, Latasha Harlins, Bobby Hutton, and so many other Black Americans is happening in other parts of the world! Sometimes I wonder whether Malcolm X was right when he said all Whites are devils."

Mr. Ngozi said, "Malcolm X changed his mind about the White devil theory when he made the pilgrimage to Mecca. There, many Whites treated him as a brother and a human being. You don't think Blacks are capable of devilry as well?"

I thought about Uncle Alonzo and said, "Okay, okay, you have a point. But how do we stop this?"

Mr. Ngozi said, "Familiarizing yourself with Black history across the diaspora is a great place to start. You have an intuitive mind. Things that seem different and separate to other people are actually the same and connected to you."

I asked him, "Do you still enjoy visiting London after all the riots that went down?"

He said, "Of course! London is one of my favorite cities in the world! It gave me a great education, and it gave my brother a home. I hope one day you'll be able to see Toronto, London, and the rest of the world."

Things got hotter in the ghetto, and I'm not talking about the weather. On the fourth day of June, another Korean shot another Black to death in a store in South Central. The story is that Lee Arthur Mitchell, a forty-two-year-old man, entered Chung's Liquor Market on Western Avenue and attempted to use jewelry to pay for a wine cooler. Tae Sam Park is the owner of the store. So, who is Mr. Chung if Mr. Park owns the store? Maybe Mr. Chung founded the store, died, and left the store to Mr. Park in his will. Mr. Park's wife didn't like the jewelry, and this made Lee Arthur mad. Lee Arthur made a motion inside his pocket, faked a movement with a gun, and said he would take the cooler, and Mr. Park shot him dead. The cops supported Mr. Park's claim that Lee Arthur pretended to be armed, and District Attorney Ira Reiner announced on the news that Mr. Park wouldn't be prosecuted.

I couldn't believe it when I heard it. Mr. Park obviously doesn't know anything about Black people. If Lee Arthur was really planning on robbing the liquor store, he would have worn a mask and made it quite clear that he was carrying a real gun. Real criminals don't make idle threats, they make good on hard action. Besides, if Lee Arthur was really carrying a gun in his pocket, Mr. Park should have been able to tell. Gun bulges look different from other kinds of bulges. Plus, not all guns fit in pockets; so, most thugs stick guns into their pants, along the waist. They also wear baggy shirts in order to hide the bulge. People seem to think a Black person with a gun is invincible.

Master Shin taught all his students how to disarm someone holding a gun. He told us only to use this move if we are a hundred percent sure we can disarm the person without getting shot or if we are a hundred percent sure the gun is a fake. I think the Canadians have the right idea. Since it's highly unlikely that any person who is not in law enforcement can get a gun, that means Canadian cops' fear of Blacks, Latinos, and other folks in the ghetto getting guns should be lower than it is here in the USA. If only cops can carry guns, their fear of folks in South Central would also decrease; but I figure that the Bloods and the Crips could still get their hands on guns via the black market, which means the LAPD would still be cowardly fools when patrolling South Central. Maybe we should just get rid of all guns.

In fantasy worlds, such as Narnia and the Redwall universe, there is no technology, which means no guns. Perhaps C.S. Lewis,

Brian Jacques, and other fantasy authors believe that technology causes more harm than good; or maybe the medieval era was better for humanity. Personally, I believe that people should take martial arts lessons to defend themselves; Master Shin also gives us mental and spiritual training to become well-rounded human beings. I doubt the LAPD is very spiritual.

If Al Capone and Bruce Lee faced each other in a fight, who would win? My guess will always be Bruce Lee.

Reverend Edgar E. Boyd, who preaches at Bethel AME Church on South Western Avenue, set up a boycott of Chung's Liquor Market. Denise Harlins, Latasha's aunt, took part in the protests. That also inspired me to take action. I gathered all the kids and teens at the rec center and told them my idea.

Wanda said, "You want us to boycott Lee's Gas Station and Convenience Store?"

I said, "Yes. Mister Lee is just as bad as Missus Du, Mister Park, and the other Korean shopkeepers. He eyes us whenever we buy gas and walk into his store, thinking we're gonna steal something. And the grapevine says he just purchased a Glock. That means the next time a Black person walks into his store, they'll most likely leave on a gurney."

Andre said, "I think it's a great idea. He'll lose money and won't be able to keep his store open. Then, we'll walk in and give him our demands."

Imani said, "We'll say, 'Mister Lee, if you want Black people to continue shopping at this store, these are the conditions: You will treat us like human beings, not criminals. You won't give us the evil eye nor have any of your Korean boys follow us while we walk through your store. You will hire Blacks to help you run your gas station and store, Blacks who can tell you the difference between good people and hardened criminals. You will also get rid of your Glock because guns just lead to more trouble. If you cannot follow these simple conditions, then you can sell your store and leave South Central.'"

Everyone applauded and I said, "Imani, write that down into a contract or something. It's just the thing we need to show Mister Lee after a month or so that we mean business." Wanda, Andre, Imani, and I went to see Dr. Murray during the week, before church starts on Sunday. He's always welcoming to all people who want to talk to him. We met him in his office. Dr. Murray has pictures of his family on his desk and pictures of Rev. Richard Allen, Rev. Vernon Johns, Dr. King, Rev. Jesse Jackson, and Rev. Al Sharpton on his walls. His degrees are also posted high on the wall behind his desk. Dr. Murray has a bachelor's degree in history from Florida A&M University and a Ph.D. in religion from the Claremont School of Theology. Dr. Murray is part of the historians' club, and I'll be joining after I graduate from college. We also saw a mother carrying a baby and a Crip gangster sitting on the chairs in front of Dr. Murray's desk. Dr. Murray has this habit of letting one meeting flow into the next so people often sit through hours of "private sessions."

The mother looked at her watch and said, "I'm gonna be late for work! Bye, Doc, I'll try to schedule another meeting with you!"

Dr. Murray said, "Missus Clark, feel free to come down here anytime."

The Crip gangster said, "I better run, too. Don't want the fellows to come looking for me."

Dr. Murray said, "Ernie, if you want to get out of the Crips, I can try and help."

Wanda scoffed and said, "You can't just *leave* the Crips. Joining a gang is a lifetime contract. Our dad was a Blood, and he remained one until the day he died."

Andre said, "The best way to get outta the life is to get outta the city."

Dr. Murray said, "Running away doesn't solve your problems."

Ernie said, "Neither does getting killed for doing stupid stuff."

Then, he left.

Dr. Murray asked the four of us, "What's this wonderful idea you have?"

We sat down on the chairs and told him about our boycott idea.

Dr. Murray said, "I think that's a wonderful idea! This reminds me of the Housewives' Leagues from back in the thirties and forties."

Andre asked, "Are you that old, Doctor Murray?"

Dr. Murray laughed and replied, "I'm old but spry. The Housewives' League was before my time. It was founded in nineteen-thirty in Detroit, Michigan. Fannie Peck was the founder, and she told the Blacks of Michigan to patronize Black-owned businesses because making sure Blacks only bought items from Black businesses would ensure that these businesses wouldn't go bankrupt during the Great Depression. As the name suggests, housewives and women participated in the league. They even boycotted stores that wouldn't hire Black workers or treat them with respect. The ladies told Black people, 'Don't shop where you can't work.' The Housewives' League soon had chapters nationwide. They disbanded in the nineteen-sixties thanks to the achievements of the Civil Rights Movement, but their message can still be used today."

I said, "Yeah. We'll make a list of all the businesses in South Central that don't hire Blacks or treat us with respect."

Andre said, "We can print them on flyers and distribute them in church."

HEAL THE HOOD

Imani said, "Then, people will know which shops to avoid."

Wanda gave Dr. Murray a lined piece of paper with store names on it.

She said, "These are all the businesses that Black kids at the rec center say are owned by racist Koreans. There might be more."

Dr. Murray took the list and said, "I'll contact other members of the church and ask them if there are other stores where our people are treated with disrespect."

In church on Sunday, Dr. Murray had the deacons and ushers distribute pamphlets to the congregation. The pamphlets were printed on red, black, green, and yellow paper. Red, black, and green are the colors of the Pan-African flag, but yellow is also considered a Pan-African color since Ghana used yellow in its flag after it declared independence from Great Britain. Red, black, green, and yellow are on several other African flags and Caribbean flags. I suppose it's meant to create solidarity between Black people around the world. When I saw all the names of the stores that disrespect Black people, I couldn't believe how high the number was. I couldn't believe how many people despise Blacks; but now that I have this list, I know which stores to avoid.

Blacks stopped shopping at Mr. Lee's and got their gas, candy, and soda from other places. Mr. Lee's store was practically empty every single day. I bet he had planned on making a lot of money during the summer, but those plans were now dashed. Devin said that when Mr. Lee was locking up, he grumbled that he would probably sell his store since none of the Crenshaw residents were shopping there anymore. He also grumbled that he hated our neighborhood and was happy to have an excuse to leave.

Some people stopped getting liquor at Mr. Hwang's store, but the serious winos are still chug-a-lugging his supply. The chances of Mr. Hwang going bankrupt are pretty slim.

Dr. King said, "The ultimate measure of a man is not where he stands in moments of comfort and convenience, but where he stands in times of challenge and controversy."

The challenges and controversies revolving around the beating of Rodney King and the deaths of Latasha Harlins and Lee Arthur Mitchell and so many others are really testing Crenshaw and every hood in South Central and maybe the nation, but the boycott of the Korean stores is definitely the ultimate measure for us. Since we decided to boycott the stores just like the Blacks of Montgomery, Alabama, boycotted buses, I am sure Dr. King, Rosa Parks, and other civil rights leaders would be pleased.

Rosa Parks said, "To bring about change, you must not be afraid to take the first step. We will fail when we fail to try."

My friends and I decided to take the first step in boycotting the Korean stores, and it has led to many more steps to show the Koreans we mean business. If we never bothered to try boycotting the stores, then the Koreans would have already won.

Malcolm X said, "If you don't stand for something, you'll fall for anything."

We all had to take a stand against the Koreans' racism, since we had been accepting it since the 1960s. But when you fall, you can choose whether or not to get back up. This boycott was our way of getting back up.

Malcolm X also said, "Be peaceful, be courteous, obey the law, respect everyone; but if someone puts his hand on you, send him to the cemetery."

Some Blacks, including me, were kind, respectful, courteous, and peaceful to Korean shopkeepers, but the Koreans kept disrespecting all of us because of the actions of gangsters. They took it too far when they murdered Latasha and Lee Arthur, but I don't want to take a Korean sword from the dojang and decapitate Mrs. Du or Mr. Park no matter how sweet that sounds. Truth be told, if I did murder Mrs. Du or Mr. Park, it wouldn't bring the people they've murdered back to life; and if I murder Mr. Lee, it would just prove him right about Blacks and lead to many other Koreans following his bigoted path. I don't want to send Mr. Lee to the cemetery but I would get plenty of satisfaction by sending his store to the cemetery. People haven't been resurrected since Biblical times, but Mr. Lee's store could be resurrected. It could be transformed into a friendly place where anyone can get gas and candy without it being poisoned by racism.

chapter six

Summertime means sleeping in and watching television all day for most folks. It's like what the chorus of DJ Jazzy Jeff and the Fresh Prince's new rap song, "Summertime," states:

> *Summer summer summertime*
> *Time to sit back and unwind*
> *Summer summer summertime*
> *Time to sit back and unwind*
> *Summer summer summertime*
> *Time to sit back and unwind*

For me, summertime means more time at the dojang, which means more green in my pocket. During the summer, I work at the dojang during the week, and I relax on the weekends. In the summer of 1991, I spent more time with Joshua. We visited the Santa Monica Pier, the LA Zoo, Disneyland, the beach, et cetera; but our first date was at the movies because I wanted to check out Spike Lee's latest movie, *Jungle Fever*. The soundtrack was released a month ago in May and all the songs except one were written by Stevie Wonder. The titular song, "Jungle Fever", is about an interracial relationship between a Black man and a White woman. Stevie Wonder has been blind since the day he was born so he doesn't know the difference between Black,

HEAL THE HOOD

White, Red, Brown, or Yellow people; but I can totally identify with the song's lyrics since I'm dating a Yellow boy.

> *She can't love me, I can't love her*
> *'Cause they say we're the wrong color*
> *Staring, gloating, laughing, looking*
> *Like we've done something wrong*
> *Because we show love strong, get real, come on*
> *Calling us names too bad to mention*
> *But we pay them no attention*
> *For color blind are inner feelings*
> *If we feel happiness*
> *And know our love's the best, forget their mess*
>
> *I've got jungle fever, she's got jungle fever*
> *We've got jungle fever, we're in love*
> *She's gone Black-boy crazy, I've gone White-girl hazy*
> *Ain't no thinking maybe, we're in love*
> *She's got jungle fever, I've got jungle fever*
> *We've got jungle fever, we're in love*
> *I've gone White-girl crazy, she's gone Black-boy hazy*
> *We're each others baby, we're in love*
>
> *Everyone's created equal*
> *Hell with all you ignorant people*
> *Trying to stereotype us*
> *You really ought to quit*
> *'Cause you don't know jack, you make us sick*
> *Get off my jock, you're trying to ride me*
> *Because I got my girl beside me*

You'll only make yourself look stupid
I love you're trying to dis
'Cause we've got happiness, I bet you're pissed

I've got jungle fever, she's got jungle fever
We've got jungle fever, we're in love
She's gone Black-boy crazy, I've gone White-girl hazy
Ain't no thinking maybe, we're in love
She's got jungle fever, I've got jungle fever
We've got jungle fever, we're in love
I've gone White-girl crazy, she's gone Black-boy hazy
We're each others baby, we're in love

I took a bus to Koreatown and Joshua picked me up in his cream-colored 1978 Cadillac Eldorado. I usually watch movies at Cinemark Baldwin Halls, which is just a twenty-minute walk away from my house; but I didn't want to advertise to the hood that I'm dating a Korean. Seeing a movie in Koreatown is still a bad idea since the Koreans already give me and Joshua dirty looks when they see us together. So, we decided to catch a show at the Paramount Theater. Joshua said that he's been there before, and that it's very luxurious.

I asked him, "Where'd you get this car?"

Joshua explained, "My dad is friends with a man who owns five car dealerships in LA County, including a used-car dealership. He sold this car to my dad at a discounted rate."

As Joshua drove, I asked him, "What does your father do for a living?"

Joshua explained, "He owns a nightclub in Koreatown and a grocery store in Watts. Both businesses are great cash cows."

I asked, "What about your mom?"

Joshua said, "She was a saleswoman at a clothing store, but she died from a car crash when I was eight. The driver that hit her car was drunk."

I said, "I'm sorry. I can't imagine not having a mom. My dad and uncle grew up without a mom as well."

Joshua said, "Really? That's something I have in common with them."

I asked, "Do you love cars?"

Joshua said, "Of course."

I said, "That's another thing you and my dad have in common."

When the movie started, we saw the Universal logo circling the Earth, and a picture of a Black guy was shown. I immediately recognized him. His picture had been shown several times on the news last year and the year before that. Then a caption said, "In memory of Yusuf K. Hawkins March 19, 1973 – August 23, 1989."

Yusuf Hawkins was a sixteen-year-old Black teenager from Brooklyn. On the night of August 23, 1989, he traveled to Bensonhurst with three of his friends because they were interested in a used 1982 Pontiac that was for sale. Unbeknownst to them, a group of Italian Americans were lying in wait for African American and Latino guys whom they believed were dating a neighborhood girl. The girl had invited African American and Latino guests to her eighteenth birthday party, but either scenario wasn't okay with the racist White boys because they didn't want any non-White intruders in their community. So, Yusuf and his friends walked into an ambush. It was believed there were between ten to thirty Italian boys and at least seven wielded baseball bats. Yusuf was shot in the chest twice, one bullet went through his heart, and he died. The NYPD investigated the situation and stated that Yusuf was not involved with any of the girls in the neighborhood.

Yusuf's death was the third killing of a Black guy by White mobs in New York during the 1980s. Willie Turks was killed on June 22, 1982 in Brooklyn and Michael Griffith was killed on December 20, 1986 in Queens. Obviously, the news showed lots of protests by the Blacks of New York in the wake of Yusuf's death. Rev. Al Sharpton led the protests; Al Sharpton is a famous preacher like Dr. King, Rev. Jesse Jackson, and Dr. Murray.

Joseph Fama, the guy who fired the gun and killed Yusuf, was convicted on the charge of second-degree murder on May 17, 1990. The next day, Keith Mondello was acquitted of murder and manslaughter charges and convicted of twelve lesser charges, including rioting, menacing, discrimination, unlawful imprisonment, and criminal possession of a weapon.

Some other members of their gang were also tried by the courts. In August 1990, John Vento was convicted of unlawful imprisonment and received a sentence of two to eight years. Five months ago, on January 11, 1991, Joseph Serano was convicted on the charge of unlawfully possessing a weapon and sentenced to three hundred hours of community service.

Since Keith Mondello was acquitted for murder and manslaughter and Joseph Serano received a light sentence, the Blacks of New York continued to protest. They held protests in Bensonhurst, the scene of the crime. Shortly before a planned march on January 11, 1991, Rev. Sharpton was stabbed and wounded by Michael Riccardi in a Bensonhurst schoolyard. Rev. Sharpton recovered from his wounds, while Michael Riccardi was convicted of first-degree assault and received a sentence of five to fifteen years in prison. Rev. Sharpton wanted the cops and the courts to go easy on Michael Riccardi, but

HEAL THE HOOD

I certainly didn't want the courts to go easy on Michael Riccardi and neither did my friends and family. The courts have been going easy on White people since the British created the Thirteen Colonies. White people have been slipping through the system for centuries. They aren't afraid of breaking the rules because they're rarely made to face the consequences. This has me wondering whether Mrs. Du will face the consequences for killing Latasha and whether the four cops will face the consequences for beating Rodney King. I know Whites slip through the system but do Asians slip through, too?

In *Jungle Fever*, Wesley Snipes, another fine Black actor, plays an architect named Flipper Purify. He has a wife and daughter, but he begins an affair with an Italian American woman named Angie Tucci. When Flipper's wife finds out he is cheating on her, she kicks him out; and when Angie's dad finds out she is dating a Black man, he beats her with his belt. Flipper and Angie get their own apartment and move in together, but they still encounter racism. A memorable moment is when two cops harass Flipper because they think he's attacking Angie. Angie tries to tell the cops that she and Flipper are just friends, but they almost don't believe her. When I saw the cops, I realized I recognized them. They were the same cops who murdered Radio Raheem in another Spike Lee movie, *Do the Right Thing*. I was sure those two cops wouldn't have minded killing another Black man. In the end, Flipper and Angie end their affair once they realize they are incompatible.

Another interracial couple featured in the movie is Paulie Carbone and Orin Goode. Paulie was Angie's former fiancé and his friends ridiculed him for losing his girl to a Black man, but Paulie asks out Orin, one of his Black customers, even though his dad doesn't approve. Paulie is beaten up by his friends for asking Orin out, but he still shows up at Orin's house for their date.

When Joshua drove us to Koreatown, I asked him, "Anyone give you a hard time about us?"

Joshua said, "Some of my friends and classmates have. But I tell them to shut up because they don't know what they're talking about."

I asked Joshua, "What do they say?"

Joshua said, "I'm afraid you'll get offended."

I said, "Not as long as *you* don't say anything offensive."

Joshua said, "Alright. Some of the guys think I asked you out 'cause none of the girls in my neighborhood want to go out with me, and I'm desperate for a date. Some other guys think I just want to hit third base with you. Plenty of my friends have crushes on Whitney Houston, Janet Jackson, Naomi Campbell, and other Black women celebrities. They think all Black girls have big butts and big breasts and that they have their legs open for every Tom, Dick, and Harry. But I told them that not all Black girls have big body parts or are whores. They said you're definitely not like most Black girls because most guys can't tell what your body looks like since you don't dress half-naked."

Even though I don't dress half-naked, guys can still tell I have a big butt and big breasts by how my clothing outlines my body parts. Guys talk about my body all the time, but I have never heard Joshua talking about my body behind my back. Then, I thought about when we sparred in the dojo, and how Joshua always smiled when I tackled him and vice versa. I thought he was smiling to be a good sport. Now I realize that he was smiling because we grabbed and held each other in places that most other couples are unaware about. When we tackled each other, Joshua must have gotten a good feel of my body. Apparently, he *had* been studying my body but in an unconventional way. I'm not sure if I should be impressed or disgusted.

After a moment of silence, I told Joshua, "During the era of slavery, many White masters and overseers had Black mistresses or concubines. Anne Moody stated in her autobiography that up until the nineteen sixties, plenty of White men in Centreville, Mississippi, had Black mistresses. That's what they think we're all good for, sex."

Joshua said, "For the record, I don't feel that way."

I asked him, "So you're not interested in sex?"

I was playing with him, which might be a bit mean, but I wanted answers.

Joshua said, "When I hit third base for the first time, I want it to be with a girl I really care about, a girl who's as beautiful on the inside as she is on the outside."

I didn't say much after that.

Then, Joshua said, "Flipper went White-girl hazy and Angie went Black-boy crazy. We kind of have the same thing going."

I laughed and said, "Yeah, you've gone Black-girl hazy and I've gone Yellow-boy crazy!"

We both laughed and laughed and laughed.

For our next date, we decided to hit the beach in Malibu. Personally, I thought Malibu was too bougie, but Joshua insisted we go. The drive from Koreatown to Malibu takes about forty minutes, but that's only if you leave early. When we got to Malibu, there were few people on the beach; so, Joshua found a good spot to set up our blankets and umbrellas. I took off my sweater and sweatpants and took *The Color Purple* out of my purse. *The Color Purple* is one of my all-time favorite novels. It's about a Black woman named Celie who has been abused and taken advantage of by men, almost her entire life. Other Black women – her sister, Nettie and her friends, Sofia and Shug Avery – help her find the strength to get away from her abusive husband, Mister, and build a new life for herself. My girls always have my back because we know how powerful sisterhood is. Mister isn't the only abusive Black man in history. There are many abusive Black men in Crenshaw and other hoods in LA; but if any man thinks he can get away with beating me, I'll give him an all-expense paid trip to the emergency room.

I don't wear a two-piece bathing suit because I don't want guys eyeing me like I'm a piece of meat, but my one-piece purple bathing suit still had guys eyeing me, including Joshua.

I started to read but Joshua asked, "May I put sunscreen on you?"

I told him, "I can do it."

Joshua said, "But the sunscreen will make it hard for you to hold your book properly. Plus, that book is in good shape. Getting sunscreen on it will just ruin its condition."

I couldn't argue with logic like that, so I said, "Alright. But don't think about touching my ass."

Joshua smiled and rubbed sunscreen on my legs, arms, and shoulders. I had to admit that it felt nice and he didn't try to touch my ass. Joshua swam in the ocean, while I continued reading. For lunch he got us hotdogs and around four o'clock he said it was best if he took me home. I told him he could drop me off in Koreatown, but he insisted on taking me back to Crenshaw.

As we walked to the parking lot, I told him, "Crenshaw is a tough hood and most of my neighbors won't be happy to see you. You know, Korean shopkeepers shooting Black people and all."

Joshua said, "Yeah, but I didn't shoot Latasha Harlins or Lee Arthur Mitchell."

I asked him, "Are you okay with what Missus Du did to Latasha Harlins or what Mister Park did to Lee Arthur Mitchell?"

Joshua said, "No! Shooting someone in the back of their head is very cowardly. If Missus Du didn't feel safe in South Central, she should have sold her store to a Black family. If she didn't like Black people, she should have shut down Empire Liquor instead of staying in a place where her hatred grew. If she knew martial arts like us, she could have protected herself more easily and without taking lives. Missus Du stated she hates Black people and even said some racist stuff like all Black people don't work and they use welfare money to buy liquor."

I angrily asked Joshua, "When did she say that racist stuff?"

Joshua said, "My dad is friends with a guy who's friends with Mister Du. Missus Du told her husband that the reason Blacks are criminals is because they're too lazy to do real work. She said you all spend welfare money on liquor, which is why all Blacks are winos."

I gruffly replied, "I assume Missus Du thinks all Blacks are junkies, too."

Joshua said, "Probably. But I know your parents aren't like that."

I asked, "Do you think I'm 'one of the good ones'?"

Joshua said, "You're not *one* of the good ones, Hatima. There are many good people in the hood, and I can tell because of the wonderful person you've become. Parents aren't the only influence in kids' lives. Your neighbors and friends and your friends' parents must have all played a hand in raising you. You were right, Hatima. Latasha was killed because she was Black. Lee Arthur was killed because he was Black. I thought about what you said and realized that you could have easily been shot, too. Then, I would have never gotten to take you out."

That was so insightful. I immediately hugged Joshua.

I convinced Joshua to drop me off at Denny's and walked back to my house. During the summertime, days are longer than the nights; so, it takes a while for it to get dark. Mama and Daddy want me in the house before dark because gangsters do most of their shooting at nighttime. As I walked back, I wondered about telling my family and Wanda about Joshua. I know Grandma wouldn't approve because she told me I should never bring a White boy home. Even though she never said anything about bringing a Korean boy home, I'm sure her disapproval extends to Koreans as well. Mama and Daddy take pride in our Black heritage; so, they may consider me a traitor to our race. Wanda's always talking about how fine Black men are, and I have had my crush on a few Black male celebrities: Bobby Brown, Mr. T, Malcolm-Jamal Warner, Will Smith, and Michael Jackson. Some people say Michael Jackson is a traitor to our race since he now has white skin. Some people accused him of bleaching his skin, but he claims he has a skin disorder called vitiligo. I checked the school library, and I read that vitiligo is a skin disease that can turn a Black person's skin white. Only about one percent of the world's population suffers from it, so I wondered why God let Michael Jackson be part of that one percent. I have a copy of his autobiography, *Moonwalk*, and it has pictures of him from when he was a kid up to the *Bad* era. The plastic surgeries he had on his nose and his Jheri curl made him look sexy. Even though he now looks White, he's still sexy to me and to a lot of other Black girls in South Central.

When Joshua and I went to the Santa Monica Pier, we rode the Ferris wheel in the evening. LA always looks so beautiful at night. From the top, I could see the LA skyline.

I said, "La La Land is beautiful, isn't it?"

Joshua said, "Yeah, beautiful."

HEAL THE HOOD

Joshua was looking at me when he said it. He put his arm around me and leaned toward me. I leaned toward him and – what do you know? – we had our first kiss. His lips were soft. My first kiss didn't send a jolt of electricity through my body and the world didn't stop rotating, but it was still nice.

On July 12, a new movie titled *Boyz n the Hood* was released in theaters. It was directed and written by a Black man named John Singleton and the main setting was South Central LA. When film crews came to the hood last year to shoot the movie, Daddy drove Wanda and I to where a scene was being filmed. We got to meet Ice Cube, and he gave us his autograph. I also asked John Singleton for his autograph because I had a feeling that this movie would turn him into one of the greatest filmmakers in LA.

I went with Joshua, Wanda, and Marcus Miller – Wanda's date who is still sporting a Jheri curl even though many Black guys, including Michael Jackson, have dropped the hairstyle – to see the movie the day after it debuted. I convinced them that we should see the show at the Paramount Theater because it seemed only right to see John Singleton's debut film in a luxurious setting. They bought that even though I knew it would be more logical to watch the movie at Cinemark since it's located in the hood, the same setting as the film. We had to get there early because movie theaters get crowded on Saturdays.

When Marcus drove me and Wanda to the movie theater, Wanda said, "I'm so glad I get to meet this mystery boyfriend of yours."

I told her, "He's not my boyfriend."

Marcus said, "But you want him to be."

I said, "I'm still not sure if it would work out. When you see him, you'll know what I mean."

When we got to the theater, Marcus bought four tickets. Then, Joshua showed up in his Cadillac, picked a parking spot, got out, and walked to us.

Marcus asked, "Yo, dude, can we help you?"

Joshua said, "I'm the fourth guy. I'm Hatima's date."

Wanda said, "Say what?"

I said, "Wanda, Marcus, this is Joshua Yang. We both teach hapkido at Master Shin's Dojang. He's been taking me out since the summer started."

Marcus said, "Hatima, you crazy!"

Joshua said, "I know that the tension between Koreans and Blacks is very high."

Marcus exclaimed, "Hell yeah! Your people killed Latasha Harlins! And they only got that Korean woman on manslaughter charges. It was murder, ya hear, murder!"

I explained, "Murder is planned, while manslaughter happens in the spur of the moment. If Soon Ja Du had been planning to kill Latasha for days or weeks, then it would be murder."

Marcus snorted and said, "I'm sure she was planning on putting a bullet in some Black dude or dudette. So, she *should* be on murder charges!"

Wanda said, "Lee Arthur Mitchell's murderer walked away scot-free. We hate it when some people can walk through this world like they're made of grease, with no worries, no punishments."

Joshua said, "I know that, and I apologize for the racism my race has inflicted on yours. But I'm not like that and neither is my dad."

I asked, "Does your dad hire Black people to run his Watts store?"

Joshua said, "No, but only because he's closer to the people in our neighborhood than the people in Watts. Besides, Mister Yoo is finishing up his degree at Cal State LA and plans on getting another job soon so maybe my dad will be more open-minded to hiring Blacks."

Then I asked, "Is your dad is okay with you dating?"

Joshua said, "Not exactly. I still haven't told him."

Wanda said, "Hatima hasn't told her parents either so that makes you even."

I asked her, "How do you know I haven't told my parents?"

Wanda explained, "'Cause all of South Central would have heard your daddy's tirade. The roof hasn't been blown off your house yet. It means they still don't know."

Marcus said, "I'm sure y'all will want to keep this a secret. Unless y'all wanna end up like Romeo and Juliet?"

I remembered how Mama didn't want my middle name to be after Grandma Juliet because of what happened in Shakespeare's classic tragedy, but there was a still a good chance Romeo and Juliet's romantic curse would affect a pair of nineties' lovers: Joshua Yang and Hatima Parker. So, I asked Marcus, "What makes you think our story will have a tragic ending?"

Marcus said, "'Cause this is America. I know they spread the lie that racism ended after Doctor King told us about his dream and the Jim Crow signs were removed; but LA never had Jim Crown signs, and our oppressors still got away with bringing us down. They're still getting away with it, and us Blacks need to stand together."

Joshua asked, "Why can't I stand with you?"

Marcus snorted and explained, "'Cause you're part of the problem, not the solution."

Joshua said, "Oh, just because Missus Du and Mister Park are

Korean and I'm Korean that makes me a racist? You can't punish all the Koreans for the crimes of a few."

I exclaimed, "That's enough! It's a good thing we're seeing this movie. It will shed some light into what really goes down in the hood."

The movie started with gunshots and a message came on the screen.

> "One out of every twenty-one Black American males will be murdered in their lifetime ... Most will die at the hands of another Black male."

The movie is set in 1984 South Central LA. It starts with an elementary school kid named Tre Styles who lives with his mom in Inglewood. Tre is smart but has anger issues, so his mom sends him to live with his father, Furious Styles. Tre's father is the only Black father on the block in their South Central hood. Tre's two best friends are Ricky and Doughboy, two brothers with different fathers – that's a very common thing in the hood. Ricky loves to play football, but Doughboy and his friend Chris keep getting into trouble and get arrested for stealing when they're kids.

Then, the movie jumps seven years into the future when Mrs. Baker is holding a party in her backyard to celebrate Doughboy being let out of jail. Anyone can tell by the blue clothes he wears and the heat he carries that Doughboy is an official member of the Crips. Tre is a smart guy with a good job at the Fox Hills Mall, and Ricky is a star running back for the Crenshaw High School football team and hopes to attend USC on an athletic scholarship. Ricky also has an infant son since he got his girlfriend pregnant, which is another regular occurrence in the hood.

HEAL THE HOOD

Tre's dad has some wonderful insights about life in the hood. When he took Tre and Ricky to Compton, he explained how gentrification works and told them about the importance of keeping everything in the hood, Black. That means Black-owned business and Black money. If a Black family owned Empire Liquor, they wouldn't have seen Latasha as a threat. They would have seen her as a young girl trying to buy some juice. If a Black man owned Mr. Chung's Liquor Market, they would have accepted Mr. Mitchell's jewels as payment because they could easily get cash for it at a pawnshop. Also, an old man tells Furious that gangsters are bringing the property values in the hoods down by selling drugs and shooting each other, but Furious explains that drugs come into the country via planes and ships. Since Black people in the hood don't own any planes or ships, we're not the ones transporting that shit into the ghetto.

Furious also reminds the man that drugs aren't a problem as long as they stay in South Central, Compton, Harlem, Bed-Stuy, South Side Chicago, and all the other hoods, but when they find their way to Beverly Hills, Iowa, Wall Street, and other places where there are hardly any Black people, that's when the drug epidemic is seen as a problem. Furious also explains that the reason there are gun stores and liquor stores on every corner in a Black community is that they want us to kill ourselves. The best way to kill off a group of people is to take away their ability to reproduce themselves. Everyone knows it's teens who are getting killed in the hood. Furious explains that we all need to think about our futures, instead of playing into the oppressors' hands.

Unfortunately, the movie takes a sad turn when Ricky gets shot by the Bloods. At first, Tre joins the Crips to avenge Ricky's death; but he tells them to let him out of the car. I was glad he could see that the cycle of violence had to end sometime and somewhere.

Doughboy and his friends kill the Bloods who killed Ricky though Doughboy knows this would just lead to his own death. The next day he tells Tre that he saw on television about how we live in a violent world, but the television only talks about violence in foreign countries, not the violence in the ghetto.

Doughboy says, "Either they don't know, don't show, or don't care about what's going on in the hood. They had all this foreign shit. They didn't have shit on my brother, man."

The epilogue reveals that Ricky was buried the next day, and Doughboy was murdered, two weeks later. In the fall, Tre goes to Morehouse College and his girlfriend, Brandi, goes to Spelman.

The tagline of the movie is, "Once upon a time in South Central LA … It ain't no fairy tale."
Life in the hood is not a fairy tale because fairy tales always have happy endings. Tre and Brandi get happy endings, but Ricky and Doughboy do not. I hope this movie raises awareness about what goes on in the hood so that people will do more to help change things.

When we left the movie theater and went outside, Joshua asked, "Is life really that bad in the hood?"

Wanda exclaimed, "Of course it is! What? You think John Singleton and the rest made it up to make the movie more exciting and heartbreaking?"

I said, "Wanda, calm down. The fact that Joshua is asking questions is a good thing. It shows that this movie has him thinking about the hood." Then I told Joshua, "Yes, life in the hood is that bad. Tre, Ricky, and Doughboy were raised in a tough but occasionally nurturing environment and so are we."

Joshua asked, "Why'd the Bloods have to shoot Ricky? He wasn't a Crip."

Marcus said, "Yeah, but he still repped them."

I explained, "Ricky was wearing a blue jacket at the street races. He also wore a blue shirt at his brother's 'Welcome Home' party. Tre drives a blue Volkswagen Beetle. The Crips represent their part of the hood, and they all show their support. This keeps the Crips off their back but can draw the ire of the Bloods."

Joshua said, "Doughboy wore a 'Beat It' t-shirt when he was a kid. If he listened to the Gloved One's song, why didn't he understand the message?"

I explained, "Michael Jackson tries to get his point across through music, like lots of other musical artists. He said in his autobiography that gangsters are little more than rebels who want respect, and he had a point. Gangsters want respect, money, power, and protection. Those are the reasons why so many guys join gangs. My uncle is a gangster."

Joshua said, "Really?"

I said, "Yep, Uncle Alonzo is a Blood. The main reason he became a gangster was because he and Daddy needed money to pay the bills after Grandpa was injured at Reliance Steel. Daddy joined the Marines and had his checks mailed back home to help Grandpa, but Uncle Alonzo knew they needed more money, so he started robbing people. He stole stuff and fenced it on the street. He did a stint in juvie and when Daddy came home from Vietnam, he didn't approve of Uncle Alonzo's lifestyle. Uncle Alonzo joined the Bloods when it was formed and became a serious hustler. He went to San Quentin seven years ago on charges of grand theft, armed robbery, and resisting arrest. When he got out after three years, he re-joined the Bloods and is now cruising in a red Pontiac."

Joshua said, "Whoa! Do any families in South Central make enough money to support their families?"

Wanda said, "Some make it, others don't. When a family isn't making it, their kids usually join a gang. Gangsters make enough money to pay bills *and* buy cool stuff, like luxury cars, fancy suits, and the latest electronics. But, in the end, the system doesn't give a damn about people like us."

Joshua asked, "Don't your parents tell you to do good in school?"

I said, "Of course they do. Our parents know the best way to get out of the hood is through education. They love and support us one hundred percent."

Marcus said, "Doughboy's mom didn't support him. He was a smart dude, but he didn't get the proper amount of support from his mom. She was always praising Ricky's athletic ability and, as a result, Ricky became a star athlete, and Doughboy became a gangster."

Joshua said, "I liked Furious. He's a smart man but too bad Tre's mom missed out on Tre's childhood."

I said, "Tre could have left the hood and gone to live with his mom, but he chose to stay with his dad and his boys. Furious was also smart enough to leave the hood, but he decided to stay and give back to the community. We need more guys like them."

Joshua hung his head and said, "I'm sorry I was insensitive to what's been going on in your neighborhood. This movie is important and every person on Earth should see it."

Chapter Seven

At the dojang on Monday, I saw a Black guy named Jared Wilson come out of the boys' locker room with a box of his stuff: his uniform, some deodorant, and some posters of Bruce Lee and Chuck Norris.

I asked Jared, "Yo, Jared. You're leaving the dojang?"

Jared said, "Yeah, I'm leaving for college in the fall."

I said, "Cool. Which college are you going to?"

Jared said, "Cornell University."

I said, "Ivy League. But I wouldn't expect anything else from a guy like you. Besides, we need more Black people in the Ivy League."

Jared went outside to put his box of things in his car. He usually drives a Black 1970 Dodge Charger, but today he was driving a white 1990 Buick Riviera.

I exclaimed, "Whoa! *This* is a car!"

Jared said, "I'm glad you like it. Because I got accepted into Cornell, Mom and Dad decided to reward me on a job well done. Cornell's school colors are carnelian and white. Since there aren't many carnelian Buicks, my parents got me a white Buick."

I asked, "Are you still gonna study law?"

He said, "Of course, after I get my bachelor's degree. With all the injustice being meted out to our people, attorneys are still a must in the fight for equal rights."

Just then, Joshua waved to us and crossed the street, but he stopped on the other side of the car, leaned, and stood back up with a sour look on his face.

He said, "Jared, you should see this."

Jared and I both walked to the other side of the car, and we saw "NIGGER-MOBILE" scratched on the driver's side door. It looked like the perpetrator did it with a key. I was immediately angry. They had no right scratching Jared's lovely car.

Jared quietly said, "I'll take it down to the mechanic and see if he can fix it."

I asked, "Jared, don't you want to find the people who did this?"

Jared said, "I doubt we'll be able to find them. There's no evidence linking anyone to this crime."

Jared got into his car, but I got into the passenger seat. I asked him, "Do you want your parents to know about this?"

Jared said, "No, but if we take it to our usual mechanic, then my parents will find out."

I said, "You can take it to Oscar's Garage. He can fix anything."

Jared asked, "Is this garage in the ghetto?"

I did not like how Jared said the word "ghetto." He said it like it was tainted, cursed, and dirty.

I said, "Yes, but Mister Brown is the best mechanic in all of South Central. He'll fix your car as long as you pay the bill."

Jared asked, "Does Mister Brown have a lot of experience fixing luxury cars?"

I replied, "Are you kidding? Do you know how many gangsters and drug dealers are riding large? They bring their Benzes, BMWs, Lexuses, Pontiacs, et cetera to be fixed at Oscar's Garage all the time."

Jared admitted, "But I'm afraid something bad may happen to me if I venture into the ghetto."

I told Jared, "Don't worry. You're with me, which means no one will bother you."

That was a bit of an exaggeration since *some* people respect me; but Uncle Alonzo is a Blood, so other gangsters in the hood usually don't bother me because they wanna stay on his good side. Sometimes Crips bother me. The last time they did was shortly before school ended. I was walking to the rec center when a blue Oldsmobile followed me slowly.

The Crip driving the car said, "Yo, baby, where's a girl as fine as you walking to?"

I replied, "Nunya bizness."

The Crip driver said, "Oh, that's cold."

I kept walking, but they kept following me.

The Crip driver asked, "Ain't you Alonzo Parker's niece?"

I said, "Yeah, so?"

The Crip driver stated, "A pretty girl like you should be taken care of by the Crips, not the Bloods."

I stated, "I don't need to be taken care of by any gangbangers."

I kept walking and refused to answer the Crip driver when he tried to keep the conversation going. When I got to the rec center, Mrs. MacNevin, one of the ladies who helps run the center, came up to the blue Oldsmobile and stated, "If you gentlemen are causing trouble, I'll have to ask you to leave."

The Crip driver said, "We ain't causing no trouble."

Mrs. MacNevin looked behind the Oldsmobile and said, "Look at that, a police car."

A squad car stopped next to the blue Oldsmobile and a White cop asked, "Is there a problem?"

Mrs. MacNevin asked the Crip driver, "Well, is there?"

The Crip driver said, "Nah, me and my boys were just leaving."

The Crips left and the cops followed them. That was the probably the first time I had ever seen the cops show up at the right place at the right time.

Jared drove to Crenshaw and I directed him to West Jefferson Boulevard.

Mr. Brown came out of his garage, saw me with Jared, and said, "Hatima Parker! Your daddy's gonna have your behind when he finds out you're hanging with drug dealers!"

I told him, "Relax, Mister Brown. Jared is *not* a drug dealer."

Mr. Brown asked, "What does he do? Rob people? Extort people? Pimp out girls?"

Jared's face became angry, and he shouted, "Do you honestly think the only way for a Black man to get a nice car like this is to commit crimes? I'm going to become an attorney one day so that I can put the real criminals behind bars!"

I told Mr. Brown, "Jared's parents work legit jobs and live in a bougie neighborhood not far from here."

Mr. Brown asked, "Really? What do they do for a living?"

Jared said, "My dad's a cardiothoracic surgeon at the UCLA Medical Center. My mom's a civil engineer for AECOM."

Mr. Brown asked, "Part of the Black bourgeoisie, huh?"

Before Jared could respond, I asked, "Can you fix the driver's side door?"

Mr. Brown walked from the passenger side to the driver's side and saw the racial slur.

He said, "Lord, have mercy."

Jared asked, "Can you fix it?"

Mr. Brown said, "Sure. But I hate it when people think Black people don't deserve their success."

Jared said, "They probably thought I was a criminal like most Black guys in the ghetto."

I exclaimed, "Jared, not all people in the ghetto are criminals! My mom and dad are honest, hardworking members of society. So is Mister Brown and Wanda's mom, Missus Brooks."

Jared said, "Sorry, but the Black people who are criminals make it tougher for honest, hardworking Blacks. That's why I want to be an attorney; I'll put away the real criminals and defend the innocent."

In a week, Mr. Brown repaired Jared's Buick, and when we examined it, it looked brand-new.

I told Jared, "Can't go to Cornell with a messed-up car. Ya gotta show those Ivy League folks that you mean business."

Jared said, "Thanks, Hatima." Then he turned to Mr. Brown and asked, "How much do I owe you?"

Mr. Brown gave him the price, and Jared took out a blank check from his wallet. Then he wrote down the cost of repairs on the check and handed it to Mr. Brown.

I asked, "Do all rich kids get blank checks?"

Jared explained, "My parents gave me the check to pay for the repairs, but they told me not to wave it around in the hood."

I said, "That's true. Don't want anyone to rob you. People are always looking for ways to make extra cash. A popular way is gambling."

Jared asked, "Do your parents gamble?"

I said, "Of course not. Gambling is a sucker's game."

Since I helped Jared fix his car, he invited me to have dinner at his parents' house. I asked if I had to dress fancy, and he said that I could wear what I wanted. So, I wore my baggy overalls, a graffiti-print t-shirt, and an LA Lakers cap. I took a bus to Westwood and walked to 740 Thayer Avenue. As I walked down the streets, I felt like I was in a different world. The houses were much bigger than the ones in Crenshaw. Some houses in Crenshaw have two-stories and garages but Westwood's two-story houses also had garage doors bigger than the ones in South Central. Since the garage doors were huge, that signaled to me that these people made enough money to own a lot of cars. The money I make teaching at Master Shin's is not enough for a down-payment on a car *and* the price of gas. The number one priority for Daddy's Ford is that it gets him to work. Since Mama carpools, I'm the one who needs to find alternate means of transportation. The Westwood houses look like they have more than three bedrooms, while the maximum number of bedrooms in a house on my block is three. Michael Jackson and the rest of the Jackson family have stated that they lived in a two-bedroom house in Gary, Indiana. There is no way that all nine Jackson kids would have fit in one bedroom; I'm sure some of them slept in the living room, probably on a sofa bed.

As I walked down the street, some people looked at me funny. Not funny ha-ha, but funny funny. They probably think I'm here to cause trouble. Maybe wearing my cap backwards is a bit much, but in America everyone has the right to freedom of expression so, I should be able to wear my cap any way I want. I kept walking until I got to the right address.

I knocked and a five-foot-ten Black man with black-and-gray hair opened the door.

I said, "Good evening, Doctor Wilson. I'm a friend of Jared's and he invited me to dinner."

Dr. Wilson shook my hand and said, "Come in, Hatima. Welcome, welcome."

HEAL THE HOOD

The best way to describe the house is huge – the stairs, the kitchen, the living room, the dining room, the parlor, the bathrooms, the bedrooms, the backyard, everything!

Point number four of the Black Panther Platform is,

> "We want decent housing, fit for shelter of human beings. ... We believe that if the White landlords will not give decent housing to our Black community, then the housing and the land should be made into cooperatives so that our community, with government aid, can build and make decent housing for its people."

How come poor Black people live in small houses with barely enough rooms to house our families? There are families as large as the Jackson family in my hood, and there obviously aren't enough rooms for them in the mini houses of Crenshaw. Why can't we all have big houses with lots of bedrooms and bathrooms, large kitchens, dining rooms, and living rooms with the latest television sets, and pools in the backyard? How come people seriously think that the money in a person's bank account determines how much their life is worth? People should get housing based on necessity not money or social class.

My parents don't rent our house. They own it, but other folks in the hood ain't as lucky.

Dr. Wilson led me to the dining room, and I asked what we were having.

A Black woman in a maid's uniform came out of the kitchen and told me, "We're having baked chicken, mashed potatoes, jasmine rice, and pecan pie."

I told her, "Sounds delicious."

Then, Jared came into the dining room, gave me a high-five, and said, "Hatima, so glad you could make it."

I said, "Thanks for inviting me."

A Black woman of Grandma's height walked in and said, "Pleasure to meet you, Hatima. Jared says you're the best martial artist at Master Shin's."

I said, "I don't like to brag but it's true."

Jared said, "This is my mom."

I said, "Pleasure to meet you, Missus Wilson."

I kinda towered over her, but Mrs. Wilson didn't seem intimidated by my height.

Then, a Black girl with dreads who looked my age and a pre-teenage boy sporting a low-cut fade walked in.

Jared said, "These are my siblings, Stella and Kenny."

I said, "Nice to meet you." I held out my hand, but Stella didn't shake it at first. She's the same height as her mom.

Kenny shook it vigorously and asked, "Have you seen anyone get shot?"

Mrs. Wilson exclaimed, "Kenny!"

Kenny explained, "She's from the ghetto so I have to know."

I said, "I hear gunshots every night and, now and again, my family and friends find dead bodies on the street or in alleyways; but it's not all bad."

Kenny asked, "Is everyone in South Central LA in a gang?"

Jared exclaimed, "Kenny!"

Kenny said, "I wanna know."

Dr. Wilson said, "'Wanna' is not a word."

I said, "I'm not in a gang. Most gangs recruit guys but sometimes girls join up."

Kenny asked, "Is it true that if you wear red or blue a gang will beat you up?"

I explained, "The Bloods – whose color is red – and the Crips – whose color is blue – both have territories in Crenshaw. So, some folks usually avoid wearing red and blue if they aren't with a set. Some others wear red and blue to show their support even though they're not members."

Jared looked at my mostly red graffiti shirt and asked, "If you're not a member of the Bloods, why do you wear red?"

I explained, "To show that we're supposedly under the Bloods' protection and to make sure the Bloods don't have an excuse to shoot us."

Stella asked, "Why would anyone in your neighborhood support the Bloods if they're criminals?"

I explained, "We don't 'support' the Bloods. We pretend we're okay with what they do because sometimes joining the Bloods is the only profitable option for Black kids."

Stella asked, "Don't you all go to school?"

I told her, "A little more than half of Dorsey High students graduate. The other half drop out because the work is boring, and the textbooks are outdated. *A lotta* teachers don't care about us, and gangbangers make more money than most other folks in the hood."

After we sat down, Stella asked, "Are you still in school?"

I said, "Yeah. September is my senior year. As long as I keep my grades up, pass all the tests, and get a nomination from a US Representative or a US Senator, I can go to the Naval Academy next year."

Dr. Wilson asked, "You want to be in the Navy?"

I explained, "No, I want to be a Marine. My paternal grandfather was a Montford Point Marine and my dad was a Marine in Vietnam.

I want to continue the family tradition and get a good education."

Mrs. Wilson said, "The US military academies are tough to get into. Their acceptance rates are as low as the Ivy League's. Are your grades high enough?"

I said, "I get straight-As in all my subjects, but my favorite subjects are English, history, and other humanities subjects."

Mrs. Wilson said, "Sounds like you have a good average. Have you taken the SAT or ACT?"

I said, "Yeah. I got a score of seven hundred and twenty on the math section of my SAT and a score of eight hundred on the verbal part."

Stella asked, "You got a perfect score on the verbal part?"

All the other Wilsons cheered for me.

Dr. Wilson said, "A perfect score on the verbal part of the SAT is a wonderful accomplishment. Even Jared and Stella didn't get perfect scores on the verbal and math sections of the SAT."

Then, the maid walked into the dining room with platters of food. The food all looked great.

Dr. Wilson said, "Thank you, Cynthia. This looks like it will be delicious, as usual."

We all sat down.

As everyone took portions of food, Mrs. Wilson asked, "What score did you get on the ACT?"

I said, "A thirty-four."

Jared said, "Your SAT score is in the ninety-fifth percentile while your ACT score is in the ninety-fourth percentile. Most people believe colleges prefer the SAT over the ACT but that's a lie. Colleges value either one of those scores equally. Have you decided which test scores you'll submit in your college applications?"

I said, "Not yet. Guess I'll go with my instincts."

As we ate, I asked Dr. and Mrs. Wilson, "Where did you both study?"

Dr. Wilson said, "I got my bachelor's degree and MD at Freeman University. Then, I came to LA to complete my residency at the UCLA Medical Center."

Freeman University is an HBCU in Atlanta; it's considered part of the Black Ivy League and it is one of the schools I'm gonna apply to.

Mrs. Wilson said, "I got my bachelor's degree at Prairie View A and M University and my master's degree at Cornell."

I told Jared, "So that's why you wanna go to Cornell. It's your mom's alma mater."

Jared said, "That's right. I love my parents, and I want to follow in their footsteps."

I said, "The only people I know who went to college are the clergy of First AME; my elementary, junior high, and high school teachers; and the head of our neighborhood funeral parlor. Mister Ngozi is one of a few African teachers we have at our school. He's also the only teacher who studied in England. He got his bachelor's degree at the University of Nigeria, Nsukka, and he got his master's degree at University College London."

Dr. Wilson said, "I've never heard of the University of Nigeria, Nsukka; and African universities aren't ranked very highly versus American and British schools; but I've heard of University College London. It's one of the best schools in the UK."

Stella asked, "If Mister Ngozi studied at a top school in the UK, what's he doing teaching in the ghetto? Isn't he overqualified for a school like Dorsey High?"

Now, Stella's attitude has been rubbing me the wrong way since she stepped into the dining room; so, I told her, "Mister

Ngozi specifically applied to inner-city schools when he moved to LA. He knew that we kids in the ghetto need more help than you bougie kids. Society may have turned their backs on us, but Mister Ngozi and Principal Edwards never will. They've instilled a love of learning into many students, students who were already planning on dropping out of school before they came to Dorsey. It was already decided that I would be a dropout cum blue-collar or pink-collar worker cum criminal cum murder statistic before I was born. It was decided that you and your siblings would be high school graduates cum college graduates cum lawyers cum doctors cum engineers cum businesspeople cum whatever suits your fancy. Are you aware that the only reason you can go to college is 'cause your school is better equipped than mine and your parents can afford to pay your college tuition? My dad is a baggage handler at the airport, and my mom is a waitress so, obviously, being able to pay college tuitions was never an option for them. Since I do extremely well in school, a scholarship will be part of my future. But Dorsey doesn't have enough supplies to properly educate its students so maintaining a straight-A average is hard for a lot of other kids. That means academic scholarships aren't an option for most students. Some people in the hood call the Black bourgeoisie sellouts, and I always thought that was a wrongful accusation. But you, Stella, fit the description of a sellout; you have no sympathy for people in the hood or the obstacles we must overcome. Who do you think you would be if you had my parents? Who do you think you would be if selling drugs sounded like a great way to help pay the bills? Like Uncle Phil said on *Fresh Prince*, before you judge someone, you find out what they're all about."

The Wilsons stayed silent for a moment; then, Jared slapped his sister upside her head.

Stella exclaimed, "Ow! What was that for?"

Jared explained, "For being a classist."

Dr. Wilson said, "Jared, I don't think classist is a word."

Jared said, "Classism is a word. Since Stella thinks that she's superior to Hatima because you and Mom are rich, then she's a staunch supporter of classism."

Stella said, "But we donate to charities that help poor people."

I asked her, "Have you actually gone down into the hood to be among the poor?"

Stella said, "No. Mama's old hood in South Central is dangerous, and she's told us so."

Mrs. Wilson explained, "I don't want you coming with me to South Central until you're emotionally ready. If there's one thing a lot of folks in my old hood hate, it's affluent African Americans."

I asked, "Do they think you're sellouts?"

Mrs. Wilson said, "They've never called me or my husband sellouts to our faces. Some are impressed by our success, but others are angry. I believe jealousy fuels their anger."

Stella said, "If they got off their lazy butts when they were in high school, they could have become successful, too. But few people are willing to put in the hard work required to be successful."

Mrs. Wilson said, "Stella, that's an unfair accusation. People can't lift themselves from their own bootstraps when they can't even afford boots. People have opened doors for me, your father, your brothers, and you. But not that many people open doors for people in the ghetto. Plenty of my classmates were shot and killed before they reached their senior year. Others had to drop out to support their families."

I said, "That's what happened to my parents. Grandma Flora May raised Mama herself because Mama's no-good daddy ran out on Grandma. He moved to Chicago, and Grandma moved to LA.

Grandma works as a janitor in a brokerage firm and that salary is barely enough to pay rent, the bills, and groceries. There were welfare checks, but they were unreliable. So, Mama dropped out of high school to work as a waitress at the Beverly Hills Hotel's Polo Lounge. She could have become a teacher, a nurse, or a social worker. But since her daddy abandoned her and Grandma was paid such a pitiful salary, Mama wasn't destined to succeed. Grandpa Gabriel was injured at Reliance Steel and couldn't work. So, Daddy and his twin brother, Uncle Alonzo, dropped out of school in order to support their home. Daddy joined the Marines, fought in Vietnam, and became a baggage handler at the airport when he came home; but Uncle Alonzo went down a dark path from which there is no return. If Reliance Steel's sick pay wasn't lousy, Daddy could have been successful as well. I'm sure you two faced many obstacles as well, Doctor and Missus Wilson; but you managed to overcome them and find success. You two had something my parents didn't: luck."

Dr. Wilson said, "I did have certain advantages other kids didn't. My dad was a professor at Howard University, and my mom was an elementary schoolteacher. They gave me extra homework to make sure I maintained straight-As. My dad had a friend who was a professor at Freeman, and he put in a good word for me when I applied there. One of my med school professors had a brother who worked at the UCLA Medical Center, and he helped set up an interview for me since I was determined to get a good residency position."

I told Dr. Wilson, "You've helped popularize one of my least favorite sayings: 'It's not *what* you know, but *who* you know.' Rich people always know more influential people than poor people, which is one of the reasons why they get so much more. This entire system is messed-up."

Mrs. Wilson said, "You're right, Hatima. The system isn't perfect, but we all have to do our best to change it."

After dinner, Dr. Wilson told me, "Hatima, I'll drive you home."

I said, "It's okay, I can take the bus."

Dr. Wilson said, "Nonsense. No reason you should waste money on bus fare."

Dr. Wilson led me into their garage. Jared's Buick was there along with a Rolls-Royce Silver Spur and a red Toyota Camry. Damn! The Wilsons are definitely loaded if they can afford three sweet rides. He opened the door to the driver's side of the Rolls-Royce, and I went into the passenger side. Then, he pressed a button on the dashboard and the garage doors opened automatically.

We drove through Westwood and, about half an hour later, we were in Crenshaw. I can't believe how close Crenshaw and Westwood are. It reminds of me how simple it was to travel to Narnia from England; in *The Lion, the Witch and the Wardrobe,* Narnia is easily accessible through a wardrobe; but at the end of the novel, the Pevensie kids learn that getting back to Narnia won't be as easy; and by the end of *The Voyage of the Dawn Treader,* they are banned from Narnia until the day Aslan destroys the Narnian universe. I can't believe that it takes thirty minutes to travel to another world or, as Dorothy Gale puts it, somewhere over the rainbow. The tornado ride from Kansas to Oz must have taken longer than the drive from Crenshaw to Westwood. I'm glad that Dorothy and her aunt and uncle moved to Oz later in the series. Life is brighter in Oz than it is in Kansas. The future also seems brighter in Westwood than it does in Crenshaw.

I told Dr. Wilson my West Boulevard address and the best way to get there without getting caught in the gangs' crossfire. Then, a police car came up behind us, whirred its sirens, and Dr. Wilson pulled over. I immediately put my hands on the dashboard.

A White cop shone his flashlight on Dr. Wilson's face and asked, "Where are you headed?"

Dr. Wilson kept both his hands on the steering wheel, looked the officer dead in the eye, and calmly said, "I'm dropping this young lady off at her home."

The cop asked, "Do you live here?"

Dr. Wilson said, "She lives here in Crenshaw, but I live in Westwood."

Another White cop walked to the passenger side and looked at me through the window. I kept both my hands on the dashboard; Mama and Daddy told me to keep my hands on the dashboard so that the cops can see I don't have a weapon, or that I'm not trying to reach for one. They also told me to try and get a good look at the cops' badges; all LAPD badges have an officer's rank and number on it. When I looked at the second White cop's badge, I saw that it said "POLICE OFFICER" at the top and that the number said "416."

The first officer asked Dr. Wilson, "What's your name?"

Dr. Wilson replied clearly, "Doctor Jeremiah Wilson. May I ask what your names are?"

The first officer said, "I'm Officer Greene and my partner over there is Officer Wayne."

I looked at Officer Greene's badge and saw that it also said "POLICE OFFICER" at the top and "714" at the bottom.

I thought, *Officer Greene, number Seven-One-Four. Officer Wayne, number Four-One-Six.*

Officer Greene asked Dr. Wilson, "What are you a doctor of?"

Dr. Wilson explained, "I'm a doctor of medicine. I work as a surgeon at the UCLA Medical Center."

Officer Greene looked like he didn't believe Dr. Wilson. I didn't blame him since the only doctors in the hood work at the community clinic. Once their residencies end, they usually apply for better-paying jobs at hospitals. But a few doctors divide their time between the clinic and hospitals because they want to give back to the community.

Officer Greene asked, "How do you know this young lady?"

Dr. Wilson said, "She and my son study martial arts together. My son invited her to our house for dinner."

Officer Greene still gave Dr. Wilson a mean look. I knew he thought Dr. Wilson was a gangbanger or drug dealer because those are the only kinds of people who drive Rolls-Royces in the hood.

Officer Greene said, "Step out of the car."

Dr. Wilson asked, "Why?"

Officer Greene explained, "We need to search the car."

Dr. Wilson said, "You can't search this car without a valid warrant. If you try to, I'll be more than happy to bring this to court with help from my friends at Webster and Cunningham."

Officer Wayne, who had been silent until now, asked, "Webster and Cunningham? The Webster and Cunningham Law Firm in Downtown LA? That's where your lawyer friends work?"

Dr. Wilson said, "Yes. Do you want me to call them on my cell-phone?"

Cell-phones were invented back in the 1970s, but only rich people can afford them. Us poor folks use pay phones when we don't have access to a landline.

Officer Greene asked Dr. Wilson where his cell-phone was, and Dr. Wilson said it was in the glove compartment. Officer Wayne opened the compartment, took out the cell-phone, and looked at it closely. I was wondering what the fuck he was doing. Did he think the phone would magically turn into a gun? Then Officer Wayne gave the phone to Dr. Wilson and let him dial his lawyer. Dr. Wilson spoke to his lawyer and gave the cell-phone to Officer Greene. Officer Greene talked to the lawyer over the phone. Then, his face changed, like he just ate spoiled milk.

Officer Greene gave Dr. Wilson his cell-phone back and said, "You're free to go, Doctor Wilson."

Officer Greene looked angry as he spoke, and I knew why. Dr. Wilson had made a fool out of him by lauding his bougie lifestyle. Officer Greene felt he had been cheated out of an opportunity to humiliate, beat, and, possibly, imprison another Black person for no reason.

Dr. Wilson drove me to my house and told me, "Don't worry, Hatima. My wife is friends with a woman who's a police officer, and she'll help me file a complaint."

I said, "Folks in the hood been filing complaints for as long as I can remember, and this shit ain't getting any better."

Dr. Wilson said, "Please don't swear or use ghetto talk. If you want people to respect you, speak proper English."

I told him, "Mr. Ngozi is always telling us to speak Queen's English. Then, we make fun of each other using mock British accents."

Dr. Wilson laughed.

I got out of the Rolls-Royce and he told me, "Good night, Hatima Parker."

I told my parents about dinner with the Wilsons during Monday night dinner. I mentioned how big their house was, that they had three cars, and that they hired a maid named Cynthia to clean their house and cook their food.

Mama asked, "Is Cynthia Black or White?"

I said, "Black."

Mama said, "I'm sure she's paid a better salary than the maids who worked in the South."

Daddy asked me, "Any other Blacks live in Westwood?"

I said, "I didn't see any other Black people. It's mostly White people, but I'm sure there are a few more Blacks in Westwood."

Daddy said, "The low number of affluent African Americans is a wrong that needs to be righted."

I asked them, "Would either of you like to dine with the Wilsons?"

Daddy said, "It's summertime. That means lots of tourists are coming to LA on vacation, which means more shifts, which means more money."

Mama said, "Summertime also means more guests at the Beverly Hills Hotel. More guests mean more customers at the Polo Lounge every day. So, I'm also very busy."

I think my parents are coming up with excuses because they feel they would both be out of place in a bougie neighborhood. Shoot, I don't think they've ever ventured into Leimert Park, and it's right next to Crenshaw. Will Smith felt out of place in Bel-Air in the first episode of *Fresh Prince*. Uncle Phil even told Will to act like Carlton, but when Uncle Phil had his partners from the law firm over for dinner, Will acted like himself: a guy straight out of the West Philly hood. He flaunted his street-smart personality to the law partners and embarrassed his aunt and uncle. The funniest moment of the dinner was when Ashley rapped the blessing. That was so hilarious! Everyone else in Crenshaw thought Ashley had a real gift with words and a future career as a rapper and songwriter. Uncle Phil reprimanded Will for embarrassing him, but Will pointed out that he was sent out West and forced to adapt to a new lifestyle without his own input. Uncle Phil pointed out that being on the streets may be cool when you're seventeen, but at Uncle Phil's age it's a waste. Then, Will accused Uncle Phil of forgetting where he came from, but Uncle Phil pointed out the bigotry he had to face when he was young and explained how his hard work got him to Bel-Air. He wasn't interested in hearing Will's story, and I think that makes him a snob; but when Will played a classical piece of music on the piano, Uncle Phil saw there was more to Will than his street-smarts and love of hip-hop.

Arnold and Willis Jackson also felt out of place when they moved from Harlem to Park Avenue in the first episode of *Diff'rent Strokes*. Willis even wanted him and Arnold to move back to Harlem and live in their friend's overcrowded apartment, but Mr. Drummond pointed out to Willis that he didn't even try to get to know him or Kimberly. Arnold also pointed out that their mama asked Mr. Drummond to look after her boys when she passed away. Mrs. Jackson wouldn't have given custody of her kids to a man who didn't want them. Willis decided to give his and Arnold's new life in the Park Avenue penthouse a chance. Willis and Arnold adjusted to their new home and new family and Mr. Drummond finally adopted them later in the show.

Will Smith, Willis Jackson, and Arnold Jackson all felt out of place in Bel-Air and Park Avenue because they figured they didn't belong in those bougie neighborhoods. Will's mom works at a Philly post office and Willis and Arnold's dad worked as a janitor at the UN HQ and their mom was Mr. Drummond's maid. But Will is now living large in a Bel-Air mansion with his lawyer uncle and professor aunt. I'm sure he thinks about his mom and boys in Philly and the new friends he made in the hoods of California. Will's mom worked hard but it was not enough to get them outta the hood. What about Will's boys from the California hoods? Since a lot of them suffer from below average intelligence, high school diplomas aren't part of their futures. Now, I don't like how Will's friends from the hoods are depicted as unintelligent clowns 'cause we ain't all like that. I'm not like that; Imani ain't like that; Wanda ain't like that; and Ben Carson wasn't like that. In an episode of *Diff'rent Strokes*, Arnold feels guilty that he and his brother have everything their mother never had for herself. But Willis points out that their mom would be happy with what Mr. Drummond has given them because parents often give up their own dreams so that their kids have one.

Mama and Daddy work hard to make sure I can achieve my dreams. When their dreams for better educations were crushed, they held onto the hope that their child would have everything they never had. I *gotta* make it if I want Mama, Daddy, and even Grandma's hard work to mean something.

One day I was reading a *Jet* magazine in my room. Larry Fishburne, Ice Cube, and Cuba Gooding Jr. were on the cover, and a headline even said, "*Boyz N The Hood* Shows Danger, Pain And Love Make Men Out of Boys."

Just then, New Edition's "Boys to Men" started playing in my head. Danger, pain, and love does turn some boys to men, but it does the opposite for others. Daddy and Uncle Alonzo are perfect examples.

The phone rang, and my thoughts were shattered. I went to the living room, picked up the phone, and said, "Parker residence, Hatima speaking."

Dr. Wilson said, "Hi, Hatima. Can you come to my neighborhood?"

I said, "Sure."

Dr. Wilson said, "Great. I'll come pick you up."

Dr. Wilson hung up. I wasn't sure what he wanted me for, but I got my purse and put my magazine and some books in it. I went outside and sat on the steps. About half an hour later, Dr. Wilson's Rolls-Royce drove up.

I got into the passenger seat, said "Hi" to Dr. Wilson, and we drove away from my house. When we drove through Crenshaw, folks in the hood kept eyeing us. They probably thought he was a gangbanger or drug dealer and that I had officially joined the Bloods; but when word of that got to Mama and Daddy, they would clear things up in the hood.

Soon, we got to the Wilsons' house. There weren't as many kids playing on the streets as the ones in Crenshaw. Maybe they were inside watching television, at day camp, or had jobs. When I got out of the car and we walked into the house, Dr. Wilson led me to the living room. Their living room had a television set, a videocassette recorder, and a stereo system. Their television set was a new model, which I wasn't surprised by since rich people always buy the best stuff. I looked up at the walls and saw pictures I didn't see the first time I was here because the Wilsons had been repainting their living room walls and all the pictures had been taken down. There were pictures of Dr. King, Malcolm X, Nelson Mandela, Mahatma Gandhi, Frederick Douglass, Jackie Robinson, Muhammad Ali, Jesse Owens, Althea Gibson, the Black Panthers, John Brown, Abraham Lincoln, Lyndon B. Johnson, John F. Kennedy, and Bobby Kennedy.

My family doesn't have pictures of Jackie Robinson, Muhammad

Ali, Jesse Owens, or Althea Gibson. But without them, Black people wouldn't be respected on a baseball diamond, a boxing ring, a racetrack, or a tennis court. My family also doesn't have pictures of John Brown, President Lincoln, LBJ, JFK, or RFK, but everyone knows how important they are to Black history. During Black History Month, most guys do their reports on Jackie or Ali, totally unaware of the other Black athletes that broke down racial barriers. Tennis isn't a popular sport in the hood since basketball courts are the main sport venues, but some girls have done reports on Althea Gibson since there are few Black female athletes for us to look up to. Daddy said that Grandpa told him and Uncle Alonzo stories about how Jesse Owens won four gold medals at the 1936 Summer Olympics in Germany, but Hitler refused to shake his hand and congratulate him. I'm sure that was a great morale booster for Black Americans! There are a lot of other famous Black athletes who paved the way for other athletes: Joe Louis, Ernie Banks, Jim Brown, Wilt "the Stilt" Chamberlain, et cetera.

Everybody on Earth knows who Gandhi is. His non-violent methods led to India's independence from British rule. Gandhi was one of Dr. King's greatest inspirations, so without Gandhi's words, Dr. King's words would never have been. Malcolm X's White devil theory doesn't fly with a lotta Black folks because every African American respects John Brown, Abraham Lincoln, LBJ, JFK, and RFK. John Brown was an abolitionist who thought liberation for slaves was moving too slowly. So, he decided to raid a place called Harpers Ferry in Virginia. The raid was unsuccessful, and he was put to death. Frederick Douglass said, "I could speak for the slave. John Brown could fight for the slave."

Malcolm X even said, "If John Brown were still alive, we might accept him."

Malcolm X was one of the biggest haters of White people, but John Brown must have really loved Blacks and valued their freedom so much for Malcolm X to show him respect like that.

Everybody knows Abraham Lincoln freed the slaves. The Emancipation Proclamation didn't free the slaves at first. So, Abraham Lincoln wrote and signed the Thirteenth Amendment, which ended slavery forever – his reward: a bullet in the back of his head.

JFK and RFK supported the Civil Rights Movement. JFK was friends with Dr. King and even started writing out the Civil Rights Act, but he was assassinated before he could sign it. Thank God that Lyndon B. Johnson signed the Civil Rights Act into law. LBJ also signed the Voting Rights Act and the Fair Housing Act, proving that JFK's concern about civil rights was still very much alive even though he was dead. RFK was an Attorney General and a Senator. I heard he even visited poor neighborhoods and tough hoods to bring about positive changes to the areas, but a few years after JFK was assassinated in Dallas, someone shot his little brother right here in LA in the kitchen of the Ambassador Hotel.

Whenever any person, including non-Black people, stands up for Black people, they get shot down. There might be some people willing to take a stand against the cops and Mrs. Du, but they're probably afraid they would get shot down, too.

A White woman with brown hair, red lipstick, a white blouse, blue corduroy slacks, a gun on her hip, and a police badge dangling around her neck, walked into the living room. Her badge said "DETECTIVE" at the top and "2430" at the bottom.

I immediately put my hands up. Mama and Daddy explained to me what my rights are just in case I'm ever unlawfully arrested. I have the right to remain silent; anything I say can and will be used against me. I have the right to an attorney during questioning; if I can't afford one, the court can assign me one. Since I'm seventeen that makes me a minor, which means I can call my parents and have them with me before I answer any questions. The cops are supposed to tell us our rights but sometimes they don't. This counts as police misconduct but, like I've said before, our complaints aren't taken seriously.

The cop said, "Whoa, Miss Hatima Parker! My name is Detective Crawford. I'm not here to arrest you or shoot you; I just want to help settle the situation that happened between you, Doctor Wilson, Officer Greene, and Officer Wayne."

I asked, "What kind of detective are you?"

Officer Crawford explained, "I work in the Gang and Narcotics Division of the Detective Bureau." Then, she gave me a funny look and asked, "Are you going to put your hands down?"

I said, "No."

Officer Crawford asked, "Why not?"

I explained, "As soon as I put my hands down, you'll beat me or shoot me. Then, you'll tell your fellow cops that you thought I was a threat and that you were scared for your life. But you can still shoot me even if I don't put my hands down. Everyone knows your life matters more than mine. It always does."

Officer Crawford sighed, shook her head, and said, "I can see you have a negative opinion of the LAPD. Look, Hatima, I'm not going to hurt you. I just want to make sure the cops stationed in Crenshaw are actually doing their jobs instead of harassing folks." She pointed to the couch and asked, "Can we please sit down?"

I finally put my arms down 'cause they were getting really tired. I sat on one end of the couch while Detective Crawford sat on the other side.

She stated, "Officer Greene wanted to search Doctor Wilson's car without a warrant. But a police officer can also search a car without a warrant if they have probable cause. I ran a background check on you since Officer Greene claimed you looked mighty suspicious."

I said, "Probably because I was wearing baggy overalls, a graffiti shirt, and a backwards cap. But everyone in the hood wears those clothes so that's not a good enough reason to stop someone."

Detective Crawford ignored my comment on racial profiling. Instead, she said, "Your background check revealed that your uncle is Alonzo Parker, a high-ranking member of the Bloods. Is this true?"

I said, "Yeah, but my family and I don't want anything to do with Uncle Alonzo. He's nothing but trouble, and Daddy has forbidden him from talking to me and vice versa."

Detective Crawford asked, "Has he interacted with you anytime during the past few months?"

I read that it's illegal to lie to the cops. Uncle Alonzo talked to me the day Latasha Harlins died, but I don't want the cops to think that I'm intentionally doing anything with Uncle Alonzo or the Bloods.

So, I said, "No."

Detective Crawford asked, "Are you sure?"

I said, "Absolutely positive."

Detective Crawford gave me a look that said she didn't completely believe me. Then, she asked, "Do you have any idea where your uncle stores drugs, stolen items, and other contraband?"

I exclaimed, "How the Hell would I know that?! My family doesn't want anything to do with my uncle's dirty business, so we don't know where he keeps his drugs and stuff!"

Detective Crawford didn't react to my tirade, but I had fucked up. Mama and Daddy told me to always speak quietly and calmly to cops. When a Black person talks in an angry voice, the cops may see it as a threatening action and start shooting.

Detective Crawford asked, "Have either of your parents had recent contact with your uncle?"

Daddy hasn't grumbled about Uncle Alonzo seeing him in quite a while.

I said, "No."

Detective Crawford said, "Okay. If Officer Greene or anyone else stops you again, it may be because of your uncle. They're probably hoping that any close connections you have with him can help us take him down."

I said, "The cops will just use my blood relation with him as an excuse to harass me or beat me or shoot me."

Detective Crawford took a card out of her shirt pocket and gave it to me.

She said, "If any cops harass you, call me. I'll help straighten it out."

I asked, "Why should I trust you? Why would you care about me?"

Detective Crawford said, "Your background check also revealed that you've applied to Annapolis. Do you want to be with the Navy or the Marines?"

I immediately said, "The Marines. My grandpa and dad were both Marines. They both fought for and served this country, and I wanna carry on the tradition. Now I'm questioning about whether or not this country is worth fighting for."

Detective Crawford asked, "Have you received a nomination from a Senator or Representative?"

I said, "Not yet."

Detective Crawford said, "Your background check also revealed that you've won several martial arts tournaments."

I said, "Yeah. Since the Marine Corps Martial Arts Program is first-class, I gotta be ready for all kinds of combat training. I spend most of my time helping Master Shin train other kids at his dojang."

Detective Crawford asked, "Are you talking about Master Shin's hapkido school in Koreatown?"

I said, "Yeah."

She exclaimed, "I studied under him, too!"

I said, "Really?" *Never imagined I would have something in common with a cop.*

Detective Crawford said, "Boys said that girls couldn't be martial artists, but I was determined to prove them all wrong. I kicked plenty boys' butts when I was a kid."

I said, "I've been in a few fights, strictly self-defense because I know assault and battery is a crime."

Detective Crawford asked, "What are you going to major in at Annapolis?"

I said, "History. I want to be an Africanist."

Detective Crawford said, "That dream is more original than most I've heard. Most kids say they're going to be doctors, lawyers, engineers, teachers, police officers, firefighters, or businesspeople. But it takes all kinds of people to make the world go round."

After Detective Crawford left, I realized she was the first cop I had met that I felt comfortable around. Black folks in the hood believe in the Black Panthers' statement that all cops are pigs. But I know that not every single police officer in the USA and the planet is a pig, just like how not every Mexican is an illegal immigrant or how every Black person is a thief, wino, junkie, and/or deadbeat parent. But, until I met Detective Crawford, I hadn't met a cop who had treated a Black person decently. I just knew there had to be some nice cops. But why would I believe that if I had never seen it? People say seeing is believing, but maybe we also need more faith about goodness.

Now, no one has seen God in almost two thousand years, but people have seen what He does. He makes the sun rise, He makes the trees grow, He made all the animals, and He made all the stars and knows them by name. There is proof of God's power everywhere in the world. But what proof is there that the LAPD are doing a good job? The Bloods and the Crips are still shooting at each other and innocent people get caught in the crossfire. Uncle Alonzo is still pimping girls, leading burglary rings, and heading a drug dealing empire. Should I tell Detective Crawford that I know which people in my hood are gangsters? Should I tell her that these gangsters might help the LAPD take Uncle Alonzo down?

Snitching is the worst sin in the hood. In the movie *Sister Act*, Deloris Van Cartier witnessed her mobster boyfriend kill a guy and the witness protection program put her in a San Francisco convent. Being a nun drove Deloris crazy, so she called Lieutenant Eddie Souther to put her someplace else, but he said that there's a leak in the police department and some of their witnesses end up dead. From the way Uncle Alonzo talks, I figured out that he has some LAPD officers on his payroll. That's understandable because the Bloods make *way* more money than the cops do. The reason Uncle Alonzo, Auntie Kalisha, and my cousin Malik don't live in Westwood, Bel-Air, or some other bougie neighborhood is because the folks there would ask too many questions. Some lawyers would analyze Uncle Alonzo's records and realize that he has no tax statements or tax returns since drug dealers, pimps, and thieves don't pay taxes. Then, they would undermine his entire operation and the police would lock him back up in San Quentin and throw away the key. But when Black people don't cooperate with the cops and help them take down the gangsters, are we not contributing to the problem?

Dr. Wilson drove me back to Crenshaw. While he was driving there, we saw a cop harassing Marcus. His hands were spread out on the police car, and the cops were patting him down. I'm pretty sure Marcus isn't a gangster because I haven't seen him hanging out with the Bloods or the Crips. Marcus is also one of the few kids in the hood who has a father. His dad is a construction worker, and his mom works at the post office. Boys often grow up into carbon copies of their dads; since Mr. Miller is a hardworking and responsible man, Marcus has also grown into a hardworking and responsible man. Plus, even though Wanda's dad was a gangster, I highly doubt Wanda would want to go down the same path her mom did.

Dr. Wilson stopped his Rolls-Royce, parked, got out, and asked, "Excuse me, officers, but is there a problem?"

The White cop who patted down Marcus said, "Yeah, a liquor store just got robbed a half an hour ago. We're stopping anyone who fits the description."

The White cop's badge said "POLICE OFFICER" at the top and the bottom said "2560."

The second cop was Black. The top of his badge also said "POLICE OFFICER" but the bottom said "2200." The Black cop said, "The storeowner said the thief was African American, five foot seven, had cornrows, wore a black hoodie, and wore Adidas sneakers."

I looked at Marcus. Marcus is five foot nine and sports a Jheri curl. He was wearing an LA Dodgers jersey and Nike sneakers. The only part of the description that he fit was his black skin.

Dr. Wilson asked, "Officers...?"

The White cop replied, "I'm Officer Hawthorne and he's Officer Jones."

Dr. Wilson asked, "Officer Hawthorne, does this young man look like he fits the description?"

Officer Hawthorne said, "He's Black, and he looks suspicious."

Dr. Wilson said, "He's not wearing a hoodie."

Officer Jones said, "He could have taken it off."

Dr. Wilson said, "He looks like he's five foot nine, not five foot seven. He has a Jheri curl, not cornrows. I highly doubt he could unbraid his hair, curl it, and then be back on the streets in half an hour. He's also wearing a pair of Nikes, not Adidas."

Officer Hawthorne asked, "And who are you?"

Dr. Wilson replied, "Doctor Jeremiah Wilson. I'm a surgeon at the UCLA Medical Center. If you don't stop pestering this man, I'll be more than happy to bring you both to court on charges of racial profiling and obstruction of justice."

Officer Hawthorne gave him a mean look and told Officer Jones, "Come on, let's get outta here. It's highly unlikely we'll find the thief anyway. You know how sneaky these people are."

Dr. Wilson asked Officer Jones, "Brother, are you going to let him talk about us that way?"

Officer Jones said, "I'm just doing my job."

Dr. Wilson said, "You don't seem to be doing it very well. If you sit back and watch your fellow officers disrespect our people, then you're part of the problem not the solution."

Officer Jones said, "I want to help people, not cause more harm."

I blurted out and sarcastically said, "I'm sure the cops who beat up Rodney King thought the same thing. Beating up a man for speeding and driving while intoxicated is a great way to make the world a better place."

Officer Jones said, "Ever since George Holliday released that videotape, he's made every LAPD officer look like a fool. We're not all like those cops who beat Rodney King."

I asked, "Would you have beaten up Rodney King if you were there that night? Or just stood there and watched him be almost killed without saying nothing?"

Officer Jones took a breath, let it out, and said, "I would have had to restrain him because he was under the influence of alcohol, but I'm not one hundred percent sure that I would have beaten him. Maybe I would have because the gangsters I've encountered over the years have me made me fearful for my life. But beating a Black man bloody who has no affiliation with gangs shows how far the LAPD has gone off the deep end. I don't support what those cops did to Rodney King because there has to be better ways to bring peace to the hood."

Dr. Wilson said, "Then, don't support your partner's dirty tactics. Use that brain and your heart. There's a reason why many Black people call Black cops Uncle Toms."

Officer Jones got into the passenger side of his police car, and Officer Hawthorne drove away.

Marcus said, "Thanks, Doctor Wilson. Hatima, how you know him?"

I replied, "His son Jared and I study martial arts together."

Marcus said, "Cool. See you around, Doc."

Marcus was starting to walk away but Dr. Wilson asked, "What's your name, son?"

Marcus replied, "Marcus Miller."

Dr. Wilson said, "Marcus, you should file a complaint."

Marcus said, "I should, but I won't. Filing complaints ain't gonna do shit. Black folks have been filing complaints for decades and dirty cops still oppress our people."

Dr. Wilson said, "Then, *I'll* file a complaint. I'm sure the LAPD will listen to what I have to say."

Marcus scuffed and asked, "You think you're special just because you a doctor? You think the cops saw you as little more than a nigga to them?"

Dr. Wilson sternly said, "Don't use the n-word. It is a derogatory term that has been used against our people for centuries and it isn't any less hurtful when a Black person says it."

I told Dr. Wilson, "Doc, Officer Greene and Officer Wayne didn't see a respected medical doctor when they stopped you, a few days ago. All they saw was a Black man in a fancy car. In their eyes, if a Black man is driving a fancy car in the hood then they better stop him because it's probably stolen. Or maybe he's a gangbanger and he has drugs or stolen stuff in the trunk. It never occurs to them that the Black man might have a legit job that pays six figures even though this city is full of rich Black folks."

Marcus added, "Hatima is right. You may think you're aiding the struggle, but *a lotta* bougie Blacks who don't reside in South Central have no idea how bad the struggle is."

When Master Shin closed the dojang for a week in August, Joshua saw it as a chance to introduce me to his father. If he thinks this would make me take him to my hood and introduce him to my parents, he is crazy as Hell.

Joshua took me to his dad's nightclub in the afternoon. He led me into the back of the nightclub where his father kept his office.

He knocked on the door and a male voice said, "Come in."

Then, he opened the door and I saw a Korean man who looked a lot like him was behind a desk punching numbers into a calculator.

Joshua said, "Dad, this is the girl I told you about, Hatima Parker."

Mr. Yang looked up at me but didn't say anything.

I stretched out my hand and said, "It's a pleasure to meet you, Mister Yang."

Mr. Yang didn't shake my hand. He said something to Joshua in Korean and Joshua said something back. I have learned some Korean words from Master Shin, but I'm not fluent in the language. I didn't understand all the words being passed between Joshua and his dad, but I was able to deduce that Mr. Yang didn't have anything nice to say about me. When folks want to insult you, they start talking in another language if they are multilingual. The Latinos who go to Master Shin's always speak Spanish among themselves. The way they speak it and the funny looks they give the others at the dojang always has me thinking that they might be insulting us.

Dr. King preached integration – intergroup and interpersonal living – but I'm not sure if it works. The Blacks, the Latinos, the Koreans, and other ethnic groups all keep to themselves in their own hoods. Westwood is far from being a diverse neighborhood, which has me wondering if Dr. King's dream will ever come true.

Dr. King said, "We must accept finite disappointment but never lose infinite hope."

I guess I expected this meeting to be nothing but disappointment, but I haven't lost hope that Mr. Yang will see that I'm an honest, hardworking girl, not some cheap ho trying to pull a fast one on his son.

Then, Mr. Yang asked, "Joshua says you're a teacher at Master Shin's Dojang. What do you do when you're not at the dojang?"

I said, "I'm still in school. I get straight-As. I want to attend the US Naval Academy, study history, get into a graduate Africana Studies program, fight as a Marine, and become an Africanist."

Mr. Yang asked, "What's an Africanist?"

I explained, "An expert on Black history and the African diaspora."

Mr. Yang asked, "Do they actually pay people to be Africanists?"

I said, "Of course they do! Many colleges, not just HBCUs, have Africana departments and courses. Africana scholars become teachers, writers, lawyers, politicians, et cetera."

Mr. Yang said, "The American military academies feature some of the best educational systems in the world. I wish you luck getting there."

I said, "Thanks, Mister Yang."

Joshua asked his dad, "Do you have any other questions you want to ask Hatima?"

Mr. Yang said, "No, she seems like a nice young lady, unlike those other girls who live in South Central."

I didn't like how Mr. Yang gave me my props but took away props from girls in Crenshaw. I tried to keep a straight face and not show Mr. Yang that I was upset with what he said. We left the office, but I had expected more, a much longer interrogation. Well, if the interrogation had gone any longer, I probably woulda lost my cool.

Then I asked Joshua, "So, can we still date?"

Joshua said, "Yeah. Dad didn't say 'no,' which means he's okay with it."

I still had doubts about Mr. Yang. I could tell that he didn't like me all that much.

Marcus Garvey said, "If you have no confidence in self, you are twice defeated in life."

I have to continue to believe in myself regardless of what other people think of me.

Chapter Eight

Soon, summer ended. Summertime always ends too soon, but I like school 'cause I love learning new things; so, I didn't mind saying goodbye to summer.

I saw Mr. Ngozi at the Creole & Cajun Kitchen eating a po' boy sandwich; so I went to sit across from him in the booth he was dining in.

I asked him, "Hi, Mister Ngozi, how was Toronto?"

He replied, "It was wonderful. Canada is a beautiful country."

I asked, "Should we expect anything new for the upcoming school year?"

Mr. Ngozi said, "The senior class will be learning about Africa. The 'Scramble for Africa', back-to-Africa odysseys, the effects of both World Wars on the African continent, post-colonialism, apartheid, and more will all be covered."

I said, "Cool. The one African country people are obsessed with is South Africa, but it's important that people learn about other African nations to get a better understanding of the worldwide Black struggle."

Mr. Ngozi nodded in approval said, "Plus, my goddaughter is attending medical school at UCLA. She just graduated from Oxford with her undergraduate degree."

I said, "All I know about Oxford is that they make great dictionaries and thesauruses."

Mr. Ngozi laughed and explained, "The University of Oxford is located in the city of Oxford, England. It's not only one of the top schools in the UK, it's considered one of the best universities in the world. Yale has nothing over Oxford."

I asked, "If England has such great schools, why is she coming here? What's her name anyway?"

Mr. Ngozi said, "Ifechukwu Ejiofor but everyone calls her Ife for short."

He pronounced her name "Eee-fay-choo-koo" and "Eh-jee-oh-for."

I asked, "What does Ifechukwu mean?"

Mr. Ngozi explained, "It means 'the Light of God.' Ejiofor is derived from the words Eji and Ofo. Eji means 'to hold.' An Ofo is an object historically used to settle disputes and to bestow judgment. Thanks to God's light and critical judgment, Ife has made it into medical school and will soon become a successful doctor."

I said, "Wow. When Nigerians name their kids, y'all really give them a lot to live up to."

Mr. Ngozi then said, "Students at British universities usually receive their bachelor's degrees in three years, but medical school takes up to five years to complete in the UK, while it takes four years to complete an American MD."

I said, "Three years in the UK and four years here? That's a very effective academic strategy!"

Toward the end of August, a red 1970 Chevrolet Impala convertible drove up to me while I was walking home from the bus stop. When the driver rolled down his window, I saw that he was my cousin.

HEAL THE HOOD

Malik Parker had on a red t-shirt, a red sweatband around his head, a gold Heuer watch on his left wrist, and cornrows on his head. Some guys in the hood are rocking cornrows, which means braids ain't just for girls. Malik looked like the world was his oyster and he acted like his car made him King of the Hood. *Malik* is Arabic for "king"; so, I guess Uncle Alonzo and Auntie Kalisha hope he will actually become a king. The only people who become kings are folks who are part of royal families, like the British, Saudi Arabian, and Moroccan Royal Families. The only thing Malik will ever be king of is a corrupt empire. Plus, Malik is one of Malcolm X's Islamic names, El-Hajj Malik El-Shabazz. Malcolm X is one of the few civil rights leaders Uncle Alonzo respects. I guess he thinks he and Malcolm X are the same since they both have criminal records, run all-Black organizations, and use guns to defend themselves and their loved ones; but that's the only similarity between them.

Malcolm X said, "To have once been a criminal is no disgrace. To remain a criminal is the disgrace."

The Nation of Islam helped set Malcolm X on the right path; he renounced his criminal past when he got out of jail and became one of the world's greatest Black leaders, but Uncle Alonzo obviously never renounced his criminal past since he's still gangbanging with the Bloods. Plus, the NOI gives back to the Black community, while the Bloods just take from the Black community. Uncle Alonzo and Malcolm X ain't the same and Malik also has no comparison with Brother Malcolm.

Malik asked me, "Yo, cuz, you need a ride?"

I replied, "No, I don't need a ride. I'm fine walking."

Malik said, "Come on, cuz, this thing between our parents doesn't have to affect our relationship."

I stated, "We don't have any kind of relationship. We may be cousins, but the Bloods matter more to you, Uncle Alonzo, and Auntie Kalisha than your real bloods."

Malik said, "Uncle Orlando can't look past Dad's business to try and have a civil relationship. You know the brothers could still hang out, drink beer, listen to jazz at nightclubs."

I explained, "And what happens when the cops come down hard on Uncle Alonzo? If my daddy is with him, he could be considered an accessory. Either way, when Uncle Alonzo finally gets busted, Daddy wants me, Mama, and Grandma to have all ties cut from him. That way the cops can't pin any crimes on us, and we won't end up in jail."

Malik said, "I won't end up in jail. My pops taught me how to play the game. The number one rule is not to get caught; and since plenty of boys in blue are paid good money by my dad, we don't have to worry about ever getting busted."

It's not just White and Yellow skin that helps certain people slip through the system. The amount of money a person has, even if it's dirty money, also lets them slip through the system like greased pigs.

I told Malik, "You, Unc, and Auntie are just as bad as the KKK, the Nazis, the LAPD, and every other group trying to oppress the people and keep us down."

Malik asked, "You're still holding onto that stupid dream of becoming the next Rosa Parks or Harriet Tubman?"

I said, "It ain't stupid! In a year's time, I'll have my diploma; and years later, I'll have my PhD. When I become an educated Black woman, you and the rest of the Bloods better watch out. Brains always beat brawn."

Malik said, "I heard you've become friends with a doctor who lives in Westwood. Heard he helped Marcus Miller get out of a tough spot with the cops. I always figured you'd try to get on the good side of bougie folks. But all you had to do was walk next door to Leimert Park."

I crossed my arms and asked him, "What's that supposed to mean?"

Malik explained, "You can't get into the Naval Academy or any college in this country alone. You need to kiss up to rich folks, niggas and Whites. The rich niggas will help you get into an HBCU. The rich Whites will help you get into the other schools. I know you think my parents and I are crooks, but at least we're staying right here in the hood with our people. You wanna move on up outta here like the other sellouts. You wanna become an Uncle Tom because everyone knows White folks are the ones who hold the true power. White folks hold most of the power because they own most of the money. There are hardly any legit ways for Blacks to make money, and we got no choice but to do it on the other side of the law. Now, if White folks relinquished their power and let Blacks have more freedom, maybe the Bloods' enterprises wouldn't be necessary. Unfortunately, our work is needed."

Malik rolled up his window and drove away, while I rolled my eyes.

Malik, Uncle Alonzo, and the rest of the Bloods are a bunch of fools. They believe that since so many people have a low opinion about Black folks, we have no choice but to be niggas. To them, since White folks don't want us to succeed in school and legit businesses, we have no choice but to become criminals. That is a lie. God holds the power in this world and, by His grace, I will become a successful woman the right way.

When I got home, the phone rang, and I answered it.

A woman's voice asked, "Can I please speak to Miss Hatima Parker?"

I replied, "I'm Hatima Parker."

The woman's voice said, "Miss Parker, I'm Maxine Waters. I'm the US Representative for California's Twenty-Ninth Congressional District."

I couldn't believe I was talking to Mrs. Waters!

I exclaimed, "It's such an honor to talk to you, Missus Waters! I've seen you on the news! Are you calling because of my request for you to nominate me so I can get into the Naval Academy?"

Maxine Waters said, "Yes, Miss Parker. I like what you put in your letter.

> 'Dear Missus Maxine Waters,
>
> I have always dreamed of becoming a Marine and an Africanist. That is why I want to attend college at the United States Naval Academy after I graduate from Susan Miller Dorsey High School. After I graduate from the Naval Academy, I plan to pursue a PhD at another college and then serve my country in the Marine Corps.
>
> I come from a neighborhood that many people believe is dangerous, corrupt, and poisonous. Many people believe that Black people in the ghetto can't contribute positively to American society, but there is so much more to Crenshaw than meets the eye. Sure, there are Bloods, Crips, and other gangs that are constantly robbing, extorting, and murdering people. But there are also good people who run legitimate businesses, such as Missus Brooks, the mother of my best friend, who owns a restaurant called the Creole & Cajun Kitchen, and Mister Brown, the owner of a mechanics business called Oscar's Garage.

My parents are also good people; my father, Orlando Parker, is a baggage handler at the Los Angeles International Airport and my mother, Suzanne Jane Parker, is a waitress at the Beverly Hills Hotel's Polo Lounge. Unfortunately, neither of my parents has a high school diploma so their dream has always been for me to do better than they did. My parents instilled in me a love for Black history so that I would know I am capable of greatness.

Missus Waters, I know your life was tough since you were raised by a single mother, and you worked in a garment factory and as a telephone operator. But I read and heard about the work you did with Head Start in Watts, my grandmother's neighborhood. You also went to Cal State LA and received your B.A. in sociology. Even though the odds were stacked against you, you still succeeded.

I believe that, despite the odds stacked against me, I can also fulfill my dreams.

Sincerely,

Hatima Gabriella Parker.'"

I exclaimed, "I'm so glad my letter convinced you to nominate me!"

Maxine Waters said, "A friend of mine who teaches at UCLA says that a friend of hers who works at the Ronald Reagan UCLA Medical Center mentioned you wanted to go to Annapolis. I can't ignore their good judgment because it's hard to earn their approval. I reviewed your letter, and I'm impressed by how you've managed to maintain good grades and great extracurricular activities even though you live in an at-risk area."

"At-risk area" is another name for the hood but Maxine Waters didn't say it like it was a dirty word. After all, she has lived and worked in the ghetto as well and is still campaigning for better conditions in our hoods. But I can tell she probably views me as another charity case. One of the reasons I wanna be a Marine is to show what I can give to my country.

But I said, "Thank you so much, Missus Waters. I'll treasure your good word for the rest of my life."

Mrs. Waters said, "You're welcome," and hung up.

I couldn't wait for my parents to get home so I could tell them the good news! Then, I thought about what my cousin said to me. He said I was kissing up to rich folks because I needed their connections to get outta the ghetto, but I didn't befriend Jared and the rest of his family because I expected a reward. My parents always taught me to be myself and treat others with respect so I could make friends. I never expected that the Wilsons would help me achieve my dreams, but I was grateful.

But did the Wilsons help me because they saw me as a charity case?

Do they think my community is so poisonous that they have to do their part to get me as far away from South Central LA as possible?

I became a senior in the fall of 1991, which meant I was a queen of the school. I could now take the courses I liked since I had completed my math and science requirements. This meant that my schedule was full of English, French, history, geography, and other humanities courses – all AP, of course. The grades I got in senior year would fully determine my future so I needed to fill out applications to schools with great Africana programs.

The schools I applied to were Freeman University, Louisiana Agricultural & Mechanical University (LAMU), Howard University, Washington University in St. Louis, UC Davis, and Vanderbilt. LAMU is in New Orleans; Howard is in DC; UC Davis is a six-hour drive from LA; and Vanderbilt is in Nashville, Tennessee. Freeman, LAMU, and Howard are all Black Ivy League schools, which means getting in is not easy. LAMU has the highest acceptance rate of the three HBCUs, over fifty percent, so I was sure I would get in. Freeman and Howard's acceptance rates are lower than fifty percent, so getting in was not guaranteed. WashU's and Vanderbilt's acceptance rates are as low as the Ivy League's, but UC Davis' acceptance rate is much higher. That means my chances of getting into WashU and Vanderbilt were low, but I had a good chance of getting into UC Davis.

These schools all have great Africana Studies programs, so they were my back-up plan in case the Naval Academy rejected me. The Naval Academy's acceptance rate is also as low as the Ivy League's so there was a high chance I could be rejected.

Another great thing about September is the new episodes on television. There were new episodes of *Fresh Prince*, *The Cosby Show*, *Saved by the Bell*, et cetera. Since Will is from the hood of West Philly, many people underestimate his intelligence. But in "PSAT Story", Will scored in the ninety-first percentile of the PSAT, while Carlton only scored in the ninetieth percentile. Obviously, Will rubs it in Carlton's face and hilarity ensues. That got me wondering if people in Annapolis would underestimate my intelligence just because I'm from Crenshaw. Ben Carson has stated in interviews that people at Yale underestimated his intelligence, especially when he first struggled with his courses. They even told him to either drop premed as his major or transfer to another school, but he proved them wrong by graduating with honors and getting into a top medical school. I will prove any bigot at the Naval Academy wrong if they even think about suggesting my transfer to another school.

On *The Cosby Show*, the Huxtables have a streetwise relative named Pam Tucker who moves into their home. Pam is not as much trouble as Will and the Huxtables are a good influence on her. She gives serious thought into going to college even though tuition is expensive, and most kids from the hood go to community colleges instead of major universities.

Unlike other sitcoms, *Saved by the Bell* airs on Saturday mornings. *Saved by the Bell* features only one main Black cast member, Lark Voorhies. That makes her the token Black of the show. Other television shows have had token Blacks: Kim Fields as Tootie Ramsey on *The Facts of Life* and Mr. T as B.A. Baracus on *The A-Team*. Lark Voorhies plays Lisa Turtle, the fashionista of the *Saved by the Bell* group. Lisa's parents are both doctors so she can afford to buy the latest fashions. Some of my friends think Lisa is a bit of a spoiled brat, and they question whether or not she's a good representation of African American culture. Obviously, they also question if the Huxtables and the Bankses properly represent our culture.

It was the weekend so Wanda, Imani, and I hung out at the Fox Hills Mall. The main reason we went there instead of the mall in our hood was so Imani could apply for a job. She had finally convinced her mom that she could work *and* keep her grades up. Since Imani's Chuck Taylors are almost worn through and they had to really stretch the small amount of food in their fridge, Ms. Fitzpatrick finally agreed. It would be hard for Imani to concentrate on her schoolwork if she's struggling with hunger pains.

I told Wanda and Imani while we were sitting in the food court,

"The Huxtable kids and the Banks kids have parents who went to college and pull in six-figure salaries. Obviously, all the clothes, albums, electronics, and other stuff they buy is just them reaping the reward of hard work and perseverance. The same can be said for Lisa Turtle. I think the folks who work on *Saved by the Bell* are concerned that if Lisa was a girl from the hood, it might be a stereotypical view of African Americans. Besides, Black sitcoms have a variety of Black families who come from different levels of the socioeconomic ladder. What about the Evans family from *Good Times*? Raj, Dwayne, and Rerun from *What's Happening!!*? Their lifestyles in inner-city Chicago and the mean streets of LA are something we can relate to. There are also plenty of Black families who can relate to the Huxtables, the Bankses, and Lisa Turtle."

Wanda said, "Those bougie friends of yours, the Wilsons, can definitely relate to the Huxtables and Bankses. Didn't you say they have three cars and a maid?"

Imani looked up from the application she was filling out and said, "Doctor Wilson is a surgeon, and Missus Wilson is an engineer. One of their kids is headed to an Ivy League school. They sound like a mix of the Bankses and the Huxtables."

I asked them, "Do either of you have a problem with the Wilsons?"

Wanda said, "No. Doctor Wilson got my man out of a jam with the po-po. Any chance we can call him the next time the cops stop us?"

I said, "It might be better if I called Detective Crawford."

Imani asked, "Detective Crawford? You snitching to the jake now?"

I said, "No, I ain't about to snitch about my uncle, but the next time the cops stop us Detective Crawford might help us out."

Wanda asked, "Was she one of the cops who was there when Rodney King was beaten?"

I said, "If she was, she wouldn't be out in public. The news has repeated the names of the four cops who were indicted for beating up Rodney King and word has spread about the other cops who witnessed the crime. Detective Crawford ain't one of them. My instincts tell me that she might be a good cop."

Imani asked, "Is she a sister?"

I said, "No, she's White."

Wanda asked, "What makes you think we can trust her?"

I said, "We have to put our trust in some cops. It's not like we have an all-Black protection force in Crenshaw or any other South Central hood."

Wanda said, "We did have all-Black protection forces back in the day. The Nation of Islam, the Black Panthers, the Organization of Afro-American Unity."

Imani added, "SNCC, CORE, SCLC, the NAACP."

Wanda explained, "The NOI and the BPP did a better job at protecting Black folks. They refused to ask help from White people because they knew we could fix our problems ourselves."

Imani said, "SNCC, CORE, the SCLC, and the NAACP still protect Black folks. Plus, they're still around fighting the fight. Last time I checked, the BPP had disbanded, and Malcolm X's death guaranteed the collapse of the OAAU."

Wanda said, "The Nation of Islam is still around."

Imani said, "Last time I checked they weren't as popular as they were back in the sixties."

Wanda said, "The SCLC also hasn't been as popular as it was back in the sixties since Doctor King was shot. The NAACP definitely isn't doing enough to create change. Maybe an armed war is the only way to guarantee our rights!"

Some other people in the food court looked angrily at Wanda. Like I said before, White folks get uneasy when Black folks get angry. Are they afraid Wanda will take out a Glock and yell, "This is a stick-up, fools!"?

So, I said, "My sisters, please calm down! All these groups have done their part in the fight for equality. Some of these groups have been disbanded, but others haven't. Doctor King, Malcolm X, and the BPP may not be around anymore, but their words are still important. As long as we keep quoting and learning from Doctor King, Malcolm X, and the BPP's Ten-Point Platform, they'll never really disappear."

Wanda said, "I can't argue against an Africanist."

I said, "I won't officially be an Africanist until I graduate from college."

I thought about Dr. Wilson, his Rolls-Royce, and a *Fresh Prince* episode from the first season called "Mistaken Identity." In the episode, Will and Carlton drive a Benz to Palm Springs because Uncle Phil and Aunt Viv are at a retreat with Uncle Phil's legal partners. Two cops stop them, and Carlton stupidly thinks that the cops stopped them for driving too slowly and are just doing their jobs. Will knows why they were stopped, and he tries to give the cops short and easy answers to their questions, but Carlton states that they live in Bel-Air near the Reagans and that he's gonna go to Harvard Law School. Of course, the cops don't believe them. Will and Carlton try to call Uncle Phil and Geoffrey, but they're unable to give them a message about their predicament. Then, Will decides to give a confession as long as a news crew shows up with a video camera; and Uncle Phil,

Aunt Viv, and Mr. Furth, the owner of the car, see the live confession and come to their rescue.

I love Uncle Phil's speech: "I've got a few questions for you. When you got this alleged confession from these two young men, did they have a lawyer present? No, because *I'm* their lawyer. Did you notify their parents? No, because *we're* their parents. So, officer, don't tell us to wait, and don't tell us to sit down. Just open that damn cell, and let those two boys outta there, or I'm gonna tie this place up with so much litigation that your *grand*children are gonna need lawyers!"

When they get home, Carlton still can't see how he and Will were racially profiled. Obviously, Uncle Phil and Aunt Viv never gave Carlton or their kids the talk about what to do when the cops stop you.

Carlton asks his cousin, "What's your complaint here? We were detained for a few hours. Dad cleared things up, and we were released. The system works."

Then Will says, "I hope you like that system 'cause you'll be seeing a lot of it in your lifetime."

Carlton says, "Not if I bring a map."

Will explains to his cousin, "You just don't get it, do you? No map is going to save you, neither is your glee club or your fancy Bel-Air address or who your daddy is. When you're driving in a nice car in a strange neighborhood, none of that matters. They only see one thing."

Carlton tells Will as Will leaves the living room, "Maybe growing up where you did has made you a little touchy, but I think you've blown this thing out of proportion. If you look at the facts—"

Will reiterates that skin color is all that matters to those cops, and it's the only thing that will matter to many people in the world.

This shakes Carlton's confidence in the legal system as he slowly realizes that his rich lifestyle doesn't make him immune to bigotry.

I wonder if the Huxtables ever had the talk with their kids. None of the shows on *The Cosby Show* so far have dealt with racism. Since the Huxtables are respected members of their community in Brooklyn Heights, most people love them and don't have a problem with them. But what about when the Huxtables travel outside Brooklyn? There is a good chance that the Huxtable kids may encounter bigotry, and I hope they'll know how to handle such situations.

Another sitcom that deals with serious issues, including racism, is *Diff'rent Strokes*. Since Willis and Arnold are adopted by a rich White man who lives in a Park Avenue penthouse, a person might think they have nothing to worry about after that, but their skin color never changes so they're victims of racism several times, though their White dad and White sister always stand by them.

I remember an episode called "Hot Watch." Willis and Arnold found a neighbor's watch in a potted plant and decided to tell their father instead of the cops. They don't trust cops because they knew all cops treat Black kids as suspects. Sure enough, a White cop does apprehend Willis and Arnold and take them to their penthouse, telling Mr. Drummond that Willis and Arnold claim to be his sons. Mr. Drummond clears things up with the cop, and he releases them. Then, the cop finds Willis' fingerprints on an apartment knob and assumes he was the thief, but Willis explained that he and Arnold saw that the door was open, so he closed it. The lady who lives in the apartment doesn't believe him and insists on pressing charges against Willis, but that is unnecessary because the cops catch the real thieves. When the cop sees how much trust Mr. Drummond has in his sons, he lets go of his prejudice and does his job properly.

In another episode titled "Skin Deep", Kimberly gets the hots for a guy called Roger Morehouse. Willis wants to take Emily – Roger's sister – out, but Roger is against it. Arnold records Roger making racist remarks and Kimberly is sad that her new boyfriend is a bigot, but they decide to teach him a lesson by turning Kimberly Black. Usually, when White folks dress up in Blackface, it's considered racist because when Whites performers in minstrel shows dressed in Blackface, they depicted African Americans as lazy, unintelligent, and uncouth. But folks in South Central loved the "Skin Deep" episode because of the important lesson Kimberly, Willis, and Arnold are trying to teach Roger. Kimberly's skin color might have changed, but her personality doesn't. Roger has second thoughts about dating Kimberly when he sees she is Black, and Kimberly dumps Roger when she sees that he won't change his racist ways. The funniest moment is when Mr. Drummond sees that his daughter has turned Black. I couldn't stop laughing!

I love the Drummonds and the Jacksons. They teach folks how wrong bigotry is and how the world, sadly, has not changed much since the 1960s.

Stella Wilson acts so high and mighty when she's around me. Does she seriously think a cop will treat her any better than they treat me or my friends? If the cops can stop her dad, then they can stop her too. Rich Black people shouldn't go around acting so high and mighty because they're still part of the same race as us poor hood rats. The cops will racially profile them, too; the difference is they have access to top lawyers to help them out. Legal assistance and public attorneys is all us hood folks have, and some public attorneys don't make an effort to help us when we're in trouble.

In late September, Joshua told me at Master Shin's, "My homecoming dance is coming up. When's yours?"

I said, "The first week of October."

Joshua asked, "Do you wanna go?"

I said, "With my friends, yes. With you, not really."

Joshua said, "Come on, Hatima, I thought we got over our differences. I like you, and I don't care that you're Black. You like me even though I'm Korean."

I told him, "South Central and Koreatown haven't got over our skin colors. Racial tensions are still high in the hood. Blacks are still boycotting Korean businesses and phoning and mailing hate messages to Charles Earl Lloyd since he's willingly representing Missus Du in court."

Joshua said, "I'm guessing folks in your hood think Mister Lloyd is a traitor to your race for siding with a Korean woman instead of the Harlins family."

I said, "Exactly."

Joshua asked, "Do your friends and family think you're a traitor because you have a Korean boyfriend?"

I asked, "Since when are you my boyfriend?"

Joshua said, "Since we made out on the Ferris wheel in Santa Monica. We've made out *a lot* during the summer and this September. I care about you and you care about me, so why can't I be a full part of your life?"

I asked him, "Why do you wanna be a full part of my life? Aren't there any nice Korean girls you can make out with?"

Joshua said, "There are plenty of nice Korean girls, but I only care about you."

I asked, "Why?"

Joshua said, "I love your spirit. If life is a bull, you've taken it by the horns. You have such a wonderful love of life that I find attractive."

That was so eloquently put. I was speechless.

Then, Joshua said, "We can hang out somewhere else in LA after our homecoming celebrations. That sound good?"

I said, "Yeah. That sounds really good."

In October, a *Fresh Prince* episode called "Guess Who's Coming to Marry?" got me thinking. In the episode, Will's Aunt Janice is engaged to a White man named Frank and Will's mother, Vy, is angry about it. She thinks Janice has lost her mind and even forbids Will from going to the wedding.

Aunt Helen tells Aunt Janice, "I think there are a lot of fine young brothers, just as good as Frank, but you can't control who you fall in love with."

That is also true about me and Joshua. I tried to control my feelings about Joshua, but I ended up falling for him just the same. Perhaps this is part of God's plan for me.

But Vy tells Aunt Janice, "Janice, you should've told me he was White!"

Aunt Janice replies, "Vy, I am sick to death of your attitude! Now if you don't wanna be here, just leave! I mean, if you don't want me to be with Frank, so who cares?"

Vy says, "Baby, don't you have enough problems being an African American woman? You need a White husband to further complicate things? What about Frank? This isn't gonna make his life any easier. Have you thought about that? You thought about your children or the jobs and friends you may lose because some bigot fails to see the beauty in your marriage? Honey, I did not make the rules, but I do know how to play the game. For survival, Janice, please don't marry this man."

Aunt Janice tells Vy that she and Frank are aware of all the obstacles they may face, but that they can handle it; and Vy tells her sister she is making a "terrible, terrible mistake." But Will convinces his mother to attend the wedding, after he asks her that in order for everyone to love her do they all have to do exactly what she says. When Vy attends the wedding, she looks happy for her sister.

Of course, the thoughts going through my brain are whether I'm making a mistake dating Joshua.

Am I a traitor to my race?
Is Joshua a traitor to his?
Will my parents and grandmother be okay with us dating?
Could our dating lead to something more?
How many people in the world will judge us harshly because we're dating?
Could we also lose friends, jobs, and positions at colleges?

When October started, Imani called me and said her brother Hector, who was convicted for selling drugs, was back home. The Fitzpatricks live in the Chesapeake Apartments, and it ain't as bad as other apartments in South Central. But some people think that the Chesapeake Apartments are so bad that the buildings should be condemned. Ms. Fitzpatrick works as a maid at the Beverly Hilton. Imani and Hector have two different dads and neither pays child support or even spends time with them. Hector decided to start selling drugs for the Bloods and Uncle Alonzo helped Hector start his own hustle. Then, the cops busted him, and he was sentenced to the Metropolitan Detention Center for three years. But Hector has been let out after only two years, which means he will have a parole officer breathing down his neck for a year.

I went to the Fitzpatricks to say "Hello" to Hector.

When I knocked on the door, Hector answered it. He is three

inches taller than me and muscular, but just because he looks like a fighter doesn't mean he is. I've beaten him in sparring matches plenty of times, and I suggested that I could give him martial arts lessons. Before he started selling drugs, he didn't have any money for extracurricular activities, but he stated that he didn't need a girl to give him lessons even though I kicked his butt easily. Hector, like a lot of guys in the hood, tried to hide the fact that he can't fight by getting a gun but having a gun doesn't make one invincible. During drive-by shootings, gangbangers shoot out as many bullets as possible, hoping that some will find their targets, but *a lotta* gangbangers are lousy marksmen. As a result of my hapkido training, I can throw knives with great accuracy, but I'm not planning to throw a knife at a person or shoot a bullet into a person until I become a Marine.

Hector hugged me and exclaimed, "Hatima! It's so nice to see you! You still training to become the next Bruce Lee?"

I replied, "I'm not the next Bruce Lee, I'm the one and only Hatima Parker!"

Hector said, "Cool!"

I walked in and saw Imani sitting at the kitchen table, reading some bills and bank statements. I figured that she was trying to figure out how to help pay the bills. Imani was able to secure the job at the Fox Hills Mall's food court as a cashier. The money helps, but things are still very tight for them.

Hector said, "Sit down, Hatima, we have some great news."

I sat down and asked, "You found a legit job?"

I know that the conditions of Hector's parole are that he stays away from the Bloods, he stops selling drugs, he gets a legit job, and he shows pay stubs as proof of his employment.

Hector said, "Yep. I told Mister Lee I'd buy his gas station."

I said, "Really? With what money?"

Imani said, "Mister Lee is willing to accept any money our family has as a down-payment, and Hector can keep paying him from the store's profits until he's paid the whole thing in full."

I said, "That's great! Our boycott worked!"

Imani said, "Yeah, on Mister Lee's store. What about the other Korean-owned stores that still won't hire Blacks or treat us with respect?"

I said, "We keep boycotting until they give in to our demands or decide to sell. Point two of the Black Panthers' Ten-Point Platform states, 'We believe that the federal government is responsible and obligated to give every man employment or a guaranteed income. We believe that if the White American businessmen will not give full employment, the means of production should be taken from the businessmen and placed in the community so that the people of the community can organize and employ all of its people and give a high standard of living.'"

Imani said, "In this case, Korean businessmen won't give full employment or any respect for our people. It seems only fair that the Koreans should give up control of their businesses to the Black populace. We'll never truly be free until we can determine our own destinies."

Hector said, "Thanks a lot, Angela Davis and Kathleen Cleaver, but word through the grapevine is that not all Blacks in the hood are participating in these boycotts. Some say prices are too high in other stores, and the Koreans are the cheaper option. Others say they don't see what the point of boycotts are since it won't bring Latasha Harlins, Lee Arthur Mitchell, and all them other people who are dead back to life."

I said, "Only God has the power to resurrect people. Other than that, there's no way to bring victims of racist attacks back to life, but we can try to stop the cycle of hatred and bigotry that took them away from this world. Since Mister Lee is leaving the hood and Hector is taking over, the chances of a person getting killed when they buy gas, candy, or soda is now much lower. This is a spark of hope in a world full of prejudice. Remember what Bob Marley said: 'Light up the darkness.'"

Chapter Nine

Time flew as people anticipated Soon Ja Du's trial. Most people mark Halloween as an important event, but I don't. My parents never let me celebrate Halloween because, in their words, "It's the Devil's holiday."

My family are all God-fearing Methodists, which means we don't associate with the Devil. I don't mind not celebrating Halloween because I don't like to pretend to be someone I'm not. I want to be myself, and if people have a problem with that, then fuck them.

The Du family hired a Black lawyer named Charles Earl Lloyd to represent Mrs. Du in court. Dr. Wilson said Mr. Lloyd is one of LA's most successful criminal law attorneys and he's represented lots of Black people over the years. Dr. Wilson said Mr. Lloyd has also represented a score of Korean Americans in criminal cases involving other Korean Americans. When the Dus went to him, he brought in a White co-counsel named Richard Leonard. Dr. Wilson said Mr. Leonard specializes in murder cases and he and Mr. Lloyd had tried three capital cases together.

We were in the Wilsons' living room, and Dr. Wilson stated, "Mister Lloyd and Mister Leonard want to prove that the killing of Latasha Harlins was an act of self-defense by a woman who felt her life was in danger."

I told Dr. Wilson, "That's bullshit! Missus Du wouldn't have felt her life was in danger if a White girl or an Asian girl went shopping at her store."

Stella walked in and said, "If it turned out Latasha was a gangster, then Missus Du probably wouldn't have gone to court."

I exclaimed, "So you think Missus Du was justified in killing Latasha? You think Latasha's life didn't matter?"

Stella said, "Take a look at the crime rate! In 1990, the thirty-two blocks surrounding Empire Liquor had one of the highest crime rates in the city. Nine-hundred-and-thirty-six reported felonies that include five murders, nine rapes, one-hundred-and-eighty-four robberies, and two-hundred-and-fifty-four assaults. Forty percent of serious crimes go unreported since people believe the LAPD won't try to find the stolen goods. If the LAPD did a better job, Missus Du wouldn't have had to take the law into her own hands."

I looked past Stella's BS at the only thing she said that made sense. I said, "So you agree that the LAPD are doing a shitty job in the hood?"

Stella said, "Yeah. Look at you. You're trained in hapkido, and I'm sure the main reason you studied martial arts is so that you can defend yourself against thugs in your neighborhood."

I said, "A hook punch and a roundhouse kick are better options than a Glock or a Uzi in my opinion."

Word on the street is that Mr. Lloyd and Mrs. Du are receiving so much hate mail and threats over the phone that Mr. Lloyd wants to avoid a trial and have Mrs. Du plead guilty to manslaughter, voluntary or involuntary; but that means that she will serve no jail time. Roxanne Carvajal and District Attorney Ira Reiner are not fly with that. They believe that Latasha made no threat to Mrs. Du and that Mrs. Du falsely portrayed Latasha as a thief. The only plea they will accept is a charge of second-degree murder, which requires a prison sentence. Mr. Lloyd has refused to settle for that. For the record, Ira Reiner got Rodney King out of jail after his beating because he couldn't find enough evidence to prosecute him. He also sought an indictment from the grand jury to charge the cops for beating Rodney King. Ira Reiner has a great head on his shoulders.

Only registered voters can serve on juries. Grandma said difficult literary tests and unfair markers kept Blacks in the South from voting, but the Voting Rights Act put a stop to that. The jury overseeing Mrs. Du's case includes five African Americans but no Asians, which is *very* odd. The news stations, the *Los Angeles Sentinel*, the *Los Angeles Times*, and other media gave detailed stories about the trial. Reading and hearing about the trial is just as intense as reading and watching Tom Robinson's case in *To Kill A Mockingbird*.

During the trial, Ms. Carvajal called ten witnesses: Lakeshia Combs and Ismail Ali, four cops who had investigated the case, three expert witnesses, and Denise Harlins. Mrs. Du, her husband, and their son were the only defense witnesses.

Mrs. Du's testimony was sketchy. She spoke through an interpreter even though Lakeshia already told the grand jury that Mrs. Du speaks English very well. Mrs. Du appeared frail, vulnerable, and old. I thought this was done to build sympathy for her so people might see how vulnerable she felt when Latasha approached the counter. Mrs. Du claimed she thought Latasha was stealing the orange juice because of the methods shoplifters use: they often hide stuff they wanna steal in sweaters or backpacks or purses and then buy inexpensive items. Mrs. Du claimed Latasha feigned ignorance about the orange juice when she went to pay for it. That's when Mrs. Du touched her; Mrs. Du couldn't reach the backpack so she grabbed the sweater. Now that I think about it, some of Mrs. Du's testimony might be plausible. I've seen plenty of Blacks in the hood use the methods Mrs. Du described to steal stuff; but Latasha had money to pay for the orange juice and the cops didn't find any stolen stuff in her backpack. Plus, even if Latasha was trying to steal, that's still no reason to shoot and kill her!

Mrs. Du also claimed she didn't know how to fire a gun and never pulled the trigger. That was pure bullshit!

The testimonies took three days and the cross-examination was on the second day of October, but Mrs. Du wasn't sentenced until mid-November. The jury decided that Mrs. Du's decision to fire the gun was fully within her control and that she fired the gun voluntarily. They found her guilty of voluntary manslaughter. From what ex-cons have said, voluntary manslaughter carries a max prison sentence of sixteen years, but Judge Joyce Karlin rejected the jury's sentence; instead, she sentenced Mrs. Du to five years of probation, four hundred hours of community service, and a $500 fine! Folks in Crenshaw, Watts, other hoods, and beyond were happy that the jury found Mrs. Du guilty of manslaughter, but Judge Karlin obviously cared more about Mrs. Du's well-being than justice for Latasha. A Black girl is dead, and her killer's punishment is community service and forking over five hundred bucks? Judge Karlin is a professional bullshitter! The entire American justice system is fucked up!

This reminded me Anne Moody's memoir and the death of a Black boy that shook her up as well as the nation because the murder went unpunished. On August 28, 1955, Emmett Louis Till was murdered in Money, Mississippi, for whistling at a White woman. Probably for the first time in Southern history, two White men were indicted for murdering a Black person and had to stand trial. My class and I watched the first episode of *Eyes on the Prize*, which gives details about Emmet Till's murder, during Black History Month and read about Emmet Till's death from textbooks and old newspaper archives. Roy Bryant and his half-brother, J.W. Milam, abducted, tortured, and killed Emmett because they believed that Emmett had endangered Roy's wife, Carolyn Bryant. No one is sure what happened at the Bryants' store, but my class and I were able to come to our own conclusions about what happened to Emmett after he encountered Mrs. Bryant.

In the trial, Mrs. Bryant claimed that Till ordered some bubblegum. Then, when she held out her right hand for the money, Emmett caught her hand and wouldn't let it go. Mrs. Bryant claimed she tried to pull away but Emmett said, "How about a date, baby?"

Mrs. Bryant said she pulled her hand away and started walking to the back of the store, but Emmett caught her at the cash register. She stated that Emmett put both his hands around her waist and said, "What's the matter, baby, can't you take it?" Mrs. Bryant got away from Emmett, but she stated he still said horrible things. Then Emmett said, "I've been with White women before."

Mrs. Bryant said another Black boy came in and pulled him out of the store. She said she went to get her pistol, but Emmett was still on the front porch of the store. Then, he smiled, whistled at her, ran off with his friends, got in a car, and drove away.

My friends, classmates, and I were absolutely sure Mrs. Bryant was lying and that she just wanted an excuse to murder a Black person because Southern Whites seemed to have an uncontrollable bloodlust. Plus, if Emmett really spoke that way to any woman, his mother would whoop him so hard, he wouldn't be able to sit down for a month.

Mr. Breland, Roy Bryant and J.W. Milam's lawyer, asked Mrs. Bryant, "Was this Negro man who accosted you Emmett Till?"

Mrs. Bryant replied, "I don't know Emmett Till. I've never known Emmett Till, or any other Negroes, for that matter."

Mrs. Du didn't know Latasha Harlins, at least not the way Latasha's friends and family knew her. Mrs. Du claimed she knows what Black people are like based off the gangsters who have robbed stores, but she doesn't really *know* Black people.

The cops who beat Rodney King also didn't know him. I bet they also think they know Black people based on the Black criminals they've locked away, but the cops don't really *know* Black people either.

When people see the Black race, they see exaggerated stories, not people.

Dorsey High suffered from burst water mains that left parts of the school flooded. So, they had to close the school for about a week so they could fix it. My parents were concerned because they didn't want my education to be jeopardized, but I called Dr. Wilson and asked if I could go to Stella's school and observe her classes. Dr. Wilson said he didn't see why I couldn't. So, I took a bus to Westwood and walked to the Wilsons' house. Mrs. Wilson drove me and Stella to Stella's school in the Toyota Camry.

When I got out of the car, Stella said, "Welcome to University High School."

The architecture of University High School looked different from Dorsey High. It looked older and what's the word I'm looking for ... archaic. It reminded me of pictures I had seen of Ivy League schools, like Cornell.

I said, "University High School is a weird name for a school just like University College London. That's like calling a residence an 'apartment house' or a car a 'limo truck.'"

Stella explained, "I think the name is supposed to show us that high school and university are closely connected. You need good grades in high school to get into a good college. I have to take you to the office and explain that you're a visitor, so you don't get in trouble for trespassing."

The people working in the office didn't look as beat-down and stressed out as the people in the Dorsey High office. They looked happy and perky.

Stella explained I was a visitor, and they took note of that on their computers. A secretary asked me who I was and why I was here.

I explained, "Dorsey High has some burst water mains, and it's gonna take a while to clean up the mess and fix the pipes. I decided I wanted to observe some classes here at Uni to see the differences between the teaching style here and the teaching style at Dorsey."

The secretary took note of that and said, "Okay, have a nice stay."

I said, "Thanks."

I accompanied Stella to all her classes. In her gym class, the uniforms and balls all looked brand-new, but the White kids were not as good at playing volleyball as the Black kids at Dorsey. The uniforms had pictures of a Native-American in a headdress on them. Stella explained that their school mascot is the Warrior. Since this school had a Native-American as its mascot, I was already starting to get bad vibes.

In her history classes, Stella's classmates had the latest textbooks, which state that George H.W. Bush is the President, while Dorsey's textbooks state that Jimmy Carter is the President.

Stella's history teacher is a White woman named Mrs. O'Hara. Stella said she's pretty cool for a teacher. Mrs. O'Hara rocked her black hair in a ponytail and wore red glasses.

She said, "Alright, class. We've studied several aspects of

American history, including Black history. Given the tense racial climate plaguing our city, does anyone believe that Doctor King's dream has been fulfilled?"

A White girl with brown hair and brown eyes raised her hand, and Mrs. O'Hara pointed at her and said, "Yes, Brenda."

Brenda stated, "I believe that Doctor's King's dream has been fulfilled. There are Black kids, Latino kids, Asian kids, and White kids all sitting here together."

I said, "But White kids still outnumber all other races in this school, same thing about Westwood. It's still a predominantly White community with some sprinklings of non-Whites. This school is far from being diverse."

Brenda squinted at me and asked, "Who are you?" She sounded kinda snooty.

I said, "Hatima Parker."

Stella explained, "Hatima's school in Crenshaw has been closed for a few days due to burst water mains. So, she decided to come here and observe our classes."

I said, "I plan to become a Marine and an Africanist. Part of my future ambition is taking note of how racism, both overt and covert, still plagues the US and the rest of the world."

Brenda asked, "Have you encountered any racism since you got here? Last time I checked all the races get along in this school."

I explained the obvious, "This school has a Native-American as its mascot. Mascots are usually animals. Having a Native-American as your mascot is your way of telling the Native tribes that they're still viewed as animals and savages."

Mrs. O'Hara said, "Many students and teachers have voiced open dislike about our school's mascot, me included. I'm sure one day the mascot will be replaced with a more appropriate one."

I asked, "What about Latasha Harlins? Do y'all seriously think Judge Karlin gave Missus Du a fair sentence?"

A White boy with blond hair and blue eyes raised his hand and Mrs. O'Hara said, "Yes, Rupert."

Rupert said, "Missus Du was just defending herself, which is her right as an American citizen. The Second Amendment states that all US citizens have the right to bear arms. That means we have a right to defend ourselves."

I said, "People can defend themselves without guns. Ever heard of karate, kung fu, taekwondo, hapkido, capoeira?"

Rupert said, "I guess Missus Du didn't know karate. Besides, she has a family, you know. Their lives would be turned upside down if she was killed or imprisoned."

I said, "Latasha has a family as well. She has an aunt, a grandmother, a little brother, and a little sister who loved her. The only reason she doesn't have a mom is because of the Second Amendment. Her mother was shot to death at a club, and her murderess claimed she was threatened by Crystal Harlins. The murderess received a five-year prison sentence for manslaughter, which made her eligible for parole in two years. Latasha was mad that her mom's killer received a short prison sentence, so she decided to become a prosecuting attorney when she grew up. She went to Westchester High School to receive a better education than what was offered at other inner-city schools, but none of that mattered to Missus Du. She got to get married, have a family, open up businesses, et cetera. Well, Latasha will never have any of that because Missus Du took away her life. Latasha's dreams and ambitions mattered, but people are buying the bullshit that Missus Du is the real victim."

Rupert said, "I heard Latasha was always getting into fights, and her grades were slipping. She would have never gotten into law school so it's not like she was going to amount to anything."

I yelled, "Say what?!"

Stella said, "Now that was uncalled for."

Mrs. O'Hara said, "Class, settle dow—"

I said, "No, Missus O'Hara, let Rupert continue flapping his gums and using that peanut he calls his brain."

A Black kid sporting a high-top fade raised his hand and Mrs. O'Hara said, "Yes, Victor."

Victor asked, "If Rupert doesn't believe that Latasha can become a lawyer, does that mean he believes Hatima can't become a Marine and an Africanist?"

Mrs. O'Hara said, "That's a good question."

Rupert said, "Well, Hatima, I haven't heard of lady Marines."

I stated, "There are plenty, I've seen them on the news. Sexism is still an issue in our world and the low number of women in the US Armed Forces is proof of that."

Rupert said, "Women don't need to be on the front lines because they should be back at home looking after their men and kids."

The guys laughed, except for Victor.

I exclaimed, "That's a sexist line most guys give me when I tell them I'm gonna be a Marine! Thanks for proving that bullshit still exists in our world!"

Mrs. O'Hara said, "Settle down, everyone!"

Then, Rupert said, "Stella said you go to school in Crenshaw, which means you live in the ghetto."

Rupert said "ghetto" the same way Jared said it, like it's a dirty word.

Rupert continued, "Are you in a gang? Are you still in school? Is your dad still around?"

HEAL THE HOOD

I said, "No, I'm not in a gang." I thought, *But my uncle and cousin are.* I continued, "I'm a senior at Susan Miller Dorsey High School, and my dream is to attend the US Naval Academy, major in history, and become a Marine after I get a PhD in Africana Studies. My dad is not a deadbeat, in jail, a wino, a junkie, nor dead. My father, Orlando Parker, and my mother, Suzy Jane Parker, have been happily married for eighteen years. My dad works as a baggage handler at the airport and my mother is a waitress. I live in a small house with three bedrooms and two bathrooms. I've never gone to bed hungry, my clothes fit me, and my parents have made sure I don't fall prey to the predators of the streets."

Victor raised his hand, and Mrs. O'Hara called on him again.

Victor said, "I don't think it's right to assume that if a person is from the ghetto it automatically means that they won't succeed. Doctor Ben Carson was born and raised in the ghettos of Detroit. His father didn't offer any child support after his parents split up. His mother worked hard to provide for her sons and ensured that they did well in school. Doctor Carson developed a love of reading that helped him maintain a straight-A average. He attended undergraduate school at Yale, got his MD at the University of Michigan, and completed his residency at Johns Hopkins University Hospital. When he completed brain surgery on kids, people kept asking where he was from. He always says he's from the mean streets of Detroit, and he takes pride in that. Doctor Carson wants his life to prove that it isn't where a person comes from but where they're going."

I said, "That was an excellent example, much better than a rags-to-riches story about a Black musician or athlete."

Then Rupert said, "A Black man is LA's mayor. Isn't Tom Bradley's political power proof that racism is a thing of the past?

Aren't Doctor Carson, Terry White, Michael Jackson, Bill Cosby, Reginald Lewis, Oprah Winfrey, and other Black peoples' success stories proof that Doctor King's dream has been fulfilled?"

I explained, "Just because *some* Black people have found success doesn't mean that a racial caste system doesn't still rule the world."

Mrs. O'Hara said, "Elaborate please, Hatima."

I explained, "This school has the latest textbooks, computers, gym equipment, et cetera. I'm also assuming that the teachers at Uni have high salaries. Now, at Dorsey High we have old textbooks that say Jimmy Carter is the President. There aren't enough balls and equipment for PE. We only have a few computers that hundreds of students are supposed to share. Teachers are paid much lower salaries so they're constantly applying for better jobs at other schools. Our teachers don't teach us that the world is our oyster because that phrase is a lie to many kids in the ghetto."

Stella said, "We also have SAT and ACT prep classes as part of our curriculum. Does Dorsey have that?"

I said, "Yeah, but SAT and ACT prep classes cost money that a lotta parents don't have. My parents were willing to spend their hard-earned money on SAT and ACT prep, but other kids' parents don't have that kinda cash. As a result, most kids at Dorsey High score lower than a thousand on the SAT and score less than thirty on the ACT. I like reading so I read extra books from the school and public libraries. My parents and grandma also teach me stuff about the past, such as life in the Deep South, the Civil Rights Movement, and Caribbean history. As a result, I've done very well at Dorsey, and college is a possible step in my future."

Victor said, "So since ghetto schools have inferior supplies, the chances of inner-city students graduating and succeeding in life is lower than it is here at Uni."

I said, "Exactly. Another factor is home lifestyles. I have a father, but plenty of my friends and classmates don't. It's always been hard for Black single mothers to raise their kids. When you add up rent, groceries, clothing, et cetera, it's very hard to break even. Now, not everyone in my hood relies on welfare because, one, they think it's embarrassing, and, two, sometimes their checks aren't mailed to them. My mother's father abandoned her and Grandma before she was born. It was hard for Grandma to support Mama on a janitor's salary, so Mama dropped out of school to help her with the bills. My dad's father was a steelworker, but he was injured on the job. Since my dad's mom died while he was a kid, Grandpa Gabriel was the sole breadwinner for the family. Grandpa couldn't work until he had recuperated so my dad and uncle dropped out of school. My dad joined the Marines and fought in Vietnam. When he was discharged, he began working at the airport. He met my mom, they fell in love, got married, and had me. My dad will never abandon me and my mom because his father never abandoned him and his brother. But since other guys have been abandoned by their fathers, they think caring about others is a waste of time."

Mrs. O'Hara said, "One of the reasons some Blacks sell drugs, rob stores, and commit other crimes is because they have families to support. Unfortunately, even today, housing discrimination and low wages make it hard for Blacks to support their families. So, crime has become the only viable option for some of them."

I said, "That's so true, Missus O'Hara."

Rupert said, "Okay, Missus Du killed Latasha even though she didn't know her whole life story. If Missus Du did know her, would she have pitied the girl or still thought the world would be better off without her?"

I said, "Missus Du might have still killed her. My boyfriend said

Missus Du said some racist things about Blacks and she repeated them to other people after her trial. She said we don't like to work, that we spend all our welfare money on liquor, that kind of stuff. If Missus Du had known that Latasha wanted to be a lawyer, she would have still thought that's an impossible dream for a hood rat. Missus Du still would have thought the world would be better off without Latasha."

Brenda asked, "What about Rodney King?"

I said, "I figured we'd get to him sooner or later. Do you think the cops were justified in beating Rodney King?"

Rupert said, "Rodney King was driving while intoxicated. He's also been arrested in the past. Robbery, assault with a deadly weapon, intent to commit great bodily injury. He's a career criminal."

I said, "Just because Rodney King has been incarcerated *once* at a minimum-security prison doesn't mean he's a career criminal. Plus, according to what I read in the *Los Angeles Sentinel*, Angela King, Rodney King's aunt, told the cops her nephew was guilty of robbing a store in Monterey Park because he wanted the cops to leave him alone. Rodney King was hungry, and his hunger drove him to try and rob Tae Suck Baik. Rodney King threw pies at Mister Baik, and Mister Baik tried to hit him with a tire iron. But in court, Mister Baik claimed that *Mister King* tried to hit him with the tire iron, forced him to open the cash register, and took the cash. Mister Baik also claimed Mister King stole some checks. The cops *did* discover a check from Mister Baik's but no cash. Another thing you should know is that Mister Baik doesn't speak English. He couldn't have understood and obeyed Mister King's orders. If Mister Baik lied, then that means Missus Du and the LAPD are also capable of lying as well. In the end, the Asian man's word won, mostly because Rodney King decided to surrender before he fought."

Rupert said, "Okay, some of that story is plausible, but Rodney King's definitely a wino. He hasn't even been arrested on DUI charges because people are trying to paint the cops who stopped him as the criminals."

Victor said, "Rupert, your brother was arrested for drunk driving last year."

Rupert said, "So? He's always taking dares because he can't stand it when someone calls him chicken."

I said, "He sounds like Marty McFly."

Stella said, "But the fact that he did drive while drunk shows that winos come in different colors and from different socioeconomic backgrounds."

I asked Rupert, "What was your brother's punishment? Was he let off with a warning? Community service?"

Rupert said, "He got community service. Since my brother has never been convicted before and Mom and Dad didn't want to see one of their kids in jail, they convinced my brother's lawyer to try and get him a light punishment. If my brother was sent to jail, even for a few months, there'd be no way he'd get into college. UC, Cal State, Stanford, Vanderbilt, Duke, and all the other top schools would be scared away."

I said, "Rodney King was driving while intoxicated and his punishment was a fractured facial bone, a broken right ankle, multiple bruises and cuts, and his clothes soaked in his blood. How come your brother's punishment didn't include broken bones and bloody clothes?"

Rupert said, "My brother doesn't have a criminal record, but Rodney King does! My brother is now an undergrad student at Stanford, and he wouldn't be there if he was sent to jail. Rodney King never went to college, and I'm pretty sure he's not planning on doing anything productive with his life. I bet those cops knew who Rodney King was and what he did in the past. They had to beat him up to ensure he couldn't hurt them or anybody else."

Victor said, "Since there are so many Blacks in prison and with criminal records, I doubt the LAPD knows the names and histories of all Black ex-cons. They beat up Rodney King because he was Black. Your brother was spared from brutality because he was White. Even today, many people think the lives of White people are more important than the lives of Black people."

It felt nice to know some rich Black folks outside of South Central hadn't turned their backs on the hood; but Brenda's and Rupert's comments were all the proof needed to convince folks in my hood that White folks, especially *rich* White folks, didn't give a damn about us.

During lunch, Stella and I ate outside. She offered to buy me lunch, but I showed her I had a turkey sandwich, a bag of barbecue chips, and a bottle of water.

I ate angrily, and Stella said, "I'm sorry for how my classmates talked about Latasha Harlins and Rodney King. Life in the hood sounds like … a trap; but my parents and Victor's parents are proof that it's possible to get out."

It didn't sound like Stella was apologizing for her classmates' racist comments. It sounded like she was trying to calm me down before I went all ghetto up in this bougie school.

I told Stella, "Most people call life in the hood a dead-end, but a trap is another good description. No matter how hard some folks in my neighborhood work, it's not enough to provide for their families, let alone enough to move out and on to a better place. Now, successful Blacks have achieved their dreams even though the odds were against them. Doctor Murray said we should never believe the lie that anyone is more powerful than God. There are forces in this world that are determined to keep Black people down. Institutionalized racism has kept many Black people from realizing their full potential, but God's love is still stronger than humanity's hatred." Then I asked Stella, "What do you want to do?"

Stella asked, "What do you mean?"

I explained, "What career path do you wanna take? What kind of degree would you like to pursue?"

Stella explained, "I want to be a journalist. I've been a reporter for the school newspaper, the *Wildcat*, since I was a freshman. There have also been underground newspapers published and delivered on campus, the *Worrier* and the *Red Tide*."

Bougie kids organized underground fight-the-power press? I said, "Cool. Knowledge is power. The news keeps people informed about world events."

Stella explained, "I'd like to be a journalist for a magazine. I'm thinking *Ebony* or *Jet* or *Essence*."

I said, "Cool. So, where are you gonna study after high school?"

Stella said, "UC Berkeley has a fantastic graduate journalism program, but since Berkeley doesn't offer an undergrad journalism program, I've applied to other schools. I've applied to San Diego State University, San Francisco State University, Columbia University, Northwestern University, UW-Madison, Howard University, and LAMU. I'm sure at least one of them will accept me."

I asked, "Then, after you get your bachelor's degree in journalism, you'll apply to the graduate journalism program at Berkeley?"

Stella said, "That's the plan. What about you? I'm assuming you've applied to other schools besides the Naval Academy."

I explained, "I've applied to Howard, Freeman, LAMU, WashU, Vanderbilt, and UC Davis."

Stella asked, "Have they mailed replies yet?"

I replied, "Not yet. But I'm hoping at least one will accept me since I need something to fall back on in case the Naval Academy says no. Have any of the schools you applied to mailed replies?"

Stella said, "Still waiting."

When I told Wanda and Imani about Uni, they wanted to check it out for themselves. They accompanied me to Westwood the next day, and Mrs. Wilson drove us all to the school.

Imani was fascinated by Uni, but Wanda just glared at everyone and everything.

When we sat down in Stella's history class, I said, "Wanda, could you maybe put on a different face? Folks here are gonna think you'll rob them or burn down the school."

Wanda said, "Maybe we should do that."

Imani said, "Whoa, Wanda. People outside the hood expect us all to become criminals. But we're all going to get into college, graduate with degrees, get great jobs, and have wonderful lives."

Wanda asked, "Who do you think you are? A rich White girl?"

Imani said, "No, but just because I'm a poor Black girl doesn't mean I won't succeed."

Stella said, "I'm a rich Black girl. I know I'm destined to succeed."

Wanda said, "The supplies and teachers at Dorsey High aren't as good as the ones here. Every kid in this school is gonna graduate and go to college because they're better prepared. This is just like those Jim Crow schools Mama told me about that were in Louisiana before the Civil Rights Movement."

Then, Mrs. O'Hara came in and said, "Good morning, everybody."

Everyone except Wanda said, "Good morning, Missus O'Hara."

Mrs. O'Hara noticed Wanda's silence, so she asked her, "Young lady, is something wrong?"

Wanda said, "Yeah, this whole world is messed-up. People say Jim Crow is dead, but I can tell Jim Crow is alive by comparing this school to our school."

I explained, "Missus O'Hara, these are my best friends, Wanda Brooks and Imani Fitzpatrick. They also wanted to check out Uni, so I invited them."

Mrs. O'Hara said, "It looks like we'll have a continuation of yesterday's talk. Yesterday we discussed whether or not Doctor King's dream came true."

Wanda said, "It hasn't."

Mrs. O'Hara said, "Elaborate, please."

Wanda explained, "The world is still divided even if the physical signs of Jim Crow were destroyed years ago."

Rupert said, "This isn't a Jim Crow school. If it were, Stella, Victor, and the other Black kids wouldn't be here. People are no longer judged by skin color."

I told Wanda and Imani, "Ladies, meet the class douchebag."

Everyone laughed, and Rupert said, "Shut up, bitch."

I immediately jumped up and exclaimed, "You wanna take this outside?"

Stella pulled me back down to my seat. Going all angry-Black-girl in a predominantly White school ain't cool.

Stella told Rupert, "You don't wanna fight Hatima. My brother said she's the best fighter in their dojang."

Rupert asked, "Don't all Black people solve problems with their fists?"

Imani replied, "We're talking about Doctor King, the king of non-violence, and you have the gall to ask if all Black people solve problems with their fists? Ever heard of Bob Marley or Nelson Mandela? Black peoples' words are more powerful than our fists."

Victor said, "Uni and Dorsey are perfect examples of class discrimination."

Mrs. O'Hara said, "Elaborate please, Victor."

Victor explained, "Poor people have always been at the bottom of the USA's socioeconomic ladder. Poor neighborhoods have always had inferior housing and schooling. Why should rich people get everything nice? Why don't we work hard to make sure people can move from the working-class to the middle-class to the upper-class with ease?"

I said, "That's how I feel. Why can't poor people get big houses? Some poor families are as big as the Jackson family, and there's barely enough room in hood houses and apartments for all of them. Why can't ghetto schools receive the same budget as bougie schools? Why can't ghetto schools have the same high-quality supplies to ensure a better learning environment?"

Rupert said, "If they work hard, they can move to a higher class and reap the benefits."

Victor said, "We just discussed yesterday how hard it is for certain people to succeed."

I said, "I'm guessing that most peoples' parents in this school support the Republican Party."

Rupert said, "My parents support them, and they believe Ronald Reagan was one of the best presidents in US history."

I said, "Yeah, Ronald Reagan's attack on the poor was the mark of a great leader."

Rupert repeated, "Attack on the poor?"

I asked him, "Where do you think all that extra money that

supported the upper-class came from? Folks in Crenshaw, South Central, Inglewood, Compton, South Side Chicago, West Philly, Harlem, et cetera were all nearly crushed by the boulder you call Reaganomics. Alex P. Keaton the young Republican may have worshiped Ronald Reagan like so many rich folks and folks who hope to be rich, but plenty of folks in Crenshaw were hoping someone would carry out a successful assassination on Ronald Reagan."

Everyone fell quiet. Blacks threaten to kill each other all the time, but I'm guessing these bougie kids never thought Blacks would band together, hoping a president's death would be inevitable.

At lunchtime, Wanda, Imani, and I took out our packed lunches while Stella went to buy her lunch.

Wanda said, "When Blacks make it out of the ghetto, they're no longer down for the cause. What a bunch of sellouts."

Imani said, "Don't call them that. Their parents worked hard to become successful."

Wanda exclaimed, "Yeah, that's why they get more opportunities while we get shit because our parents wear blue-collars and pink-collars instead of white-collars to work!"

Imani said, "Y'all know I want to be a doctor."

I said, "Yeah, yeah, a pediatrician. Good thing Howard, Meharry, Morehouse, Freeman, LAMU, and Charles Drew all have medical schools."

Imani said, "I might go to a medical school that's not all Black."

Wanda said, "I don't know why so many Black kids are eager to go to White colleges. We don't need them, and they don't need us. Besides, our schools are just as good as theirs."

I said, "We all know Black colleges are as good as White ones. But the reason the Little Rock Nine, Ruby Bridges, Vivian Malone,

James Hood, James Meredith, et cetera worked so hard to integrate public schools and universities was so that Black people could have more options. Do you seriously think that the six Black medical schools in this country have enough room for every Black medical student?"

Wanda said, "I just hope that when Imani becomes a doctor, she won't forget her friends."

Imani said, "Of course I won't. I'll come back to the hood. I'll talk to students at Dorsey during homecoming, tell them what they need to do to get into college. When Dorsey High alumni stop by for visits, it really puts a spark into the kids' lives. It grows into a fire that fuels their will to succeed."

Then, Stella came to the cafeteria table. Stella had mac and cheese, a chicken drumstick, salad, and a water bottle. Wanda, Imani, and I had sandwiches. I had a chicken sandwich while Wanda had a BLT and Imani had a salami sandwich. Wanda and I had juice boxes while Imani had a metal water bottle. I also had a bag of Doritos while Wanda had a plastic bag of her mom's cookies. Imani didn't have any dessert. Fitzpatrick's Gas Station and Convenience Store had started off well, but it looked like Imani would be eating small portions until the business made more money.

Stella asked, "Do the three of you wanna check out Jack and Jill?"

Wanda asked, "Why would someone name their kids after a nursery rhyme?"

Imani asked, "Is Jack cute?"

I explained, "This is why the two of you need to do more research about Black history. Jack and Jill of America is a Black organization that was founded in Philadelphia in 1938. It helps support Black kids through philanthropic programs or something like that."

Wanda said, "I've never heard of it."

Imani said, "Me neither."

Some of the bougie kids who go to Dorsey High are part of Jack and Jill, but my girls and I aren't close friends with them so some aspects of the lifestyle of the Black bourgeoisie are alien to us.

Stella said, "Well, I think you'll enjoy it."

After school, Stella told her mom that Wanda, Imani, and I wanted to check out Jack and Jill.

Wanda, Imani, and I sat in the backseat of the Toyota Camry, while Stella sat in the passenger seat.

Mrs. Wilson looked back at us and asked her daughter, "Are you sure you want to bring them?"

Stella said, "Yeah, I think they'll enjoy it."

Mrs. Wilson said, "Okay."

I knew why Mrs. Wilson asked Stella if she was sure she wanted to bring us. She knew we were too ghetto for Jack and Jill.

Soon, we arrived at a big building. Mrs. Wilson parked her car, and we all got out. Mrs. Wilson led us inside where we saw Black women and teens all walking around. She talked to a woman at a reception desk, took some papers, and led us down the hallway, to the right, and into a room.

I asked Stella, "What are we doing here?"

Stella said, "Most likely finding out about our assignments for Thanksgiving."

Some more Black teens came in and took their seats. Mrs. Wilson stood at the front, and another Black woman stood behind the podium.

Stella told us, "That's Missus Hamilton, the president of the LA chapter of Jack and Jill."

Mrs. Hamilton said, "Hello, ladies and gentlemen. Thanksgiving is a day we give thanks for all our blessings. But there are always people less fortunate than us who don't have as many blessings."

Then, Mrs. Hamilton wrote down on the blackboard a list of churches, community centers, and other locations in LA. FAME was on the list.

She said "These places all give free meals to poor people, and Jack and Jill have to help supply food. Thanksgiving is next week Thursday, so we have only eight days to get everything done. Remember to bring nonperishable food items here so that the adults can deliver them to the soup kitchens of LA."

Imani eyed the food, checking to see what brands these rich folks would donate. I know she and her family will eat at FAME's Thanksgiving dinner because Ms. Fitzpatrick usually can't afford to buy stuff for holiday celebrations.

I raised my hand and said, "For the record, when you celebrate Thanksgiving, you're celebrating the Pilgrims' massacre of the Native-Americans. Since it isn't cool to celebrate racism in any form, my family doesn't celebrate Thanksgiving. The rest of y'all should consider giving up Thanksgiving but don't give up helping poor folks. I think it's messed-up that rich folks only care about poor folks during the holidays."

Wanda said, "Thanksgiving, Christmas, and the Fourth of July. There are hungry people every day of the year, ya know."

Mrs. Hamilton said, "We help provide underprivileged families with meals all-year round, not just the holidays. By the way, who are you three?"

I said, "I'm Hatima Parker."

Wanda said, "I'm Wanda Brooks."

Imani said, "I'm Imani Fitzpatrick."

HEAL THE HOOD

Mrs. Hamilton asked, "Are your mothers interested in joining Jack and Jill?"

Wanda asked, "We need our mothers' permission to join this club?"

Stella explained, "Jack and Jill is comprised of mothers who want their children to grow and excel through several activities and projects."

I said, "Ma'am, our parents can't join this club because it's a restricted club for token Blacks, Black folks who became rich and successful and still think folks from the hood are beneath them."

Mrs. Hamilton quickly said, "We offer plenty of help to at-risk kids—"

Wanda cut her off and exclaimed, "At-risk kids? You think there's something wrong with us?"

Imani said, "Since we live in a neighborhood with a high crime rate, hostile policing, and substandard housing, I would say that we *are* at risk of getting killed or being stuck permanently in the cycle of poverty."

I explained, "Only rich mamas are allowed in this club. Doctors, lawyers, professors, engineers, businesswomen, et cetera. My mama's a waitress so they don't want her."

Wanda said, "My mama owns a restaurant, but it definitely doesn't bring in six figures since we still live in Crenshaw."

Imani said, "My mama's a maid so you probably don't want her, either."

Mrs. Hamilton explained, "We don't look down on those less fortunate. We just believe well-educated and hardworking Blacks are better equipped to help our people."

A guy waved his hand, and I saw that it was Victor.

I asked, "Victor, you're part of this club, too?"

Victor said, "Yeah. We help out poor folks all the time, but I'm not sure what moms who are waitresses, janitors, and small-time cooks have to teach us or offer us."

I explained, "Our mamas can teach you what really goes on in the hood. They can teach you girls not to date boys just 'cause it's considered cool."

Wanda said, "My mama can tell you what it was like growing up in the Deep South during the days of segregation."

Imani said, "My mama would say not to let hard times turn you into a hard person. My mama's probably experienced more heartache and disappointment than the rest of y'alls' mamas, but she's still the nicest person you'll ever meet."

I told everyone, "Malcolm X said, 'There can be no Black-White unity until there is first some Black unity. We can't think of uniting with others until after we have first united among ourselves. We cannot think of being acceptable to others until we have first proven acceptable to ourselves.' Y'all rich Blacks who don't live in the bougie parts of South Central still think you're better than poor Blacks, forgetting that there was once a time when we were all at the bottom of the totem pole. How are we supposed to fix things in the ghetto and make sure what happened to Latasha Harlins and Rodney King doesn't happen again if rich Blacks won't help poor Blacks get out from under a dead-end system?"

Mrs. Wilson said, "You're very verbose, Hatima, and I believe you're right."

Victor asked, "She is?"

Mrs. Wilson nodded and said, "We offer food, clothes, and other supplies to the less fortunate, but I just remembered an important quote: 'Give a man a fish and he eats for a day. Teach a man to fish and he eats for a lifetime.' If we taught helpful skills to Blacks in inner-city schools and helped inner-city parents get better jobs, then the future of the ghetto would be a lot brighter."

I said, "Perfect! We can call Principal Edwards and Mister Ngozi and the Dorsey High students who aren't part of Jack and Jill to arrange times for y'all Jack and Jill folks to come visit Dorsey High!"

Wanda said, "Now that sounds like a plan."

Chapter Ten

Dorsey High reopened the next week. When I took a good look at the overcrowded classrooms, teachers speaking in monotonous voices, the old textbooks, the un-computing computers, the chipped paint on the walls, and the missing tiles from the floor, I became boiling mad.

No wonder South Central doesn't have as many rich neighborhoods as poor neighborhoods. No wonder there are only a handful of Black folks in rich White neighborhoods. I'm sure whoever is in charge of education in California is making sure ghetto schools have inferior school supplies to ensure that we don't succeed and get outta here. It feels like the whole system is stacked against us, but it could have been worse. Other ghetto schools have constant fights between the Bloods, the Crips, and other gangsters; Principal Edwards told the gangbangers that the only reason they should step foot on school property is to receive an education. That means guns, knives, drugs, and all that other shit stays in the streets. Believe it or not, the gangbangers respect that rule and don't bring their street nonsense into Dorsey High. As a result, Dorsey High is a safe zone.

A great way for me to unwind is to listen to music and one of my favorite artists recently released a new album. Michael Jackson finally released a new album four years after *Bad*: *Dangerous*. I bought it when it came out on Tuesday. The first single, "Black or White," was released, almost two weeks ago, and the music video premiered on MTV three days later. Like all of his music videos or short films, as he likes to call them, it was spectacular. MJ danced with Zulu hunters, Thai dancers, Native-Americans, an Indian woman, and some Russians. Then, he walked through videos of fire and declared "I ain't scared of no sheets!"

"Sheets" must mean the KKK. If MJ ain't scared of the Klan, then he's either very brave or very stupid. Macaulay Culkin, the kid from *Home Alone*, did the rap, while MJ and some other kids danced. Two of the kids in that scene are part of the music group, Another Bad Creation – the name is self-explanatory. Then, Michael Jackson sang the final verse, while in the Statue of Liberty's torch. The camera panned out and showed that Lady Liberty was surrounded by other famous world monuments. The only ones I recognized were the Sphinx and the Pyramids, the Parthenon, the Taj Mahal, the Golden Gate Bridge, the Eiffel Tower, and Big Ben.

The rap goes:

> *Protection*
> *For gangs, clubs, and nations*
> *Causing grief in human relations*
> *It's a turf war on a global scale*
> *I'd rather hear both sides of the tale*
> *See, it's not about races*
> *Just places*
> *Faces*
> *Where your blood comes from*
> *Is where your space is*
> *I've seen the bright get duller*
> *I'm not going to spend my life being a color*

The song's message is that it shouldn't matter whether folks are Black, White, or any skin color. There is so much more to people than what meets the eye. The Bloods, the Crips, and other gangs are still around, decades after they were founded; hate groups like the KKK are also still around. Why? Because crooked cops and other law enforcement officials give them leeway and protection in exchange for a cut of their profits or because they're getting rid of certain groups that law enforcement despises. Legit clubs like Jack and Jill think they're part of the solution, but they're also part of the problem. These elite clubs that rich Blacks have created only cause more divisions within the Black community. Other groups, such as the NAACP, SNCC, NOI, and the BPP allowed any Blacks to join as long as they are willing to help make a difference. These groups don't care or didn't care about how many degrees a Black person had or how much money they had in their bank account. All they cared about was a person's heart and soul.

Gangs and other criminal organizations have been waging a global turf war for years. People only look at these stories from one crooked angle. The cops tell their side and try to paint all gangsters as heartless monsters, but Hector and Devin aren't heartless. They're just looking for ways to feed, clothe, and support their families. The rap states that places are what matter not races. Where your blood comes from is where your space is.

My roots are in Mississippi, Florida, Jamaica, Haiti, and Africa.

I feel a connection and solidarity with people from Mississippi like Fannie Lou Hamer, Medgar Evers, James Meredith, and Anne Moody. I feel a connection and solidarity with people from Florida like Dr. Robert Hayling and Dr. Donald Shirley. I feel a connection and solidarity with people from Jamaica like Marcus Garvey, Harry Belafonte, and Bob Marley. I feel a connection and solidarity with people from Haiti like Toussaint Louvertre, Edmonia Lewis, and James Weldon Johnson. I feel a connection and solidarity with people from the continent of Africa like Nelson Mandela, Miriam Makeba, Kwame Nkrumah, Fela Kuti, Chinua Achebe, Patrice Lumumba, Julius Nyerere, and Jomo Kenyatta.

Marcus Garvey said, "A people without the knowledge of their past history, origin, and culture is like a tree without roots."

Alex Haley said, "In all of us, there is a hunger, marrow-deep, to know our heritage – to know who we are and where we come from. Without this enriching knowledge, there is a hollow yearning. No matter what our attainments in life, there is still a vacuum, an emptiness, and the most disquieting loneliness."

Knowledge of my roots in all these states and countries lets me know who I am and, more importantly, where I am going and what I am capable of.

The final line of the rap declares, "I'm not going to spend my life being a color."

I am not just Black; I am a martial artist, a softball player, a future Marine, and a future Africanist. Daddy is not just Black; he is a great baggage handler, a loving husband, and the best father in the world. Mama is not just Black; she is a wonderful waitress, a loving wife, and the best mother in the world. Grandma is not just Black; she is the matriarch of our family and our wise head. Mr. Ngozi is not just Black; he is an alumnus of the University of Nigeria, Nsukka, and UCL and a great teacher. Andre Brooks is not just Black; he is a great basketball player and a hardworking college student. Wanda Brooks is not just Black; she is a good student who is fed up with the double standards given to Black people. Imani Fitzpatrick is not just Black; she is an intellectual and a future doctor.

We are not symbols.

We are not stereotypes.
We are not scapegoats.
We are somebodies.

On Thanksgiving, school is always closed for two days; the Thursday Thanksgiving date, and the Friday after it. That way, we get a four-day weekend. My friends know my family doesn't celebrate Thanksgiving, but they always invite me to their houses for dinner; and I always say "No, thanks," because my parents wouldn't approve of me celebrating it with anyone else. That's like a Muslim going to Christmas Dinner or a Hindu participating in an Easter Egg Hunt.

Wanda is excited because her brother is coming home for the holiday. I said I would stop by their house and say "Hi, what's up!" But things didn't go as planned.

On Thursday morning, I was walking down Coliseum Street, when I saw Devin taking out a toaster from the trunk of Malik's Chevy Impala.

I asked, "Is that toaster hot?"

Devin replied, "It will be when the toast and Pop Tarts finish cooking."

I stated, "You know that's not what I mean."

Devin shrugged and said, "I may have pinched it. So what? Mister Travis has plenty of electronics, and I'm sure he won't miss a few."

I asked him, "How do you sleep at night, knowing you're stealing from your own people?"

Devin said, "I sleep fine, knowing my moms, my sis, and my baby nephew will be taken care of. You know Alicia's baby daddy only pays child support now and again."

I explained, "He got laid off at the power plant. At least he hasn't resorted to hustling like you have."

Devin said, "If he did hustle, then I wouldn't have to hustle. Someone's gotta make the sacrifice for the family."

Then, Malik walked up to the car. He's as tall as Daddy and Uncle Alonzo, but he's a sad waste of six feet when he's on the basketball court. I had to admit that he looked good with his cornrows, diamond earrings, and his Black and Infrared Air Jordan 6's. Air Jordans cost a fortune, and only a handful of people in the hood besides the hustlers can afford them.

Malik said, "Devin, you sell that toaster. I'll stay here with my cuz."

When Devin walked away, I asked Malik, "How much hot stuff do you have in that trunk?"

Malik looked down at me and said, "None. The toaster is the last piece of merchandise we need to sell. Business is good."

I told Malik, "I don't want anything to do with your business so don't bother asking."

Malik rolled his eyes and said, "I know you don't need it. I heard Maxine Waters decided to nominate you. Looks like you'll be going to the Naval Academy after all. Hope you have fun shooting folks in foreign countries instead of Crips niggas who try to step onto the Bloods' turf."

I said, "Wars across the world are fought over land, oil, gold, diamonds, and other resources. Your fellow gangbangers fight over streets you don't even own. Marines protect the helpless while gangbangers target and murder the innocent."

Malik exclaimed, "The Crips ain't innocent!"

I replied, "But Mister Travis is! What did he ever do to you?

What right do you have to steal from him? It's messed-up how we're killing and stealing from our own people!"

Malik said, "I told you, Hatima. You do things your way, and I do them my way. I don't need you lecturing me like you're Coretta Scott King."

Devin started walking up to us and said, "The toaster's sold."

My sixth sense started tingling as a blue Camaro stopped a few feet away at the corner of the sidewalk. The window was already rolled down.

I grabbed Malik and pulled him down.

BAM! BAM! BAM! BAM!

Malik immediately said, "Oh shit!" and started applying pressure to my left shoulder.

As he sat me up, I saw the blood running down my left arm. It looked like one of the four bullets had hit me. I didn't feel pain right away, just numbness. A few feet away, I saw Devin spread out on the sidewalk. He was lying on his stomach, and his eyes were open in shock. I saw two bullet holes in his back and one in his neck. I was impressed by the Crip's marksmanship. Usually, since most gangsters have lousy aim due to lack of training, they try to shoot out as many bullets as possible, but this Crip must have had practice. If I carried around knives, maybe I could have thrown one in his face or neck. But, since bullets fly faster than knives, that would be a bad idea. Plus, the cops and courts would see me throwing a knife at a Crip as murder instead of self-defense. Then, I would be sent to jail on murder or manslaughter charges and assault with a deadly weapon charges, and all my dreams would end right there.

Malik took out a first aid kit from his car and applied a tourniquet to my left shoulder. Pretty soon, we heard sirens.

I asked him, "Are you gonna stick around or run away, cuz?"

Malik said, "I'll stick around until you get to the hospital. What else is family for?"

I said, "When Mama and Daddy see the medical bills, they'll probably kill me themselves! I don't want my family to be completely broke!"

Malik said, "I know you hate the Bloods' dirty money, but it looks like you'll need my help and my dad's help to pay your hospital bills."

I started crying because Devin was gone, just like that. Now, I have seen plenty of people get killed since I was little, including some of my friends and classmates. The last friend I saw get killed was Keisha Jones. It was shortly after New Year's. I was across the street, and I saw Keisha walking out of Mrs. Brooks' restaurant when a cream-colored 1988 Jeep Comanche 4x4 drove by. Some Latino gangsters in the truck took out their Uzis and shot a Black guy near Keisha. Since the Black guy was wearing a red bandanna and an LA Clippers jersey and had a .357 Magnum in his back pocket, he was definitely a Blood. The Black guy didn't get his gun out in time, and the Latinos shot him dead. But, like I said, a lot of gangsters have lousy aim. Since the Latinos shot out as many bullets as possible from their Uzis, Keisha had holes in her chest, arms, and legs. When I saw all that blood, I threw up, right there on the sidewalk. Mrs. Brooks called 911 and they took away Keisha's body as well as the Blood's. Keisha was in my English class, and she wanted to become a poet like Gwen Brooks and Maya Angelou. But all her dreams ended right there. Word on the street was that the Latino gangsters were part of the 18th Street Gang, a gang made up of Mexicans, Puerto Ricans, Dominicans, and other Latinos. The 18th Street Gang are one of the Bloods' rivals, which explains why they shot the Blood. But why could they not wait until he was in proximity or away from other people? Why did they not care that an innocent girl was killed in their senseless war?

The paramedics put me on a gurney, and Malik climbed into the ambulance with me; but Devin was put in a separate ambulance. I knew they would take him to the morgue because there was nothing doctors could do for him.

Michael Jackson said in his autobiography that he liked riding in an ambulance after he suffered a burn accident on his head during that Pepsi commercial. He said it was cool that the ambulance was driving fast, while the siren was wailing. I also must admit that riding in an ambulance is kind of cool. My dad can't drive over the speed limit since it's illegal, and he doesn't wanna pay extra money for speeding tickets. Plus, the cops beat Rodney King because he was speeding so they would definitely beat Daddy if they ever caught him speeding.

Malik asked, "How you feeling, cuz?"

I pinched my left arm and said, "I can still feel my arm. That means I haven't lost too much blood, and my nerves ain't dead."

One of the paramedics explained, "It's a good thing your cousin knows first aid. That tourniquet stopped you from losing too much blood."

Malik said, "*I'm* gonna lose a lot of blood when Uncle Orlando finds out what I let happen."

I told Malik, "The Crip shot me, not you."

Malik said, "Yeah, but you got caught in the crossfire because the Crip was aiming at me and Devin. Maybe you being seen with me ain't cool."

I exclaimed, "I know it ain't cool! Why do you think my dad forbade me from seeing you and Auntie Kalisha and Uncle Alonzo?

The path you're going down leads to dead-ends, disappointments, and darkness."

Malik asked, "Are you gonna say, 'Don't be a fool, stay in school?'"

I said, "Nah, that slogan has gotten corny, but I want you to do better because you *can* do better."

I was driven to Dignity Health – California Hospital Medical Center. Then, I was wheeled out of the ambulance, into the hospital, and into the emergency room. They put a plastic mask over my mouth and nose; and the doctor told me to count down from ten.

I said, "Ten, nine, eight, seven, six, five … four … thr …"

I didn't have any dreams, just blackness.

It felt like I woke up a second later, but I knew operations lasted *way* longer than that. When I woke up, I saw myself in a bed and an IV needle injected into my right arm. A machine was beeping, showing that my heart was still beating. There were also tubes up my nose. My left arm felt a little sore, but that was to be expected. I knew I was in a recovery room and not Heaven, which was a relief.

Malik was sitting next to me reading this week's issue of *Jet* magazine. It featured Magic Johnson on the cover, explaining that he was retiring after testing positive for HIV. The LA Lakers won't be the same without Magic. Since HIV has turned into a wordlwide pandemic that has already taken away so many lives, my parents and I prayed that Magic would be able to fight the disease. I wouldn't want anything to happen to a basketball player as fine as Magic, but he's not as fine as Michael Jordan.

Michael Jordan, the other MJ, is on the cover of this month's issue of *Ebony* magazine. Now he is as fine as the summertime! I'll watch him play basketball any day! Michael Jordan has made watching basketball an even bigger religious act than ever before and many people, including myself, think he's the greatest athlete to ever pick up a basketball.

Then Malik put down the magazine exclaimed, "Thank Black Jesus, you're alive, cuz!"

I replied, "Of course I'm alive! It's gonna take more than a bullet to take me out."

I overheard voices outside.

Daddy yelled, "I want you, your son, and your thugs to stay away from my daughter! I don't want you to talk with her, follow her around, or even think about her!"

Uncle Alonzo said, "Bro, relax. My boys will find the guys who killed Devin and shot Hatima. Nobody messes with my family."

Daddy said, "After you kill some Crips, the Crips will just shoot more of your boys. What happens if they think Hatima is part of the Bloods? She won't live to see Christmas!"

Auntie Kalisha said, "Orlando, everybody knows who is and who is not a Blood or a Crip. Everyone knows Hatima isn't part of our set, so they'll leave her alone."

Mama said, "Just being related to you has brought danger into our family! Hatima has a bright future, and we don't want you to ruin it for her!"

Daddy said, "From now on, I don't want you two or Malik anywhere near my wife and baby girl. Alonzo, you and I are done."

Uncle Alonzo said, "Come on, bro, you don't mean that—"

Daddy yelled, "Yes, I do! Now get outta my face before the doctors have to send you to the emergency room, too!"

Malik yelled, "Yo, fam! Hatima's alright! She's awake!"

I fully realized that Devin was gone and was never coming back. Devin used to hit on me and came on as a bit of a player, but he was still a good guy who loved his family. That's why he took on the risk of being a Blood. I started crying; my tears fueled by anger and frustration.

Mama and Daddy opened the door to my room and saw me crying. They immediately hugged me.

I felt a twinge of pain in my left arm and said, "My left arm is still sore."

They released me from my hug, and Mama asked, "Hatima, are you alright?"

I said, "No, I just got shot and one of my friends is dead. To quote Tre Styles, 'I'm sick and tired of this shit.'"

Daddy glared at Malik and asked, "What were you doing hanging out with this thug?"

Malik said, "Whoa, Uncle Orlando! I ain't some random thug, I'm your nephew! Since Hatima is my cousin, I made sure she had a tourniquet before the ambulance arrived. The paramedics even said I did a good job at first aid."

I further explained, "I wasn't hanging out with Malik. I saw Devin taking a toaster out of Malik's Chevy Impala on Coliseum Street, and I asked him if the toaster was hot. I then asked him if he had any remorse about what he was doing with the Bloods, but he didn't. Then, Malik walked to his car and told Devin to sell the toaster. We argued, and Devin walked back to us. Next, I saw a blue Camaro, and I pulled Malik down to the ground. Good thing my sixth sense went off or else all three of us would probably be dead."

Daddy said, "These damn Bloods and Crips. Folks can't even walk outside in the daylight anymore."

Just then, Grandma walked in and exclaimed, "My grandbaby!" After she hugged and kissed me, she said, "I came as soon as I got the message. The brokerage firm is going to dock my pay, but you're more important than my measly salary."

I said, "Thanks, Grandma."

Malik left with Uncle Alonzo, and I wasn't sure if I would ever see him again in this lifetime. I had to stay in the hospital on Friday and Saturday to ensure there was no further internal damage to my arm. Wanda, Andre, Imani, and Marcus stopped by to visit me.

Wanda said, "I called your martial arts school, and told Master Shin that you won't be able to work for a while. When I told him you got shot, he said he'll tell Joshua, so I'm sure your boyfriend will come and visit you if he has free time."

I said, "That's great. Maybe his words of wisdom will help."

Then I asked Andre, "How's TSU?"

Andre said, "Great. Business classes are a bit tough, but I like them. With a business degree, I'ma get me a good job with loads of cash. The loads of cash will ensure I don't have to move back to our shithole of a neighborhood after I graduate."

Imani said, "Come on, Andre, our neighborhood ain't all bad."

Andre said, "It's extremely bad! The crime rate is higher than it's ever been, and our incompetent police force can't or won't do shit about it! Fuck this shit!"

Marcus said, "You ain't gonna become another brother who turns his back on the people, right?"

Andre said, "I ain't no sellout. When I have loads of cash, I'll give some to Dorsey High, the rec center, the churches, and every other place in this neighborhood to ensure things get better. Everyone knows the real power in this world is money. Without money, you ain't shit."

I said, "God holds the power in this world, not money. That's the problem with most folks today. They worship cash more than they worship the One who made the world and gave us life."

On Friday, someone knocked on the door and I said, "Come in."

Joshua walked in with a box of Hershey's Kisses. He asked me, "Are you alright?"

I replied, "I just got shot. Do you honestly think I'm alright?"

Joshua set the box of chocolates on the bedside table, sat in the chair next to me, and stated, "I was trying to be polite. What else am I supposed to ask?"

I stated, "You might ask, 'Are you in a gang?'"

Joshua said, "I know you, Hatima, and I know you're the last person who would join a gang. I figure that you were in the wrong place at the wrong time like Ricky Baker."

Even after all these months, Ricky's death still haunts us, but I guess it haunts Joshua more than me since I've already seen people get shot and killed, and I've seen plenty of dead bodies on my way to school.

I said, "I told you my uncle and cousin are members of the Bloods. Some Crips tried to shoot my cousin and a former classmate of mine, Devin, but they only got Devin."

Joshua said, "Whoa. Why are you hanging out with your gangster cousin?"

I exclaimed, "I wasn't hanging out with Malik! I was checking on Devin! It ain't right that he quit school to join the Bloods! If his sister's baby daddy found another job and Devin's dad wasn't dead, then maybe he'd still be alive! But no one gives a damn about us!"

I started crying like a baby; people never really get over the deaths of people they care about.

Joshua held me and I cried into his shirt. He said, "Shhhh. I wish I could tell you everything's going to be alright, but I'm not Bob Marley." I laughed and Joshua continued, "But I'll stand by you. If I met your parents, I would stand with them, too."

I laughed and said, "If you wanna meet my parents, stick around until they get here. Mama and Daddy are gonna leave their shifts at the restaurant and the airport to come check on me."

Sure enough, an hour later, my parents arrived.

Daddy eyed Joshua and asked, "Who are you?"

Joshua said, "I'm Joshua Yang, and I'm your daughter's boyfriend."

Daddy repeated, "Boyfriend?"

Mama asked, "Where did you two meet?"

I explained, "At Master Shin's Dojang. We've known each other since we were ten, but Joshua asked me out months ago, around February and March. We started going on a lot of dates during the summer, and I guess things are now serious."

Daddy asked Joshua, "Are you Korean?"

Joshua said, "Yes I am, Mister Parker."

Daddy asked Joshua, "Does your daddy own any stores in Crenshaw?"

Joshua said, "No, he owns a nightclub in Koreatown and a grocery store in Watts. When I introduced Hatima to my dad, he didn't seem to have any problems with our relationship."

Mama asked, "When did your father meet our daughter?"

Joshua said, "Back in August."

Daddy asked, "And we have to wait three months before our daughter tells us about you?" He was getting as mad as a bull facing a matador.

Joshua said, "Don't blame me. Blame the times. Tensions are high between Blacks and Koreans. Hatima thought it would be better if we kept our romance a secret since our two races are at each other's throats."

Mama put her index finger and thumb on her chin, which

meant she was thinking about something. She said, "Maybe your romance is a good thing."

Daddy, Joshua, and I all said, "What?"

She explained, "If people see how close you two are, maybe our peoples may finally be able to resolve things peacefully."

Daddy said, "Suzy Jane, this is not a Shakespearian play. Romeo and Juliet thought their romance would end the feud between their families, but their romance didn't end their families' feud, their deaths did. Is that what you want?"

Mama explained, "This is the twentieth century, Orlando. Human thought has evolved. I doubt our daughter and Joshua will end their own lives just to make sure they can stay together."

I asked, "So, am I allowed to keep dating Joshua?"

Mama said, "It's alright with me because I trust your judgment."

Daddy didn't answer right away, and Mama nudged his arm.

Daddy said, "I guess if y'all are serious, you can keep dating, but don't have too much fun."

(Translation: "Don't get my daughter pregnant, Korean boy, or else…")

On Sunday, I was discharged. My left arm was in a sling and the doctors said I could take it off in a week or two, and I would have to do physical therapy.

Mama and Daddy said I didn't have to go to church, but I insisted that some time in God's house would help my recovery.

I figured hating the Crips was a waste of time not just because, in my opinion, several corrupt forces played a part in Devin's death.

Coretta Scott King said, "Hate is too great a burden to bear. It injures the hater more than the hated."

I think this means hatred poisons people's hearts and turns

them into monsters. The KKK's hatred of Blacks turned them into monsters. Adolf Hitler's hatred of Jews, Blacks, homosexuals, people with disabilities, and pretty much anyone who is different from blond-haired, blue-eyed Whites turned him and his Nazi Party into the biggest monsters in the history of the world. The Bloods' and the Crips' hatred of each other simply because they live in different parts of the hood has also turned them into monsters.

Mama, Daddy, Grandma, and I all went to the afternoon service at FAME. At church, Dr. Murray told the congregation that he wanted to give a special shout-out of praise to me and Devin. He asked me to stand up, and I did.

Dr. Murray proclaimed, "Sister Hatima was a victim of violence in her own neighborhood. Her instincts helped her save her cousin, a young man who is a member of the Bloods. Unfortunately, Devin Williams was not so lucky, and he was shot in the back and neck. Now, First AME, we are not the only ones raising money for Sister Hatima's medical bills and Brother Devin's funeral. The Black women and children of Jack and Jill are also raising money to help Hatima and Devin. They are also teaming up with the South Central chapter of Jack and Jill to raise money to help aid the schools, churches, and other establishments in our communities. Missus Hamilton, the head of the LA Jack and Jill chapter, said that Sister Hatima alerted her to affluent Blacks' apparent lack of concern for life in the ghettos. I know many of you believe all affluent Blacks who live outside of South Central are sellouts, but the reason we push our children hard in school is so that they have a chance to make it to the highest possible level of success. Now, many rich Blacks have not turned their backs on the people. Look at Doctor Ben Carson and Mister Reginald Lewis. We have been accused by the Koreans of always waiting for handouts because we're too lazy to work. But our hard work led to the building of this church! Our hard work led to the HBCUs! Our hard work led to Jack and Jill! We are a people who help ourselves. We have and will continue to fight for our fair share in the world!"

The whole congregation stood up and yelled, "Hallelujah, Doc!" and "Praise the Lord!" and "Thank You, Jesus!"

People continued clapping and cheering while the choir led us in songs. Church usually makes me happy, but I still felt sad about Devin.

Am I allowed to feel sad in the Lord's house?

After church, Mama, Daddy, and Grandma saw a squad car parked near our house. When Daddy parked the Ford next to our house, Detective Crawford got out of the driver's seat of the squad car.

I asked, "Do you wanna take me in for questioning, Detective Crawford?"

She replied, "Yes, as long as it's okay with your parents."

Detective Crawford walked up to my parents and held out her hand.

She told my parents. "The name's Detective Crawford, Mister and Missus Parker. Your daughter and I have already been acquainted."

Mama shook her hand and so did Daddy. Detective Crawford didn't appear to be intimidated by Daddy the way a lot of cops are. A lot of cops pat Daddy down to make sure he's not carrying a gun although they're probably afraid his arms are good substitutes for guns.

Mama asked, "When did you two meet?"

Detective Crawford explained, "Back in July, after Hatima and Doctor Wilson were racially profiled. I questioned her about the incident and told her to call me if any other cops harass her."

Detective Crawford mostly asked me questions about Uncle Alonzo, milking me for info about the gang I ain't a part of and don't care shit about, but I still had good instincts about her, so I didn't tell my parents and Grandma about the interrogation.

Daddy said, "I'm sorry you wasted your time, Detective. My daughter has nothing to say to the LAPD."

Detective Crawford said, "Look, I know LA has become a steaming pot ready to boil over, but withholding information from the police isn't going to help. The reason gangsters are still terrorizing this neighborhood is because a lot of Blacks refuse to cooperate with us. You don't report crimes when they happen, you don't testify in court, and you take matters into your own hands." Then, she asked Mama, "Do you want those gangsters locked away for shooting your daughter and murdering Devin Williams?"

Mama said, "Of course, but I doubt our messed-up legal system will keep them there."

Detective Crawford asked Daddy, "Do you have reservations about seeing your brother and nephew in jail?"

Daddy said, "No, he chose his path and should pay the consequences. Alonzo should have been locked away for good years ago, but he's still around. I doubt you and your fellow cops can contain him."

Detective Crawford said, "I am dedicated to serving the people of Los Angeles and providing a better police service."

I told her, "I'll tell you what I know but it isn't a lot of information."

Detective Crawford said, "Any info is helpful."

She got into her car while Mama, Daddy, Grandma, and I all changed out of our church clothes. Grandma stayed at home, while the rest of us got back into Daddy's Ford and followed her car to the police station.

The drive from West Boulevard to the LAPD Southeast Community Police Station took half an hour. Detective Crawford led us in; I saw White cops, Black cops, Latino cops, and Asian cops. I wondered how many actually cared about Devin's death. I also wondered how many had stopped Black people driving nice cars; how many had stopped Black kids who wore baggy overalls and hip-hop clothes; and how many of these cops had killed Black people simply because of our skin color.

How many good cops are there versus the racist and incompetent?

Detective Crawford led us to a waiting room and told us to sit there. I had packed two books, *Let the Circle Be Unbroken* and *The Road to Memphis*. Both were written by the same author, Mildred D. Taylor. They are sequels to *Roll of Thunder, Hear My Cry*, one of my favorite novels. All three novels are told from the point of view of Cassie Logan, a Black girl who resides in Mississippi during the 1930s and 1940s. Cassie and her family encounter racism since Mississippi is the most bigoted state in the US, but the Logans take pride in their land – four hundred acres of prime property. The land gives the Logans the courage they need to stand up to the world's prejudices. I've always loved the Logans, but I started thinking: do they really need four hundred acres? One of the reasons White folks are able to oppress the Blacks of Spokane County is because most of them sharecrop rich Whites' land. The majority of Blacks in Spokane County have to rely on White folks in order to survive. That means that if they step outta line, White folks will make them suffer. Now, if you divide the four hundred acres by forty, there would be enough land for ten families, including the Logans. The reason why so many Blacks are poor is because they haven't been given the means to become self-sufficient.

After the civil war, Union General William T. Sherman initiated Special Field Order No. 15. The Union then confiscated and redistributed over 400,000 acres of land in South Carolina and Georgia to newly freed Blacks in forty-acre plots. Yes, this is where the phrase "forty acres and a mule" came from, but no mules were given to the Blacks. Unfortunately, President Andrew Johnson, who took over after President Lincoln was assassinated, overturned Special Field Order No. 15 in the fall of 1865 and returned most of the land to the White planters who originally owned it.

One of the reasons the world is such a fucked-up place is because so many people are greedy – from poor folks to rich folks; but rich folks are definitely the greediest. Most of this country's wealth is owned by rich folks, and they barely give poor folks enough money to stay alive. That's why the rich stay rich and the poor stay poor.

Daddy interrupted my thoughts and asked, "Why do you like that Korean boy?"

Mama said, "Orlando …"

I wasn't surprised that Daddy brought up Joshua because my Daddy dislikes most Koreans. He even had a problem with me learning hapkido from Master Shin because hapkido is a Korean martial art, and Master Shin is a Korean man, but Master Shin has always talked to me and my parents with kindness and respect so we've grown to like him and respect him. I hope Mama and Daddy can grow to like Joshua as well.

I immediately said, "His name is Joshua Yang. It's not hard to forget. Blacks hated it when Whites called us 'boy,' 'girl,' 'uncle,' and 'auntie.' Coretta Scott King said, 'I don't believe you can stand for freedom for one group of people and deny it to others.'"

Daddy snorted and said, "The Koreans are free enough to disrespect and kill Black shoppers. Do Joshua's parents disrespect Black shoppers in the hood?"

I stated, "I'm not sure if Black shoppers at Mister Yang's Watts store are mistreated. Joshua said a man named Mister Yoo helped run the store, but he found another job after he graduated from Cal State LA. Now a guy named Mister Cho helps run the Watts store, but I don't know how he feels about Blacks. Mister Yang doesn't own any stores in Crenshaw as far as I know."

Daddy asked, "Is he planning on buying any more stores?"

I said, "I don't know."

Daddy said, "Tell him we don't need his business in Crenshaw. Black folks are better when left alone."

I said, "I used to think that, too. But if Koreans and Whites aren't killing us, then we're doing it instead. Maybe Doctor King's dream on interracial living isn't so crazy. One of the reasons why so many people hate us is because they don't know us, but they don't know us because we don't give them the opportunity to. Since Joshua got to know me well over these past several months and watched *Jungle Fever* and *Boyz n the Hood* with me, he's gained a better understanding of the African American experience."

Mama said, "Really? Maybe he is down for the cause. Governor George C. Wallace was one of the world's biggest racists in the sixties but he changed in the eighties."

I told Daddy and Mama, "The Koreans also suffered when they immigrated here. Xenophobia is a nationwide affliction that's just as bad as racism."

Daddy said, "Last time I checked, Koreans are considered

'model minorities.' The stereotype about all Asians is that they're smart. That means they'll all go to college, get six-figure salary jobs, and be upstanding American citizens. But what stereotypes are we stuck with?"

Mama stated, "That we're all criminals, winos, and junkies. That we all drop out of school, we all have babies before we're eighteen, and all fathers are absent in the hood."

I said, "You two may be onto something. I've never asked Joshua what his school is like, but I'm sure it's better equipped than Dorsey High. The schools that have large amounts of Asians may be better equipped because of the belief that all Asians are smart. So, the school district gives them new books, computers, and teachers who actually have a passion for teaching. Since the belief about Blacks is that we're all lowlives and our lives won't amount to much, there's no point giving us new equipment or teachers with brains."

Mama said, "That thinking is why schools in the South were inferior to White schools. Why bother giving books to a bunch of African monkeys? If we have all the same things other people do, we'd have a better chance at succeeding in life."

I said, "It isn't written anywhere that life is fair."

Daddy asked, "Are you turned off from Black guys because of fools like the Bloods and the Crips?"

I replied, "No! There are plenty of nice guys at Dorsey High, but I never experienced much chemistry with them. Plus, the not-so-nice guys only pay attention to my ass and my breasts. They obviously only have one thing on their minds."

Mama said, "You better not come home with babies for me and your daddy to raise."

I said, "You don't have to worry about that. If I get pregnant, the Naval Academy won't accept me. So, I'm staying abstinent."

Daddy asked, "So, what is it about Joshua that attracts you to him?"

Most folks might be embarrassed about having this conversation with their parents, but I've always felt close to Mama and Daddy – one of the perks of being an only child.

I said, "Joshua is cute, he doesn't mind that I can kick his butt, and he has an open mind." Daddy grumbled, and I asked, "Are you gonna make me stop dating him?"

Mama said, "Of course not. He sounds like a fine young man."

Daddy grunted, "Yeah, he seems alright."

Then, Detective Crawford said, "We're ready to question you, Hatima."

She led me, Mama, and Daddy into an interrogation room. There was one table with five chairs. My parents and I sat in the three chairs on one side and Detective Crawford and a Black female cop whose badge also said "DETECTIVE" and "4040" sat in the two chairs on the other side of the table.

Detective Crawford said, "Hatima, Mister and Missus Parker, this is Detective Hill. She works in the Robbery-Homicide Division of the Detective Bureau. Your daughter already knows I work in the Gang and Narcotics Division."

Detective Hill said, "Even though Miss Hatima Parker is a victim in this case and not a suspect, she still has the right to have an attorney present during questioning."

Daddy said, "Understood."

Detective Hill said, "Hatima Parker has the right to remain silent and leave anytime she wishes."

Daddy said, "Understood."

Detective Hill said, "Anything Hatima Parker says may be used as evidence later in court."

Daddy said, "Understood."

Detective Hill said, "Alright, let's begin." Then, she asked me to recount the events of Thanksgiving.

I told her, "I was walking down Coliseum Street and saw Devin standing next to a red Chevy Impala. He left and Malik came over. We talked and then Devin started walking back to us. I saw a blue Camaro drive by, and the window rolled down. My instincts told me to get down, and I grabbed Malik. I was shot in the left shoulder, but Devin was killed."

Detective Hill asked, "Do you remember the license plate number for the blue Camaro?"

I said, "No, I didn't see it."

Detective Hill asked, "Did the red Impala have any contraband?"

I knew Devin had sold a stolen toaster. I could have lied, but that would just make things worse. I already said that Devin was next to a red Chevy Impala and the cops must know who the car belongs to. All files and paperwork will show that Malik owns the car, and the cops know Uncle Alonzo is a leader of the Bloods. So, they must know Malik is a Blood, too.

I said, "The Chevy Impala had one stolen toaster that Devin sold. I don't know to whom he sold it to."

Detective Crawford wrote what I said on a notepad. Since there was a tape recorder on the table, I didn't see the point of that.

Detective Hill asked, "Do you know whom the toaster originally belonged to?"

I said, "A man named Mister Travis. He owns an electronics store, but I'm not familiar with him."

Detective Hill asked, "Did you know Devin was a Blood?"

I stated, "Devin told me in June that he was dropping out of school and joining the Bloods. He has a mom, a sister, and a nephew to take care of, and he figured hustling with the Bloods was his best option."

Detective Hill asked, "Do you know about any other plans the Bloods have?"

I said, "No because I'm not part of their gang."

Detective Hill said, "But your uncle and cousin are."

Mama said, "That doesn't mean Hatima is. We want nothing to do with Alonzo or his gang."

Detective Hill asked, "Then why was your daughter consorting with gangsters?"

I said, "People in the hood say 'Hey' to gangsters now and again, mostly because they fear them and don't want to get on their bad side. Malik is my cousin and I've tried to talk sense into him time and time again. I know he's too smart to be a Blood."

Detective Crawford said, "Blood is thicker than water, but despite the fact that you're family, I'm sure your cousin and uncle don't let you in on the details of their lifestyle."

I said, "No, they don't."

Daddy asked, "If you know my brother is dirty, why isn't he rotting in jail?"

Detective Crawford said, "We need good, solid evidence on all of his dirty schemes. We believe that some dirty cops are on his payroll and that he may be tied to the Mob."

The Mob is a large criminal organization, just like the gangs in the hood – but bigger.

I said, "Really? This sounds like a James Bond movie."

Detective Hill said, "This is not a movie but real life."

Detective Crawford said, "We're pretty sure Devin's murderers are Crips. Your testimony will help us get search warrants to investigate their vehicles and homes."

I asked, "Am I done?"

Detective Hill said, "Yes, you and your parents can leave."

As we left the police station, Detective Crawford said, "Life's most persistent and urgent question is, 'What are you doing for others?'"

I said, "Martin Luther King."

Detective Crawford said, "I became a police officer so I could serve and protect the people of LA from the poison that is crime, but I can't help others without cooperation from certain people."

She smiled at me, and I smiled back.

Chapter Eleven

After we left the police station, Daddy said, "We should stop by the Williamses' house. Pay our respects."

I stated, "Missus Williams hates me. I know it."

Mama said, "Hatima, why would you say that?"

I explained, "Because I saved Malik instead of her son."

Daddy said, "You didn't have time to run to Devin and pull him down. If you ran toward him, you would have died as well."

I further explained, "My instincts told me to pull Malik and myself down onto the pavement. I should have yelled at Devin to get down, but I didn't."

Daddy said, "That reminds me of when I was in Vietnam. When the Vietcong shot at us, my first instinct was always to get down; and if a fellow Marine was near me, I'd pull him down too. Unfortunately, many of my fellow Marines weren't as lucky as I was. The gunshots took them out. My fellow Marines who had families here in LA didn't hold me accountable when I told them how their loved ones died, but I still wanted them to yell at me, hit me, or do something. I wanted somebody to punish me for not saving my friends. Later, I realized that I couldn't save everyone, and that it wasn't my job to save everyone in my unit. I learned that I should be grateful for the lives I did save."

We got into the Ford and started to drive away from the police station.

I asked, "Should I be grateful that I saved Malik?"

Mama said, "Of course you should. He's family."

I said, "Not anymore. Daddy disowned Uncle Alonzo and Malik."

Daddy said, "Being anywhere near them or the Bloods is dangerous to your life. You have a bright future ahead of you, and I don't want you to become another murder statistic."

I added, "Uncle Alonzo and Malik are probably recruiting another Black guy to take Devin's place. They'll just spread more of their poison into our hood. I'm wondering if Malik's life was worth saving."

Mama said, "If you hadn't tried to save your cousin, I'm sure the Lord would have seen it as a sin. Letting your own flesh and blood die would lead to eternal damnation."

Daddy said, "Sooner or later, Alonzo's and Malik's luck will run out. Malik will get sent to juvie and maybe it will finally force him to get his head on straight. The next time Alonzo gets sent to jail will be his third strike. That means they'll lock him up and throw away the key. Alonzo is already too far gone, but I still have hope for Malik."

Daddy drove us back to West Boulevard.

Grandma asked, "How did it go?"

I told Grandma, "I told the cops about the drive-by. All I do know is the Crips were driving a blue Camaro, but I didn't see the license plate."

Grandma asked, "Since when is telling the cops anything a good idea?"

Daddy explained, "Flora May, we can't let gangbangers dictate the laws about how we live. If we don't try to let the justice system put those murderers away, then we're part of the problem as well."

Grandma muttered, "Don't know why that devil brother of yours and his demon followers aren't in jail."

Mama said, "Mama, the Bible says you reap what you sow. Soon, Alonzo will finally pay the price for his life of evil."

After we all used the bathrooms, Daddy drove us to the Williamses' house on Westhaven Street, which took about five minutes. He parked the car on the side of the street; and we got out of the car, walked onto the porch, and Daddy knocked on the door.

Mrs. Williams answered the door and exclaimed, "Orlando, Suzy Jane, Ms. Flora May, so nice of you to drop by!" She hugged them and then saw me and my sling. She exclaimed, "Hatima, I am *sooooo* glad you're here! It's comforting to know those devils didn't take away another young life."

She hugged me so tightly that I said, "Missus Williams, I can't breathe!"

She let me go and said, "Sorry, don't want to asphyxiate you!"

We all laughed and walked into her house.

South Central houses look different on the outside, but they're pretty much the same inside. Mrs. Williams has a living room, a kitchen, two bathrooms, and three bedrooms, same as our house.

Mrs. Williams pointed to the couch and said, "Y'all sit down, I'll get cookies and lemonade."

She went into the kitchen and then her daughter came out of her bedroom.

I said, "Hey, Alicia, how you doin'?"

Alicia shrugged and said, "Okay, I guess. Devin's passing finally convinced Hank to start looking for other work. He was able to get a loan from the bank to buy a used-car dealership."

I asked, "He's still set on becoming a successful businessman?"

Daddy said, "Hatima, all businesses start small. LA wouldn't be considered Heaven on Earth if this city didn't have one of the world's largest economies."

Alicia said, "Some parts of LA may seem like Heaven; but here in South Central, we're living in Hell. Gangsters recruit kids to continue their senseless wars. They always come up with lameass excuses to open fire, night or day. Gangbangers and innocent people get caught in the crossfire. I'm gonna work hard to get me and my son outta here."

I asked, "Classes at USC too much for you?"

Alicia said, "Nah. Mom and Ms. Morris help me baby-sit and care for Jamal. I've been able to juggle my class workload and time with my baby."

I pointed out, "Jamal is three going on four. I wouldn't exactly call him a baby anymore."

Alicia said, "Well, when I become a dentist in six years, I'll make enough money to move myself, my son, and Mom outta here. I'm gonna move on up like the Jeffersons, and I'm never looking back."

Mama said, "Hold on, Alicia. I admire anyone who manages to get out of the hood since my husband and I want to make sure Hatima also moves on up, but you shouldn't completely turn your back on the people. When you become successful, come back to Dorsey and speak to the young girls in the hood. Make sure they don't make the same mistakes so many others have and show them that the world can be their oyster."

I knew Mama would hit a wrong nerve when she said, "Make sure they don't make the same mistakes so many others have."

Alicia stated, "My son is a blessing. He reminds me why I'm working so hard to do well at USC. I want to provide a better life for my kids so they can provide a good life for their own kids. We have to break this cycle of poverty that most folks think is impossible to destroy."

Mrs. Williams came out with the tray of cookies and lemonade. As I ate one, I asked, "When's Devin's funeral?"

Mrs. Williams said, "On Saturday. We're inviting our neighbors, Devin's friends, and members of FAME. Do you want to come, too?"

I said, "Yeah, I wanna be able to say a proper goodbye to Devin."

When I got home, I took out the CD of the *Boyz n the Hood* soundtrack and put it in the stereo. Ice Cube started rapping "How to Survive in South Central." Despite all the tips we've been given by our parents and the martial arts training I've taken to hone my instincts, the Crips still got the better of me; but I survived, which is a major accomplishment in the hood. Sadly, for everyone who survives, there are a whole bunch of others who don't. I looked at Fannie Lou Hamer's picture and I told her, "Ms. Hamer, I'm sick and tired of being sick and tired."

When Ice Cube finished rapping, I skipped the CD down to the twelfth track, "Spirit." Force One Network's vocals remind me of the choir at FAME:

> *Spirit, spirit, hey, (Hey) do you really care?*
> *(Don't you know your brothers hungry?)*
> *Spirit*
> *(Don't you know your sister's lonely?)*
> *Spirit, hey*
> *(Don't you know there's babies cryin'?)*
> *(Don't you know your brother's dyin'?)*
> *Do you really care?*

Yo' man check out partna' over there, his ass is toh' up like,
toh' up from the flo' up (Ha haah), Oh man check out this sister with
the baby (you already knowing), Aww somebody ought to throw her
a bread crumb or somethin', her ass soundin' like windshield wipers!

Hooooooo oooh woo-woo woo ooooo,
Hoooo ooh woooooo hoo wooooo woooooo,
Does anybody, care at all?, Don't you know your brother's hungry?,
Does anybody, care at all? He's hungry and he hasn't got a prayer,
Walkin' alone by myself, I'm faced, with all the things I see,
The brother's on a one-way trip, and he's losin' everything, he's worked
for, yeah

Those lyrics could be about Devin and other young brothers in the hood. He was hungry, but he never had a prayer since there was no other way for him to get money for his family besides crime. Devin went on a one-way trip to Heaven, the one up in the skies not the one on Earth. Some people have keys to Heaven on Earth, but Devin wasn't one of them.

Then, Force One Network sings in their second verse:

Does anybody, care at all?, Don't you know your sister's lonely?,
Does anybody, care at all?, She's lonely and she's got no place to go,
The people say that what she does, is she, walks the streets alone yeah,
But some folks just don't understand, she's got no food, and she's got
no home

I don't think that those lyrics apply to me because I have a loving home, a great family, and a full stomach every night, but there are other girls, such as Imani, who have very little food. Some women, such as Alicia, don't see South Central as home because it's not full of love. There is some love, but the hood seems to be mostly full of hatred and violence. My parents say home is where you are loved. Dorothy Gale proclaimed that there's no place like home, and Kansas was her home because her aunt and uncle lived there, but in a later Oz book, she and her aunt and uncle move to Oz. Oz is also Dorothy's home because her "extended family" lives there – the Scarecrow, the Tin Man, the Cowardly Lion, Tik-Tok, Jack Pumpkinhead, the Hungry Tiger, the Munchkins, the Winkies, the Quadlings, the Gillykins, Queen Ozma, et cetera. The Pevensie siblings considered Narnia a better home than England because of all the love the Narnians give regardless of race or species. Redwall Abbey is a fantastic home for all because of all the love the mice, squirrels, voles, moles, hedgehogs, badgers, et cetera give each other. Maybe the human world could be as cool as fantasy worlds if we learned to love one another better.

Dr. King said, "Returning hate for hate multiplies hate, adding deeper darkness to a night already devoid of stars. Darkness cannot drive out darkness, only light can do that. Hate cannot drive out hate, only love can do that."

That means all the violence, hatred, and bullshit the Bloods and Blues and other gangs mete out to each other is just adding more darkness to the ghetto. To drive out the darkness, we need more light. Love produces more light than any other virtue on this Earth.

When folks in my neighborhood and the other South Central hoods die, their friends and family hire the services of the Angelus Funeral Home. The Angelus Funeral Home is located on Crenshaw Boulevard. Monday after school, Mrs. Williams asked me to accompany her to the funeral parlor on Monday, when school was out. I asked her why she wanted me to come.

She explained, "You tried to talk Devin out of the gang life. Even though he made a horrible mistake, you still tried to steer him down the right path. Alicia has classes Monday afternoon, and I don't want to be surrounded by all that death alone."

I agreed mostly because my shoulder wound meant I couldn't teach at the dojang. Plus, I remember an old saying: "Misery loves company."

Mrs. Williams needed a shoulder to cry on, and I was okay with letting her cry on mine. My right shoulder, of course. The left shoulder would forever have a scar that would remind me of Devin.

School on Monday was no fun, but Mondays are usually regarded as the worst day of the week. Garfield ain't the only one who knows how depressing Mondays can be. Kids at school avoided me like they thought *I* was mixed up with the Bloods. Some wanted to see my bullet wound, but I told them it was "Nunya bidness." Whenever somebody at Dorsey High is shot and lives to tell the tale, the survivor is treated with a certain awe because they've beaten the odds.

Mrs. Williams picked me up at my house in her Toyota, but she couldn't stop crying while she was driving. I wondered how the Angel of Death could do a job that led to so much misery for other human beings; but I'm sure the Angel of Death does it because God instructs him to.

I told Mrs. Williams, "I'll drive. My driver's manual states that you shouldn't drive when you're upset."

Mrs. Williams sniffled and said, "Okay."

She got out of the driver's seat, and I slid over. The drive to the funeral home only took about five minutes. Since people weren't off work yet, the roads weren't crowded, but they would probably be crowded when we were driving back.

We arrived, and I parked the Toyota, and we walked in. When we opened the door to the Angelus Funeral Home, there was a statue of a dog-headed person to my right. The dog-headed guy used to creep me out when I was little because I thought he was real and that he was the doorman. I learned that the dog-headed guy is Anubis, the Egyptian god of the Underworld. On the other side of the door was a replica of King Tut's sarcophagus; it looks so realistic that I thought it had an actual mummy inside it when I was little. Egypt has become a source of pride for Black folks ever since they found out that the 1960s *Cleopatra* film that starred Elizabeth Taylor as the titular queen was a lie. Mr. Ngozi explained that most of Egypt's population is Black or Arab. That meant Black folks helped design the pyramids, the Sphinx, the Alexandria lighthouse, et cetera. But some Black folks, like Mama, still have a bitter dislike for the Egyptians because they enslaved the Israelites and used slaves from other nations to build their empire. Ancient Egypt was just as bad as the American South.

Personally, I have no beef with Egypt. They don't practice slavery anymore and the pyramids are the only Ancient Wonder that are still standing today. I believe Egypt *is* a source of pride for Black people across the world. I'm also still proud to be American even though several aspects of American life represent an American Nightmare instead of the American Dream.

The Angelus Funeral Home is *not* like a haunted house. It is *not* decorated with Halloween decorations, such as jack o'lanterns, bubbling cauldrons, and skeletons of dead people hanging by ropes. It's actually a very distinguished place. The floors are squeaky clean, and the hallways are lit up brightly. There is fancy-looking furniture in the hallways and the offices. There are even chandeliers. The caskets are kept in a separate room, but even that room doesn't look scary. The lights are on and people can take a good look at the caskets so that they can properly decide on the one they want.

Mr. Grant is the current owner of the Angelus Funeral Home. His father was one of the first undertakers to work here when the Angelus Funeral Home was built on East Jefferson Boulevard in 1934. Mr. Grant stated that his father was the first member of his family to leave Texas. The Grants were slaves on a sugarcane plantation on the outskirts of Houston. After the Civil War ended, the Grants gave themselves their current surname after General Ulysses Grant and continued working on the sugarcane plantation as sharecroppers. During the Great Depression, jobs were scarce for Black people. So, Grandpa Grant hopped a train to Los Angeles, hoping to find work. Mr. Grant stated that his father was the first member of the family to leave Texas, but when Grandpa Grant moved out West, he found it hard to find a job since Blacks are the last hired and first fired. But the three directors of Angelus, L.G. Robinson, Lorenzo Bowdin, and John L. Hill, gave Grandpa Grant a job when he told them he had worked part-time as a mortician in Texas.

The Angelus Funeral Home is a very successful business, thanks to the high death rate in the hoods. Mr. Grant started working here part-time when he was in high school. Then, he got a Bachelor and Master of Business Administration degrees from LAMU and moved back to South Central to work at the funeral home full-time and became the president of Angelus when the last one died. His son, Eric, is taking business classes at USC, so that he can, hopefully, run the business after his dad retires.

Mrs. Williams knocked on Mr. Grant's door, and he told us to come in. Mr. Grant was sitting behind his desk, going through papers. Mrs. Williams and I sat in two chairs in front of his desk.

He said, "Once again, I am terribly sorry for your loss, Missus Williams. I am here to make sure you can say a proper goodbye to your son."

Mr. Grant always wears a suit and tie when he's working just like Dr. Murray, Dr. Wilson, and the male teachers at Dorsey High. When I was little, my friends and classmates believed that Mr. Grant and his employees had supernatural powers over their clients and that Mr. Grant would summon them all into an undead army. They figured that was the only reason Mr. Grant and the other morticians could stand to be around dead people. The boys then joked that the undead army could take down the gangbangers *and* the cops since bullets would have no effect on them. You can't kill an undead person twice, but I always told my friends that was absolute nonsense.

Mr. Grant has the job nobody else in our hood wants. When people search for Black leaders in our community, they'll immediately look for preachers, like Dr. Murray, and teachers, like Principal Edwards. Preachers remind people that God loves us and is the all-powerful One, not White people. Preachers can also organize people better than doctors or lawyers, as seen in the 1960s when Martin Luther King led the Civil Rights Movement. Teachers educate the young and most Black people know that without an education, you're nothing; but businesspeople are important leaders in the Black community as well. America is a land of businesses and the best way to be somebody is to have a business that rakes in the moola. The most gruesome business has always been undertaking, but the undertakers are important businesspeople, too. Death has always been a close shadow, and people are afraid that at any time, that dark shadow can take them away from the land of the living. Mr. Grant ensures folks can say goodbye to loved ones, and he reminds us that we have to continue living in order to keep the light shining.

Mrs. Williams told Mr. Grant, "I want my baby boy to be buried right."

Mr. Grant said, "Yes, of course." Then, he led us to the room where the caskets are and asked, "Which casket do you like?"

The caskets were all made out of different wood even though I think pine is the ideal wood for caskets. There were caskets made out of mahogany, cedar, walnut, oak, cherry, et cetera.

Mrs. Williams took a good look at most of them and said, "I like the California red cedar casket. Devin loved his home state."

I saw the price tag and asked, "Are FAME and Jack and Jill really gonna pay for that?"

Mrs. Williams said, "Of course they will. They told me that money isn't an issue for them."

I know money has never been an issue for rich folks and the church values spiritual things instead of material things. But material money does help Dr. Murray keep his many community projects going.

Mr. Grant asked, "Have you picked out a suit?"

Mrs. Williams said, "I was planning on buying him a new suit. He'll look dashing in a new jacket and tie."

I said, "I think Devin wants to look like himself at his funeral. I don't think he wants us to dress him up like he's a doll!"

Mr. Grant said, "Now, young lady—"

I exclaimed, "You don't think Devin would want to look like himself?! You didn't know him like I knew him!"

Mrs. Williams patted my shoulder and said, "Calm down, Hatima. You're still upset. I believe Devin would want his church suit passed on to his nephew, Jamal, since he had no kids of his own."

Devin will never be able to have kids of his own. He wasn't a teen daddy like some of the guys in our age group. I believe that says something about his character.

Mr. Grant said, "Drop the suit off here before the funeral on Saturday."

The next day after school, I stayed at home and did my homework. I wasn't planning on going outside until I heard a knock at the door.

I went to answer it, and I was surprised when I saw Joshua.

I asked him, "What in the world are you doing here?"

Joshua said, "Your friends Wanda and Imani thought I should check up on you. They figured you could use all the cheering up you could get."

I said, "That's sweet but you're in my hood now. Most folks here hate Koreans, and you may not make it out in one piece."

Joshua said, "I'll take the risk. Besides, this is probably how you feel whenever you come to Koreatown, right?"

I said, "Yeah. You and Master Shin are the only Koreans I've met there who are willing to roll out the welcome wagon. The others look at me like I'm gonna kill them or steal from them or burn their neighborhood to the ground."

Joshua said, "If you can deal with that when you come to Koreatown, I can deal with anything the Blacks of Crenshaw decide to dish out to me."

I said, "Come on in. You'll be safer in here than you will be out there."

Joshua came in and sat on my couch. He saw all the pictures of famous Black folks on the walls and said, "Your family has a lot of pride in your Black heritage."

I said, "Yep."

Then, after taking a good look at all the pictures and listening to me explain who some of the famous Blacks are/were, Joshua said something that surprised me. He said, "You should have pictures of Seretse Khama."

I had never heard of Serestse Khama and I asked Joshua, "Who's Seretse Khama?"

Joshua explained, "The Prince and first President of Botswana. When he went to school in England, he fell in love with an Englishwoman, and it caused a worldwide controversy. I'm surprised you've never heard of him."

I said, "Glad to see you know some Black history. I'll do more research on him and if he's considered a significant figure in Black history, I'll tell my parents that we should put up a picture of him."

Joshua walked around my house and said, "I like your house. It's cozy; you can feel all the love in here."

I said, "Glad you like it."

Then, Joshua went into my room. I know my parents wouldn't want me to be alone in my room with a boy, but he looked at my posters; then, he looked at my maps of Narnia, Oz, and Nonestica; and he took some books off my bookshelf.

Joshua said, "These books look well-read."

I said, "I've read them all many times. Doctor Seuss said, 'The more that you read, the more things you will know. The more that you learn, the more places you'll go.' I can travel to Oz, Narnia, London, the British countryside, the Deep South, Harlem, Toronto, the Great Depression, the nineteen fifties and nineteen sixties and many other places and time periods, thanks to books."

Joshua said, "Yeah, books are a great escape."

I asked him, "Anything else you wanna see?"

He sat down next to me on my bed and asked, "How many bedrooms and bathrooms are in this house?"

I said, "There are three bedrooms and two bathrooms. Other houses and apartments in South Central have less or more beds and baths, but Grandpa Gabriel bought this house and wanted to make sure my dad and uncle had their own bedrooms and bathroom."

Joshua asked, "Does anyone use the third bedroom?"

I explained, "Grandma does when she comes and visits during the weekend. She also shares my bathroom."

Joshua asked, "When do your parents get home from work?"

I explained, "If Daddy isn't working a late shift at the airport, he should get home in time for dinner. Mama works at the Polo Lounge at the Beverly Hills Hotel between seven a.m. and five p.m. so that she can get home in time to cook dinner. We usually eat dinner at seven."

Joshua asked, "Can I stay for dinner, so I can get to know you better??"

I said, "This is a bit short notice."

Joshua said, "I'm still hoping I can warm up to your family since my sixth sense says your dad still hates me."

I explained, "He doesn't hate you. He's just afraid that if I have a boyfriend, I won't need him anymore."

Joshua moved the palm of his right hand from the top of his head and down to his neck. Then, he blew out a long breath. That's how I knew he had something to say that I *definitely* wouldn't like. The last time he did that, it was to tell me that the cops would be keeping a closer eye on all Blacks who came into Koreatown shortly after Mrs. Du received that BS sentencing from Judge Karlin.

Joshua stated, "There's something else you should know. Mister Kim owns a Laundromat in this neighborhood, and he's planning on selling it so he can retire."

I said, "I know Mister Kim. He's one of the few Koreans in the hood who treats Black folks with respect. So, he's exempt from the boycott, and I still take our dirty laundry down there every Thursday afternoon."

Joshua said, "Yeah, well, my dad is buying the Laundromat."

I raised my eyebrows and said, "Really?"

Joshua said, "Hatima, I'm sure my dad will make sure his employees treat Black customers with respect. He doesn't want a repeat of what happened with Latasha Harlins and Missus Du."

I asked, "Does your dad have more sympathy for Missus Du than for Latasha Harlins? Did he think the sentence Judge Karlin gave Missus Du was fair?"

Joshua said, "I honestly don't know because my dad and I don't discuss race. I guess it makes him uncomfortable."

I thought, *It should.* Then, I asked Joshua, "Does your dad treat Black customers with respect?"

Joshua asked, "You mean at the grocery store?"

I said, "Yeah."

Joshua explained, "Mister Cho complains that he doesn't like doing business with all the gangsters who come into the store. I think he's afraid he'll get robbed, stabbed, or shot."

I asked, "Why doesn't your dad hire a Black guy to run the store?"

Joshua explained, "He doesn't completely trust Blacks. He's probably afraid a Black guy will give loads of freebies to folks in Watts or rob the store and burn it down."

I had heard this nonsense from Koreans plenty of times.

I asked, "Has your dad's grocery store been boycotted?"

The list of Korean businesses being boycotted is long, and I didn't double-check to see if Mr. Yang's grocery store was included. I mostly checked the names of Korean businesses in Crenshaw since

Crenshaw is my hood, not Watts. But I should have double-checked the Watts businesses since Grandma lives there. Maybe she used to buy groceries from Mr. Yang's store and stopped when the boycott started. That would be awkward; me dating a boy whose father's business diminishes my grandmother's humanity.

Joshua said, "Some Blacks are refusing to shop there, but others still are because the store is close to their homes, and the products are cheaper."

I sighed and said, "Okay, if you can convince your dad to hire a Black guy to run the Crenshaw Laundromat, I'll make the sure hood doesn't boycott his business."

When Mama and Daddy got home, Mama was happy my boyfriend stopped by, but Daddy still glared at him and refused to shake his hand.

I said, "For the record, we didn't do nothing."

Daddy said, "I trust *you*, baby girl. *Him*, definitely not."

Joshua looked my father in the eyes and said, "Mister Parker, I care about Hatima very much. I would never try to hurt her. Besides, we're not hitting third base since the Naval Academy won't let Hatima in if she has kids."

I joked, "Ya know Black girls are more fertile than other girls. Contraception or not, babies get made."

Joshua asked, "Can I stay for dinner, so I can get to know you better?"

Mama said, "Sure, I don't see why not."

Mama made pork chops and spaghetti. Joshua ate it all and asked for seconds.

Mama said, "I'm glad someone enjoys my cooking."

I said, "Mama, we all love your cooking."

Joshua said, "My dad's a pretty good cook. Since Mom died, he's had to become a skilled chef."

Daddy asked, "Your mama died?"

Joshua said, "Yeah, from a car accident, years ago."

Daddy said, "Sorry to hear that. My mama died from post-polio syndrome when my brother and I were boys."

Joshua said, "Sorry about your mom. Since it's just me and my dad we're really close. I don't know how he'll cope when I go away to college."

Mama asked Joshua, "Which colleges have you applied to, and what do you want to major in?"

Joshua said, "I've applied to UC Davis, Stanford, UW-Madison, NYU, and Penn State. I want to major in legal studies or political science. Dad says that I should major in law, medicine, business, engineering, or anything else that will result in a stable job and a six-figure salary. Dad always tells me how tough he and Mom had it when they moved to the States. Working as a dishwasher at a Koreatown nightclub and as a general helper in a clothing store was the only work Dad and Mom could get since they didn't have any degrees and most businesses outside of Koreatown wouldn't hire Koreans. A lot of Whites in LA hate Koreans and other Asians because *a lot* of soldiers died in the Second World War, the Korean War, and the Vietnam War. Whites want to blame every Asian for the wars fought in the East but not all Asians participated in the wars. Humanity is extremely good at hating others with little provocation, I'm sure you know that. Dad took over the club after the first owner died and bought the grocery store in Watts when he saved up enough money. Now, he wants to buy the Laundromat here in Crenshaw."

Mama said, "Really?"

I quickly said, "Mama, Daddy, don't worry. I told Joshua to

convince his dad to hire a Black guy to help him run the Laundromat. Remember, the Laundromat hasn't been boycotted since we ain't disrespected there. It would be a hassle to try and find another place to wash and dry our clothes."

Daddy said, "Mister Yang better hire someone who's Black, or we'll have no choice but to run him out of business."

Joshua said, "I don't think that will be necessary, Mister Parker. My dad's a nice guy."

Daddy grunted while I thought, *Is Mr. Yang only nice when he's around Koreans? Is he still nice when he's around Blacks?*

I said, "Daddy, this is just like that Sidney Poitier movie, *Guess Who's Coming to Dinner*. Sidney Poitier's character, John Prentice, was a doctor and had no intention of having sex with his fiancée, Joanna Drayton, until after they got married. Obviously, the only reason the Draytons disliked John at first was because he was Black, but the Draytons supported the Civil Rights Movement and racial equality. If they didn't let their daughter marry John, that would make them hypocrites. Even John's parents had a problem with his engagement even though Doctor King had a dream that one day Blacks, Whites, and people of all races would hold hands together at the table of brotherhood. That meant the Prentices were hypocrites as well.

Mama, Daddy, you have all those pictures of all those famous Black leaders on the walls. Some were okay with interracial relationships while others weren't. Perhaps if we focused on what makes us all the same instead of what makes us different, we'd learn how to get along. Blacks came to this country as slaves, but they helped build this country. They fought wars for this country and even died for it. And what's our reward? 'Go to the back of the bus; drink from that low water fountain; go to that rundown building, which is your new school.'

Despite Jim Crow and bigotry, some Caribbeans, including Grandpa's parents and Grandma Juliet, immigrated to the USA for a better life. Some were educated, others weren't. Some reaped the American Dream while others were given table scraps.

The Koreans also immigrated here and were also subject to bigotry, but one may argue that they haven't been dealt with such a raw deal as Blacks. Koreans are seen as 'model minorities' because they open successful businesses, are accepted into the USA's top schools, and easily land six-figure salary jobs.'

But how come Blacks aren't seen as 'model minorities' too? Why do we get the short end of the stick?"

Daddy asked, "So you're saying that we shouldn't hate the Koreans because we actually have a lot in common with them?"

I said, "Yeah."

Daddy said, "That's hard to believe when Blacks live in the hood, and Koreans live in the Hills."

Joshua said, "First of all, I live in Koreatown, not Beverly Hills nor Holmby Hills. Second, there are a lot of Blacks in affluent neighborhoods. Third, I believe the reason why Koreans are given more opportunities than Blacks is because of the stereotype that all Asians are smart. The schools that serve Koreatown get better supplies, the teachers are better paid, and we're given so many opportunities to expand our minds, like trips to the LA Philharmonic and community service programs. Because so many people believe the stereotypes that Blacks aren't very smart, that all Blacks are good at is entertainment and athletics, and that all Blacks in the ghettos are criminals, people won't see the point of giving your schools adequate equipment. Why waste money on future criminals?"

Mama said, "That's very insightful, Joshua. I said the same thing on Sunday when talking about Jim Crow schools. During the slavery era, it was illegal to teach slaves to read and write. The White masters didn't see the point in teaching reading, writing, and arithmetic to 'a bunch of monkeys.'"

Daddy asked Joshua, "Do you believe all those lies told about Black people?"

Joshua said, "No. Hatima and her friends are cool so that means there are kind, nurturing, and hardworking people in the hood; but the news always shows the negative aspects of the hood instead of the positive aspects."

When Joshua was about to leave, Daddy shook his hand and said, "You're alright, Joshua. I'm still not totally okay with you dating my daughter, but that's because I'm her dad. I can't imagine her loving any guy besides me."

Joshua said, "My dad is also afraid I'll grow closer to other people and not need him anymore; but I'll always need my dad, and Hatima will always need you."

Then, Daddy told Joshua, "That's a nice ride. A 1978 Cadillac Eldorado, right?"

Joshua said, "Yeah. Your 1980 Ford Fairmont is also a sweet ride. I can see where Hatima gets her taste in cars from."

Daddy laughed, patted him on the back, and said, "Have a good night."

Saturday was Devin's funeral.

I have been to several other funerals and people say, "The first one is always the toughest one."

But after going to my first funeral at the age of ten, the ones I attended after that were not any easier. Now I'm seventeen, and I have to see another one of my friends buried. Mama, Daddy, Grandma, and I all dressed in black formal clothes. Black is the color of mourning, but it's also a color of pride. Black is part of the AME logo and is on the Pan-African flag. The Black Panthers wore black leather jackets and black berets when they were patrolling the streets. So, wearing black clothes to a funeral also shows we Blacks have pride, not in the negative aspects of the African American experience which led to Devin's death, but the positive aspects that keep us moving forward.

Daddy drove us to FAME in his Ford. There were already a lot of cars in the parking lot, but Daddy found a spot. When we walked in, an usher gave us a program that detailed the events. I picked up a program and read it.

> Opening Sermon by Dr. Cecil Murray
> Eulogy by Mrs. Patricia Williams and Miss Alicia Williams
> Praise Songs by the First African Methodist Episcopal Church Choir
> Closing Prayers by Dr. Cecil Murray

There was a picture of Devin on the top of the program. It was his school picture from last year. Kids usually hate school pictures because they don't look anything like their usual selves, but our parents love them because professional photographers take our pictures and don't charge our parents lots of money for them. Mama said that she overheard rich people at the Polo Lounge talk about paying hundreds of dollars for family pictures. Since my parents obviously wouldn't pay hundreds of dollars for a photograph of me, school pictures are a better and cheaper option.

Devin was wearing a black suit, a blue shirt, and a red tie in his school picture, and he was smiling without showing his teeth, but the suit Devin wore in his casket was different. Mrs. Williams had bought a white suit, a black shirt, and a gray tie. I guess she didn't want any red in her son's outfit since wearing red led to his death. The people at the Angelus Funeral Home always put makeup on dead people's faces even though I don't see any point in that. Who's Devin getting primped up to see? I'm sure God and His angels don't care what clothes Devin was wearing on the day he died or even what clothes he's wearing at his funeral. I'm sure God doesn't care about makeup because He doesn't care about external beauty but internal beauty. I guess the suit and makeup are for Mrs. Williams' and Alicia's benefit instead of Devin's. They want to make sure he looks good when he's buried.

I looked around and saw a lot of my classmates and some of my neighbors. Wanda and Mrs. Brooks were there even though they attend church services at Crenshaw United Methodist Church, not FAME. Imani and Hector were there but not their mother; I guess Ms. Fitzpatrick couldn't get off work. The Fitzpatricks attend service at Baldwin Hills Baptist Church, but Devin was Wanda's and Imani's classmate too. Mrs. Williams and her kids have also eaten at the Creole & Cajun Kitchen many times. So, it made sense that the Brookses and the Fitzpatricks also came to pay their respects.

Hector's head was down, and I'm sure it's because he feels guilty about the time he spent with the Bloods. Hector could have ended up in a casket but instead, he wound up in a jail cell. Is he, like war veterans, wondering why God let him live while Devin died?

I also saw Mr. Ngozi. He looked sad ... no, "sad" isn't the right word. He looked ... disappointed. It's a teacher's job to prepare their students for the future. Mr. Ngozi makes us all believe that we can rise beyond our hood upbringing and become someone who makes a difference in the world. Some kids get the message, but a lot don't.

Devin obviously didn't accept Mr. Ngozi's lessons, and it resulted in him not making it to his eighteenth birthday.

Dr. Murray stood at the pulpit, cleared his throat, and was about to say something. But then, he grabbed his collar, cleared his throat, and looked straight ahead. Since Dr. Murray's eyes were on the entrance to the sanctuary, I turned around to see what he was so worried about.

Uncle Alonzo, Auntie Kalisha, Malik, and about a dozen other Bloods had entered the sanctuary. Uncle Alonzo was wearing a sharp red suit, and Auntie Kalisha was dressed in a skintight, strapless red dress. The other Bloods, including Malik, were wearing red t-shirts, baggy jeans, and gold chains. The Bloods, Crips, and other gangsters always attend funerals when the person in the casket is one of their own. Dr. Murray usually doesn't have a problem with it since most gangsters respect him for all the work he's done for the community and some look to him for help and guidance.

Then, Mrs. Williams yelled from the front row, "Oh, Hell no!"

Alicia handed Jamal to a woman sitting next to her and exclaimed, "Ma, there's no swearing allowed in the Lord's house!"

Mrs. Williams said, "I don't care! That demon is the reason my son is lying down in a casket!"

Uncle Alonzo said, "We didn't force Devin to do nothin'. We didn't twist his arm or break his teeth. He came to us for a job, and we gave it to him, but we're sorry he became a casualty on the streets."

Two Bloods walked up to Devin's casket and put a red bandanna and a gold chain on his corpse, but Mrs. Williams snatched the bandanna and gold chain off her son, threw them at the Bloods, and exclaimed, "Keep your filthy red attire and gold jewelry to yourselves! Devin sure as Hell doesn't need it now!"

That was the second time Mrs. Williams had cussed in the Lord's house.

Alicia looked at Daddy and Hector and asked, "Mister Parker, Hector, can you ask the Bloods to please leave?"

Daddy and Hector walked up to Uncle Alonzo and led him outside, while the Bloods stayed in the sanctuary; and everyone kept looking at them. Mama and Grandma fumbled with their purses, Dr. Murray kept pulling at his collar, and Alicia had to hold her mom back from attacking the Bloods. I'm very sure Mrs. Williams wouldn't have stood a chance against the Bloods even without their guns. No weapons are allowed in a church, and that's a rule the Bloods and Crips always follow. Other than that, you could cut the tension in the church with a sword.

Daddy and Hector came back in without Uncle Alonzo and said something to the Bloods. Then the Bloods all left the church. Daddy walked up to Mrs. Williams and said, "We took care of it."

Mrs. Williams replied, "Thank you, Orlando, Hector. The world needs more caring men like you."

Daddy came back to our pew and sat with us. Once again, I had to analyze how different Daddy and Uncle Alonzo were. Why did they go down such different paths? When did it all start?

It seemed to me that their diverging paths started after Grandpa Gabriel was injured at Reliance Steel. Daddy joined the Marines and learned many valuable life lessons. He learned about respecting authority when respect is due, punctuality, discipline, commitment, et cetera. But Uncle Alonzo joined a gang whose only similarity to the Marines is their high confirmed kills count. The Bloods only respect authority if it promises them green in their pocket. They're far from being disciplined; in fact, the best adjective to describe them is savages. The Bloods don't stand for anything meaningful, which is why their lives seem pretty worthless.

It seems that Daddy and Uncle Alonzo value different things in life. Just because they're twins doesn't mean they're the same.

Dr. Murray continued with the service. Mrs. Williams and Alicia gave a touching eulogy. The choir sang "Swing Low, Sweet Chariot" and "Oh Happy Day." After Dr. Murray's final words, Mr. Grant, his son Eric, and other guys who work at the Angelus Funeral Home closed Devin's casket and carried it outta the church. The congregation followed them out, and I saw them put the casket in a 1968 Cadillac Fleetwood Miller Meteor Coach Hearse. A hearse looks like a limo, but it's meant to carry the dead not the living. There was an actual Lincoln limo behind the hearse. The Williamses and some of their friends got inside the limo; the only other time Black people ride in limos is when they're traveling to big award shows such as the Oscars and the Soul Train Music Awards. Many kids in the hood wanna be entertainers and athletes, but only a small percentage of folks make it into those businesses. Plus, those careers can be short-term. That's why I never dreamed about a life in show business. An education is the best ticket out of the hood, and I believe it's important people are made aware that African Americans are also intellectuals.

Before Eric Grant got into the driver's side of the Cadillac Hearse, he talked with Alicia for a bit. I couldn't hear what they were saying over the crowd, but I saw the looks in their eyes. It looked like Eric and Alicia have a *thing* for each other – the better word is *spark*.

Then, Daddy interrupted my thinking and said, "Come on, baby girl, we have to follow the funeral procession to the cemetery."

The drive from FAME to Rosedale Cemetery took about fifteen minutes because of how long the procession was. Rosedale Cemetery is a beautiful spot; it has trees, shrubs, flowers, headstones, mausoleums, et cetera. It even has pyramids, which shows that Mr. Grant isn't the only person obsessed with Egypt. Rosedale was the first cemetery in LA that was open to all races and creeds. Grandma said that in Mississippi there were separate cemeteries for Blacks and Whites, like there's something sinful in burying folks of different backgrounds together, or God will automatically put all the folks in White cemeteries and all the folks in Black cemeteries in separate parts of the afterlife.

Devin was buried six feet under, just like so many other brothers and sisters from the hood. I walked over to Keisha's gravestone. It still looked the same: a gray, rectangular tombstone that said:

Here Lies Keisha Rachel Jones
February 4th, 1974 – January 3rd, 1991
A Beloved Daughter, Sister, and Friend

There are *a lotta* kids and teens buried here. I remember what that stat said at the beginning of *Boyz n the Hood* about one out of twenty-one Black males getting killed in their lifetime and that most of them will be killed by another Black male. That might not seem like a high number to most folks, but it's a very high number for us folks who live in the hood. One out of twenty-one of the Black guys in Crenshaw will be merked because some short-minded gangster can easily get their hands on guns and are uptight about shit that don't make sense. This world is messed-up. Should humans even be in charge of the planet?

I remembered that Frith, the sun god in *Watership Down*, told El-ahrairah, the Prince of Rabbits, that his people weren't destined to rule the world. When the rabbits' large numbers threatened to throw the world out of balance, Frith corrected the problem by creating predators to slay and eat the children of El-ahrairah, but Frith also gave the rabbits many gifts so that they could protect themselves from their Thousand Enemies. The most dangerous of the Thousand are humans and, of course, humans were meant to be the dominant species, not rabbits. But the rabbits and other animals hate humans because of all the damage we've done to the world. If Frith could correct the world order in *Watership Down*, then will God not help balance things in our own world?

Mr. Ngozi walked over to me and said, "I figured you'd want to visit Keisha."

I said, "Yeah."

Mr. Ngozi asked, "Are you feeling okay?"

I said, "No."

Mr. Ngozi said, "I think you may not want to attend church at First AME tomorrow since Devin's funeral was held there. If your parents allow it and you want to, you can attend service at my church, Saint Vibiana's Cathedral."

I said, "A Catholic church? I'm not sure my parents will let me be exposed to all that."

When Mr. Ngozi first moved here, some folks had a problem with his Christian denomination. Ya see, a lotta people hate Catholics. I remember learning in history class that when John F. Kennedy was elected President, most folks had a problem with that because he was Catholic. People were afraid the Pope would have a say in American politics, which is ridiculous since Western countries like the USA have separated the church from the state. Now that I think about it, maybe that wasn't such a great idea. If the laws of the Bible and the laws of the USA were one and the same, then this country would be a better place for all people. Of course, that means Muslims, Jews, Hindus, and other religions wouldn't be welcome and that wouldn't be cool.

It seems the main reason people hate Catholics is because Catholics are said to worship the Pope more than they worship Jesus, but Mr. Ngozi explained that he *respects* the Pope since he's a religious leader. Dr. King, Rev. Jesse Jackson, Rev. Al Sharpton, and Dr. Murray are all respected religious leaders, but people don't worship the ground they walk on. God is the only person worthy of worship.

Mr. Ngozi said, "I'll explain to your parents that I'm contributing to your education. A lot of Igbo people and other Nigerians go to Saint Vibiana's. After church, we can go to my friend's house, and you can learn more about Nigerian history and culture."

My parents respect my dream of becoming an Africanist. If taking a trip to a Catholic church will bring me closer to my dream, then they'll have no choice but to agree.

Chapter Twelve

The next day, I wore my purple church dress and white shoes – my sling matched my shoes. My braids were tied in a ponytail with a Pan-African hair tie. I figured this was a great time to show pride in my heritage.

Mr. Ngozi drove onto West Boulevard in a 1982 Honda Civic. It's the same car he drives to and from school in.

I opened the passenger door and got in.

Mr. Ngozi asked, "Ready to worship the Lord?"

I said, "I'm always ready to love God."

The drive from my house to St. Vibiana's took about half an hour. When we got there, I was a bit shocked by how big the church was. I had seen it a few times on the news but seeing it in person was a different experience. It was *big*; it seemed to be the same size as FAME, maybe a little bigger. It had me wondering how many Catholics this church could fit.

When Mr. Ngozi parked, I asked him, "How many people fit in this church?"

Mr. Ngozi said, "Oh, a lot, but they all come here at different times. The Cathedral has masses throughout the week in the morning and afternoon. On Sundays there are services at eight a.m., eleven a.m., and two p.m."

I asked him, "We could have come to the eleven a.m. or two p.m. services?"

Mr. Ngozi said, "It's 'mass' not 'service.' But people are always afraid the Devil is going to get them before they get to church so a lot of people come for the eight a.m. mass."

I said, "Reminds me of Grandma and other members at FAME. They all *love* to go to church early on Sunday morning to avoid the Devil's trap."

Mr. Ngozi led me inside. The church was air conditioned, just like FAME. If ACs weren't installed in buildings in LA, there would be disaster. Inside, there was a small diorama of the Nativity of Jesus. Since it's December, everyone has brought out their Christmas decorations. The diorama has Mary kneeling next to the manger; the shepherds looking down at baby Jesus; and baby Jesus holding his arms out like He wants someone to pick Him up. The shepherds are White and so is Jesus – Jesus has blond hair and blue eyes. I snorted, knowing that even though Jesus can change His form at will He wouldn't have taken the form of a White boy in Ancient Israel. The Romans ruled Ancient Israel; so if Jesus were a White man, the Israelites wouldn't have listened to Him. They would probably think Jesus was a spy for the Romans trying to lead them astray. It's equally stupid to think Jesus is Black. Many people in the hood have pictures of Black Jesus on their living room walls, and there are murals of Black Jesus in the hood; but considering how bad the Egyptians treated the Hebrews, I'm sure taking the form of a Black man would have also been a bad idea.

I think people want Jesus to be a certain color so they can be at ease in the belief that God favors their race over others. I thought about the works of the master of Christian allegory, C.S. Lewis. Aslan takes the form of a lion, but He changes His form a few times in the Narnia books. In *The Horse and His Boy*, Aslan takes the form of a cat to ease and protect Shasta/Cor. In *The Voyage of the Dawn*

Treader, He takes the form of a lamb. As a lamb, Aslan asks Edmund, Lucy, and Eustace to come eat breakfast, but they ask how to get to Aslan's Country. Then, Aslan changes into His lion form and tells them there is a way into His country through all worlds. The Great Lion said the way to His country is across a river and that He is the great Bridge Builder. I'm guessing it means a person must cross the River Jordan to get to Heaven. If the Pevensie siblings and their cousin, Eustace Scrubb, went to church every Sunday, then they would constantly be told how to get to Heaven/Aslan's Country. In the final Narnia book, *The Last Battle*, Aslan changes form again. He is described as no longer looking like a lion. He becomes so great and beautiful that even C.S. Lewis can't describe Him. Dr. Murray and NOI imams state that God or Allah is beyond comprehension. I guess that means there are aspects of God's personality that we shouldn't try to figure out because we'll never be able to truly figure Him out.

    Mr. Ngozi led me into the sanctuary. It was as big as FAME's, maybe a bit bigger. We sat in the third row from the front. I took out my Bible and started reading about the birth of Jesus, but I was interrupted when three Black people sat down next to Mr. Ngozi. Mr. Ngozi greeted them warmly, and I took a close look at what they were wearing. Mr. Ngozi was wearing a suit and tie but two of the Nigerians were wearing African clothing. The third Nigerian was wearing a military jacket that had a few medals on it.

    Mr. Ngozi told me, "Hatima, these are my friends Doctor Elijah Igwe, Missus Ijeoma Igwe, and their son Captain David Igwe." Mr. Ngozi pronounced their last name "Eeeg-way" and Mrs. Igwe's name as "Eee-juh-mah".

    Dr. Igwe's shirt looked like a dashiki. It wasn't tucked in, and it was down to his thigh. Parents in the hood tell their kids to tuck in their shirts because loose, untucked shirts look sloppy. Plus, loose shirts give the cops a reason to stop you. Some convicts' prison uniforms are comprised of untucked shirts and baggy pants since belts aren't allowed in prisons; so, some gangsters wear baggy clothes 'cause they think showing off prison fashion makes them look cool. Now the cops figure that *all* people who dress like that are gangsters and now our freedom of expression is being taken away. The hat Dr. Igwe was wearing looked like the kind a person wears when it snows, but everyone knows we don't get snow in LA. Mrs. Igwe was wearing a purple dress that covered most of her body except for her neck and shoulders with a matching purple headscarf. She certainly dresses better than Auntie Kalisha, and I thought her style was similar to Mama's.

I shook Dr. and Mrs. Igwe's hands warmly, while hoping they wouldn't ask about my sling. They didn't. I guess Mr. Ngozi already told them about my injury, and they didn't wanna say anything about it.

Dr. Igwe said, "We have heard so much about you, Hatima. Obi says you're one of his best students and that you plan to be a Marine and an Africanist."

I replied, "Yep. But just in case the Naval Academy rejects me, I've applied to other schools with great Africana Studies programs."

Mrs. Igwe said, "David graduated from West Point Military Academy some years ago with a bachelor's degree in management. Then, he received his MBA from Georgia Tech."

Dr. Igwe said, "A year after he graduated from Georgia Tech, the US initiated Operation Just Cause, and eight months later, the US invaded the Persian Gulf. David fought well and was given high honors by his commanding officers."

Mrs. Igwe said, "David needs to serve another year before he can leave the Army. A friend of his from Georgia Tech said he may be able to set up an interview for him with the CEO of a brokerage firm in Chicago."

I said, "Cool. My best friend's brother, Andre, is studying business at TSU. That way, just in case he doesn't get into the NBA, a business degree will set him up with a job and salary that will get him out of South Central."

I shook David's hand, but he refused to look me in the eye.

We all sat down, and the preacher walked onto the stage. He was a White man with long, white robes and a Cross around his neck.

He said, "Peace be with you."

The congregation replied, "And also with you."

The preacher said, "For any newcomers here with us this morning, I am Father Samuel Rogers. Welcome to the Cathedral of Saint Vibiana."

I remembered that Catholic preachers are called fathers and brothers. Popes seem to be at the top spot of the Catholic hierarchy. Father Rogers preached about when Jesus first brought His disciples together. He explained that other people ridiculed Jesus for befriending tax collectors, thieves, and the other rejects of Hebrew society.

But Jesus said, "Do the healthy need a doctor? No, the sick do."

That means Jesus will always be willing to help those who are lost and set them on the right path. I thought about how a lotta people in the world want to turn their backs on the hood, but Jesus would want people to offer help to the hood – proper help, not the BS the cops do. I think that the food drives Dr. Murray organizes, the lectures successful alumni give kids at Dorsey High to set us on the right path, and the activities the rec center offers so that kids won't fall prey to predators on the streets are proper help. There's a song on Michael Jackson's *Dangerous* album called "Heal the World." Well, my world is comprised of my hood, and I believe we should all help heal the hood. That ain't an impossible goal, right?

After the service, I asked the Igwes, "What are the names of your clothes?"

Dr. Igwe explained, "My wife and I are wearing traditional Igbo attire. This shirt I'm wearing is called an *Isiagu*. The hat I'm wearing is an *okpu agu*."

Mrs. Igwe said, "My mother made this dress herself. She weaves dresses back in Port Harcourt."

I'm guessing Port Harcourt is somewhere in Nigeria.

Mrs. Igwe continued, "My mother made enough money weaving dresses to send me here to school. I studied journalism at Freeman University and Columbia University."

I asked Dr. Igwe, "Where did you study and what did you major in?"

Dr. Igwe said, "I studied at the University of Ibadan and at Bristol Dental School."

Then I said, "Let me guess. After you both finished studying in England and New York, you decided to move LA because of the warm weather and tropical setting?"

Dr. Igwe said, "We actually moved back to Nigeria, met each other, fell in love, and got married. But since life wasn't getting any better in Nigeria, we immigrated to Los Angeles. My husband got a job with the Los Angeles Dental Clinic and I got a job as a reporter for the *Los Angeles Sentinel*. David was born shortly after."

Mrs. Igwe added, "Los Angeles is also a diverse city. Blacks, Whites, Asians, and Latinos all live together; but we learned that life can still be unkind."

I said, "Yeah. LA has gotten crazier, ever since Rodney King got beaten and Latasha Harlins got killed."

Dr. Igwe said, "We pray that justice will prevail. Soon Ja Du may not have been sufficiently punished, but there's little doubt the police officers who beat Rodney King will be brought to justice. I trust you've seen the videotape?"

I said, "Yep, they're playing that tape more on TV than *A-Team* and *Diff'rent Strokes* reruns."

Mrs. Igwe said, "Plenty of people in Nigeria have been victims of police brutality, especially those who speak out against the government, but those officers were never punished for their crimes."

I explained, "Nigeria is a military dictatorship while the USA is a democracy. President Babangida and President Bush are two very different people."

David asked, "Are they?"

Those were the first words I heard David say. He had stayed quiet throughout mass and didn't look at the priest. Instead, he looked down at his hands or his feet. Daddy has told me a lot about PTSD and Survivor's Guilt, and I'm sure David is suffering from both. I wonder if he's really up for another year in the Army.

I said, "Well, Mama and Daddy aren't huge fans of his because he's a Republican and because he signed a bill to increase taxes even though he said, 'Read my lips: no new taxes.' Did President Babangida make and break promises, too?"

Mr. Ngozi explained, "President Babangida was said to be a key participant in many military coups. He was a part of the Supreme Military Council so there's really not much surprise in the fact that he was able to overthrow Major General Muhammadu Buhari in 1985. We civilians have learned not to get our hopes up after each coup because each leader is as bad as the last one."

I said, "No wonder you all fled to the USA, the UK, Canada, and other places."

Dr. Igwe said, "We didn't all leave. Only a small portion of Nigerians live outside of Nigeria. Most have stayed because they refuse to give up on Nigeria, and they want to do their part to bring about change."

I said, "They sound like the man in the mirror."

Mr. Ngozi, Dr. Igwe, and Mrs. Igwe all laughed. Even David gave a small smile. But I wasn't making a joke, I was making a point.

We went outside, which was a relief because the air conditioning had made the church feel like the inside of an igloo. The sun warmed me up and took the chill off my bones. Then, I started to wonder how hot it gets in Nigeria. Is it as hot as LA or hotter? Either way, if I ever go there, I'll have to pack plenty of sunscreen and caps. I followed Mr. Ngozi to his car and got in the passenger seat. When he got into the driver's seat, he didn't start the car right away.

I asked, "Are we gonna leave?"

Mr. Ngozi said, "Soon."

Then, a sweet black Oldsmobile Cutlass Supreme car drove by. It looked like a 1970s model. Mr. Ngozi drove out of his parking spot and followed the Oldsmobile. He drove on the freeway and through South Central, near Crenshaw, but he didn't drive into our hood. When he made a turn from Crenshaw Boulevard onto Stocker Street, I immediately knew where we were. I already mentioned a bougie Black neighborhood named Leimert Park that's next to Crenshaw. Well, not far from my hood, there's another bougie Black neighborhood called View Park-Windsor Hills. The proper term is "affluent African American neighborhoods/communities", but I just call them bougie Black neighborhoods. Dr. Murray also lives in

Windsor Hills. He also drives an Olds Cutlass Supreme, but his is fire engine-red. The Olds was a Father's Day present the congregation gave him a few years ago. A lot of preachers ride large in Royces and BMWs, but the congregation knows Dr. Murray doesn't like to show off like that. Becoming a pastor sounds like a potential career with *great* benefits!

The Igwes' Oldsmobile stopped and turned into a garage on Valley Ridge Avenue, and Mr. Ngozi parked his car on the street near the house.

I got out of the car and said, "I've never been to this part of South Central before."

Mr. Ngozi said, "This neighborhood is zoned to Crenshaw High and Thomas Jefferson High. Dorsey High doesn't serve this neighborhood."

I said, "I'm glad they're still part of the hood to some extent. Turning your back on poverty doesn't help solve it. Rich and poor folks in LA have often been kept separate since the beginning of time. But I told the folks at Jack and Jill that when rich people turn their backs on poor people, they're contributing to the problem of poverty instead of solving it."

The Igwes got outta their Oldsmobile and walked to their front door, and Dr. Igwe opened the door and led us inside. From the outside, the house looked bigger than my West Boulevard home. It was even bigger on the inside.

I immediately asked, "How many beds and baths are in this house?"

David said, "There are three bedrooms and two and a half bathrooms."

I replied, "Really?"

David asked, "Why is that surprising?"

I explained, "My house has three beds and two baths, but it isn't this big."

David smiled and said, "I'll show you the rest of the house."

The kitchen and living room were huge by my standards. The bedrooms and bathrooms were also spacious, but I absolutely *loved* the backyard! They didn't have a pool in the backyard, but they had a patio with outside furniture, a garden, and a putting green. I know Wanda, Andre, Imani, Hector, Alicia, and the other people I know in our hood would want to know how a house that has as many beds and baths as the ones in Crenshaw can be this luxurious. Well, our parents always tell us the secret to getting the finer things in life is to get a good education. My parents told me that when I was little, but I always figured there had to be more to it than that.

All my teachers at Coliseum Street Elementary School have degrees, but they're all either living in houses like mine or in apartments smaller than my house. Mr. Ngozi also lives in a small, one-story house in Crenshaw, but I'm sure the teachers at Uni make enough money to live in bigger houses.

In television, movies, and Black magazines, the wealthiest Blacks who aren't entertainers and athletes are usually doctors, lawyers, engineers, professors, and businesspeople. That's why most of the smartest kids at Dorsey are planning to major in medicine, law, engineering, and business. Imani said that if I get a doctorate in African Studies, then I can get a high-paying job at a college and live in a big house in a nice neighborhood. She also said we could become neighbors.

I'm not completely sure if I can turn my back on the hood. What if I'm so busy teaching at a college that I don't have time to come back to my roots? I can't imagine living anywhere besides South Central. Maybe I should buy a house in Leimert Park or View Park-Windsor Hills.

David led me back inside, and I saw his mom had brought out pots and pans. She was stirring some white stuff that looked like mashed potatoes in one pot and also stirring some vegetables in another pot. At least, I thought it was vegetables. It looked like a mix of collard greens and meat.

I asked Mrs. Igwe, "What are you cooking?"

Mrs. Igwe replied, "Pounded yam and *egusi* soup."

I said, "Oh-kay."

Mrs. Igwe laughed and said, "I bet you've never had this dish before."

I said, "No. I know African Americans are said to eat only soul food, but my family only eats soul food on the weekends when Grandma visits and cooks for us. According to statistics, obesity and diabetic rates are highest among African Americans. One of the reasons that's true is because of the soul food a lot of us eat, but my parents cook healthy meals during the week, and I practice martial arts."

Mrs. Igwe said, "Well, this dish is considered healthy by Nigerian standards."

I helped Mr. Ngozi and David set the table. When I brought out the forks and knives, David said, "Take out the serving spoons and knives but leave the forks."

That sounded strange, but I did what he told me.

When the food was ready, Mrs. Igwe scooped the soup into a big serving bowl and put the pounded yam on a serving plate. She set the food on the table.

Then she asked me, "Hatima, since you're our guest, why don't you say the blessing?"

I said, "Sure."

We bowed our heads and I prayed, "God is great, God is good, Let us thank Him for our food, Amen."

Mr. Ngozi and the Igwes all repeated, "Amen."

They scooped some soup onto their plates, and I scooped some onto my plate, too. They cut off portions of the pounded yam with their knives, and I did the same. Then, Mr. Ngozi and the Igwes put their hands in the yam, made a ball, dipped the ball in the soup, and ate it. I couldn't believe they were eating with their hands! Grandma would have a fit if she saw me eating with my bare hands. She would remind me of how in the slavery era slaves often ate meals with their hands because the masters and overseers wouldn't give them utensils. Slaves were considered nothing more than animals. Dogs, cats, horses, cows, et cetera don't need utensils to eat so why should slaves? But this appears to be the norm for Nigerians. I then thought that another reason slaves ate with their hands could be because of their African traditions. So, I ate the yam and soup with my hands. I felt a bit giddy that I wouldn't get a whipping for acting inappropriately.

The doorbell rang, and Mrs. Igwe said, "I'll get it." She quickly washed her hands and went to answer the door. Then, I heard her exclaim, "Ife! So glad you could make it!"

A female voice replied, "I wouldn't miss a good home-cooked meal!"

Mrs. Igwe walked into the dining room with a pretty young woman wearing a blouse and jeans. Some people might think that's tacky, but I thought she looked good.

Mr. Ngozi got up and exclaimed, "I'm always happy to see my goddaughter!"

Ife said, "Uncle Obi, I'll always make time to visit you!"

They hugged and when they separated, I said, "Nice to finally meet you. Mister Ngozi has talked plenty about you. Getting into med school is no small feat."

Ife said, "Thanks. Who are you?"

I replied, "Hatima Gabriella Parker."

I don't know why I included my middle name. Maybe being around rich folks made me wanna show pride in my heritage. My parents put a lot of thought into my name, and I am proud of it.

I wiped my hand on a napkin, and Ife shook it. She sat down in an empty chair and put some food on her plate.

She asked, "Are you planning on becoming a doctor, too?"

I said, "No way! Charging poor people money is torture in my opinion. When I got shot, my immediate thought wasn't whether I would live or die. My first thought was that my parents might end up broke when they got the medical bills. But if I was a Canadian, my thoughts might be different. Mister Ngozi says taxes help pay for most of Canada's healthcare, which means Canadians don't end up bankrupt when they visit a hospital. We need a system like that in the US. Maybe I should write a letter to the US Department of Health, but since Americans value money over anything else the Health Department would probably throw my letter in the garbage."

Ife said, "You seem very verbose."

Mr. Ngozi said, "That's why she's one of my best students. She plans to attend school at the US Naval Academy and major in history. Then, she'll attend a grad school to get her PhD in African Studies."

I said, "The plan is to become a Marine and an Africanist."

Ife asked, "Why do you want to be a Marine?"

I explained, "My granddaddy was a Montford Point Marine, and my daddy fought with the Marines in Vietnam. I want to carry on the tradition and do my part for this country."

Ife asked, "Who are the Montford Point Marines?"

I felt like I had been slapped in the face and punched in the gut!

I asked, "You never heard of the Montford Point Marines?"

Ife replied, "No. Were they special Marines?"

I said, "Yeah, they were special! The Montford Point Marines were the first African American Marines in the US Armed Forces. Most folks know about the Tuskegee Airmen but not the Montford Point Marines. The Montford Point Marines raised the expectations for Black folks and paved the way for future Black Marines. Without the Montford Point Marines, President Harry Truman probably wouldn't have desegregated the US Armed Forces in 1948. If you wanna stay in the States, ya gotta learn some Black history. Marcus Garvey said, 'The Black skin is not a badge of shame, but rather a glorious symbol of national greatness.' The quote is better if you switch the word *national* with *international*. The Black skin is a symbol of international greatness. Even Aunt Viv told Will Smith on an episode of the first season of *Fresh Prince* that he can read the books, wear the t-shirts, put up the posters, and shout the slogans, but if he doesn't know all the history behind all that stuff, then he's trivializing the entire struggle. That's a message that all Black folks across the diaspora need to learn."

Ife smiled and said, "I can now see why you're a wonderful student. You really seem passionate about the history and culture of the African diaspora."

I said, "And I'm always trying to learn more. Do you mind if I ask you a few questions?"

Ife asked, "About what?"

I explained, "About your life. What do your parents do for a living?"

Ife said, "My parents own a farm in Igboland. They almost lost it during the Biafran War, but they managed to keep it and thrive."

I said, "I know about the Biafran War. Tribal and religious tensions led to the Igbo tribe seceding from Nigeria and creating their own country called Biafra. A lot of my classmates didn't understand why Nigerians can't all get along since you're all Black."

Ife said, "Just because we're all Black doesn't mean we're all the same. Nigeria is made up of many tribes, the largest being the Hausa, the Yoruba, and the Igbo. During colonialism, the British were said to favor the Hausa tribe more because they were always eager to follow instructions unlike the Igbo tribe. The Igbo tribe would always ask questions and sometimes challenge the Brits who were issuing the instructions. I, for one, don't see any problem with challenging authority; it shows that some folks wouldn't bow and kowtow to the British. But the Hausa is an Islamic tribe so they and the Fulani tribe refused to convert to Christianity; they weren't going to kowtow to the British when it came to their Muslim faith."

I said, "I know about that. Mister Ngozi has said that the Muslims live in the north of Nigeria while the Christians live in the south."

Ife said, "That's right. Most of the Igbo and Yoruba converted to Christianity and accepted the perks of colonialism, but most of the Muslims remained adamant about their culture. When Nigeria gained independence from Great Britain in nineteen-sixty, all the tribes had their own ideas on how the country should be run."

I said, "Kind of like the USA. All the races and religions got their own ideas on how this country should work. Confrontations have led to conflicts and that's always chaotic."

Ife said, "Even today, Nigeria still has a lot of tribal and religious tensions. The military coups aren't helping either. A lot of Nigerians have immigrated to the United Kingdom, the United States, Canada, Switzerland, Australia, and other countries."

I asked, "Are you gonna stay in the USA or go back to the UK or move back to Nigeria after you get your MD?"

Ife said, "I want to move back to Nigeria and use my knowledge to help my people. If every Nigerian who is college-educated stays in the West, things won't get better in Nigeria."

I stated, "That's called brain drain. Mister Ngozi told us about that; you moving back and using your education to help your people is brain gain. That reminds me of how Doctor King and Missus Coretta Scott King had to decide between staying in the Northern states or moving back to the South after they got their degrees; but they both agreed that the South was their home, and they wanted to do their part to create change. And the world is so glad they decided to move south of the Mason-Dixon Line."

Ife said, "You make fabulous connections. You'd make a great professor or journalist or diplomat."

I said, "People have talked to me about being a professor, and it sounds like a cool job. The only way Blacks will move up in the world is through education, but I'm not all that interested in journalism because of the slimy paparazzi. My friend Stella Wilson wants to be a journalist for *Ebony* or *Jet* or *Essence,* and she knows she needs a journalism degree for that. Diplomats get to travel the world, and I know that would be *extremely* cool, so it's a definite possibility."

Mr. Ngozi said, "A master's or PhD in African Studies can open up a world of possibilities."

I said, "Thanks for the heads up, Mister Ngozi." Then I asked Ife, "Besides the fact that med school in the UK takes five years, why'd you decide to get your MD in the States instead of at a British school?"

Ife explained, "I want to see as much of the world as I can. Since I've studied in England, I can imagine myself going back there in the future. And since I'm studying in LA, I can imagine myself visiting this city again and again in the future."

I asked, "Did you see the sights of London, while you were in the UK?"

Ife exclaimed, "Of course I did! London is one of the most visited cities in the world, and many Nigerians want to see London before they die! When my workload was light, my friends and I usually took the train from Oxford Station to Paddington Station."

I joked, "Paddington Station? Did you see any bears looking for homes?"

Ife laughed and so did Mr. Ngozi and the Igwes.

Ife stated, "No, I didn't see any Peruvian bears eating marmalade sandwiches, but I did see a stand selling Paddington merchandise, including books and stuffed Paddington Bears. I purchased one of the teddies because I adored Paddington when I was a kid. Then, my friends showed me all the sights of London. I saw Trafalgar Square, Buckingham Palace, Piccadilly Circus, and Big Ben during my first London weekend. On my next London weekend, we visited Madame Tussauds. Another weekend, we visited St Paul's Cathedral. On another weekend, we visited the Tower of London. London has so many sights that you won't be able to see them all in one weekend, but there are other tourist attractions in other parts of the UK: Stonehenge, Puzzlewood, Edinburgh Castle, Saint Fagans National Museum of History ..."

I said, "I've heard of Stonehenge, but I haven't heard of the other locations you mentioned. I'm guessing Edinburgh Castle is in Edinburgh, Scotland."

Ife said, "Yes it is. Puzzlewood is in the Forest of Dean in Gloucestershire and Saint Fagans is in Cardiff, Wales. Plus, I recommend you visit the University of Oxford. The architecture is exquisite."

I nodded and said, "Okay, I'll put those locations on my bucket list, but have you seen the sights of LA and California?"

HEAL THE HOOD

Ife said, "I moved here in late August, and Uncle Obi took me to Disneyland. It was so much fun! I've also visited Santa Monica, the Hollywood Walk of Fame, and the LA Zoo during my not-so-busy weekends."

I said, "You should come to Dorsey High and talk to my classmates."

Ife asked, "Really? Why?"

I explained, "You can explain to my classmates that hard work and dedication can lead to great results. My friend, Imani Fitzpatrick, wants to be a pediatrician, but she's not sure she'll make it into med school because of her hood background. Were your parents rich?"

Ife said, "They were wealthy landowners, but I've had several classmates who came from poor backgrounds and made it into medical school. I'd love to come to Dorsey High, but my parents didn't like the idea of me visiting Uncle Eli and Auntie Ije here in South Central. Venturing into South Central for any other reason would be unacceptable to them."

I became angry. This reminded of when Mr. Ngozi's relatives decided to stay in fancy hotels instead of with him during their summer vacation. I knew they all wouldn't fit in his house, but *some* of them could have stayed there since he lives alone and has extra room. His relatives believe that my neighborhood is poisonous, dangerous, and a place to be avoided.

I told Ife, "Not everyone in the hood is a criminal. A lotta people, like my parents, work hard to provide their families with good lives. Some people fall prey to the predators of the street, but my girls and I haven't. We're smart, motivated, and going places. If more rich folks cared about poor folks, then more people in the hood would realize what they're capable of."

Mrs. Igwe stated, "I work on the border between Crenshaw

and Leimert Park. There are bad aspects, such as the gangs, guns, and drugs; but there are the good aspects, such as the schools, the churches, and the legitimate businesses. One of the reasons I wanted to become a journalist was to show people that there are two sides to every story."

I said, "Exactly, Mrs. Igwe, exactly."

As I helped Mrs. Igwe clear the table and wash up, which was not easy since my left arm was in a sling, I asked her, "Which Nigerian newspaper did you work at?"

Mrs. Igwe said, "I wrote for the *Daily Times* in Lagos."

I asked, "What was that like compared to writing for the *Los Angeles Sentinel*?"

Mrs. Igwe explained, "Over the years, Nigerian newspapers have been harassed by the ruling dictators. Journalists are often bribed with money to write positive stories and kill negative ones, but I refused all bribes and the government and authorities didn't like my articles. They harassed my husband at the dental clinic and my mother in Port Harcourt. We saw that life in Nigeria was becoming unethical, and we decided to leave and move to the US because there were many Black newspapers I could work for. When we moved here, I applied for several jobs and I accepted a job at the *Sentinel*; it's the oldest, largest, and most influential Black newspaper in the Western USA. I feel so honored to be part of a strong and pround tradition."

Later, Mr. Ngozi drove me home to my house on West Boulevard. The drive gave me some time to think. People talk about Africa like it's the worst place in the world, but Africa can't be all bad if so many Africans have been able to get high-quality education and high-paying jobs. Mr. Ngozi, his siblings, Dr. and Mrs. Igwe, Corporal David Igwe, and Ife Ejiofor all got into top schools here in the US and England. How come so many Nigerians can get into the world's top schools, but most African Americans can't get into the top American schools? Educational systems in African countries are said to be of lower quality than the ones in the US. If that's true, then how come there are so many successful Nigerians? Nigerian Americans seem to be reaping more of the American Dream than African Americans. Jealousy is said to be one of the seven deadly sins, but I was starting to feel it.

To try and fight off the green-eyed monster, I asked Mr. Ngozi, "What's the educational system in Nigeria like? Is it really so bad?"

Mr. Ngozi said, "It's better than some other African countries, but still considered inferior to Western schools."

I asked, "If that's true, how come so many of your friends and family got into British and American universities? Why do they have better jobs and make more money than most of the folks in the hood?"

Mr. Ngozi said, "That's a complicated answer."

I told him, "Give me your best opinion."

Mr. Ngozi sighed and said, "Well, the British weren't all racists who believed all non-White people were inferior. Those who weren't racist put their hearts and souls into developing Nigeria's infrastructure, including our educational system. The Nigerian universities were at their prime during colonialism, but they've deteriorated since the dictators took over, and the schools are no longer on the same level as Western universities. Nigerians know degrees from Western schools are the only way we'll be able to build our nation into something wonderful. We, as a people, were taught at a young age that without education you're nothing in this world.

Education, originally the White man's knowledge, is a collective aspiration that leads to individual and family success. My parents told me and my brothers that if we dropped out of school, they would kick us out and disown us, but many African Americans don't carry this same ethic. Some African Americans truly believe they won't succeed so dropping out of school isn't a big deal for them."

I cut in and said, "But there are African Americans who also preach the importance of education. If Doctor and Missus Wilson's kids dropped out of school, I'm sure they'd kick them out, too."

Mr. Ngozi asked, "What about your parents? If you dropped out of Dorsey High would they be okay with it?"

I said, "Definitely not, but they wouldn't kick me out immediately because they wouldn't want me to be prey to gangbangers and drug dealers and pimps. But Missus Brooks did tell Wanda and Andre that if they drop outta school, she's kickin' them out! She also doesn't have time for dropouts."

Mr. Ngozi laughed and said, "If more African American adults preached the importance of education and the school district showed more concern for inner-city youth, then the number of college-educated Blacks would increase immensely."

I stated, "It isn't written anywhere that life is fair."

Chapter Thirteen

Soon, my sling came off, and I could teach at the dojang again – being able to make my own money is important to me. There are plenty of folks in my hood who sit around doing nothing either 'cause they can't find a job or are too lazy to get a job.

After I taught sword fighting at Master Shin's, Joshua came up to me and said, "The winter holidays are coming up. That means two weeks off from school."

I said, "I know. I could use the break."

When I had my sling, I was treated as a charity case by *a lotta* people, except Wanda, Imani, and Mr. Ngozi. My teachers kept asking me if I needed to take a day or two off from school "because of the trauma I must be going through." I told my teachers I was fine and that I could finish my assignments and study for my tests without special treatment. I know most kids would have jumped at the chance to get a day off school with teachers' consent, but I wasn't about to fall behind in my schoolwork. If I want to get into the Naval Academy or any other college, I have to maintain good grades. Wanda and Imani helped carry my lunch tray and my school bag, which I was okay with. They never suggested I ask for special treatment or ask me to recount what happened to Devin. My girls kept their cool, and I appreciate them for it.

Joshua said, "How about on Friday night you come to my dad's nightclub? I make sure my dad's deejay has the hottest tracks so that people won't say the club is weak."

I like dancing, not professionally but for fun. Plus, my parents would want me to have some fun if it was a way to rehabilitate myself. I haven't gone dancing at any of the South Central clubs 'cause my parents say I'm too young, and those clubs are too wild. I'm not even allowed to attend parties at my classmates' houses unless there are adult chaperones and the family ain't affiliated with gangs. But with or without gang affiliation, gangbangers usually come along and crash the party. Then, the result is usually more corpses for Mr. Grant to bury; but I'm sure Koreatown clubs don't have these problems 'cause I have never heard of Korean gangsters.

I told Joshua, "Dancing at your dad's nightclub would be fun. I'll have to ask my parents, but I'm sure they'll say yes."

Mama and Daddy agreed. So, I went through my closet to find an outfit to wear to Mr. Yang's club. I have blouses, but they aren't made for dancing and immediately look unattractive when covered in sweat. I have leather jackets, but that might look too gangster. I took out my unisex military outfit that looked exactly like Janet Jackson's "Rhythm Nation" outfit. In my opinion, it's the perfect mix of formal and rebel. I also took out my Black fedora, a signature piece of Michael Jackson. He always wears fedoras when he performs live or when he's just walking around a city anywhere in the world.

When Joshua came to pick me up and saw my outfit, he asked, "You're part of the Rhythm Nation?"

I explained, "Any person who does their best to fight against social injustices is a part of the Rhythm Nation."

Joshua was dressed in a gold vest and Black Hammer pants.

I said, "It looks like it's Hammer time!"

HEAL THE HOOD

We both laughed, and Mama and Daddy came out of the kitchen. Mama told Joshua, "You look dashing this evening."

"Dashing" is an adjective you use when someone wears a formal outfit like a suit and tie. I know Mama was trying to be polite 'cause she likes Joshua, but Daddy kept eyeing him sternly and said, "Hatima's curfew is ten p.m. Not a minute later."

Joshua said, "I know, she told me. I'll have her home in time. Don't worry."

Then, Daddy said, "Maybe it's best if *I* pick Hatima up. This hood gets extremely dangerous at night, and I don't want anything to happen to you."

I see Daddy still wants to be the number one guy in my life, and he wants to make sure nobody messes with Joshua. Some guys at school keep harassing me about how I picked Joshua's Yellow ass over their Black asses. As I suspected, they call me a traitor to our people and say that I'm sympathizing with the enemy. I've stated that Joshua isn't their enemy and pointed out that the Laundromat is now owned by Joshua's dad. Mr. Yang, with a lotta coaxing from his son, hired a Black guy named Ronnie McClure to run the Laundromat. Plus, it was hard to hire a fellow Korean because their dislike of South Central has increased since Mrs. Du's trial. Even though Judge Karlin didn't properly punish Mrs. Du, the Koreans are aware that Blacks may attack other Koreans in the hood to avenge Latasha and Lee Arthur. A lotta Korean stores have been robbed and some, including the Dus' store, have been firebombed. Even though Mr. Yang isn't completely down for the cause, Joshua appears to be. I'm sure Dr. King, Frederick Douglass, and Nelson Mandela would be pleased that at least one Korean has had a change of heart.

Joshua told Daddy, "Hatima will be with me. She can direct me toward the safest routes to make sure we don't encounter trouble.

I've been through this neighborhood with my dad plenty of times. I think I'll be okay."

Daddy scrunched his face in thought and then said, "Okay."

I said, "Thanks! Bye, Ma, bye, Daddy!"

Joshua opened the passenger side of his Cadillac for me, and I said, "You don't need to do that."

Joshua explained, "I want your dad to see I'm a gentleman, not some guy who wants to take advantage of you."

I rolled my eyes and got into the passenger seat, while Joshua closed the door, walked to the driver's side, got in, and started the car.

As Joshua drove us to Koreatown, I saw plenty of folks in the hood eyeing us suspiciously. I knew they were wondering why I'm dating a Korean boy. They probably thought I was a gold-digger after Mr. Yang's money or that since many Black guys in this hood are dead, criminals, in jail, or absent, I was turned off from Black guys. They definitely don't believe in Dr. King's dream.

When we got to Koreatown, Joshua parked his car, got out, walked over to the passenger side, and opened my door for me. I let him 'cause it was kinda sweet. He held out his left arm, and I held onto it with my right hand. Then, we walked into his dad's nightclub. Since Mr. Yang is Joshua's dad, he doesn't have to pay the entrance fee and, since Joshua is my boyfriend, neither do I. The bouncer eyed us strangely, which I expected, but he didn't say anything.

We got in and heard the Korean deejay spinning Black music on his turntable. Prince's song, "1999", was playing when we walked in. How many people will play this song on December 31, 1999? I immediately started dancing to the lyrics:

HEAL THE HOOD

I was dreamin' when I wrote this, forgive me if it goes astray
But when I woke up this mornin', could've sworn it was judgment day
The sky was all purple, there were people runnin' everywhere
Tryin' to run from the destruction, you know I didn't even care
Say two thousand zero zero party over, oops, out of time
So tonight I'm gonna party like it's nineteen ninety-nine
I was dreamin' when I wrote this, so sue me if I go too fast
But life is just a party and parties weren't meant to last
War is all around us, my mind says prepare to fight
So if I gotta die I'm gonna listen to my body tonight
Yeah hey, they say two thousand zero zero party over, oops, out of time
So tonight I'm gonna party like it's nineteen ninety-nine
Yeah, yeah, hey

Joshua tried to dance to Prince, but I could see he didn't have natural rhythm. The next song that came up was Prince's "Little Red Corvette."

I guess I should have known
By the way you parked your car sideways
That it wouldn't last
See you're the kinda person
That believes in makin' out once
Love 'em and leave 'em fast

I guess I must be dumb
'Cause you had a pocket full of horses
Trojan and some of them used
But it was Saturday night
I guess that makes it all right

And you say what have I got to lose?

And honey I say
Little red Corvette
Baby you're much too fast
Little red Corvette
You need a love that's gonna last

I immediately started dancing like Prince did in the music video, including the splits. Joshua cheered for me after I did Prince's moves and so did the other people in the club, who were all Koreans. I was the sole Black face, and I guess that immediately made me cool. The next song was "Parents Just Don't Understand" by DJ Jazzy Jeff and the Fresh Prince. I rapped along with Will Smith while breaking it down on the dance floor.

You know parents are the same
No matter time nor place
They don't understand that us kids
Are going to make some mistakes
So to you, all the kids all across the land
There's no need to argue
Parents just don't understand

I remember one year
My mom took me school shopping
It was me, my brother, my mom, oh, my pop, and my little sister
All hopped in the car
We headed downtown to the Gallery Mall
MY mom started bugging with the clothes she chose

HEAL THE HOOD

I didn't say nothing at first
I just turned up my nose
She said, "What's wrong? This shirt cost $20"
I said, "Mom, this shirt is plaid with a butterfly collar!"
The next half hour was the same old thing
My mother buying me clothes from 1963
And then she lost her mind and did the ultimate
I asked her for Adidas and she bought me Zips!
I said, "Mom, what are you doing, you're ruining my rep"
She said, "You're only sixteen, you don't have a rep yet"
I said, "Mom, let's put these clothes back, please"
She said "no, you go to school to learn not for a fashion show"
I said, "This isn't Sha Na Na, come on Mom, I'm not Bowzer
Mom, please put back the bell-bottom Brady Bunch trousers
But if you don't want to I can live with that but
You gotta put back the double-knit reversible slacks"
She wasn't moved - everything stayed the same
Inevitably the first day of school came
I thought I could get over, I tried to play sick
But my mom said, "No, no way, uh-uh, forget it"
There was nothing I could do, I tried to relax
I got dressed up in those ancient artifacts
And when I walked into school, it was just as I thought
The kids were cracking up laughing at the clothes Mom bought
And those who weren't laughing still had a ball
Because they were pointing and whispering
As I walked down the hall
I got home and told my Mom how my day went
She said, "If they were laughing you don't need the,
"Cause they're not good friends"

For the next six hours I tried to explain to my Mom
That I was gonna have to go through this about 200 more times
So to you all the kids all across the land
There's no need to argue
Parents just don't understand

If my parents bought me wack clothes like that, girls would be jumping me before and after school more often, even though I have a black belt in hapkido and can easily give them all one-way tickets to the emergency room. The next song the deejay played was Bobby Brown's "Every Little Step."

I can't sleep at night, I toss and turn
Listenin' for the telephone
But when I get your call I'm all choked up
Can't believe you called my home
And as a matter of fact, it blows my mind
You would even talk to me
Because a girl like you is a dream come true
A real life fantasy
No matter what your friends try to tell ya
We were made to fall in love
And we will be together, any kind of weather
It's like that, it's like that
Every little step I take
You will be there
Every little step I make
We'll be together
Every little step I take
You will be there

HEAL THE HOOD

Every little step I make
We'll be together

I danced like Bobby B and his homeboys in the music video. Most folks thought that Ralph Tresvant's first solo album would be New Edition's most successful side project; but Bobby Brown threw those thoughts out the window with his masterpiece album, *Don't Be Cruel*. Ralph Tresvant's solo album, *Ralph Tresvant*, is cool, but it ain't as cool as Bobby's. Next, the deejay played Bobby Brown's signature hit, "My Prerogative."

Everybody's talkin' all this stuff about me (Now now)
Why don't they just let me live (Oh oh oh)
I don't need permission
Make my own decisions (Oh)
That's my prerogative

They say I'm crazy
I really don't care
That's my prerogative
They say I'm nasty
But I don't give a damn
Gettin' girls is how I live
Some ask me questions
Why am I so real
But they don't understand me
I really don't know the deal
About a brother
Trying hard to make it right
Not long ago

Before I win this fight
Sing!

Everybody's talkin' all this stuff about me
Why don't they just let me live (Tell me why)
I don't need permission
Make my own decisions (Oh)
That's my prerogative
It's my prerogative (It's my prerogative)
It's the way that I wanna live (It's my prerogative)
I can do just what I feel (It's my prerogative)
No one can tell me what to do (It's my prerogative)
Cause what I'm doin'
I'm doin' for you now

The next song was Janet Jackson's "Miss You Much", from her album *Janet Jackson's Rhythm Nation 1814*. It was one of the hottest albums of last year and this year. I even saw her perform live at the Forum last year! That was one of the greatest days of my life! Janet sang in her instantly recognizable voice.

Shot like an arrow thru my heart
That's the pain I feel
I feel whenever we're apart
Not to say that I'm in love with you
But who's to say that I'm not
I just know that it feels wrong when I'm away too long
It makes my body hot
So let me tell ya baby I'll tell your mama
I'll tell your friends

HEAL THE HOOD

I'll tell anyone who's heart can comprehend
Send it in a letter baby tell you on the phone
I'm not the kinda girl who likes to be alone
I miss ya much I really miss you much
I miss ya much baby I really miss ya much
I'm rushing home just as soon as I can
I'm rushing Home to see your smiling face
And feel your warm embrace
It makes me feel so g-g-g-good
So I'll tell ya baby I'll tell your mama
I'll tell your friends
I'll tell anyone who's heart can comprehend
Send it in a letter baby tell you on the phone
I'm not the kinda girl who likes to be alone
I miss ya much I really miss you much

I danced like Janet and her back-up dancers in the music video. I even did the chair routine, and everyone in the nightclub cheered for me. The next song was Janet Jackson's "Rhythm Nation" – good thing my outfit matches the song.

Five, four, three, two, one
Yeah yeah yeah yeah, yeah yeah yeah
Bass bass, bass, bass
With music by our side
To break the color lines
Let's work together
To improve our way of life
Join voices in protest
To social injustice

A generation full of courage
Come forth with me
People of the world today
Are we looking for a better way of life
We are a part of the rhythm nation
People of the world unite
Strength in numbers we can get it right
One time
We are a part of the rhythm nation

This is the test
No struggle no progress
Lend a hand to help
Your brother do his best
Things are getting worse
We have to make them better
It's time to give a damn
Let's work together come on, yeah
People of the world today
Are we looking for a better way of life
We are a part of the rhythm nation
People of the world unite
Strength in numbers we can get it right
One time
We are a part of the rhythm nation

People of the world unite
Are we looking for a better way of life
We are a part of the rhythm nation
People of the world unite

HEAL THE HOOD

Strength in numbers we can get it right
One time
We are a part of the rhythm nation

I did all the dance moves, just like Janet and her soldiers. This is a great song to play, considering all the bullshit going on in LA and the world. I decided to take a break because I was sweating like crazy.

I sat at a table and asked Joshua, "Can you please get me some water?"

Joshua went to the bar and came back with two glasses of ice water. I drank it all down. Then, Hi-Five's number one hit, "I Like the Way (The Kissing Game)" was spun by the deejay.

All summer long we've been together
And I never felt so good
'Cause when I'm with you
You're such a good time, yes, it is

And when you get next to me
You make my heart beat fast
You throw me bad when you smile
And when we're alone, I know we're in love
'Cause I can't get enough, 'cause

'Cause I like the way
You kiss me when we're playing the kissing game
I like the way
You keep me looking forward to another day

Joshua asked, "Have you tried to get gigs as a back-up dancer?"

I said, "There are plenty of dancers from the hood. Most of the folks are trying to make it into show business 'cause of the money, but only the best and most exceptional talents make it into showbiz. Even if a person makes it into showbiz, their career might only last a few years. Since so many people put more work in getting into show biz, their schoolwork suffers. By the time they realize they aren't getting a big break, it's too late. They discover they have no education and are unqualified to do anything else. That's why we need more Black intellectuals, to prove that Black people are capable of so much more."

Joshua said, "You know, I have a friend who wants to be a musician. He plays the piano, the sax, and the double bass. He wants to play jazz, rock, pop, all that stuff. He's planning to get into a performing arts school or a college with a music program, but his guidance counselor told him that showbiz will never accept a Korean pop musician and he should stick to classical music. My friend doesn't like the fact that people only see Asians as doing intellectual and cultured stuff. My friend wants to show he has a creative side that can touch the world as well as any other musician."

I said, "Huh. I thought since Asians are always seen as smart, they would always be told that they can do or achieve anything they want to. That's a terrible thing to tell someone; that they shouldn't study the music they love simply because of people's expectations for their race."

Joshua said, "Exactly. We have to learn to rise above people's expectations."

After we rested, we got back on the dance floor.

The deejay spun MC Hammer's record "Lets Get It Started." I love it when Hammer raps.

HEAL THE HOOD

They said it couldn't happen, that rap wouldn't last
The beat is in effect like the oil in your gas
Cause it's makin lots of money from top to bottom
Whatever in effect, Yo, be-boys have got em
Nobody knows how a rapper really feels
A mind full of rhymes, and a tongue of steel
Just put on the hammer, and you will be rewarded
My beat is ever booming, and you know I get it started

Rap was invented in the South Bronx in New York City. It soon spread to the other four New York boroughs, then to other US cities, and around the world. Rap has become an important trait of Black culture because Black people have always used music to express ourselves. Rap used to be fun, and now its gun. There are different sub-genres of hip-hop, but the genre that has taken over the airwaves and television is gangsta rap. Gangsta rap evolved from hardcore rap, and it tells and shows folks all the shit that goes down in the hood. Obviously, plenty of folks have a problem with this, but rappers ain't afraid to preach the truth. MC Hammer's style is pop-rap. His raps remain fun instead of gun and they're great to dance to.

In fact, he's one of the few rappers who can dance. Hammer even challenged Michael Jackson to a dance contest once, but no one knows if it will ever happen.

The next song was Hammer's best, "U Can't Touch This".

Give me a song or rhythm
Making 'em sweat that's what I'm giving 'em
Now they know when you talk about the Hammer
You talk about a show that's hyped and tight
Singers are sweatin' so pass them a mic

> *Or a tape to learn what it's gonna take*
> *And now he's gonna burn*
> *The charts legit either wo'k hard*
> *Or you might as well quit*
>
> *That's word because you know*
> *You can't touch this (oh oh oh oh oh oh)*
> *You can't touch this (oh oh oh oh oh oh)*
> *Break it down*
> *(Oh oh oh oh oh oh oh oh oh oh)*
> *(Oh oh oh oh oh oh oh oh oh)*
> *Stop Hammer time*

I did the Hammer dance and so did Joshua. Since he was wearing Hammer pants, he *had* to do the Hammer dance. Joshua got the dance right, so we looked cool together, and everybody else in the club clapped for us. Next, the deejay put on "Billie Jean." When Michael Jackson performed this song on *Motown 25,* eight years ago, he debuted the Moonwalk. Then, his career went into orbit, and he hasn't come down since.

> *She was more like a beauty queen from a movie scene*
> *I said don't mind, but what do you mean, I am the one*
> *Who will dance on the floor in the round*
> *She said I am the one, who will dance on the floor in the round*
>
> *She told me her name was Billie Jean, as she caused a scene*
> *Then every head turned with eyes that dreamed of being the one*
> *Who will dance on the floor in the round*

HEAL THE HOOD

People always told me be careful of what you do
And don't go around breaking young girls' hearts
And mother always told me be careful of who you love
And be careful of what you do 'cause the lie becomes the truth

Billie Jean is not my lover
She's just a girl who claims that I am the one
But the kid is not my son
She says I am the one, but the kid is not my son

For forty days and forty nights
The law was on her side
But who can stand when she's in demand
Her schemes and plans
'Cause we danced on the floor in the round
So take my strong advice, just remember to always think twice
(Don't think twice, don't think twice)

She told my baby we'd danced till three, then she looked at me
Then showed a photo my baby cried his eyes were like mine (oh, no!)
'Cause we danced on the floor in the round, baby

People always told me be careful of what you do
And don't go around breaking young girls' hearts
She came and stood right by me
Just the smell of sweet perfume
This happened much too soon
She called me to her room

Billie Jean is not my lover
She's just a girl who claims that I am the one
But the kid is not my son

I did the Moonwalk during the bridge, and all the Koreans couldn't stop screaming just like Michael Jackson's fans during his concerts. It's a stereotype that all Black people can dance so most folks believe all Black people can do the Moonwalk. But I'm one of a handful of people in Crenshaw who can Moonwalk. Wanda, Imani, Andre, Hector, Malik, and my parents can't Moonwalk. When they try to Moonwalk, it looks like they're trying to wipe dog shit off their shoes.

The deejay spun "Smooth Criminal" next. Some people in the hood think that Michael Jackson's "Smooth Criminal" music video is better than his "Thriller" music video. I also think "Smooth Criminal" is superior to "Thriller."

As he came into the window
It was the sound of a crescendo
He came into her apartment
He left the bloodstains on the carpet
She ran underneath the table
He could see she was unable
So she ran into the bedroom
She was struck down, it was her doom

Annie, are you ok?
So, Annie are you ok
Are you ok, Annie
Annie, are you ok?

HEAL THE HOOD

So, Annie are you ok
Are you ok, Annie
Annie, are you ok?
So, Annie are you ok?
Are you ok, Annie?
Annie, are you ok?
So, Annie are you ok, are you ok Annie?

Annie, are you ok?
So, Annie are you ok?
Are you ok, Annie?
Annie, are you ok?
So, Annie are you ok?
Are you ok, Annie?
Annie, are you ok?
So, Annie are you ok?
Are you ok, Annie?
You've been hit by
You've been hit by
A smooth criminal

People always wonder who Annie is, and if she's okay, and it has become one of the unsolved mysteries of the universe along with Amelia Earhart's disappearance and Jack the Ripper's identity. I can't do the "Smooth Criminal" lean and neither can anyone else in the hood. People figure Michael Jackson uses invisible wires or magnets or something to do the dance move during his concerts.

Soon, Joshua said, "It's nine-thirty. I need to get you home."

We left the club and Joshua opened the passenger's side of his

Cadillac for me. I got in, he closed the door, and then he went around to his side.

The car drive from Koreatown to Crenshaw is shorter than the bus ride between the two neighbourhoods. It usually takes about twenty minutes, but we had a delay.

As Joshua drove into the hood, a White plainclothed cop stepped in front of his car and said, "Sorry, sir, you can't drive through here."

Joshua asked, "Why not?"

The cop explained, "There's been a murder in a bar. My fellow officers are looking for the perpetrator so we've cordoned off the area."

Joshua explained, "But I have to get my girlfriend home. She has a curfew."

The cop said, "I'll give you a police escort home. Where does your girlfriend live?"

Joshua told him my address and the cop got into his cruiser. Joshua followed him until we got to my block.

Joshua got out and walked around to open the passenger door for me.

When I got out, I asked the cop, "Who got killed in the bar?"

The cop, whose badge said "DETECTIVE" and "85" stated, "A man by the name of Darnell Matthews. Do you know him?"

I said, "No, Detective, I don't."

Detective 85 said, "We'll do our best to find Mister Matthews' murderer. Until then, stay safe."

Joshua walked me inside, and we saw Daddy sitting on the couch, reading the *LA Sentinel*.

I exclaimed, "Daddy, there was no need for you to wait up for us!"

Daddy said, "I had to make sure you got home by ten."

Joshua said, "I brought her home on time, Mister Parker. See, I kept my promise."

Daddy said, "So you did."

Then, Daddy shook Joshua's hand and gave him a warm smile.

Joshua said, "Good night, Mister Parker. Good night, Hatima."

I said, "Good night, Joshua, and thanks for a lovely evening."

When Joshua went out the front door, Daddy saw Detective 85.

Daddy asked, "What's that cop doing here?"

I explained how Darnell Matthews was killed in a bar and that Detective 85 wanted to escort us safely home. Joshua was talking to Detective 85, most likely explaining where he lived. Then, Joshua got into his car and Detective 85 got into his, and the squad car drove down our street, while Joshua's Cadillac followed. Detective 85 was most likely giving Joshua a police escort outta the hood.

Daddy said, "I doubt that cop helped you out of the goodness of his heart. He's probably keeping a close eye on us to make sure *we* aren't involved in the murder. That's what happens when your brother's a crook."

I stated, "Daddy, I don't think that was on Detective Eighty-Five's mind at all. He didn't ask for my ID, so he doesn't even know my name. Therefore, he doesn't know who we're related to."

Daddy asked, "Since when do you defend pigs?"

I frowned and stated, "Not all cops are pigs. Detective Crawford is a cop and she has a great head on her shoulders. We have to cooperate with nice cops so that the dirty cops don't get away with mistreating our people or doing a lousy job at catching criminals."

Chapter Fourteen

At Christmas, most of my neighbors drive to their houses with pine trees tied to the tops of their cars and usually need help getting their trees into their houses. Others string up lights on their roofs and hang wreaths on their doors. Others buy turkeys, sweet potatoes, powdered ginger, apple cider, et cetera to create their holiday feasts, but my family never participates in that stuff 'cause we've never celebrated Christmas. When I was six, I wrote a list of the toys I wanted and asked my parents what Santa Claus' address was.

Then Daddy told me "Baby girl, Santa Claus isn't real."

I exclaimed, "What?!"

Mama explained, "He's a made-up person that's used to explain to children about the importance of giving."

Daddy said, "Besides, do you really believe a White guy is gonna come to Crenshaw and gives gifts to children? Santa would be a plum fool if he thought he could step foot in South Central without the hood rats snatchin' all his gifts."

Then, Mama said, "Hatima, Christmas is a materialistic and consumerist holiday."

I didn't understand what *materialistic* and *consumerist* meant until I got older. Materialistic means people are more obsessed with the lights, decorations, foods, television specials, et cetera instead of the story of Jesus' birth and His importance. Consumerist means people are more obsessed with getting presents instead of giving presents. Some kids in the hood have up to twenty gifts on their Christmas lists. The kids who know St. Nick ain't real give the lists to their parents. So, these kids must think that their parents are magically given enough money to get as many gifts as there are in Santa's make-believe workshop. Some parents in the hood are given Christmas bonuses, such as my parents, but others aren't.

Grandma states that Santa Claus steals all the credit that Jesus Christ should be getting, but if Jesus came to South Central and gave toys to the kids, I'm sure his popularity would increase. Dr. Murray stated that Jesus Himself is the greatest gift God gave us, but some kids started grumbling about how the greatest gifts they can get are more food, better clothes, vermin-free apartments, and paid bills. Even Imani wonders whether or not Jesus cares about poor kids in the ghetto.

Since people think about the needy more during holidays, FAME's food bank is always overflowing with nutrition from cheerful givers. Daddy offered to drive the Fitzpatricks to FAME so that we could fit the boxes of food into the trunk of the car. I rode in the passenger seat next to Daddy and Ms. Fitzpatrick, Hector, and Imani sat in the back. They were silent while Daddy drove us to FAME. The Fitzpatricks have been receiving food from food banks for as long as I have known them, but I guess they still feel embarrassed about not having enough money for necessities.

At FAME, there was a *looooong* line to get food. I hoped that there would be enough for the Fitzpatricks even though it's cruel to be mean to other poor folks. If the news did more segments on the church's charity drives, maybe folks in LA would do more to help out South Central. Rodney King was obviously suffering from alcoholism, but the cops' response to that was to beat him bloody. Why did they not offer a helping hand to him? Why did they not try to get him into an alcohol-rehab program? Latasha Harlins lived in poverty. Why do the Koreans lack sympathy for poor Blacks? Don't they see that giving legit jobs to Blacks is the first step towards decreasing the crime rate? Don't they know that it's a stroke of luck that poverty hasn't strangled them, too?

When we got to the front, Daddy explained that we were there to help the Fitzpatricks get their donations. We've never needed food from the church's food bank, and I feel a little ashamed about that. My family easily has something that so many others don't. The Fitzpatricks were given two cardboard boxes full of cereal, canned vegetables, flour, oatmeal, powdered milk, et cetera. Daddy carried the first box and Hector carried the second. They put the food in the Ford's trunk, and Daddy drove them back to Chesapeake Apartment. When we got there, Daddy and Hector unloaded the car and carried the food into their apartment.

As we put the food away, I asked Hector, "How's the gas station and convenience store?"

Hector said, "Business is rising. I don't wanna move into my own place until I'm sure Mom and Imani are well-taken care of."

I'm hoping that by this time next year, the Fitzpatricks won't have to line up at FAME to get food. What they received today isn't enough food for a holiday feast but at least they won't starve on Jesus' birthday.

I looked at their living room. They've never been able to afford a tree, but sometimes they've had presents. When Hector was selling the rock, he made sure Imani and his mom had slammin' presents. Now I'm wondering if Hector's new business will result in presents this year.

My family's holiday season is complete without a tree, presents, or a traditional Christmas dinner 'cause we celebrate Kwanzaa instead of Christmas. There are plenty of other Black families in South Central who celebrate Kwanzaa, but they celebrate it in addition to Christmas. Mama, Daddy, and Grandma have assured me that there are plenty of other Black people in the LA hoods who celebrate Kwanzaa instead of Christmas.

Since I am an Africanist-in-training, I feel I should mention some cool facts about Kwanzaa.

- Kwanzaa was invented by Dr. Maulana Karenga in 1966.
- Kwanzaa is derived from the Swahili phrase *matunda ya kwanza*, which means "fruits of the harvest."
- Kwanzaa is celebrated between December 26th and January 1st.
- Dr. Karenga believes Jesus is psychotic and that Christianity is a "White" religion. (Obviously, my parents and grandmother disagree.)
- There are seven principles of Kwanzaa a.k.a. *Nguzo Saba*, which consists of "the best of African thought and practice in constant exchange with the world."
- The official colors of Kwanzaa are red, black, and green, the same colors of the Pan-African flag.

On Christmas Day, my family observes Jesus' birthday by reading New Testament verses about His birth. So, I guess, in our own spiritual way, we celebrate Christmas. We just don't celebrate the greedy gift-getting part of Christmas. Grandma is always happy when we bring church into our home; she raises her arms and yells, "Hallelujah!" Then, we put on some Christmas carols on the record player. My favorite Christmas album is the Jackson Five's album, but the vinyl has been worn out, so the quality of the music has faded.

On Christmas Day, Imani stopped by and asked me, "Do you notice anything different about me?"

I analyzed Imani from her head to her feet. When I saw her feet, I gasped! She was wearing a new pair of Reeboks and not just any Reeboks, but the new 1991 Reebok Blacktop Basketball Pumps!

I exclaimed, "Girl, those are the latest Reeboks! Wanda is gonna be so jealous because her Reeboks and mine are the '89 line!"

Imani laughed and said, "Hector got them for me! Now that I'm rocking the latest style, I can finally retire those old-ass Chuck Taylors!"

It looks like Imani had a good Christmas.

On December 26, 1991, I dressed up in a red, black, and green dashiki shirt and a plastic ankh necklace. Mama wore a green African dress with a red *kaftan,* a pull-over woman's robe, and a black head-wrap. Daddy wore a gold and black dashiki shirt with a bead necklace. Then, we transformed our dining table into a Kwanzaa table.

Mama covered the table with a kente cloth. Then Daddy placed a mat on the floor next to the table. The *mkeka*, a.k.a. the mat, symbolizes our traditions, history, and foundation on which we build. Even the Bible states that we should build our house on a firm foundation.

I placed a Gullah sweetgrass basket on the table and put potatoes, tomatoes, carrots, okra, corn, et cetera in the basket. This is *mazao*, the crops, which symbolize African harvest celebrations and the rewards of productive and collective labor. I thought about colonialism. When Nigeria was a British colony, Nigerian tribes didn't reap most of the rewards of their harvest 'cause most of the profits went straight to the White British officials. During the slavery era, the slaves' reward for their hard labor was raggedy clothes and barely enough food to stay alive. The women's rewards were becoming the masters' and overseers' mistresses. When Grandma and her father were sharecroppers, they were rarely rewarded for helping their White boss create a bumper cotton crop. Their low salary meant they were stuck in a cycle of terrible poverty.

The corn or *muhindi* in the basket symbolizes children and the future we embody.

Then, Daddy placed the *Kikombe cha Umoja*, a.k.a. the Unity Cup, on the table. It symbolizes the foundational principle and practice of unity, which makes all else possible.

Next, I placed the *Kinara* or candleholder at the center of the table. Mama placed a red candle on one end of the *Kinara*, and Daddy lit it with a match.

I waved a miniature version of the Pan-African flag like how people wave miniature American flags on the Fourth of July.

Daddy said, "The first principle of Kwanzaa is *Umoja*. What does *Umoja* mean, baby girl?"

I replied, "*Umoja* means 'unity' in Swahili. We have to strive for and maintain unity in the family, community, nation, and race."

Daddy said, "This has been a tumultuous year, and the future will continue to be this way if Black people worldwide don't stand united against the forces that threaten our destruction."

Mama stated, "Marcus Garvey said, 'Up, you mighty race, accomplish what you will.'"

Grandma showed up later in a tie-dyed African dress that looks like it came straight outta the 1960s. Now that the whole family was here, Kwanzaa could really begin. Daddy played Bob Marley's hit song, "One Love." Bob Marley's melodic accent sang.

Adaeze Nwosu

One love, one heart
Let's get together and feel all right
Hear the children crying (One love)
Hear the children crying (One heart)
Sayin', "Give thanks and praise to the Lord and I will feel all right
Sayin', "Let's get together and feel all right
Whoa, whoa, whoa, whoa

Let them all pass all their dirty remarks (one love)
There is one question I'd really love to ask (one heart)
Is there a place for the hopeless sinner
Who has hurt all mankind just to save his own?
Believe me

One love, one heart
Let's get together and feel all right
As it was in the beginning (one love)
So shall it be in the end (one heart)
Alright, give thanks and praise to the Lord and I will feel all right
Let's get together and feel all right
One more thing

Let's get together to fight this Holy Armageddon (one love)
So when the Man comes there will be no, no doom (one song)
Have pity on those whose chances grow thinner
There ain't no hiding place from the Father of Creation

Sayin', one love, one heart
Let's get together and feel all right

HEAL THE HOOD

I'm pleading to mankind (one love)
Oh, Lord (one heart) whoa

Give thanks and praise to the Lord and I will feel all right
Let's get together and feel all right
Give thanks and praise to the Lord and I will feel all right
Let's get together and feel all right

We celebrate seven principles on the seven days of Kwanzaa. The second principle is *Kujichagulia*. Daddy always makes me recite all the principles to make sure the Swahili lessons my parents and other Pan-Africanists have given me are intact – turns out, they are.

I stated, "*Kujichagulia* means 'self-determination.' We have to define and name ourselves as well as create and speak for ourselves."

Daddy stated, "My daddy put a lot of thought into my and my brother's names. Your grandmother put a lot of thought into your mama's name. And your mother and I put a lot of thought into your name. Your name means 'fate.' That means you and God Almighty are the only ones who have the power to determine your path in life. The US government, the cops, and the gangbangers don't determine your fate because they ain't all-powerful. Understand?"

I replied, "Yes, Daddy, I understand."

He's told me this a thousand times, and I don't mind the repetition. Too many folks in the hood think crooked politicians, racist cops, and soulless gangbangers have the power to determine what they're gonna be in life. As a result, many people in the hood feel powerless.

The next day, Mr. Ngozi visited us and celebrated the third principle with us, but I could tell from the look on his face that he had an important lesson to teach us.

"The third principle is *Ujima*." I stated, "*Ujima* means 'collective work and responsibility.' That means we have to build and maintain our community together and make our brothers' and sisters' problems ours, so we can solve them together."

Daddy stated, "Marcus Garvey founded Pan-Africanism because he believed all Black people across the world have a common struggle and a common purpose. Kwame Nkrumah, Malcolm X, W. E. B. Du Bois, Stokley Carmichael, and Maulana Karenga also believed this. Dr. King visited Ghana after the nation gained independence from British rule. Even though Dr. King never became an official Pan-Africanist, the Ghanaians' victory further inspired him to fight for equal rights for African Americans through non-violence. As we all know, Malcolm X was Dr. King's polar opposite and believed Blacks should use violence in self-defense in order to achieve their civil rights. Malcolm X made the pilgrimage to Mecca in nineteen-sixty-four and visited several African nations."

Mr. Ngozi said, "Brother Malcolm also visited Nigeria. My uncle met him in Lagos and even had his picture taken with him. He still has that picture in his office."

Daddy stated, "The African nation of Liberia was founded by free Blacks from the United States who wanted to return to their roots, build their own nation, and control their own destiny away from their oppressors'."

Mr. Ngozi asked, "Do you think that was the first back-to-Africa odyssey in the history of the Americas?"

Daddy asked, "There was another odyssey before the founding of Liberia?"

Mr. Ngozi stated, "Hatima, I taught you this in school. Tell your parents about the Black Loyalists."

I stated, in the same way I would give a presentation, "Over three thousand Black Loyalists settled in what is now the Canadian provinces of Nova Scotia and New Brunswick. They were promised land, liberty, and prosperity because they sided with the British during the Revolutionary War. The British had to relocate the Black Loyalists outside of the newly named United States because the Americans would try to snatch their 'property' back, but the Black Loyalists were treated terribly in Nova Scotia and New Brunswick. There were few jobs for them, no land, and most of them starved to death. About twelve hundred of them gave up on British North America and sailed to Africa in seventeen-ninety-two. There, they founded the nation of Sierra Leone. But the British didn't give them complete rule and independence, which led to some conflicts over the years. Sierra Leone finally achieved independence from British rule in nineteen-sixty-one."

Mr. Ngozi asked, "Are any of you thinking of moving back to Africa?"

Mama said, "Not really."

Grandma said, "Moving to the West Coast was a challenge on its own. Moving to Africa is a horse of a different color. Even though we *look* Black, Afro-Americans and Africans are as different as the sun and the moon. Marcus Garvey, Dr. King, and others say we need to stand together, but it's highly unlikely that Africa, the Caribbean, and the USA's Black population will *officially* stand together to ensure a brighter future for the Black babies of the world."

Daddy said, "I thought about moving to Africa back in the seventies. This country really hates Blacks; look at what the KKK, the White Citizens' Councils, the LAPD, and the Koreans do to us.

Maybe all Blacks should move back to Africa because race mixing doesn't seem to be working."

Mr. Ngozi asked, "Do you know any Blacks from the hood who have settled in Africa?"

Daddy said, "Yeah, the McDaniels settled in Ghana, a few years back; and they're happier there than they were here. Ghana is a beautiful and peaceful country. Since all the people look the same racism is nonexistent."

Mr. Ngozi asked, "What about President Rawlings? Do you think he's any better than President Bush?"

Daddy said, "Well, he's made some bad choices, but I'm sure he'll get things back on track."

I said, "Daddy, President Rawlings took the presidency through a coup d'état, just like the Nigerian 'presidents.' His new economic policies led to an economic crisis in nineteen-eighty-three. Do you really believe that just 'cause he's Black, he has a better interest in his nation's well-being?"

Mr. Ngozi stated, "The problem with most African politicians is that they only care about their big houses, fancy cars, and vaults full of cash. When a leader only cares about him or herself instead of their people, their rule just leads to disaster."

Daddy asked Mr. Ngozi, "Do you think African Americans should move back to Africa or stay here?"

Mr. Ngozi asked, "Do you really think this country and Africa are the only places Blacks can thrive? Ever heard of the United Kingdom, Canada, Australia, Germany, Switzerland, Japan?"

Daddy exclaimed, "I ain't moving to Germany, Switzerland, or Japan! They don't speak English, and who knows how many Blacks are in those countries?"

Mr. Ngozi stated, "This is part of the problem. Most African

Americans can't imagine living anywhere else. They always make up excuses about different official languages, the lack of fast food joints, TV show availability, et cetera. If you hate the USA so much, move to Canada. I think Canada is the best option for unhappy African Americans for several reasons. First, one of Canada's official languages is English so communication won't be a problem. Second, Canada embraces diversity while the USA embraces assimilation, but I warn you; racism and other forms of bigotry are still an issue in the Great White North. Third, Canada is more progressive, from their tax-paid healthcare system to their strict gun control laws."

I asked, "What about the UK?"

Mr. Ngozi said, "The UK suffered from a shortage of workers after the Second World War, so they called on British 'citizens' from the colonies to make up the deficit. As a result, the UK became a top location for several people emigrating out of their countries. Immigrants in the UK aren't just from former British colonies, but other areas of the world as well. This explains why the UK has one of the most diverse populations in the world. The UK also has a great educational system and it remains the most popular country for international students to study in. Similar to Canada, the UK also has great healthcare that's mostly paid for from taxation and strict gun control laws. The UK has a very high economy, although not as high as the USA. But, today, the UK has a large population inhabiting a small amount of land. The entire United Kingdom could fit in the state of Texas or the province of Ontario. The UK has one of the highest population densities in the world, and overpopulation is a problem, especially in big cities. Canada's population is smaller than the USA's and the UK's, so it's not yet overpopulated. There's lots of room throughout Canada although most people live in the southern parts of the country because the climate is warmest in those areas."

Daddy asked, "Are you totally against Black Americans moving to Africa? What? You think we're not good enough for Africa? You think we lost our blackness?"

Mr. Ngozi could hear the anger and wounded pride in Daddy's voice and explained, "I don't think you and your family would be happy in Africa because you don't understand how low the quality of life is. Now, my father is a doctor and my mother is a teacher, so my family lived in a big house in Lagos. But what kind of housing do you think poor Nigerians live in?"

I replied, "Slums."

Mr. Ngozi said, "That's right. There's a slum in Lagos called Makoko that is built over a swamp. There's no electricity, no running water, no garbage pickup. Since you live in an American ghetto, Makoko is the only place you could afford to live in if you decided to move to Nigeria."

I looked at our television, Betamax, and stereo; I looked at the kitchen, with our stove and fridge; then, I looked at the doors leading to the bathrooms. Folks in Westwood may think I'm living in poverty, but in the eyes of Nigerian slum dwellers, I'm living in the lap of luxury. I wonder what else I've taken for granted.

Mr. Ngozi continued, "What do you plan to do when you move to Nigeria? You and your wife don't have high school diplomas or college degrees, which means the best jobs in Nigeria will be denied to you."

Daddy asked, "Any chance we can take up farming?"

Mr. Ngozi said, "It's true that in Nigeria and the African continent that a man's wealth is determined by how much land and how much cattle he owns, but do you think the banks will give you a loan without incentive?"

Daddy repeated the last word, "Incentive?"

Mr. Ngozi shook his head and said, "Sadly, bribery and knowing influential people helps many people move up the socioeconomic ladder in Nigeria. You and your family don't have any relatives or close friends in Nigeria, and you're not affiliated with any Nigerian tribe. In the eyes of many Nigerians, you're nothing. Plus, Nigeria has suffered from several coups in the past, and I'm sure that there will be coups in the future due to Satan's evil and his strong hold on the world. Do you still think moving to Nigeria is a good thing?"

Daddy swallowed and said, "Not really."

Mr. Ngozi said, "The KKK wants all Blacks to move back to Africa because they believe America is a 'White man's country.' There are many bigots who don't believe diversity works. Our best revenge is to prove them wrong. America is our country, and we're going to make the most of it."

I stated, "We won't be terrorized out of America. There are a lot of great countries out there, but America is great, too. It doesn't always show a bright side but there's still plenty of goodness to fight for."

Grandma exclaimed, "Amen, Mister Ngozi! Amen, Hatima!"

The next day we celebrated the fourth principle of Kwanzaa, *Ujamaa*.

I stated, "*Ujamaa* means 'cooperative economics.' We have to build and maintain our own stores, shops, and other businesses and profit from them together."

Coincidentally, my family received a telephone call that would help the principle of *Ujamaa*.

Mama answered the phone and said, "This is the Parker residence. I'm Missus Suzy Jane Parker. Who's calling?"

The person on the other end of the line answered and Mama said, "Really?" She had a concerned look on her face, like when I got shot or when I get an injury during martial arts matches and softball games. She said, "Thank you for calling us, Detective Crawford."

I asked, "Why did Detective Crawford call? Those Crips who killed Devin ain't walking away scot-free, are they?"

Mama said, "No, it was about Uncle Alonzo and Malik."

Daddy asked, "Did they get arrested or killed?"

Mama explained, "Alonzo killed a Crip and a cop. The cop was patting the Crip down when Alonzo shot him and the Crip. Someone heard the gunshots and called the cops. The cops stopped Uncle Alonzo while he was driving, searched him and his car, found his gun, and arrested him. He's been charged with first-degree murder. If Alonzo can convince his lawyer that he didn't premeditate the murder with malice afterthought, then the charges will be changed to second-degree murder and aggravated assault."

Daddy said, "I hope the cops and courts won't buy that bullshit."

I said, "Daddy, I can't believe you're rooting for the LAPD and our wacky justice system."

Daddy said, "Alonzo deserves to go back to San Quentin for life. He's nothing more than a monster who's taken and ruined too many lives."

Grandma added, "I agree. The community will be better off without that devil!"

I asked, "What about Malik?"

Mama said, "Oh yes! Malik has been arrested on charges of breaking and entering and grand theft. The LAPD found some businesses in Inglewood full of stolen stuff. Undercover cops and witnesses claim they've seen Malik break into stores, steal precious goods, store it in these illegit hood stores, and fence them on the street. I'm sure his lawyer will also try very hard to drop those charges, too."

Daddy said, "It's about time Malik saw how the world really works. He thinks he's bad? There are plenty of badder guys in Central Juvenile Hall, and I'm sure he'll receive a fine education from them on how deadly a gangster's life is."

I asked, "What about Auntie Kalisha?"

Mama rolled her eyes and said, "That ho will probably hook up with another Blood. She's an opportunist who hooks up with the man with the best deal. She fucks any man who'll 'treat her right' and buy her all sorts of expensive shit."

I asked, "How long is Malik gonna be locked up?"

Daddy said, "My estimate is a year at the most. He might get out in six months on parole if he exhibits good behavior."

I said, "But with Uncle Alonzo in jail and Auntie Kalisha fucking some other guy, that means Malik's well-being is gonna fall on our shoulders."

Mama clarified, "Not *our* shoulders, Hatima. You'll be at college studying for your degree. Your daddy and I will have to look after Malik."

Grandma asked, "Will I have to help raise the gangster as well?"

Mama told Grandma, "Mama, some of your tough love might help us out. The hood makes many young men disrespect their elders, but you can show Malik why he should show respect when it's due."

I said, "I'll still come home for the holidays. I can do my part to set Malik on the right path."

Daddy said, "We'll cross that bridge when we have to face it."

The fifth principle of Kwanzaa is *Nia*, which is also a popular name for Black girls in American hoods.

I stated, "*Nia* means 'purpose.' We have to make our collective vocation the building and developing of our community in order to restore our people to their traditional greatness."

Mrs. Brooks, Wanda, and Andre visited us on the fifth day of Kwanzaa.

Wanda told me, "I know Alonzo and Malik are your family and that we should feel some sadness about them being locked up. I feel sorry for Malik 'cause he's still young and still has the opportunity to be a good guy, but Alonzo is all bad and he deserves to be locked up in the big house for life!"

Andre said, "We can rebuild and redevelop our community better with Alonzo gone. Crenshaw used to be a beacon of hope for Blacks back in the day, and it can still be again."

Then, Daddy played Harry Belafonte's "Jump in the Line."

Shake, shake, shake, Senora,
Shake your body line
Shake, shake, shake, Senora,
Shake it all the time
Work, work, work, Senora,
Work your body line
Work, work, work, Senora,
Work it all the time

My girl's name is Senora
I tell you friends, I adore her
And when she dances, oh brother!
She's a hurricane in all kinds of weather

Ok, I believe you!
(Jump in the line, rock your body in time)

HEAL THE HOOD

Ok, I believe you!
(Jump in the line, rock your body in time)
Ok, I believe you!
(Jump in the line, rock your body in time)
Whoa!

Shake, shake, shake, Senora,
Shake your body line, whoa!
Shake, shake, shake, Senora,
Shake it all the time
Work, work, work, Senora,
Work your body line
Work, work, work, Senora,
Work it all the time

Mama shrieked with joy as Daddy pulled her into a dance. When they were dating back in the 1970s, this song *always* put Mama in a good mood. My parents danced to this song at their wedding, so it's their song. I laughed as the King of Calypso kept telling us to rock our bodies in time. Now, in the hood, people rocking their bodies usually leads to babies in nine months if a person ain't careful. But it's the holidays so certain rules are ignored.

The sixth principle of Kwanzaa is *Kuumba*.

I stated, "*Kuumba* means 'creativity.' We have to do as much as we can to leave our community more beautiful and beneficial than we inherited it."

This ties back to Andre's speech yesterday about how *Nia* will be possible with Uncle Alonzo locked up. *Kuumba* will also be possible in Crenshaw because we can heal the hood and make it more beautiful than it is now.

I put in Michael Jackson's *Dangerous* CD and flipped to "Heal the World."

> *There's a place in your heart*
> *And I know that it is love*
> *And this place could be much*
> *Brighter than tomorrow*
> *And if you really try*
> *You'll find there's no need to cry*
> *In this place you'll feel*
> *There's no hurt or sorrow*
>
> *There are ways to get there*
> *If you care enough for the living*
> *Make a little space*
> *Make a better place*
>
> *Heal the world*
> *Make it a better place*
> *For you and for me*
> *And the entire human race*
> *There are people dying*
> *If you care enough for the living*
> *Make it a better place*
> *For you and for me*

I like how he and a little girl sing at the end:

> *Heal the world we live in, save it for our children*
> *Heal the world we live in, save it for our children*

HEAL THE HOOD

Heal the world we live in, save it for our children
Heal the world we live in, save it for our children

We gotta heal the hood for the kids living here today and the kids who will live here in the future. I don't want kids in the present and the future to deal with the same shit that we're dealing with now – the gangsters, the cops, and the Koreans. It has to stop before we fuck ourselves into extinction.

The seventh and final principle of Kwanzaa is *Imani*. You guessed it. My homegirl, Imani, is named after the seventh principle of Kwanzaa.

My family celebrates New Year's Eve and New Year's Day in addition to Kwanzaa because it ain't a materialistic or consumerist holiday. It's actually very spiritual 'cause folks reminisce about the good things that happened during the year and make New Year's Resolutions so that they can try and improve stuff in their lives.

But making resolutions isn't always great because many people don't see them through. My family talks about the blessings of the past year and what they hope to accomplish this year. Since I'm the only member of my family with big dreams, I'm usually the only one who has ideas of accomplishments. What I hope to accomplish is acceptance into the US Naval Academy or any of the other schools I've applied to. My family has the same dreams for me, so I have back-up.

We stayed up late, counted down the seconds until midnight, and screamed, "Happy New Year!"

After we hugged each other, Grandma read some verses from the Bible, and Daddy played "Auld Lang Syne" on the record player.

Since we went to bed late, we all slept in, and when we woke up, we all ate a brunch meal comprised of pancakes, bacon, pork ribs, and cornbread – I guess rich folks aren't the only ones who eat brunch.

The Fitzpatricks came over for dinner in the evening. I hope this New Year would ensure nothing but success for Fitzpatrick's Gas Station and Convenience Store.

Daddy lit the final candle on the *Kinara*.

Then, I proudly stated, "*Imani* means 'faith.' We need to believe with all our hearts in our people, our parents, our teachers, our leaders, and the righteousness and victory of our struggle."

Hector put his fist in the air in the Black Power salute, and Daddy played Marvin Gaye's hit song, "What's Going On."

Mother, mother
There's too many of you crying
Brother, brother, brother
There's far too many of you dying
You know we've got to find a way
To bring some lovin' here today, eheh

Father, father
We don't need to escalate
You see, war is not the answer
For only love can conquer hate
You know we've got to find a way
To bring some lovin' here today, oh oh oh

Picket lines and picket signs
Don't punish me with brutality
Talk to me, so you can see

HEAL THE HOOD

Oh, what's going on
What's going on
Yeah, what's going on
Ah, what's going on

In the mean time
Right on, baby
Right on brother
Right on babe

Mother, mother, everybody thinks we're wrong
Oh, but who are they to judge us
Simply 'cause our hair is long
Oh, you know we've got to find a way
To bring some understanding here today
Oh oh oh

Picket lines and picket signs
Don't punish me with brutality
C'mon talk to me
So you can see
What's going on
Yeah, what's going on
Tell me what's going on
I'll tell you what's going on, ooh ooo ooo ooo
Right on baby
Right on baby

Chapter Fifteen

School started soon, and the only thing people were gossiping about was the fact that Uncle Alonzo and Malik were still in police custody and their trials would start in a few weeks.

Detective Crawford had informed me and my parents that at the arraignments, the charges against Uncle Alonzo were first-degree murder, assault with a deadly weapon, and resisting arrest, while the charges against Malik at his arraignment were breaking and entering and grand theft. The grand juries met on the first Friday of the winter semester. This is one of the few times in my life that I'm glad that racial bias is a large part of the criminal justice system. The Bloods represent every part of the Black experience that other races fear. Uncle Alonzo is the stereotypical Black man; a gangster, a drug dealer, a pimp, an ex-convict, uneducated, et cetera. Even though Uncle Alonzo and his lawyer will claim that Uncle Alonzo wasn't there when he shot that cop and that Crip, the LAPD will defeat that testimony by showing that the bullets from Uncle Alonzo's Glock match the bullets in the dead bodies. Malik actually pleaded guilty at his arraignment so it doesn't look like he and his lawyer will be lying. It's two Bloods' words against the cops, and the cops are sworn officers of the law. So, the jury will automatically believe the cops' words over Uncle Alonzo's and Malik's. Malik must have figured that out and that's why he decided not to start off lying.

HEAL THE HOOD

Detective Crawford said the jury being put together will be diverse despite several attempts to exclude Black and Latino jurors. I'm pretty sure that any non-Black jurors will find Uncle Alonzo and Malik guilty because all Black people are born suspects. The Black and Latino jurors will also find them guilty because they want thugs outta the hoods.

At dinnertime I asked Mama and Daddy, "What if Malik doesn't wanna stay with you two? What if he wants another legal guardian?"

Mama stated, "Malik's only other option is foster care. I know that most people think foster homes are scary places because of *Annie* and *Oliver Twist*, but some foster homes are nice places."

I asked, "Does Auntie Kalisha have any other relatives, any sisters or brothers or a ma and a dad or an aunt or an uncle?"

Daddy states, "Her only other relative was her mama. She never knew her daddy because he left when she was a baby. She grew up in Dallas, Texas. Her mama worked as a maid for a White family, but I'm sure the salary was barely enough to live on. Kalisha wore second-hand clothes and sometimes went to bed hungry. She was obsessed with getting the key to the good life. So, she concluded that the key to the good life was to marry a rich man, but she wanted to get away from Texas So she saved up enough money for a one-way bus ticket to LA. But most of the rich Black men in Leimert Park, View Park-Windsor Hills, and other bougie Black neighborhodds wouldn't give her the time of day because she has a nasty attitude."

I said, "Yeah, she doesn't think she should work. She thinks men should take care of her 'cause she thinks she's a Black queen."

Mama said, "Kalisha ain't Cleopatra, and if she was given a kingdom, she'd lead it to ruin."

Daddy said, "The only other rich Black guys around here are

the gangbangers. Kalisha was attracted to Alonzo's money and power and became his bitch."

Mama said, "Of course, Kalisha's mama didn't approve of Alonzo and refused to come to the wedding, but she came to LA when Malik was born so she could see her grandson. Such a shame she died from a brain aneurysm when Malik was ten."

I said, "Yeah, that's sad."

Daddy said, "When Malik gets out of juvie, he'll have to obey the rules of this house. No gangbanging, no drug dealing, no guns, no messing with tramps, none of that mess. If Malik can't follow these rules, then he can find a nice foster family to take him in."

I said, "He'd probably be shuffled from foster home to foster home until he turns eighteen. Most adults want to adopt babies because it's easier for them and the child to adjust, but no adults are gonna adopt a teenage ex-con. Malik better figure out how lucky he is to have other family besides his parents. He should be grateful."

Daddy said, "I doubt he'll figure out how grateful he is. I'm sure Malik will put up a fight when he gets here, but we'll cross that bridge when it comes."

Uncle Alonzo's and Malik's trials were held two weeks after their arraignment. That was pretty fast, even for a city that lives life in the fast lane. I guess the justice system wanted Uncle Alonzo and Malik in jail, ASAP. The trial was held on a Friday afternoon, which meant I could go with my parents. I called Master Shin and explained to him that I couldn't work that day. I told him about the trials because I had told him about my uncle and cousin before. I wanted to clarify that I wasn't joining the Bloods and didn't plan to teach hapkido to Malik because he already knows karate and he would just use his martial arts skills to cause more pain for others.

The first time I talked to him about them, Master Shin stated, "So many people rely more on guns than on their bodies and minds. What most people see as *progressive*, I see as *problematic*. There are few people who still cling to the old ways and the path of the true warrior."

So, I asked, "What, exactly, is a true warrior?"

Master Shin stated, "A true warrior is a person who dedicates their life to defending those who can't defend themselves."

I asked, "Are the men and women in the LAPD true warriors?"

Master Shin stated, "Some of them are, and some of them aren't. Some police officers protect the people while others harm the people."

I asked, "What about the Marines and the other people in the Armed Forces?"

Master Shin stated, "Some protect others while others only protect themselves by seeking the myth of the glory of the war."

I repeated, "The myth of the glory of war?"

Master Shin stated, "Some people join the Marines and other branches of the Armed Forces because they want to be seen and treated as heroes. But they don't give a damn about the oppressed people they're supposedly protecting."

I said, "I don't care about medals and awards and all that stuff. I just wanna do my part for the USA. I wanna carry on the tradition Grandpa Gabriel started."

Master Shin said, "You have a good heart, Hatima. Remember, never lose sight of who you are."

At the courthouse, Uncle Alonzo was brought in wearing an orange jumpsuit and handcuffs. One of the few things people know about prison is that all the prisoners are dressed the same way, like school uniforms, but prison uniforms are tackier than school uniforms. Trust me, orange jumpsuits will *never* be in style.

The LAPD presented the evidence against Uncle Alonzo; and Uncle Alonzo's lawyer, a fellow brother, tried to defend him with lameass excuses.

"The gun found in my client's car belonged to someone else who was trying to frame him. … My client hasn't been found guilty of any crimes in almost five years. That should be sufficient proof that Mister Parker has distanced himself from the criminal element. … Racial bias has led to many Black men being imprisoned. This has led to the disenfranchisement of Black women and children. If Mister Parker is convicted, how will his wife and son cope without him? Rodney King and Latasha Harlins didn't deserve what was meted out to them and neither does Mister Parker."

I rolled my eyes and almost gagged. What right does this jackass lawyer have to compare my uncle to Rodney King and Latasha Harlins? Uncle Alonzo is a gangster, but Rodney King isn't and Latasha Harlins wasn't. Uncle Alonzo hasn't been found guilty of any crimes since he was released from San Quentin in 1987 because most folks in the hood are too scared to testify or snitch.

The jury deliberated for half an hour and then they came back in. A Black man stood up and said, "We the jury find Alonzo Parker guilty of first-degree murder, assault with a deadly weapon, and resisting arrest. We unanimously agree that he deserves the death penalty."

The judge banged his gavel and said, "I hereby sentence Alonzo Parker to death row at San Quentin."

Mama started crying. I was sad too. California, along with a lot of states, has capital punishment as a legal penalty. Therefore, the jury and/or judge may be given the option of imposing the death penalty on murderers. This is Uncle Alonzo's third and worst strike. Even though he'll one day be dead, hatred itself will remain alive and claim more lives.

When the guards escorted Uncle Alonzo outta the courtroom, he looked at Daddy, and said, "So much for family."

What did Uncle Alonzo expect Daddy to do? Lie for him in the courtroom? Help smuggle him out of the country from the LA International Airport? Uncle Alonzo chose his own path, and he'll be paying for it with his life.

Next, Malik was escorted into the courtroom. He was wearing an Armani suit because the Bloods were able to pay his bail and get him home to Inglewood. Uncle Alonzo was denied bail, so he was incarcerated at the Metropolitan Detention Center. MDC holds inmates before and during court proceedings as well as people who have been found guilty of crimes. The LAPD presented the evidence against Malik, but since Malik had already pleaded guilty at his arraignment I didn't see the need for all the formalities. Malik's lawyer's excuses weren't *completely* lame; he mainly stated that Malik deserved a second chance and pleaded with the judge and jury not to give him a harsh sentence.

The jury deliberated for half an hour and then came back in.

A Latino man said, "We the jury find Malik Parker guilty of breaking and entering and grand theft."

The judge banged his gavel and said, "I hereby sentence Malik Parker to one year at Central Juvenile Hall."

One year in juvie sounded *a million times* better than death row at San Quentin. I theorized that Malik could be eligible for parole by July if he behaved himself in there. Malik was handcuffed and escorted outta the courtroom by the guards.

When he saw us, he said, "Ma didn't bother to come, huh?"

Mama said, "No, dear. I believe seeing you in handcuffs would be too much for her."

I immediately thought the only reason Auntie Kalisha wasn't here was because she was busy fucking some other gangster. I'm sure that once she hears that her man is on death row and her baby boy has been locked up, she would start filing for divorce papers. There's no way she's waiting until Uncle Alonzo is dead before she starts fucking other men. Defendants remain on death row during appeal and habeas corpus procedures, which may continue for years. Plus, I'm sure Auntie Kalisha wouldn't wanna be bothered with her son now, since she refuses to take responsibility for anything or anyone. To Auntie Kalisha, Malik is now a problem that she'll be more than happy to dump on my parents. Auntie Kalisha is a mindless and heartless whore, and I hope one day she gets what she deserves.

After the trials, we all left the courthouse and got into the Ford. I was surprised that I was sad about Uncle Alonzo's death sentence. I thought a life sentence in jail is punishment enough. But with him locked up, things should get better in Crenshaw and other LA hoods, but Uncle Alonzo's and Malik's incarcerations mean the LAPD will be harder on Blacks in the hood. Uncle Alonzo and Malik have proved what so many people think of Blacks – that we're all gangsters, thieves, murderers, and drug dealers. When the cops stop, harass, beat, and kill other Blacks, some who are criminals and others who are not, Uncle Alonzo and Malik are gonna be the ones they remember. They'll picture my uncle and cousin when they harass other Blacks and believe they're justified in labeling *all* Blacks as criminals.

While we were driving home, a siren went off. I looked behind the Ford and saw a squad car. I thought, *This is a real bitch.* My uncle and cousin have just been incarcerated and now the cops are gonna harass Daddy, the Parker brother who has never messed with gangs and their senseless street wars.

Two White cops walked to our car. With horror, I realized that the cops were Officers Greene and Wayne. Yep, the same ones who stopped Dr. Wilson because he was driving a Rolls-Royce. Dr. Wilson's job and connections helped put the cops in their place but, unfortunately, Doc Wilson ain't here. What if the cops beat and arrest Daddy to get back at me?

Officer Wayne looked at me through the left back window, and Officer Greene questioned Daddy.

"Where are you off to, boy?"

Boy?

Grandma said that in Mississippi a Black man is a boy unless he's a senior citizen. Then, he is an uncle.

Daddy told Officer Greene, "There are no boys in this car. I'm a man."

Officer Greene narrowed his eyes and said, "Lemme see your license and registration."

I didn't think that was a good idea. But Daddy showed Officer Greene his license and the Ford's vehicle registration. When Officer Greene saw Daddy's license, an evil smile crept onto his face. I'm sure the Wicked Witch of the West, the White Witch, the Queen of Hearts, Captain Hook, Cluny the Scourge, and Slagar the Cruel all have similar smiles.

Officer Greene said, "Outta the car, boy!"

Daddy stepped out with his hands in the air; and Officer Greene forced Daddy down onto the hood of the car, put his arms behind his back, and handcuffed him.

Mama exclaimed, "What are you arresting my husband for? He hasn't done anything wrong!"

Officer Greene took out his gun and pointed it at Mama! Then, he told his partner, "Show that little girl we mean business."

Officer Wayne took out his gun and pointed it at me! I raised my arms in the air to show I wasn't packing, and Mama put her arms in the air, too. I was so scared I was sure everyone could hear how loud my heart was beating!

Daddy said, "There's no need to point those weapons at my wife and daughter! They haven't done anything wrong!"

Officer Greene stated, "We know who your brother is. He's just been sent to death row. Looks like you'll get to join your brother in the big house."

Just then, someone across the street asked, "What's going on?"

I looked and saw that it was Mr. Brown. He was wearing his mechanic's uniform, and it was covered in oil and grease.

Officer Wayne pointed his gun at Mr. Brown and said, "This is none of your concern, boy!"

Mr. Brown exclaimed, "Boy? I'm a man who's gonna make sure you pigs get what you deserve!"

Officer Greene led Daddy to the squad car and shoved him in the back seat, and Officer Wayne followed. Officer Greene got in the driver's seat, and Officer Wayne got into the passenger's seat, and then they drove away.

Mr. Brown came over to the passenger's side of the Ford and asked Mama, "Are you and Hatima alright?"

Mama said, "My man has just been brutalized and arrested! Of course, I'm not fine!"

Mr. Brown asked, "Can you drive?"

I said, "I can. Mama's not in a good mood to drive."

Mr. Brown said, "I'll drive you home. Then, we can help get Orlando out of jail."

Mama asked, "How will we get him out of jail?"

Mr. Brown said, "He'll need a damn good lawyer."

I said, "Dr. Wilson has friends at the Webster and Cunningham Law Firm. If I call him, I'm sure he can get a good lawyer to represent Daddy."

Mr. Brown drove us back to West Boulevard. Then, I called Dr. Wilson and told him what happened to my dad.

Dr. Wilson exclaimed, "I'm so sorry about what has happened to your father, Hatima! I'll call my friends at Webster and Cunningham and make sure your dad has the best lawyer in LA!"

I called Detective Crawford and told her what happened to Daddy.

She said, "I'll look into this and try to help your father."

Then, Mr. Brown picked up the phone, dialed a number, waited for someone to answer, and said, "Doc Murray? It's Oscar Brown, owner of the Crenshaw garage. Brother Orlando Parker has been brutalized and racially profiled. We may need your help to get him out."

Later, there was a knock at the door. I opened it and saw Dr. Wilson standing next to a Black man about an inch taller than him.

Dr. Wilson said, "Hatima Parker, I'd like you to meet Mister Henry Caldwell, attorney-at-law."

I replied, "Welcome, Mister Caldwell. Please, come in."

Dr. Wilson and Mr. Caldwell sat on the couch.

There was another knock on the door. I opened it, and Dr. Murray came into our house. He said, "This is a calamity! Racial profiling is a sin that too few care about! But don't worry, Sister Parker and Sister Hatima. I called up some Black cops I know and asked for information about Brother Parker. They told me his crimes are resisting arrest and assaulting police officers."

I said, "That's a goddamn lie!"

Dr. Murray exclaimed, "Don't use the Lord's name in vain, young lady! *We* know they're lying, but the other cops and the justice system probably don't think they are. Don't worry, the AME church will move mountains to make sure your daddy's set free."

Then, Dr. Murray sat on the couch, and Mama offered our guests cookies and lemonade. The reverend, the doctor, and the lawyer all introduced themselves to each other.

Dr. Murray asked Dr. Wilson, "Where did you study?"

Dr. Wilson said, "I got my undergrad degree and MD at Freeman University. I moved to LA to complete my residency at the UCLA Medical Center."

Dr. Murray asked Mr. Caldwell, "Where did you study?"

Mr. Caldwell stated, "I got my bachelor's degree at Howard and my law degree at the University of Chicago."

Dr. Murray said, "Very impressive."

Mr. Caldwell asked Dr. Murray, "Where did you study, Doctor Murray?"

Dr. Murray stated, "I got my B.A. in history at Florida A and M University. Then, I got my PhD in religion at the Claremont School of Theology."

Mr. Caldwell said, "Very impressive. I've read in the papers about the projects you've created to improve the ghettos of LA. It's very admirable work."

Mr. Caldwell didn't say ghetto like it was a dirty word. My instincts told me he was cool.

Dr. Murray asked, "Do you provide free legal aid for those less fortunate?"

Mr. Caldwell said, "Of course I do! Webster and Cunningham may charge hundreds of bucks an hour, but I haven't forgotten my roots. I grew up on the mean streets of North Philly, but I decided to make a difference through the law. I told myself that when I became a lawyer, I would offer free legal aid to those who can't afford good lawyers. So, I'll be more than happy to represent Mister Orlando Parker, and it won't cost anyone a dime."

The phone rang, and I answered it.

Detective Crawford said, "It's me again. Officer Greene may not be able to get your dad incarcerated for any gang-related crimes, but he claims your dad assaulted him and his partner and resisted arrest."

I shouted, "That's bullshit, Detective Crawford!"

Detective Crawford said, "I know it is, Hatima! But I outrank Officer Greene, and I can help release your dad. Plus, a lot of the uniformed officers are not the sharpest swords in the armory. They've tried to charge innocent Blacks with bogus crimes like this, and Officer Green has done it plenty of times. He hasn't always been successful. So, there's still hope."

I asked, "What can we do?"

Detective Crawford explained, "Bring in pay stubs, tax receipts, anything that can prove your father works a legit job."

I told everyone what Detective Crawford said.

Detective Crawford said, "Hatima, I'll work hard to make sure Officer Greene and Officer Wayne aren't allowed back on the streets."

Then, Dr. Murray said, "I also requested for an emergency message on the radio to be sent. The message asks for any member of the congregation who is able to come to First AME this evening. We're going to do a Saturday morning march."

I asked, "You expect people to march on a Saturday morning?"

Dr. Murray stated, "There are better ways to spend Saturdays than on a couch watching cartoons."

I stated, "*I* don't have a problem with the march, but some other kids may not be interested in something that threatens their Saturday mornings."

Dr. Murray said, "Child and teenage activists in the fifties and sixties didn't mind making sacrifices for the greater good. That's the problem with kids today. Y'all need to sort out your priorities."

That night, Black people of all ages showed up for the emergency meeting. Grandma received a ride to West Boulevard from Watts from a neighbor. She was also boiling mad. There was enough anger on our street to burn down Crenshaw.

Grandma said, "So help me, Jesus. Those corrupt cops better hope I don't get my hands on them! This mess has been happening in Mississippi and California and throughout America for too long! No more, I say! No more!"

I drove us to FAME. Mr. Brown had to check his garage, and I promised we would be okay on our own. Dr. Murray went to FAME to prepare for the Friday night sermon. Dr. Wilson and Mr. Caldwell left to do their own business.

At church, Dr. Murray stated in his strong voice, "A member of our congregation, Orlando Parker, has been arrested simply because he's a strong Black man who is related to a felon. Mister Henry Caldwell has agreed to represent Mister Parker and make sure he's released."

Officer Greene stated that he was certain Daddy stole the Ford, forged the vehicle registration, and is a member of the Bloods. Mama called Daddy's co-workers and bosses so that they'll testify that he's a legit employee at the airport. Mr. Caldwell said the cops have forty-eight hours to charge somebody with a crime and the charge has to be backed up with hard evidence. Folks in Crenshaw, starting with Mr. Brown, are also ready to testify that Daddy has never messed with the Bloods or their dirty businesses.

Dr. Murray continued with his speech. "We have protest signs waiting to be painted in. At nine a.m. tomorrow, we will march to the police station. We will show the LAPD that we refuse to be terrorized!"

The congregation shouted out, "That's right!"

Dr. Murray exclaimed, "We've helped build this city's economy! We deserve some respect!"

The congregation replied, "Tell the truth, Doc!"

Dr. Murray concluded, "Blacks live, work, and are educated in this city! We are human beings, but they treat us like animals! No more Rodney Kings or Latasha Harlinses! No more, I say, no more!"

I wasn't sure if it was cool for Dr. Murray to replace the line, "No more beatings!" with "No more Rodney Kings!" or to replace "No more killings!" with "No more Latasha Harlinses!" Rodney King hasn't appeared much in person to talk about his beating. I don't think he wants to be a symbol or an icon. Shoot, since he has a history of drinking and hasn't kicked the habit, I definitely doubt he's gonna become the next Dr. King, Malcolm X, Huey Newton, or Frederick Douglass. But I still think it's important for Rodney King to tell his side of the story so that people won't see this shit from one fucked-up angle.

After Dr. Murray's speech, some people stayed behind to color in the protest signs. I started wondering about the baby boomers a.k.a. the Civil Rights generation. How many times did they paint protest signs in this very church? How many times did they march on the streets of LA? How many stores and businesses did they boycott? How many times were they arrested for civil disobedience?

I started to really wonder if the techniques used to achieve civil rights in the 1950s and 1960s would work in the 1990s. I mean, the boycott has had a few successes but most Koreans are still here disrespecting our people. Obviously, Dr. King's dream hasn't been achieved and the BPP's Ten-Point Platform isn't as well-respected as the Ten Commandments since all this BS is still happening.

What about Uncle Alonzo, Malik, the Bloods, the Crips, and other gangbangers? Do they not care that they have become traitors to their people? Do they not care that they have become part of the problem instead of the solution? Dr. King, Malcolm X, the BPP, Frederick Douglass, Marcus Garvey, Booker T., and Dr. Du Bois stated that we all have to stick together in order to achieve freedom. Unfortunately, the gangbangers don't even know what that means.

I woke up at seven o'clock the next morning. I didn't feel sleepy, just sick to my stomach. I used my bathroom, brushed my teeth, and took a shower. But when I looked at myself in the mirror, I thought about Michael Jackson's No. 1 hit, "Man in the Mirror." The girl in my mirror wants to be a Marine and an Africanist. Was Officer Greene a Marine or in any other branch of the US Armed Forces? Was he taught to protect the helpless but decided bullying the helpless was more fulfilling? The Marines are supposed to protect the American Way in order to ensure our future, but was Officer Greene's American Way what I was supposed to be fighting for? Was Officer Greene's racist ways why he was considered the right recruit for law enforcement?

I went back to my bedroom, put cream on my body, brushed my cornrows, put on a Black Panther Free Breakfast t-shirt and jeans, and went to the kitchen. I poured some milk and cornflakes in a bowl, but I didn't bother heating up the milk. The milk was cold but that matched the temperature of the rest of my body. Mama soon joined me for breakfast, and I could tell she had been crying. The only times she sleeps alone is when Daddy is working a late shift at the airport. I bet Mama prayed to God that she wouldn't suffer the same heartbreak as Grandma – the pain of not having a man because the world has worked so hard to break apart Black families.

Grandma soon joined us. She saw our sad faces and said, "Don't give up before the battle's over. Orlando needs our help to get him out of jail. We're gonna offer our prayers to Jesus and pray for mercy. Understand?"

I glumly said, "Yeah, understood."

Mama nodded but said nothing.

Later, Mr. Brown showed up and said, "We gotta get to the church on time in order to take part in the march."

The march! I wonder how many times that was said in the 1950s and 1960s. How much hope did the baby boomers have that the world would change? Does America of today look any different from the America of yesterday?

Mister Brown drove us to church in his car, a classic 1964 blue Cadillac Coupe DeVille. Mama and I went to the church basement and picked up two protest signs. Mama's sign said, "FREEDOM FOR ALL!" My sign said, "LAPD, WE DON'T WANT BRUTALITY!" Our destination was the LAPD – Southwest Community Police Station, the same place where I gave a statement against the Crips who killed Devin.

Someone tapped me on my shoulder, and I saw that it was Joshua and his dad!

I exclaimed, "Joshua and Mister Yang, what are you two doing here?"

Joshua said, "Dad and I heard about this march over the radio last night. We decided to come here and help."

Mr. Yang stated, "Joshua believes it's about time Koreans showed sympathy to the plight of our Black customers. You seem like a nice young lady, Hatima, and Joshua says your parents are good people."

People stared in wonder at the Yangs. I'm sure they were wondering what Koreans were doing in a Black church. I, for one, thought Mr. Yang was doing this to create positive PR for his Watts store and the Crenshaw Laundromat, but I decided not to be too picky.

Since everyone was staring at us, I proudly announced, "This is my boyfriend, Joshua Yang. His dad, Mr. Yang, is the new owner of the Crenshaw Laundromat. They both agree that the way cops and Koreans treat Blacks is despicable. They want to do their part to fix our messed-up world."

This was the first time Grandma saw Joshua. She just humphed and refused to talk to the Yangs. Yep, dating a Korean boy is just as bad as dating a White boy.

Mama, Grandma, Joshua, Mr. Yang, Dr. Murray, about thirty other people, and I all marched to the police station. The walk took over forty minutes, and every step counted. Every step we walked took us closer to bringing Daddy home.

When we got to the police station, all the protestors chanted, "LAPD, we don't want brutality!"

If the LAPD can't find any hard evidence by tomorrow afternoon, they would have to release Daddy.

We all stood there for hours, waiting for any of the cops to talk to us. The cops had formed a perimeter around the police station. They had all their guns, batons, and helmets. Master Shin would say this isn't a fair fight because the cops are armed while the protestors aren't. I think Dr. King faced bigotry without guns, knives, and other weapons to prove that armed conflicts aren't the only ways to solve the world's problems. I read in some books that Gandhi – since all I know about him is that he helped liberate India from British rule and that he inspired Dr. King – was non-violent. Gandhi stated that it was important for the oppressed to rise above their oppressors' anger, not to add fuel to it. If Blacks back in the 1950s and 1960s faced the KKK with guns and knives, it just would have added more fuel to the fire. But when they were non-violent, it was obvious to everyone who read the papers or watched the news that there was no need to attack the protestors. Perhaps the cops were justified in arresting Blacks back then because Jim Crow laws were still legal and Blacks entering White areas was illegal, but there was no need for cops to fire hoses and sic dogs on protestors, especially the kids. Will the LAPD fire their weapons on us? Will they even be arrested for it?

We stayed there for hours until lunchtime. Then, we dispersed to go get something to eat.

The next day, after service, we marched again. In the afternoon, Detective Crawford and Mr. Caldwell came out with Daddy. We all cheered! When Daddy saw me and Mama, he immediately ran to us and hugged us.

Detective Crawford came to us and said, "All your friends and neighbors testified that Mister Parker never associated with the Bloods because he hated his brother's business. Oscar Brown also testified that Mister Parker neither assaulted Officers Greene and Wayne nor did he resist arrest. His co-workers and bosses at the airport vouched for him, and those tax returns and pay stubs helped as well. The detectives who are trying to take down the Bloods and Blues stated that they had never seen Orlando near any gang-related crime scenes. They have case files with several gangsters in them, and your father is not on the list. With no evidence to convict him, your father was released. Officers Greene and Wayne have been suspended for a month. After their suspension, they'll be demoted to filing records. It'll probably be safer for them if they never set foot in Crenshaw."

I asked, "Shouldn't they be fired for their incompetence?"

Detective Crawford said, "My superiors think that would be too harsh a punishment. Baby steps, Hatima, baby steps."

You win some, you lose some.

chapter sixteen

After Daddy came home, he seemed happy, sad, and angry all at once. When we got home, Daddy gave me some money to go to a movie and get a pizza afterwards. He told me to stay out as late as I wanted. I went out the door but snuck over to my parents' bedroom window. They had turned on some music, but it didn't completely drown out the other noises in there.

Later, I told Daddy my thoughts about my dream.

I stated, "I'm not sure I wanna be a Marine anymore."

Daddy gestured for me to sit at the dining table. Then he said, "Explain."

I said, "In *Boyz n the Hood*, Tre's father, Furious Styles, fought in Vietnam, but he must believe he wasted his time because he told his son to never join the Army. Furious says a Black man has no place in the White man's Army."

Daddy said, "Good thing you're joining the Marines, not the Army."

I laughed a little and said, "Come on, Daddy, I'm being serious. Point number six of the BPP's Ten-Point Platform states, 'We want all Black men to be exempt from military service. We believe that Black people should not be forced to fight in the military service to defend a racist government that does not protect us. We will not fight and kill other people of color in the world who, like Black people, are being victimized by the White racist government of America. We will protect ourselves from the force and violence of the racist police and the racist military by whatever means necessary.' Grandpa fought the Axis powers in the Pacific, but his reward was the continuation of being a victim of Florida's and LA's racist system. You fought in Vietnam and the cops treat you like a criminal instead of as a war hero. If I fight for the Marines, bigots will still treat me like I'm worthless."

Daddy asked, "True, but why do you think your grandfather and I fought with the Marines? Do you think we were seeking eternal glory? Do you think we thought Blacks fighting and dying for their country might be a small step toward racial equality?"

I replied, "The bravery exhibited by Blacks during World War Two led to President Harry Truman desegregating the Armed Forces in nineteen-forty-eight. President Richard Nixon decreased the number of young men drafted to fight in Vietnam. But what about today? A lot of cops were in the Armed Forces before joining the police force. A lot of them were in the Army but some were Marines. Was Officer Greene a Marine?"

Daddy said, "As a matter of fact, yes. Officer Crawford said he was a Marine during the Lebanese Crisis in the early eighties. After he was discharged, he joined the LAPD."

I asked, "Did he promote the American Way in Lebanon? Did he protect the American Way on the streets of Crenshaw?"

Daddy grabbed my shoulder and said, "Hold on, baby girl. Officer Greene is an example of a bad Marine. He didn't honor any codes except his own personal one. Detective Crawford did a further investigation into his past. He was a bully when he was a kid. He always enjoyed beating up other kids, especially Asians, Latinos, and Blacks. Detective Crawford says that if the Marine Corps knew about that, they never would have let him join. Detective Crawford said the LAPD needs to screen new applicants better, do thorough investigations into their pasts and backgrounds to see if they truly believe in the American Way. But just because Officer Greene was a bad Marine, doesn't mean all Marines are bad. Just because Officer Greene was a bad Marine, doesn't mean you won't be a great one. Remember your name means 'fate.' Only you and God have the power to determine who and what you're gonna be. Understood?"

I nodded and Daddy hugged me.

Soon, January ended, and February started. February is my favorite month 'cause it's Black History Month. As a future Africanist and an African American teenage girl, I feel obligated to explain the history of this hallowed month. Carter G. Woodson declared in 1926 that the second week of February would be Negro History Week. This week coincides with the birthdays of Abe Lincoln and Frederick Douglass, two men who did their part to bring liberty to Blacks. In 1976, the USA's Bicentennial, Negro History Week was expanded into Black History Month – thanks to President Gerald Ford.

Grandma, Mama, and Daddy said their teachers always assigned Negro History Presentations for that week when they were kids. Grandma did her reports on the antebellum South's slavery system: cash crops, house slaves versus field slaves, successful and failed attempts at running away, et cetera. Mama always did her report on Black women, including Harriet Tubman, Sojourner Truth, Ida B. Wells, and Bessie Coleman. Daddy did his reports on Caribbean history and famous Afro-Caribbeans, including Toussaint Louverture and the Haitian Revolution, Harry Belafonte and the evolution of calypso, and the tense political climates in Haiti and Jamaica.

On the second Saturday of February, Joshua and I went to see a movie at Cinemark Baldwin Hills. At this point, I could care less what people said about us behind our backs. No one ever insulted us to our faces 'cause we can kick anybody's butt with ease. We're a power couple, like Ossie Davis and Ruby Dee.

Joshua and I saw *Mississippi Masala*. The movie is about an African American man named Demetrius Williams and an Indian American woman named Mina who fall in love in Mississippi, but their families and friends are against their romance. It turns out that Mina's family is from Uganda, which is in Eastern Africa. The British brought in Asians to help build the railroads and these Asians adopted Uganda as their country. The British did the same thing with Jamaica and other Caribbean islands that were part of their empire. When the Afro-Caribbeans refused to work in the sugarcane fields after slavery was abolished in the British Empire, the British brought in Indians to do the labor as indentured workers. Today, tensions are still high between Afro-Caribbeans and Indo-Caribbeans.

When General Idi Amin became the military dictator of Uganda, he kicked out all the Asians. He believed Africa is only for Black people. I know some African Americans may agree, but I think that's just as racist as saying America is only for White people. The Asians have all contributed to Ugandan society, but Idi Amin thinks it's okay to kick them out simply because they originated on another continent? Where did they plan on going? Mina's father, Jay, was called a bootlicker by his fellow Indians because he and his family chose to stay in Uganda. Do people in foreign countries also insult and degrade emigrants who decide to settle in America, Canada, the UK, and other countries? Did Grandpa's parents' friends insult them for moving to the US instead of staying in the Caribbean? Do Joshua's relatives insult him and his father for staying here in America instead of Korea? *Mississippi Masala* showed how racial minorities treat each other in the US. Demetrius and Mina's romance reminds me of my relationship with Joshua. We have so much in common, but all most people can see are our differences.

At Dorsey High, all the kids in humanities classes were eagerly planning and designing their projects.

Wanda, Imani, Marcus, and I all did research in the school and Baldwin Hills Branch Library. Wanda decided to do her presentation on Reconstruction, its successes and failures, and why its failures led it to being dubbed "an unfinished revolution." The Civil Rights Movement has often been called the Second Reconstruction. I figure if Abe Lincoln wasn't assassinated and his successors, Andrew Johnson, Ulysses S. Grant, and Rutherford B. Hayes, had made good on the promise of forty acres and a mule, maybe a Second Reconstruction wouldn't have been necessary.

Imani's presentation is on Paul R. Williams, a Black architect, who designed many buildings in LA. He designed First AME Church, Second Baptist Church, the Angelus Funeral Home, the 28th Street YMCA, and the Beverly Hills Hotel, among many more buildings. It's hard to imagine what La La Land would look like without Paul R. Williams.

Marcus's presentation is on Black musicians who have broken racial barriers in music. His presentation includes jazz musicians such as Duke Ellington and Ella Fitzgerald, rock 'n' roll musicians such as Chuck Berry and Little Richard, R&B and soul musicians such as James Brown and Motown acts, and pop musicians such as Michael Jackson and Prince.

My presentation is on back-to-Africa movements. I'll start with North America's first back-to-Africa odyssey, the Black Loyalists' exodus from Nova Scotia and their resettlement in the British colony of Sierra Leone. Then, I'll conclude on today's back-to-Africa odysseys, African Americans moving to Ghana.

Personally, I believe Mr. Ngozi has a point. Moving back to Africa may not be the best option since no African country is going to accept millions of Black Americans into their borders. Ghana is the size of a US state, and all the Blacks in the US wouldn't fit in their country. Mr. Ngozi said that despite how much the British and other Europeans developed African nations' infrastructures and economies, Africa is still an impoverished continent. Mr. Ngozi said some parts of Nigeria don't have indoor plumbing and that the electricity is shut off during certain times of the day and night. The quality of electricity that is provided to buildings with power lines is pitiful, according to Mr. Ngozi. Plus, Nigeria's government, along with several other African nations, is comprised of greedy, arrogant, and incompetent fools who don't give a damn about the people they're supposed to lead.

This has me thinking about my favorite fantasy novels and the styles of government in them. A common fantasy cliché is that most magical kingdoms are ruled by monarchies. Some rulers are cool, others are a'ight, while others are as incompetent as Nigeria's military dictators and America's politicians. The Queen of Hearts is a merciless dictator who decapitates people, and she's a classic Disney Villain. The Wizard of Oz hid in a secret room in the Ozian Royal Palace, but he did a bad job of running the country since wicked witches, Khalidahs, and giant spiders caused havoc throughout the land. Narnia has had great rulers and merciless dictators. The White Witch and Lord Miraz were among the worst tyrants Narnia had, but the Pevensie siblings and Caspian were wonderful rulers. I guess it was okay for them to sit on the thrones of Narnia since Aslan

Himself chose them, approved them, and oversaw their coronations. If God says some man or woman will make a great president, then the rest of us should believe Him since God never makes mistakes.

But does this mean that humans can't make the right choices on our own? According to fantasy authors, democracies are just as problematic as some monarchies because the leaders nominated and elected are sometimes incompetent fools? My head is spinning.

Mr. Ngozi scheduled our presentations for the final week of Black History Month. My presentation is on the final day, Friday, the 28th. Since this year is a leap year, that means the next day, February 29th, is Leap Day. But it doesn't matter whether or not it's a leap year because February is always the shortest month of the year. Many Blacks, including Daddy and Mrs. Brooks, think it's an insult to us to have our sacred month for only twenty-eight or twenty-nine days, but I think it's also insulting for people to only think about Black history for one month. People should care about Black history all-year long. I certainly care about it all year; of course, I have to in order to become a successful Africanist.

February is also when a favorite holiday takes place: Valentine's Day. February 14th was on a Friday so that meant I could stay out till ten o'clock at night. Joshua said he had planned a date at a fancy restaurant. At the dojang, he told me to wear a dress because the restaurant had a strict dress code.

I told Joshua, "I don't want you to spend too much money on me."

Joshua said, "Hatima, you are totally worth it. How else am I gonna show you how much I care about you?"

He gave me a cute smile, and I started smiling and giggling.

I said, "Joshua, it's hard for me to say 'no' to you. The only other guy I can't say 'no' to is my daddy."

Joshua asked, "Is your dad one hundred percent okay with us dating?"

I said, "Yeah. You marched with us when he was arrested so that means you're down for the cause."

After Joshua drove me home, I saw Daddy arranging roses in a vase on our dining room table.

Daddy said, "Valentine's Day is the one day a year when a man seeking a courtship can *really* show the woman of his dreams how much he cares about her."

I said, "You mean to tell me that before Valentine's Day, Mama still wasn't giving you the time of day?"

Daddy walked to the couch and sat down; so, I sat down with him. He was gonna tell me about his and Mama's love story, and I always liked to hear it.

Daddy explained, "Your grandmother was hurt real bad by your mama's no-good baby daddy. Plus, other men were nice to her until they saw Suzy Jane. As soon as they saw Flora May already had a kid, *BOOM*, they were out of there faster than Jesse Owens. Your ma had to drop out of school at age sixteen to help your grandma with the bills. Flora May always wanted your mama to get a diploma and a degree 'cause that was the only way Black people who didn't have any musical or athletic talent could move up in the world. But Flora May's salary combined with welfare checks that didn't always come wasn't enough to pay for rent, power, water, gas, food, and second-hand clothing. So, your mama got her waitress job at the Polo Lounge, but she always relaxed on the weekend by going to nightclubs.

I was discharged from the Marines in nineteen-seventy-two after four years of service. I was twenty-one years old and was looking for love. My brother was with the Bloods and was looking for trouble; so, we never hung out again. I was at a club called the Hot Spot drinking a beer when I saw the hottest girl in all of LA. She was tall, fit, and had a great smile. I introduced myself to her, but she told me to leave her alone. I just wanted to get to know her, but she'd already decided that all men were no good based on her daddy and most of the other men in Watts.

I kept pestering her and pestering her until she stopped coming to the Hot Spot. But my boys were able to tell me which club she was hanging at, and I resumed pestering her there. She finally agreed to go on a date with me if I promised to leave her alone for two weeks. We saw *Blacula*, a horror film about an African prince who was turned into a vampire. Horror films are great to watch with women because they usually bury their faces in their dates' chests when they see a scary scene. Your mama wasn't as scared as I thought she would be, but we still had a great time.

After that, your mama warmed up to me. We went on more dates and grew closer, but our Valentine's Day date cinched our bond.

I reserved a table for us at this ritzy Hollywood restaurant. I spared no expense; the money I made from working with the Marines was really paying off. Since your mama figured out that a man wouldn't spend that much money on a woman unless he cared about her, she finally saw that I was serious.

The only obstacle for us to overcome was Flora May. Everybody in South Central knew my brother was stealing, pimping, and killing for the Bloods. Flora May figured I *had* to be with the Bloods too, not because my twin was with them, but because she always wanted to find something wrong with *all* men. But I told Flora May that I had an honest job working at the airport and had saved up cash from my time with the Marines. Then, she started dogging me about *what* exactly I did in Vietnam. She'd heard on the news that some soldiers harassed Vietnam civilians. Yeah, some fools did that but not me. When your grandma couldn't find anything wrong with me, she finally gave me consent to date her daughter.

A few months later I proposed to her, we got married, and you were born in '74."

I've always thanked God for Daddy. Most of my friends don't have fathers. Some fathers that are present in the hood are great parents, but others are not. A lot of girls hope to find men who aren't like their deadbeat dads, but they're usually unlucky. Some boys who grow up without fathers vow to always be there for their future kids, but other boys believe their fathers had the right idea, and that caring about other people, including your own flesh and blood, is a waste of time. Their mantra is "Look out for only yourself."

That's the problem with our world. Too many people care only about themselves. One of the many great things about the people my friends and I are doing our Black History Month projects on is that they all put other people's needs before themselves. The world is a better place because of it – not perfect but better.

I immediately got bad vibes when Joshua and I stepped into the restaurant. The White *maître d'* gave us hard looks; seriously, his face looked like it was made of stone.

The *maître d'* looked Joshua in the eyes and ignored me.

He said, "Welcome, sir. Do you have a reservation?"

Joshua said, "Yes. It's under, 'Joshua Yang.'"

The *maître d'* said, "I'll need to see some ID."

Joshua showed his driver's license. The *maître d'* looked at it and then looked at me.

Joshua explained, "She's my girlfriend."

The *maître d'* stated, "Really? What an unusual sight."

Joshua stated, "Don't insult my girlfriend."

The *maître d'* said, "I apologize. This way, sir and ma'am."

Just because the *maître d'* called me "ma'am" doesn't mean he really sees me as one. What did he think I was gonna do? Shoot everybody and rob the place? I'm wearing a pretty blue dress with my white church shoes. I had my cornrows done at Ms. Esther's Hair Salon and put in some Vaseline to make it look extra nice. Mama even put some makeup on me but not too much – the key to wearing makeup is to give off the illusion that you're not wearing any. But the *maître d'* still thought I was a thug. Just like how Officers Greene and Wayne thought Dr. Wilson was a thug even though he was wearing nice clothes and spoke in a polite manner. No matter what we look like or sound like, all Black people will immediately look like thugs to all bigots.

Dinner was nice. I had never heard of some of the dishes on the menu, but I didn't mind trying new things.

After dinner, Joshua parked his car in a parking lot not too far from the restaurant.

Then he said, "I'm sorry about how that asshole treated you."

I said, "I've learned not to let stuff like that rile me. You have to know when to pick your battles."

Joshua said, "We don't have to ever go back there. I'm not paying any more of my money to bigots."

I said, "Fine by me."

Then, Joshua leaned toward me and kissed me. His left hand stroked my right cheek, and I felt goosebumps. My right hand was around his neck and my left hand was on his right shoulder. He opened his mouth wider and our tongues found each other. As we

French kissed, my left hand strayed down from his shoulder to his shirt. I unbuttoned it and felt his chest. The only other time I had seen Joshua with his shirt off was when we were at the beach; so, I already knew he was muscular. But I had never touched his bare chest before. As I stroked his chest, his hands tried to unzip my dress.

Just then we heard sirens and immediately stopped our make-out session, which would have turned into a car-sex session. We both turned toward the sound and saw two Los Angeles Fire Department fire trucks, two police cars, and two ambulances driving down the street. My guess is there was a fire somewhere in the area and that means there could also be injured or dead people. Cops immediately show up at anyplace where 911 has been dialed, but they only have the authority to do anything if the fire was a result of arson.

Joshua immediately buttoned up his shirt and said, "I'm *soooooo* sorry for getting carried away like that. I would never intentionally try to mess up your life."

I stated, "Just because a girl has sex with her boyfriend doesn't mean her life is ruined."

I zipped up my dress while Joshua said, "You told me that the Naval Academy won't accept you if you're pregnant. Plus, our parents would hound us forever if we slipped up like that."

I exclaimed, "Joshua, I'm not angry at you! We're almost adults and our hormones are raging!"

Joshua asked, "Do you *wanna* have sex? You always seemed adamant about that."

I said, "I've completed most of my application. I also need to complete the interview with a 'blue and gold' officer to ensure my acceptance."

Joshua asked, "Are you planning on having sex if your application gets rejected?"

HEAL THE HOOD

I exclaimed, "What?! I'm not planning on getting a rejection!"

Joshua said, "But you might. The Naval Academy only accepts ten percent of applicants. Your GPA, test scores, and extracurricular activities are great, but you could still get rejected. If you are, does this mean our entire relationship is just a back-up plan?"

I repeated, "A back-up plan?"

Joshua stammered, "Th-th-that may not have come out right—"

I shouted, "You're damn right it didn't! Joshua Yang, this relationship is *not* my back-up plan if my Naval Academy application falls through! My applications to other colleges *are* my back-up plan! *Why* would I treat you as a 'back-up plan'? I love you!"

Joshua asked, "You love me?"

I immediately started blushing. Grandma said I might make a good lawyer if I could control my big mouth a little better.

I said, "Yes, I love you."

Joshua said, "I've loved you since I was ten. None of the other girls I met were as amazing as you. I refused to give up until I asked you out on a date. Now, I can't imagine my life without you in it."

I immediately leaned in and kissed Joshua passionately. He kissed me back, but we didn't try to undress each other. Joshua's Cadillac isn't an ideal place for sex. I've always thought that having sex in cars is tacky and not very private.

On Saturday, I went to shoot hoops at the rec center.

When I took a break, Imani came over and asked me, "How was your date with Joshua?" I told Imani about the racist *maître d'*, and she said, "This is why I can't wait until I'm a doctor. Then, I won't have to deal with racist BS."

I stated, "Imani, I was wearing my best dress and shoes, and I had my hair done. The *maître d'* still thought I was a troublemaker because of my skin color. It doesn't matter what we wear, how we talk, or what we do. Most people will just see as niggers."

Imani exclaimed, "Hatima Gabriella Parker, I don't ever want to hear you using the n-word! We're people, not criminals. You're going to become a fine Marine and Africanist. Besides, look at the Wilsons and the Malones. They're proof of what Black people can accomplish if you work hard enough."

The Malones are Victor and his family. Mr. Malone is the chief financial officer for Capitol Records and Mrs. Malone is a lawyer. Imani and Victor have been dating since November, but Wanda doubts if the relationship will last. Imani and Victor haven't officially called themselves boyfriend and girlfriend. Judging by the way those Jack and Jill folks looked at me and my girls, I know they think that we're inferior to them. Victor hasn't even *told* his parents about him and Imani dating. I guess they won't approve because Imani is from the ghetto, while the Malones are from Holmby Hills. I can't believe those bougie folks judge people by where they come from instead of where they're planning on going. Imani is a straight-A student and plans on becoming a doctor. Everyone knows being a doctor ain't no easy goal.

I asked Imani, "When is Victor gonna tell his folks you two are dating?"

Imani replied, "He promised he'd tell them soon."

I stated, "That's what he said three months ago."

Imani snapped, "What's *that* supposed to mean?"

I explained, "It seems to me Victor is almost ashamed of dating a hood girl. He knows his parents will think he's lowering himself or something."

Imani exclaimed, "I can't believe you just said that!"

I stated, "Why don't I just drive you to Holmby Hills and see what the Malones have to say?"

Imani asked, "Do you have access to your daddy's car?"

I said, "Yeah, he has the day off."

We went back to my house, and I asked Daddy if I could borrow the Ford. He asked why. I explained that Imani and I were gonna visit her boyfriend's family in Holmby Hills.

Daddy repeated, "Holmby Hills?"

I said, "Yeah. Imani met him when we first visited the Jack and Jill folks back in November."

Daddy gave me the car keys and said, "Don't get into trouble."

I got into the driver's side, and Imani got into the passenger's side of the car.

I asked Imani where the Malones lived and she said, "Two-Six-One Baroda Drive. I'll point out the house when we get there."

The drive from West Boulevard to Baroda Drive took less than twenty minutes. Baroda Drive is a mega-mansion neighborhood, which means it's a big step up from Westwood and a *huge* step from Crenshaw. Imani pointed out the house, and I parked the Ford.

We got out, walked up to the gates, and I pressed the intercom.

Imani said, "They might not be home. Maybe we better leave."

I asked, "Are the Malones working today?"

Imani said, "No."

I said, "Then they must be home. If you wanna be a success in this world, ya gotta stand up for yourself."

A British voice spoke through the intercom and asked, "Who is it?"

Imani said, "Imani Fitzpatrick and Hatima Parker. I'm dating Victor, and I was hoping I could finally meet his family."

The British voice said, "Come in."

The gates opened automatically, and we walked in. All I could think was, *Damn!* The Malones' mansion is *huge!* Three families can easily live here.

Imani and I walked across the pathway, and a White man wearing a suit and bowtie was standing outside the house.

He said, "Welcome, Miss Fitzpatrick and Miss Parker. I'm Frederick Redmond, the Malones' butler."

I stuck out my hand and said, "Pleasure to meet you, Mister Redmond." I thought, *A Black family with a White butler! That is what I call progress!*

Mr. Redmond said, "You can just call me Frederick. I'm a servant in this household."

I asked, "Can we call you Freddy?"

Frederick stated, "No, Frederick is fine."

I said, "Okay, Frederick."

Imani asked, "Are the Malones in?"

Frederick said, "Yes, I'll tell them you're here."

The mansion was even bigger on the inside! The living room was *waaaaay* bigger than my family's living room. The furniture also looked expensive. The furniture in my house is mostly second-hand and shabby.

Frederick said, "You ladies can sit down here while I get Mister and Missus Malone."

We sat down on the couch; I'm sure it cost at least ten grand.

Then Imani said, "When I'm a doctor, I'll have a house just like this one."

I stated, "Doctors make six-figure salaries, not seven or eight figures. When you become a doctor, you'll most likely get a house like the Wilsons' Westwood home or a house in Leimert Park or View Park-Windsor Hills. You'd need to study business and move up the corporate ladder to get a mansion like this."

A Black man as tall as my dad walked in followed by a Black woman as tall as me.

I stood up, stuck out my hand, and said, "Good day, Mister and Missus Malone. I'm Hatima Parker and this is my friend, Imani Fitzpatrick."

They shook our hands.

Mr. Malone said, "Hatima is Swahili for 'fate.' Imani is Swahili for 'faith.'"

I exclaimed, "A lot of people know what Imani's name means because it's the seventh principle of Kwanzaa! But *a lotta* people don't know what my name means!"

Mr. Malone explained, "I'm fluent in Swahili, so I'm knowledgeable about the names in the language family."

They sat down in chairs across from us, and Mr. Malone asked, "Who are you two, and why are you here?"

Imani explained, "I'm dating your son, Victor."

Mrs. Malone said, "Victor never told us about you. Do you live in Holmby Hills?"

Imani said, "No. Hatima and I live in Crenshaw."

Mrs. Malone repeated, "Crenshaw."

She didn't say "Crenshaw" like it was a poisonous word, but there was no emotion when she said it. Does that mean she thinks our hood means absolutely nothing?

Mr. Malone asked, "What do your parents do for a living?"

Imani said, "My mom is a maid at the Beverly Hilton, my brother owns a gas station and convenience store in Crenshaw, and I work as a cashier at the Fox Hills Mall food court."

Mrs. Malone asked, "What about your father?"

Imani said, "My father and my brother's father aren't part of our lives."

Mr. Malone asked, "What are your future aspirations?"

Imani stated, "I want to be a pediatrician."

They nodded their heads in approval.

Mrs. Malone asked, "Which schools have you applied to?"

Imani said, "Stanford, UC Davis, LAMU, Freeman, and Howard."

Mr. Malone asked, "How long have you and Victor been dating?"

Imani said, "Since November."

I immediately cut in and said, "They weren't sure you'd approve of their relationship because Imani is from the hood, and y'all live in the Hills. But Imani is the smartest girl in our class. She's set to become valedictorian and receive affirmative replies from the schools she's applied to."

Mrs. Malone said, "I don't see any reason why you and our son can't keep dating. You seem like a fine young lady."

Imani breathed out a sigh of relief and said, "Thank you."

Then, Mrs. Malone asked me, "Hatima, what are your future aspirations?"

I stated, "I wanna be a Marine and an Africanist. I've applied to the US Naval Academy and just need to do an interview before I learn whether or not I'll be accepted. But I've applied to other colleges with great Africana programs: LAMU, Freeman, Howard, UC Davis, WashU, and Vanderbilt."

Mr. and Mrs. Malone both nodded in approval.

Then, Mr. Malone asked, "What do your parents do for a living?"

I stated, "My dad is a baggage handler at the airport, and my mom is a waitress at the Polo Lounge at the Beverly Hills Hotel."

Mrs. Malone said, "The US Naval Academy has an excellent academic program and a low acceptance rate. It's like the Ivy League except for all the uniformed officers and lessons in the art of war."

Mr. and Mrs. Malone laughed.

HEAL THE HOOD

I asked, "If y'all live in such a big house, how come Victor isn't in a private school?"

Mr. Malone explained, "Private schools are all full of spoiled rich kids, and they're predominantly White. University High has a diverse student population and excellent academics. We believe our kids would learn more about the real world in a public school than a private school."

I said, "That reminds me of what people say about the hood and the Hills. They say South Central is the real world and the Hills is a fake dream world."

Mrs. Malone said, "What's real about life is *what* you choose to do and *who* you choose to do it for."

Mr. Malone asked Imani, "Imani, do you want to be a pediatrician because you care about kids or you care about money? Do you care about the high praise doctors get or the importance of saving human lives?"

Imani scrunched her face in thought and said, "I always wanted to be a doctor because they seem to hold the greatest power over human life after God. The money is something extra. But my brother and I have gone to bed hungry, our clothes have been bleached from too many washings, and we often share our apartment with rats. Being rich seems like the best ticket out of that kind of life."

I cut in and said, "Yeah, but my parents aren't rich, and we're doing alright. We have a TV, a Betamax, a stereo, lots of food, nice clothes, et cetera."

Imani said, "Yeah, y'all aren't rich, but you're still doing better than my family."

I tried to ease any resentment Imani might have against me and my parents by saying, "We still live in the hood and *I'm* the only member who has a chance of getting out. But getting a six-figure salary isn't the only way to the good life."

Just then Victor came into the living room. When he saw us, he exclaimed, "Imani! Hatima! What are y'all doing here?"

From the way he sounded and the look on his face, you would think we saw him bare-butt naked.

I explained, "Imani thought it was high time your parents knew about your romance. They're okay with it."

Victor sighed in relief and said, "Cool."

My sixth sense still goes off when I'm around bougie folks.

In the final week of February, we gave our presentations. For my presentation, I had a poster of pictures and typed words that detailed the founding of Sierra Leone, the founding of Liberia, the life of Marcus Garvey, and the McDaniel family. I explained that the Black Loyalists left Nova Scotia and New Brunswick for Sierra Leone because they were angry at the conditions under which they lived in the soon-to-be Canadian provinces, but when they got to Sierra Leone, they still weren't allowed to govern their own affairs. The Sierra Leone Creole people settled in Freetown, and their culture is a mix of American, British, and African cultures and values. The Creole people held prominent leadership positions in Sierra Leone until the end of colonialism. Dissatisfaction with the way the country was run led to military coups that started in the late 1960s, and this led to a chain reaction that resulted in the Sierra Leone Civil War, which started almost a year ago.

Liberia is the only country in Africa that was colonized by the United States. The American Colonization Society believed free African Americans would be better off in Africa than the USA. Slavers and advocates of slavery feared free Blacks because of the hope they represented for slaves; but if all free Blacks moved to Africa, there would be little chance of slaves revolting. Unfortunately, the Americo-Liberians set up a political and economic system like the only one they knew – the antebellum South. The Americo-Liberians ran wealthy plantations and businesses and exercised overwhelming political power over Liberia's other tribes. The Americo-Liberians considered themselves superior to the indigenous Africans, the way White people see themselves as superior to Blacks. Stella Wilson has *a lot* in common with the Americo-Liberians, in my opinion. But things went downhill when a military coup led by Master Sergeant Samuel Doe of the Krahn Tribe overthrew and killed President William Richard Tolbert Jr. Future elections were viewed as fraudulent and now Liberia is fighting a civil war – the African continent seems to have *a lotta* coups and civil wars. But Liberia is still a source of pride for many Blacks across the world. Liberia was the first African colony to declare independence, which makes it Africa's first and oldest republic. It even managed to stay independent during the Scramble for Africa, showing that the Europeans respected the sovereign nation. Liberia was also a founding member of the League of Nations, the United Nations, and the Organization of African Unity.

When Marcus Garvey founded Pan-Africanism, he urged Blacks in the Caribbean, North and South America, and Europe to move back to Africa because that's where our roots are. Pan-Africanism inspired the Black Power Movement, so the Nation of Islam and the Black Panthers also supported Pan-Africanism. As mentioned before, Dr. W. E. B. Du Bois, Dr. Maulana Karenga, Fela Kuti, Kwame Nkrumah, et cetera are also proponents of Pan-Africanism. Pan-Africanism can be seen today in the worldwide support Black people are giving to the Blacks of South Africa. I wonder if Nelson

Mandela will become an official proponent of Pan-Africanism.

I then explained how, in the present day, plenty of Black Americans have decided to move back to Africa, including the McDaniels. Dr. McDaniel found it hard to get tenure at the universities he worked at, and Mrs. McDaniel stated that she kept being passed over for promotions at the brokerage firm she worked at. Before that, the McDaniels faced plenty of racism in the Ivy League because many students and teachers believed they didn't belong there. They were upset at how racism was still a problem in American society so they decided to move to a place where they wouldn't have to worry about that: the Republic of Ghana. Dr. McDaniel teaches at the University of Ghana and his wife helped found the Ghana Stock Exchange. They said they're happy living in a country where everyone looks like them and they're glad that their kids won't have to face the same prejudice they did. But Ghana's educational system is nowhere near the same level as the USA so the McDaniel kids will most likely come to the US to get their degrees. Plus, the political climate is still tense so a lotta Ghanaians are emigrating and resettling in the West. This shows that it's more common in the present day for Africans to leave the African continent, not the other way around.

I concluded my presentation by telling my classmates, "Outside of Africa and the Caribbean, Blacks will almost always face racism in one form or another. Running away from our problems may seem cowardly but these Black Exodusters weren't really running away *from* their problems. They chose to leave the Americas because they believed they could make a difference in the land of our ancestors. What about you? Do you wanna move back to Africa or stay here in the USA? Which places in the world can you make the most difference?"

As for the other presentations, some weren't very original, in my opinion. One guy compared the Jim Crow system to apartheid – like no one on Earth has already figured out that Dixieland and South Africa have so much in common or that the USA is just as corrupt as some African nations. Another girl compared and contrasted Martin Luther King and Malcolm X – which people have been doing since the 1960s.

Some were great, and I'm not just talking about my friends'. One girl talked about the three NAACP National Conventions that were held at Second Baptist Church in 1928, 1942, and 1949.

Another guy compared Frederick Douglass's newspaper, *The North Star*; Ida B. Wells's newspaper, *The Chicago Conservator*; and LA's very own Black newspaper, the *Los Angeles Sentinel*. Frederick Douglass used his newspaper to preach against slavery; Ida B. Wells' newspaper documented lynchings; and, in the present day, the *LA Sentinel* has documented slum lords, lack of affirmative action, police brutality, et cetera.

The one I liked best besides my friends' presentations was Raquel Curtis' presentation called "Am I Next?" On her poster she had pictures of Emmett Till before and after his death, the four girls killed in the Sixteenth Street Baptist Church bombing, Johnny Robinson and Virgil Ware, James Powell, Matthew Johnson Jr., Bobby Hutton, Edmund Perry, Yusuf Hawkins, Latasha Harlins, and Gavin Cato.

Raquel told us in detail about their deaths.

James Powell was a fifteen-year-old Black boy who was shot and killed by New York Police Department (NYPD) officer, Lieutenant Thomas Gilligan, in Harlem on July 16, 1964, two weeks after President Lyndon B. Johnson signed the Civil Rights Act. His death sparked riots in Harlem, Manhattan and Bed-Stuy, Brooklyn, but a grand jury decided not to indict Lieutenant Gilligan for murdering James Powell.

Matthew "Peanut" Johnson was a seventeen-year-old Black boy who was killed by Officer Alvin Johnson – whose ancestors might have owned Matthew's ancestors during slavery – in San Francisco on September 27, 1966. Matthew Johnson was joyriding in a stolen car with two other guys. After their car stalled, the three teens ran from the cops, but Officer Alvin Johnson chased Matthew Johnson and yelled, "Stop! Hold it, or I'm going to shoot!"

Matthew Johnson kept running, and Officer Alvin Johnson shot Matthew Johnson four times and killed him almost instantly. His death sparked the Hunters Point Uprising, but a coroner's jury ruled about a month later that Officer Alvin Johnson committed "justifiable homicide."

Edmund Perry was a seventeen-year-old Black boy who was shot and killed on June 12, 1985 by an NYPD officer named Lee Van Houten because Edmund Perry and his brother, Jonah Perry, jumped the cop and beat him. Even though Edmund Perry was unarmed when he was beating the cop, some people still thought his death was justified. Others didn't think Edmund Perry's death was justified, not just because he was unarmed, but because he was an honors student at a bougie prep school and was set to attend college on a scholarship. Edmund Perry's death is the inspiration for Michael Jackson's hit song and music video, "Bad." Some kids in the hood understand the song and the music video's message: "Don't give in to peer pressure. You don't need to be tough and cold to be considered down for the hood; you can always walk away." Officer Van Houten was cleared of any culpability in Edmund Perry's murder.

Gavin Cato was a seven-year-old Black boy from Brooklyn who was struck and killed by a car driven by a Jewish man named Yosef Lifsh on August 19, last year. His car was part of a motorcade for Rabbi Menachem Mendel Schneerson, a Hasidic Jewish leader.

HEAL THE HOOD

Gavin Cato's death sparked the Crown Heights Riots last summer. My friends and family all watched the news, hoping Yosef Lifsch would face punishment for taking the life of a boy who never reached double digit birthdays, but the grand jury saw no reason to indict Yosef Lifsch.

Society saw them as monsters, as savages, as troublemakers, as threats that needed to be eliminated. Apart from Bobby Hutton, who was holding a gun in the photo, and Emmett Till's mutilated corpse, the others looked like sweet and lovable kids.

Raquel said, "There are no more birthdays, graduations, or weddings for these kids. There may not be tomorrows for us either. When all these kids were killed between 1955 and 1991, Black kids across the USA asked, 'Am I next?' We don't have to become murder statistics. We have to show the world that we aren't monsters. We have to show the world that we are people who deserve life, liberty, and the pursuit of happiness."

I started applauding, and everyone joined in. The applause grew louder, and I exclaimed, "Preach the truth, my sister!"

Chapter Seventeen

In March, my scheduled interview with a blue and gold officer took place. My interviewer was Major Davis.

When Major Davis walked into my home, I saw he was a Black man who looked like he was in his mid-forties. He wore a blue dress uniform with a white cap. The uniform had a lot of medals on it, and I wondered how many people he killed or saved to earn those medals.

I was wearing black slacks and a white blouse; Daddy told Mama that no Marine officer would be able to take me seriously if I wore a dress.

Major Davis looked at me and asked, "Hatima Gabriella Parker?"

I said, "That's me, sir."

I stuck out my right hand, and he shook it firmly.

Major Davis asked, "Does your first name have a meaning?"

I said, "Yes, it means 'fate' in Swahili."

Major Davis said, "How nice."

I led him to the couch, and we sat at opposite ends of the couch.

Mama set down a tray of lemonade and cookies and asked Major Davis, "Would you like to eat or drink anything else?"

Major Davis said, "No, Missus Parker. This looks just fine."

Mama's smile looked too big for her face. I guess Mrs. Brooks' face looked the same way when college recruiters interviewed Andre.

Major Davis took off his hat, set it on the table, and the interview commenced.

Major Davis asked me, "Why do you wish to attend a service academy?"

I replied, "My dad was a Marine and so was his dad. In fact, my grandfather, Gabriel Parker, was a Montford Point Marine. They were the first Black Marines in the Armed Forces, but I'm guessing you already knew that."

Major Davis said, "I did."

Then, I added, "Not a lot of kids in South Central go to college. At the Naval Academy I wouldn't just have the chance to train as a Marine, but I'd also receive a quality education that's as good as the Ivy League."

He asked me a whole bunch of questions. There were a lot, but these were the ones that stood out.

Major Davis asked, "When did you first develop an interest in attending a military academy?"

I said, "I wanted to become a Marine, but my parents and grandmother wanted me to go to college. Attending the Naval Academy seemed like the perfect compromise."

"Are you financially able to attend other colleges?"

"I've applied to Freeman, Howard, LAMU, UC Davis, WashU, and Vanderbilt. I've received affirmative replies from Freeman, Howard, LAMU, and Vanderbilt but I've received no replies from UC Davis and WashU. They're most likely still scanning my application among many others. Since I have a high GPA and scored high on the SAT and ACT, I don't think I'll have any problems getting scholarships and grants. But, just in case, my parents have promised to pay part of my tuition, and I also let the schools I applied to know I may need on-campus jobs to earn extra cash for other necessities, such as public transit."

"What are your parents' occupations?"

"My dad is a baggage handler at the LA International Airport, and my mom works as a waitress at the Beverly Hills Hotel's Polo Lounge."

"What grades have you received during your high school career?"

"I get As and A-pluses in English, French, history, geography, and other humanities subjects. I received A-minuses in math and science."

"Do you give back to your community?"

"I told you about my daily schedule. I help train kids, including Black kids from South Central, in hapkido because martial arts teaches many valuable skills. Kids are taught to use violence as a last resort and that there are better ways to resolve problems than with a gun. I also talked to Doctor Cecil Murray, the senior pastor of First African Methodist Episcopal Church, about organizing boycotts against Korean businesses that don't treat Blacks with respect. I also give advice to kids at the rec center when I go there to play ball."

"Do you have any outstanding achievements you'd like to share?"

"I've competed and won several martial arts tournaments. I'm also a member of the Dorsey High softball team. We haven't won a state championship, but we've done well."

"A background check into your medical history has shown that you suffered a bullet wound in your left shoulder. Will this injury impair you from fully participating at the Naval Academy?"

"No. My shoulder feels fine, and I can still write, fight, and play softball."

"Further investigation into your background has shown that

your uncle, Alonzo Parker, is on death row at San Quentin for first-degree murder and your cousin, Malik Parker, is incarcerated at Central Juvenile Hall for breaking and entering and grand theft. Were you ever involved with any of your uncle's or cousin's criminal schemes?"

"No. My dad forbade me from talking to them, but Malik always struck a conversation with me when he was in Crenshaw. I tried to talk him out of staying with the Bloods, but he didn't listen. Plus, the Crip who shot me was aiming at my cousin and another boy, Devin Williams. Malik and I survived, but Devin was killed. Lots of innocent people are caught in the crossfire of senseless gang wars in South Central."

When the interview was completed about an hour later, Major Davis shook my hand vigorously and said, "Ms. Parker, you have wonderful grades, a perfect score on the verbal section of the SAT, and you participate in impressive extracurricular activities. I think you will be a valuable asset to the Naval Academy and the United States Marine Corps."

I gave Major Davis a huge smile and exclaimed, "Thank you so much, sir! You're helping me achieve my dream, and I'm so happy you gave me a chance!"

Mama and Daddy shook Major Davis' hand as well and thanked him for stopping by. Then, he put on his hat, said goodbye, and left.

Daddy said, "We should keep our fingers crossed."

Mama said, "We should offer prayers to Jesus. It's because of Him that Hatima has made it this far."

Daddy said, "I can't believe my baby girl is graduating from high school in a few months. She's gonna get the one thing we wanted to get but were unable to."

I walked over to the Brookses' house to tell them the good news. Then, I called Imani and Stella, and Stella invited me to her friend Brenda's birthday party, the next Saturday. I wasn't sure I wanted to go to a rich White girl's birthday party, especially an arrogant rich White girl, but I didn't have any other plans for that Saturday, so I accepted. I decided to buy Brenda a copy of Anne Moody's memoir, but what I really needed was a book about race relations in the present day. Brenda, the foolish White girl who seriously believes Black people don't have problems today and sees racism as a thing of the past. I still can't believe she can't see the racial profiling that was the cause of Rodney King's beating and Latasha Harlins' murder.

On the day of the party, I decided to dress in my jeans, dashiki, and TSU cap Andre gave me. Say it loud, I'm Black and I'm proud.

Daddy dropped me off at Brenda's Brentwood house. I expected the house to be huge and it was, and that same anger I had when I first visited the Wilsons came back. Brenda claims Black people have no problems, but the shitty apartment Imani lives in and the bullets we hear and dodge near our homes is a problem. I'm sure Brenda doesn't have a full understanding about life in the hood 'cause she doesn't live where I live.

Daddy said, "Don't let these bougie kids get the better of you."

Daddy drove away, and I knocked on the door. A White man with brown hair and brown eyes answered the door and asked, "Who are you?"

I explained, "I'm a friend of Stella Wilson's and Stella is a friend of your daughter. I actually visited University High School a few months ago, and I encountered Brenda in Stella's history class."

The White man said, "Okay …" From the way he was looking at me he was probably profiling me. I guess he thought I was there to start trouble.

I then said, "Nice to meet you, Mister ...?"

He responded, "Blake." He walked into his house, but he left the door open. Then, he came back and said, "Stella confirmed your story."

I walked in and Mr. Blake followed me. I guess he wanted to keep an eye on me and make sure I didn't steal anything. I walked toward the noise of other kids, which was in the backyard. Like the Wilsons, the Blakes had a pool, but it was bigger and no one was swimming in it. It definitely wasn't a pool party. I put my gift on a table that had lots of other gifts.

Stella walked up to me and said, "Girl, I would like to congratulate you again on your Naval Academy interview. I'm sure you're gonna get in!"

I said, "Thanks, Stella."

Then, Stella yelled, "Yo, everyone, this is Hatima Parker!"

The other kids, who were mostly White, rushed toward me and shook my hands to congratulate me on my interview. Some White kid asked if I had applied to and been accepted to other colleges, and I told them about the affirmative replies I received from Freeman, Howard, LAMU, and Vanderbilt. Most of them congratulated me, but some glared at me including the spawn of Satan himself, Rupert.

I asked Rupert, "You gotta problem with a Black woman getting into schools that aren't HBCUs?"

Rupert said, "Yeah, I do. Affirmative action is the reason Blacks get into the Ivy League, and I'm sure Annapolis and Vanderbilt are using the same bullshit policies!"

Brenda said, "Rupert, that's a terrible thing to say!"

Rupert said, "I know some schools are trying to be more diverse, which means they're letting in Blacks, Latinos, and Asians. Unfortunately, some of these applicants aren't as qualified as hardworking White students."

I asked, "Are you planning to go to the Naval Academy or Vanderbilt?"

Rupert explained, "I applied to the business and economics programs at UC Berkeley, UPenn, Yale, Vanderbilt, the University of Washington, Santa Clara University, and NYU. I received affirmatives from NYU, UW, and Santa Clara but rejections from UPenn and Yale. Vanderbilt and UC Berkeley haven't mailed replies yet."

I said, "Then, there's still a good chance you'll get into Vanderbilt. Don't lose hope."

Rupert exclaimed, "Well, I am losing hope! I know UPenn and Yale rejected me because of affirmative action! A bunch of Blacks who aren't as qualified as me got in because of skin color! That's straight-up racist!"

I couldn't believe my ears. I asked, "You think affirmative action is racist? You think the Black applicants aren't as qualified as you? What score did you get on your SAT?"

Rupert said, "A fifteen hundred."

I said, "I got fifteen-twenty."

Rupert said, "That's bullshit!"

I said, "I ain't lyin'! What score did you get on the ACT?"

Rupert said, "Thirty-two."

I stated, "I got a thirty-four!"

Rupert said, "You're a grade-A bullshitter!"

I repeated, "I ain't lyin'!"

Then Victor came, stood beside me, and stated, "Rupert, it's racist of you to assume that Hatima got lower scores than you did. It's racist to believe that affirmative action only cares about skin color without regard to grades. It's racist to believe that all Blacks should only apply to HBCUs."

I said, "This country is going straight to Hell with people like you at the helm. You claimed racism was nonexistent in Missus O'Hara's history class, but you seem totally oblivious to the fact that *you're* a racist."

Rupert said, "I don't bomb Black churches, burn down houses in South Central, or hang Blacks from trees."

Victor explained, "That's one way of being racist. Thinking affirmative action is bullshit is one way to be racist. Believing a Black girl from the ghetto won't get into highly selective schools is another way."

Brenda said, "Hatima, if you can't chill, you need to leave."

I asked, incredulously, "Why do *I* have to leave? Why can't Rupert leave?"

Victor explained, "Brenda is one of those White people who gets scared when a Black person gets angry. She believes you'll use your martial arts training against her."

I said, "That's bullshit! I only use martial arts when someone *physically* attacks me. When someone *verbally* attacks me, I fight back with words."

Victor said, "If Hatima leaves, then I leave."

Stella said, "Me too."

I was surprised that Stella would stand by me instead of with a girl she's probably been friends with since kindergarten.

Brenda asked, "How come everything is suddenly about race?"

I repeated, "*Suddenly* about race?"

Victor said, "Girl, race has and will probably always be a part of American life!"

I said, "I hope the book I got you will knock some sense into you."

I walked away from the party and so did Stella and Victor.

They walked toward a parked red 1990 Ford Mustang GT. To be clear, the Wilsons didn't have that sweet ride in their garage the last time I was there. You might think Victor had to get a job and work hard to earn some money for this Mustang, but Imani told me that his parents bought it for him as a reward for passing his driver's test. It must be nice to have a CFO and a lawyer for parents. My reward for passing my driver's test was lunch with Mama, Daddy, and Grandma at Denny's. I got to eat a double cheeseburger and chocolate cake with a strawberry milkshake to wash it down, but that delicious meal seems laughable to Victor's car.

I realize how different I am compared to Stella and Victor. Victor has his own car, while I mostly rely on the bus to get me across LA. Stella and her siblings know they'll get into college and their parents will be able to pay their tuitions, but I have to rely on scholarships, grants, jobs, and, possibly, student loans to pay my tuition if I don't get accepted into the Naval Academy. Most of Dorsey High's senior class knows that college isn't where they're gonna be in September. They'll be working nine-to-five like all blue-collar workers. But Stella, Victor, and I still have Black skin. We all have to face the same bullshit, no matter where we live or which career we choose. As long as there are people like Brenda and Rupert, it's our job to stick it to 'em.

Victor got behind the wheel, Stella claimed shotgun, and I sat in the back.

As Victor drove away, he asked, "Where to?"

I said, "I dunno."

Stella said, "We should get something to eat since we didn't eat at the party."

Victor asked, "What about Pizza Hut?"

I said, "That'd be cool."

Victor drove to the nearest Pizza Hut, which was twenty minutes away. We got a booth and ordered a medium Meat Lover's Pizza.

As we chomped on our slices, Victor said, "I'm sorry about our friends' BS. It feels like LA has traveled back in time to the nineteen-sixties."

Stella said, "I just wish things would go back to normal."

I asked, "What normal? Blacks getting beat and killed even though they didn't do anything wrong? People remaining oblivious to what goes on in the hood? That's the normal you want?"

Stella explained, "I meant that I wished race was no longer a serious issue. Thanks to Rodney King and Latasha Harlins, the whole world thinks the USA hasn't changed since the sixties."

I couldn't believe what I was hearing. It sounded like Stella was blaming Rodney King for his beating and Latasha Harlins for her death.

I exclaimed, "Rodney King didn't beat himself bloody and Latasha Harlins didn't pull the trigger on the gun that killed her! The cops and Missus Du are the ones you should be blaming!"

Stella rolled her eyes and said, "Not this shit again!"

Victor said, "Stella, your lack of concern for Rodney King and, especially, for Latasha Harlins is astounding! Latasha Harlins is a Black girl who looked just like you, but you can't shed a single tear for her! Rodney King was a Black man who looked like your dad, but you believe he got what he deserved!"

Stella exclaimed, "Rodney King is a wino, and Latasha was a thief! They were both criminals that got what was coming to them!"

I asked, "Did Emmett Till and Bobby Hutton get what was coming to them? Did the four Black girls from Birmingham deserve to get blown up for standing up for their rights?"

Stella asked, "Who's Bobby Hutton?"

I rolled my eyes and said, "I ain't surprised you've never heard of L'il Bobby. I'm guessing your opinion of the Black Panther Party must be low."

Stella stated, "They were a bunch of gangsters and ex-cons pretending to be activists and revolutionaries! Their leader was arrested and most of them accepted bribes from cops! They hindered the Black struggle instead of helping it!"

Victor said, "Stella, the BPP is more complicated than that." I explained about the Ten-Point Platform, the community programs, and the death of Bobby Hutton.

Stella said, "Bobby should have known what was coming to him when he opened fired on those cops!"

I explained, "Stella, Bobby was unarmed and almost naked when he surrendered. How can you justify murdering an unarmed teen in his boxers? If we don't find peaceful ways to liberate our people, an armed revolution is going to commence. Look at the American Revolution, the French Revolution, the Haitian Revolution."

Victor said, "Revolutions happen when the world needs to change and, hopefully, a revolution will commence here in LA when those four racist cops are brought to court."

I told Stella, "Your dad and I were stopped by two racist cops the first time he dropped me off in Crenshaw. They almost didn't believe your dad when he said he was a doctor."

Stella said, "That's what happens when gangsters ride large in luxury cars. They have all the cops thinking the only way Blacks can live a luxurious lifestyle is through crime."

I said, "Okay, I'll give you that. But have you been followed around in stores or asked to hand over your purse?"

Stella said, "Yeah, at the Fox Hills Mall. In an accessory store, I had to hand over my purse to a salesclerk because she said it was bigger than the other customers'."

HEAL THE HOOD

I asked, "Were the other customers White?"

Stella said, "Yeah, so?"

I repeated, "'Yeah, so?' Stella, that salesclerk asked you to hand over your purse because she thought you were gonna shoplift."

Stella asked, "Why would I shoplift? Do you not know where I live?"

Victor said, "We know where you live but that salesclerk didn't. All Blacks look the same to Whites. She probably thought you were a girl from South Central, since there are more Blacks in the hood than in the Hills."

Stella said, "That salesclerk must be stupid to think I'm like Hatima and her friends!"

Stella seemed more upset about being viewed the same way as me and my friends than being racially profiled.

I told Stella, "Bitch, you are unbelievable."

I grabbed my purse and left.

Victor came after me and said, "Whoa, Hatima. I can drive you home, you know."

I said, "I am *not* riding in the same car as that sellout. One minute she's showing me off because I seem set for the Naval Academy. Next, she's furious at being seen as the same person as me and my friends. Is there something wrong with me, my friends, my family, or my hood? Do I look broken?"

Victor said, "Of course not! Stella has to believe that racism isn't an issue in our world anymore because it gives her a false sense of security. When we see pictures of Emmett Till's mutilated corpse and activists being hosed and bitten by dogs, it scares the bejesus out of us. Stella doesn't wanna live with the fear that the KKK might lynch her or a racist cop might shoot her because she's Black. That would mean nothing has changed since the March on Washington and the signing of the Civil Rights Act. That would mean that death is still a constant shadow in our world."

I thought about Grandma, who has lived with the fear of the KKK and other racist Whites since she was a child. Mama and Daddy grew up in the 1960s so I'm sure the fear of what happens to activists was a part of their lives as well; but pretending there isn't a problem won't lead to a solution.

I told Victor, "Stella needs to sort out her priorities."

Victor smiled, and we walked to his Mustang.

Chapter Eighteen

My birthday, as I said before, is at the end of April, and I looked forward to turning eighteen, becoming an adult, being the first in my family to graduate from high school, and going off to college. Major Davis said that my name wasn't taken off the list so there's still a good chance that I'll attend the Naval Academy

One event that my friends, my family, and I were all looking forward to almost as much as my birthday was the trial that would determine the fates of the four cops who beat Rodney King. Since Missus Du was let off easy by the judge for murdering an unarmed teenage Black girl, there was a good chance that the jury or judge wouldn't see Rodney King's brutal attack by cops as a serious crime.

The news stated that the trial would take place in Simi Valley, a predominantly White city. I hoped that meant that the jurors wouldn't all be White, but hoping was a waste of time on that issue. Nine of the jurors overseeing the trial were White. There was one Latina, one Asian-American woman, and one biracial guy. Deputy District Attorney Terry White was the chief prosecutor. It was comforting that a high-ranking brother was trying to prove that the four cops were just as bad as the real criminals they were supposed to protect LA from. Emmett Till's, Medgar Evers', and Tom Robinson's faces kept popping into my head. The trials that oversaw Emmett Till's and Medgar Evers' murder cases and Tom Robinson's false crimes were put in the hands of all-White juries. Despite all the evidence, Roy Bryant and J.W. Milam got away with murdering a Black teenager and Byron De La Beckwith got away with murdering a good man who was just trying to help Black folks in Mississippi reap the American Dream. Tom Robinson was also convicted for raping Mayella Ewell even though all he was guilty of was feeling sorry for an abused and mistreated White woman.

When I visited the Wilsons, I watched some television with the Doc. During the commercials, I asked Dr. Wilson about the mostly-White jury overseeing the trial. I thought we left this nonsense behind in the 1960s.

Dr. Wilson explained, "Mister Holliday's videotape has solved the problem of excessive force utilized by police officers by making it impossible to deny that the LAPD severely beat up a suspect. The video has also simultaneously undermined the criminal case that was created. Defense attorneys have an opportunity to question jurors ahead of time about the prosecution's evidence. Prospective jurors are often asked if they have formed conclusions based on news accounts, but they can't be asked to give opinions about evidence they've never seen. Can you see where I'm going with this?"

I replied, "Yeah. Mister Holliday's video has been seen by almost everyone in the USA and the world. It's evidence, but it's also part of the news. Defense attorneys can ask jurors if they have opinions about the news when they're actually asking them their opinions about the evidence. Those no-good sons of bitches!"

Dr. Wilson didn't even reprimand me for swearing. His son wasn't in the house, his wife was at work, and Stella was working on an article up in her room.

Dr. Wilson said, "Asking jurors how they feel about evidence is illegal, but I doubt the defense attorneys will be punished for it. All prospective Black jurors most likely decided the cops were guilty the first time they saw the tape. Then, they were all excused by Judge Weisberg. This may not be the fifties and sixties, but people are still using the same sly tricks."

The trial took six days to complete. Deputy DA White kept showing the videotape 'cause it was the best evidence the prosecution had besides Rodney King's testimony. Actually, Deputy DA White was *supposed* to call Rodney King to the stand 'cause every Black person in LA knew that it was an important part of the plan to stick it to the man, but he never did. The news explained that White was afraid that Rodney King would have said something that didn't fit together with what the other witnesses said. Since Rodney King was drunk and had multiple skull fractures, he might not be able to recall what happened to him last year in perfect detail and might say the wrong thing.

I thought that was ridiculous! Rodney King didn't have to name names. All he had to do was talk about the excruciating pain he felt; the broken bones, the bruises, the blood, et cetera. That should have created sympathy for him and the Black struggle.

Melanie Singer testified that Officer Powell hit Rodney King's head and face even though Rodney King was on his knees and not resisting arrest. She said that when Officer Koon saw Officer Powell hitting him, he told them to stop and that it was enough. She also said that Officer Briseno also tried to stop Officer Powell from hitting him. Michael Stone, Officer Powell's lawyer, said Powell didn't bust up Rodney King's face. He stated that Rodney King hit his face on the pavement. Plenty of people in the hood have tripped and landed face-first on the pavement, but their faces never looked as bad as Rodney King's!

John Barnett, Officer Briseno's lawyer, singled out Officers Powell and Wind as the out-of-control pigs. Officer Briseno kicked Rodney King in the video, but Mr. Barnett twisted the evidence by claiming that Officer Briseno was trying to protect Mr. King by keeping him down with his foot.

In the video, Officer Powell hit Rodney King repeatedly with his baton and kicked him. In fact, Officer Powell hit Rodney King more than five times.

Officer Powell testified that he did all this because, "I was completely in fear for my life, scared to death."

I am sick and tired of that excuse! Rodney King is not Superman, Batman, or even Bruce Lee. He's just a tall Black man who has alcohol issues. I remembered that Victor said that Rupert's older brother was also caught speeding by the cops, but he got off easy. How come the cops didn't see Rupert's brother as a huge threat? Rupert's brother plays football, so he must be in great physical shape. He probably could have beat up the cops if he had anger issues.

Twenty minutes before the beating, Officer Powell sent a computer message and said, "Sounds almost exciting as our last call. It was right out of *Gorillas in the Mist*."

Officer Powell's lawyer tried to make up a lameass excuse, but Deputy DA White said that Officer Powell's message "shows motive and also bias by Mister Powell against Rodney King because he is Black." In other words, the statement was racist.

Officer Powell's comment sounded racist to me and every other Black person in LA since Blacks have been called apes and monkeys since the slavery era.

Officer Wind was a rookie cop, while Officer Powell was his supervisor. He beat Rodney King because Officer Powell did. Officer Wind must have thought that since his mentor was beating up a Black man for speeding and drunk driving, it was okay for him to do it too. If there's one thing worse than wolves, it's sheep. Officer Wind never testified so I guess being a sheep meant his actions weren't as bad as the others; he reminds me of why it's important to think for yourself.

Every Black person in the world was sure that all four cops would get convicted. The tape had been played repeatedly, and their excuses were nothing more than cowardly lies.

On my eighteenth birthday, the jury gave their verdict. I was at school and Principal Edwards interrupted classes to give us the announcement.

Principal Edwards stated, "Students and staff of Susan Miller Dorsey High School, I just heard the results of the trial against the four LAPD officers who beat Rodney King. Unfortunately, the verdict is not guilty. I repeat, the jury found the four cops not guilty."

I remembered when Dr. Murray told the congregation at FAME on Sunday morning, "Even in anger, be cool." It was a warning of what to do if things turned out badly, but I had a feeling few would heed it.

My classmates yelled, "That's straight-up bullshit!"

"We all saw what those pigs did on the tape!"

"Whaddaya expect from a non-Black jury?"

Point nine of the Ten-Point Platform states,

We want all Black people when brought to trial to be tried in court by a jury of their peer group or people from their Black Communities, as defined by the Constitution of the United States. We believe that the courts should follow the United States Constitution so that Black people will receive fair trials. The Fourteenth Amendment of the US Constitution gives a man a right to be tried by his peers. A peer is a person from a similar economic, social, religious, geographical, environmental, historical, and racial background. To do this the court will be forced to select a jury from the Black community from which the Black defendant came. We have been and are being tried by all-White juries that have no understanding of 'the average reasoning man' of the Black community.

The Black Panthers spoke the truth! Even though Rodney King wasn't a defendant, not having any Blacks jurors resulted in his pain being seen as a joke. An all-Black jury would have found those cops guilty, but the defense attorneys knew that and resorted to dirty tricks to make sure that Blacks wouldn't be on the jury. Of course, a jury comprising of one racial, economic, social, and religious group would all come to the same conclusion and their answer would be biased. Diverse juries bring about different opinions and see a story from several angles. Latasha Harlins' murder trial had a diverse jury with the exception of no Asians; but Judge Karlin still saw Mrs. Du as the victim, not Latasha. Maybe she was trying to make up for the lack of Asian input in the jury's decision. Perhaps diverse juries are what all trials need to ensure that all the USA's racial, economic, social, and religious groups have a say in matters.

I thought about Gavin Cato, Latasha Harlins, Yusuf Hawkins, Michael Griffith, Edmund Perry, Willie Turks, Eula Mae Love, Mark Clark, Fred Hampton, Bobby Hutton, Matthew Johnson, James Powell, Johnny Robinson, Virgil Ware, Addie Mae Collins, Denise McNair, Carole Robertson, Cynthia Wesley, and Emmett Till. I thought about Dr. Martin Luther King Jr., Malcolm X, and Medgar Evers. I even thought about Tom Robinson, a fictional character who felt so real to my tenth grade English class, and about T.J. Avery, another fictional character from the Logan Family series who was given the sole blame for a crime two White boys helped him commit. They all lost their lives and the USA didn't give a damn about them.

Mayor Tom Bradley himself said, "Those four pigs don't deserve to wear police uniforms."

President Bush himself said, "It was sickening to see the beating that was rendered, and there's no way, no way in my view, to explain that away."

The mayor of LA, a Black man, and the President of the United States, a White man, both agreed that those cops are despicable human beings, but words are powerful things. Lawyers, journalists, pastors, politicians, et cetera are all masters with words. The cops' lawyers were able to convince the jury that Rodney King was the dangerous presence that night and that the cops were justified in beating him almost to death.

When Kunta Kinte and countless others were stolen from Africa and brought here as slaves, the slavers were able to justify what they did by claiming that Africans were dangerous savages. Africans were said to be cannibals and heathens, but in America they would become civilized by Christianity and the English language.

Kunta Kinte and countless others had families, friends, and, most importantly, lives. Kunta had wonderful plans for his future, but they were ripped away from him when he was enslaved. He had a mother, father, and three younger brothers whom he never saw again during his lifetime, but the human spirit is hard to kill, and words are powerful things. Kunta's daughter Kizzy, her son Chicken George, his children, and their children all kept his story alive. If Alex Haley hadn't listened to his Grandma Cynthia's stories with rapt ears in Henning, Tennessee, the rest of the world would have never known about Kunta Kinte's heroic defiance of slavery, a defiance that inspires us even today.

Was Emmett Till also seen as a dangerous person? I read in a book that he was stocky and muscular, one hundred and fifty pounds, and was five-foot-four. Michael J. Fox is the same height Emmett Till was. Did his muscular form convince Carolyn Bryant, her husband, his half-brother, and the rest of Mississippi that Emmett Till was the dangerous presence in the store? If he was really such a vicious monster, then he probably would have been able to defend himself from Roy Bryant and J.W. Milam; but Roy Bryant and J.W. Milam both walked away from Emmett Till's murder without so much as a scratch on them. Murdering Emmett Till was like murdering a puppy.

Were the six kids from Birmingham also seen as vicious monsters? Three of the girls killed at the Sixteenth Street Baptist Church were fourteen, but one was only eleven. What kind of sick person sees four little girls as monsters? Perhaps the girls were killed because of the threat school integration represented to segregationists. Four dead girls meant four less students at White schools, but I know that the KKK couldn't kill every single Black child in Birmingham. Plus, the Sixteenth Street Baptist Church was a meeting place for civil rights activists. I'm sure the KKK were hoping the destruction of the church would mean the end of the protests, but the Black activists could hold their meetings in other places if every church in Birmingham was bombed.

All Johnny Robinson did was throw some rocks. Did the cop who kill him really think Johnny was gonna stone those White kids to death? Officer Parker could have arrested Johnny instead of killing him, but Johnny would most likely have been sent to jail on trumped-up charges. What about the White kids who insulted and attacked Johnny and his friends? How come they were never seen to be at fault? I'm sure it's most likely because insulting and attacking Blacks wasn't a crime back then but a regular occurrence.

Virgil Ware was riding on his brother's bike. How is that threatening? Michael Lee Farley most likely thought shooting Virgil is no different than shooting a duck, but Larry Joe Sims' heart wasn't into the situation. Larry should have thrown the gun away or smashed it to pieces. He should have walked away and made Michael Lee do the same. If Larry Joe Sims hadn't given into peer pressure like Officer Wind did, then Virgil Ware would still be alive.

The cops who killed James Powell, Matthew Johnson, and Edmund Perry all stated that they felt threatened by the Black teens they killed. Lieutenant Gilligan stated that James Powell lunged at him with a knife. The SFPD claimed that Matthew Johnson's death wasn't race related, but an excusable shooting of a suspected criminal by a law enforcement officer who never intended to kill Matthew Johnson in the first place. Even though Edmund Perry and his brother, Jonah Perry, beat Officer Van Houten, Officer Van Houten could have called for back-up. Shoot, if Officer Van Houten knew martial arts, then taking down two Black guys who had no guns would have been no problem. The pigs' testimonies were designed to create maximum sympathy for the police by painting *themselves* as the victims.

Yusuf Hawkins was just trying to buy a new car. He wasn't dating an Italian girl, but those Italian guys decided to kill any Black guys who came to their Brooklyn hood to make sure an interracial relationship wouldn't continue. Were those Italian guys afraid that since all Blacks are vicious monsters that the Black guy dating the Italian girl would hurt her in some way?

Bobby Hutton was one of the few victims of police brutality who posed a threat to the cops. The Black Panthers shot at the cops first and started a battle. Even though Bobby Hutton walked out with his hands up and almost nude, the cops still saw him as a monster not a human being; but if the cops' considered things from the Panthers' point of view, they would understand why the BPP did what they did. They were tired of Blacks being oppressed and decided to wage war on the cops. In all the fantasy books I've read, tyrants are always afraid that the people they oppress will rise and fight back. I'm sure the police departments and the feds were also afraid that Black people would unite and aim their guns at their oppressors. That's why the FBI did too good a job at dismantling the Black Panthers.

In *To Kill A Mockingbird*, even Scout Finch believed that it was possible Tom Robinson could have beaten and raped Mayella Ewell – although Scout doesn't understand exactly what rape is – because Tom Robinson was a muscular man. But Tom Robinson's left hand was damaged beyond repair by a cotton gin when he was a kid, so he couldn't have been Mayella's attacker. Mayella's attacker was a left-handed man, her own father, Bob Ewell. Mayella was so desperate for companionship that she tried to seduce a married Black man and her father beat her because of it. In order to pretend that the incident never happened, Bob and Mayella lied to Maycomb's sheriff and said Tom Robinson was the attacker. Throughout history, Black people are often seen as little more than scapegoats.

My tenth grade English teacher, Mrs. Preston, once asked us, "If Tom Robinson's case was held in the present-day, would he have been acquitted by the jury?"

A few kids said "yes", but most of us, including myself, said "no." The USA has hardly changed since the 1930s and Los Angeles, California has proven time and time again that it's just as bad as Maycomb, Alabama; Birmingham, Alabama; Spokane County,

Mississippi; Leflore County, Mississippi; Jackson, Mississippi, et cetera.

A lot of emotions built inside me after Principal Edwards' announcement; disbelief, sadness, fear, et cetera. But the one emotion I really felt was rage.

Chapter Nineteen

South Central remained a boiling pot of racial and class tension since Mr. Holliday's videotape was shown, last year in March. That day when I first heard Dr. Murray tell us about Rodney King's beating and Mr. Holliday's video now felt like a long time ago. My family, friends, and community hoped the video would lead to real change but, like fools, we got played.

Last year in June, three cops were accused of demolishing apartments inhabited by Blacks and Latinos, but the pigs were acquitted by an LA jury. Then, in August, three Korean markets were firebombed, including Soon Ja Du's store. Since Judge Karlin let her off with a light punishment, I thought the Dus' store being bombed was a fitting punishment. There were plenty of protests in November when Mrs. Du was granted probation, but a lot of people, especially teens, were frustrated and tired. Quotes from Dr. King, Medgar Evers, Frederick Douglass, and even Malcolm X, Marcus Garvey, and the Black Panthers weren't so helpful. Words didn't seem to be stopping racists from terrorizing us so maybe action would help.

Students ran outta Dorsey High, yelling how messed-up America is and how the world doesn't give a damn about us. I agreed wholeheartedly and walked home to West Boulevard, and I noticed the sad and mad looks on many people's faces. I'm sure people looked like this when Medgar Evers, John F. Kennedy, Malcolm X, Dr. King, and Bobby Kennedy were assassinated back in the 1960s.

Mama and Daddy were still at work. Since it was Wednesday and softball season, I would usually have stayed at school for practice, but I didn't feel like catching, throwing, and hitting softballs. I would rather throw down and beat up those cops who brutalized Rodney King. I'm pretty sure my martial arts skill would help me take them down easily, but I was planning on heading to FAME because I heard on the radio that Dr. Murray was leading a rally that was intended to launch "Operation Cool Response."

I looked up at the pictures of famous Black people on the walls. Dr. King never carried a weapon, not even a pocketknife.

He said, "I believe unarmed truth and unconditional love will have the final say in reality."

Well, the four cops who beat Rodney King were armed, and Missus Du was also armed when she shot Latasha Harlins. It took me a while to figure out what "unarmed truth" means. I believe it means when you try to bring about positive change without the use of swords or guns. When the UK and other European nations colonized the world, they were armed with guns, cannons, and other weapons as well as the Bible. The Bible is truth; it's a manual that teaches everyone how to live life God's Way; but since the Europeans had weapons, their truth was backed up with arms. As a result, colonialism, while developing the infrastructures of the rest of the world, also created several more problems since, in the end, the Europeans were still conquerors. Some have even called them dictators, albeit benevolent dictators.

Malcolm X had a gun, and I saw a picture in a textbook of Malcolm X pointing a gun out of a window. He only believed in violence when it was used as self-defense. But did he know boxing and other forms of hand-to-hand combat? Did he know how to fight without a gun? According to testimonies from his siblings, Malcolm Little was a lousy boxer when he was a kid. That is the most annoying thing about guns. A lotta people use them when they know they can't fight. Take away a gangbanger's gun, and he turns into a coward. I'm not saying Malcolm X was a coward because, just like Dr. King, he wasn't afraid to speak his mind. But is shooting at our oppressors the solution or just another big problem?

Brother Malcolm said, "You're not to be so blind with patriotism that you can't face reality. Wrong is wrong, no matter who does it or says it."

Just because a cop wears a badge doesn't mean they stand for what's right; just because someone has a law degree doesn't mean they believe that everyone is equal under the American legal system. The cops, the lawyers, the juries, the judges, the Koreans, and every single person who has played a part in getting away with terrorizing and murdering Blacks is guilty in the eyes of the Lord.

I looked at the pictures of all these famous Blacks who made a difference in the world. What good did it do? Dr. King, Malcolm X, Medgar Evers, et cetera were all gunned down. The worst stuff always seems to happen to the nicest people. What if peace and self-defense doesn't work? What if violence and offense is the only way to fix the world? If every bigot on the planet were eradicated, would that mean peace is finally possible?

I packed my *nunchaku* and knives in a hidden compartment in my backpack. If the cops searched me for weapons, they wouldn't be able to find them because the bulk of my books would hide the bulk of the hidden compartment. Then, I went to the Brookses' house and knocked on the door. I had a hunch that Mrs. Brooks might close the restaurant early because of the verdict.

Sure enough, Mrs. Brooks answered the door after I knocked.

She asked, "Hatima, are you alright? Are you heading somewhere?"

I said, "Yeah, to First AME for the rally Doctor Murray has planned. Can you drive me?"

Mrs. Brooks replied, "Of course! Wanda and I are going to the rally as well."

We all got into Mrs. Brooks' Volkswagen, and she drove us to FAME. There were lots of other cars parked in the parking lot, but Mrs. Brooks was still able to find a spot.

We went inside the church, which was already half-full. Everyone looked mad as heck and would probably have been cussing the LAPD, the justice system, and the entire planet Earth if they weren't in church.

Soon, FAME filled up; it almost looked like a typical Sunday service except no one was wearing suits and dresses, and everyone had frowns and glares on their faces.

Now, get this: Mayor Tom Bradley himself showed up.

But Wanda yelled, "Since when do we let coons into God's holy house?"

Other people agreed with her and yelled, "You're nothing but an Uncle Tom! Uncle Tom Bradley!"

Soon, almost everyone was chanting, "Uncle Tom Bradley!"

I thought that was a bit unfair since politicians don't have that much power when people do a closer analysis. Queen Elizabeth II is a figurehead, which means the British Prime Minister is the one who calls the shots in Britain. Abraham Lincoln's Emancipation Proclamation didn't force the South to give up slavery; it took two more years of war and the Thirteenth Amendment to end slavery. But, in the end, Abraham Lincoln was shot in the head. John F.

Kennedy was also President, but he had no power over the Klan, the White Citizens' Councils, or other bigots, so he was also shot in the head.

Every politician on this planet is still a human being. Humans are blood, flesh, and bone. They can still die. As much as they try to act it, they ain't superhuman.

In *The Chronicles of Narnia*, Aslan is the only character who appears in all seven books. Kings, queens, warriors, and even the Friends of Narnia came and went, but Aslan wasn't going anywhere. Mayors, governors, presidents, kings, queens, et cetera come and go, but Jesus ain't going nowhere.

Dr. Murray calmed everyone down with prayers and gospel songs; but it's gonna take more than prayer and singing for bigots to stop brutalizing and murdering our people.

Then, Eric Grant stood up and exclaimed, "Prayer isn't going to stop cops, Koreans, and other bigots from murdering us!"

I replied, "I'm so glad the prospect of new customers for your daddy's business hasn't made you relish death!"

A lot of people laughed, and even Dr. Murray smiled.

Then, Mrs. Brooks said, "We have to put our faith in the Lord because we sure as heck can't put our faith in law enforcement and the government!"

Some ladies exclaimed, "That's right, Sister Brooks! Preach the truth!"

Then, Imani ran into the church and yelled, "Parker Center is burning! We need help ASAP!"

Dr. Murray exclaimed, "Calm down, Sister Imani. What happened at Parker Center?"

Imani explained, "Lots of people, including myself, went to a protest at Parker Center in Downtown LA 'cause that's where the

LAPD's HQ is. But the protest turned violent and people made their way through the Civic Center, attacked cops, and set cars on fire! The LAFD were shot at while trying to put out the fires. Some of us managed to get outta there; then, I remembered the rally that was being held here. Please, Downtown needs all the help it can get!"

The fact that my surname had the same name as the LAPD's HQ just made me sick to my stomach.

Then, Doctor Murray said, "Someone turn on the radio so we can hear about damages being caused in other parts of the city. Church family, divide into groups of five. We'll all have to go out into the eye of the storm."

Mrs. Brooks, Wanda, Imani, and I created our own team, and Dr. Murray told us to go to Lake View Terrace. Rodney King was beaten by those pigs in Lake View Terrace, so protestors marched south on Osborne Street to the LAPD Foothill Division HQ. According to the radio, they threw rocks, shot bullets, and set fires.

As we were driving through LA, the night seemed blacker than usual. Even though there were lighted buildings, the world seemed to have a layer of darkness covering it. I got goosebumps on my arms; the darkness seemed to be spreading, extinguishing all light and goodness in the world. I felt the same way the Narnians must have felt after the Last Battle: that the world was coming to an end. I was sure things would be hellish when we got to Lake View Terrace, and I was right.

At Lake View Terrace, we saw cops in riot gear: helmets with plastic face coverings, shields, and batons. Those batons looked just like the ones that almost killed Rodney King, and now the pigs were using them to beat the protestors.

The protestors carried signs that said, "NO JUSTICE FOR A BROTHER."

The Los Angeles Fire Department (LAFD) was putting out fires, and Mrs. Brooks, Wanda, Imani and I got outta the car to ask the firefighters if we could help. For the record, the LAFD have been met with good reviews by the Black folks of South Central. Firefighters are often neutral in the race war since their job is to deal with fires, earthquakes, and other disasters, not criminals. But in the news, firefighters and even paramedics have been threatened by the Bloods, Crips, and other gangsters. This has me wondering if firefighters have now become swine officials, just like the LAPD.

The cops were beating folks bloody. One cop beat a woman in her face until she stopped moving. I wasn't sure if she was dead or not. Then, the cop handcuffed her and tried to put her into his cruiser. I followed my instincts: I picked up a rock, threw it at the guy's plastic face covering, and got a bull's-eye. That distracted the cop long enough to drop the woman and be set upon by three angry rioters.

Wanda followed my lead and started throwing rocks at the cops, but her aim wasn't as good as mine; Wanda neither knows martial arts nor does she play sports, so her marksmanship is lacking. Mrs. Brooks and Imani ran to the fallen rioters and helped get them away from the fighting. They took them out of the melee and carried them to ambulances where paramedics were ready to offer aid. It reminded me of those Red Cross volunteers. I wonder if any of them will come to LA.

When the cops arrested the rioters who hadn't run away or been taken to hospitals, Mrs. Brooks, Wanda, Imani, and I went back to Crenshaw. I was definitely gonna get it from my parents, but I'm sure they would know I was heading to FAME for the rally by listening to the radio.

Mrs. Brooks stopped her car in front of my house and said, "Good luck, Hatima."

I nodded my thanks, walked to the door, unlocked it, opened it, and prepared to see my parents' angry faces, but the house was dark. I turned on the lights and checked the living room, the kitchens, the bedrooms, and the bathrooms. There was no one else in the house.

I turned on the television to hear more news about rioting in LA. The news showed that a few hundred demonstrators showed up at the LAPD HQ in Parker Center. When Imani said people were protesting at Parker Center, I imagined a few dozen, not hundreds; but that was a good thing. It showed that many people saw the verdict as bullshit and a betrayal of the justice system. They were demanding that Chief Gates resign, and I agreed with them. He was just as incompetent as our mayor. Then, the people started to storm the building. I couldn't believe it! They were trying to force their way into the building! But the cops held them off.

I kept watching the news as a whole bunch of activist organizations added their outcries about the verdicts: the NAACP, the American Civil Liberties Union, the American Jewish Congress, the Los Angeles Gay and Lesbian Community Services Center, and the Gay & Lesbian Alliance Against Defamation Los Angeles. They all saw the acquittal of the four pigs as a travesty.

The news also recounted what happened to a White man named Reginald Denny. He was a White truck driver who decided to stop at a traffic light, but he was dragged out of his truck and beaten to a pulp by a Black mob. A concrete fragment slammed into Mr. Denny's temple and a cinder block landed on his head. News helicopters recorded the beating like how George Holliday recorded Rodney King's beating. But a Black man rescued Reginald Denny. Bobby Green Jr. watched the assault live on his television and rushed to the scene, which is a few blocks away from his home and drove Mr. Denny to the hospital in Mr. Denny's eighteen-wheeler truck.

Another beating caught on camera was right around the corner from where Reginald Denny was beaten. A Latino man named Field Lopez was ripped from his truck and robbed of his money. One attacker smashed his forehead open with a car stereo, while another tried to slice his ear off. After Mr. Lopez lost consciousness, the crowd spray painted his torso and genitals Black, but a Black minister named Rev. Bennie Newton prevented others from beating Mr. Lopez any further.

Rev. Newton wedged himself between Mr. Lopez and his attackers and told the mob, "Kill him and you have to kill me too."

From one point of view, Mr. Green's and Rev. Newton's bravery and determination is inspiring. After all, beating up Whites and Latinos who aren't part of the LAPD is wacky since they haven't done anything wrong to our people. On the other hand, it seems people will have more sympathy for Reginald Denny, a White man, than for Rodney King, a Black man. They may even have more sympathy for Reginald Denny than for Field Lopez. Field Lopez is a Latino, and Latinos have also been racially profiled. They also live in ghettos, like East LA and parts of Inglewood. Like I said before, Black lives don't seem to matter as much as White lives. Brown lives also don't seem to matter as much as White lives.

It looked like history was repeating itself. In August 1965, a Black man named Marquette Frye was pulled over by the cops for speeding while drinking and driving. Marquette's brother, Ronald, was a passenger in the car, and he walked to their house to take their mother, Mrs. Frye, to the place where Marquette was arrested. But then, shit went downhill, and Mrs. Frye jumped on a cop's back when he drew his gun. Then, Marquette was hit on the head. All three Fryes were arrested, but things went out of control when angry mobs formed on the scene of the crime. Rumors spread that Marquette's mother was assaulted by the cops, and a rumor even spread that Marquette's pregnant girlfriend was assaulted even though she wasn't at the scene of the crime; and Blacks took to the streets less than an hour later.

The Watts Riots resulted in thirty-four deaths and damage of over forty-million dollars' worth of properties. The National Guard came in to help stop the rioting, but five days of fighting, looting, and burning took its toll on LA, and things got worse about three years later.

I looked at Dr. King's face on the wall. When he died on April 4, 1968, riots erupted in over one hundred US cities, including LA. His death was also seen as a travesty of justice, and every single Black person on the planet agrees.

During the Watts Riots, Grandma and Mama stayed inside their apartment and didn't leave until the riots were over. Since Grandma missed five days of work, that was a huge cut in their budget, but during the MLK riots, Mama took part in the rioting. Like most people, she idolized Dr. King and believed firmly in his dream. So, Mama was as mad as a raging bull when she heard on the news that Dr. King was shot while standing on a balcony in Memphis, Tennessee. Mama threw some rocks and bottles at store windows but had to run home when the LAPD swarmed into South Central.

Here we are, reliving the same shit that went down in the 1960s. In *Watership Down*, the rabbits state that there is a great evil in the world that comes from humans. They say humanity will never rest until humans have spoiled the Earth and killed the animals. Shoot, we won't rest until we've destroyed our world and killed every living creature on the planet, including our own species.

Then, I looked at Jesse Jackson's face.

He said, "Leaders must be tough enough to cry, human enough to make mistakes, humble enough to admit them, strong enough to absorb the pain, and resilient enough to bounce back and keep moving."

Is Uncle Tom Bradley tough, humble, strong, and resilient enough to remain the mayor of La La Land? I've never seen Tom Bradley cry, but that wouldn't be cool to see on the news. He has *definitely* made *a lotta* mistakes, and he has never humbled himself enough to admit all his faults. Is Tom Bradley strong enough to absorb LA's pain and resilient enough to keep us moving toward the Promised Land?

Dr. Murray is tough, humble, strong, and resilient. FAME's large congregation and community projects are a testament to that. Dr. King, Malcolm X, Medgar Evers, the Black Panthers, Gandhi, Abe Lincoln, the Kennedy brothers, et cetera were all tough, humble, strong, and resilient. Even death couldn't scare them away from their mission for equality.

When Jesse Jackson ran for president back in the 1980s, he lost. A lot of people thought a Black president was too good to be true, so some didn't get their hopes too high. But if America did have a Black president, I doubt things would get better. LA has a Black mayor, but racism is still a plague in this city, from the hood to the Hills. If the US had a Black president, I think things would probably still stay the same. After all, a Black president can't keep track of *every single* African American in the USA. Only God can do that. I doubt a Black president could do much when cops accused of brutality are acquitted by bogus juries. Only God can mete out punishments because He is all-knowing and all-powerful. Despite the acquittals, I still love God. I'm sure that when those four cops face the Lord on Judgment Day, He'll sentence them to eternal damnation. Yep, Jesus is the best judge, jury, and executioner. I take comfort in that.

Chapter Twenty

By eleven o' clock that night, Mama and Daddy still didn't show up. Uncle Tom Bradley pledged to "take whatever resources needed" to stop the violence. He said that assistance would come from the county sheriff's department, the California Highway Patrol, and police and fire departments from neighboring cities. My instincts told me that all the pigs in the world wouldn't stop LA's day of reckoning.

It was getting late, and I needed sleep. I collapsed into my bed and drifted off to sleep wondering what exactly was wrong with humanity.

When I woke up the next morning, I went to my parents' bedroom and banged on the door. They didn't answer so I opened it and, sure enough, they weren't there. Then, I realized that if they had returned during the night, they would have woken me up so that I would know they were alright.

I called the airport and the Beverly Hills Hotel, but I couldn't leave any messages because their voicemails were full. I tried not to think the worst, but I had read how bad the Watts Riots, the MLK Riots, and other riots back in the day were. Shoot, I saw on the news how severely damaged Crown Heights was after the riot back in August. My parents might become casualties of a new riot.

I turned on the television. They showed images of the four

acquitted cops. The cameras showed them congratulating each other and hugging their attorneys. From the way they were smiling, you would think they won backstage passes to a Michael Jackson concert.

It made me sick. It reminded me of the pictures and videotapes I saw of Emmett Till's murder trial. Mr. Bryant and Mr. Milam shook hands, slapped their lawyers' backs, and then kissed their wives. Somebody handed them cigars, and Mr. Milam lit his up immediately. Emmett Till's murderers and their friends, family, and associates *celebrated* the two demons' murder of a boy and their impunity. It made me sick and made my entire class mad as Hell. Now, history has repeated itself.

The Declaration of Independence will not protect us.

The US Constitution will not protect us.

The Civil Rights Act will not protect us.

We are a people who must help ourselves.

The news showed more on the aftermath of the verdicts. The first fires were set yesterday before the sun went down. An hour after the verdict, a store was busted up by some kids, and the violence was spreading like the plague.

I immediately packed my knives, sticks, and *nunchaku* into my bag. Then, I picked up my metal sword and stepped out of my house. I am eighteen. This means I'm officially an adult, and adults can think for themselves. I was sure nobody would show up at Dorsey High. I imagined most of my classmates and even some of my teachers were participating in the riots. Well, there was about to be another rioter.

I have two *bonguk geoms*. A *bonguk geom* is a Korean sword like the Japanese *katana*; it is a curved, single-edged sword with a circular hilt that is superior to the swords medieval knights used. The other swords I used at the dojang were wooden, so I asked Master Shin why he gave me such a dangerous weapon.

Master Shin explained, "Weapons are as good or evil as the people who wield them. I know you plan on becoming a Marine, but I'm certain you won't take away life needlessly. If there's one thing you are, it's good."

That reminded me of what Squire Julian Gingivere told Matthias in *Redwall*. The Squire explained that despite how beautiful Martin the Warrior's meteorite sword is, it was still just a sword. A sword holds no magical spells or special powers – Excalibur is an exception. The Squire also said what Master Shin said, that a sword is only as good or evil as the person who wields it.

I went to Wanda's house and knocked on the door.

She replied in a deep, gruff voice, "Who is it? I must warn you. I'm armed!"

I said, "Yeah, girl, with your mama's shovel. Open the damn door!"

Wanda opened it. She was wearing a football helmet, a bullet-proof vest, and had a shovel in her right hand.

I laughed and asked, "Girl, where did you get a bullet-proof vest?"

Wanda explained, "Willie, one of my mom's cooks, got us bullet-proof vests because he knew we would need protection if LA erupted into chaos. Turns out, he was right."

I walked inside, and Wanda closed the door with all the locks. The curtains were drawn so her house looked dark.

I asked, "You're afraid someone's gonna come and rob you?"

Wanda replied, "Yes. Mama told me to watch over the house and to make sure no strangers get in. Since you ain't no stranger, Hatima, you're welcome here anytime."

I said, "Great, Wanda. Since we're like sisters, I'm gonna need your help."

Wanda asked, "To do what? Tear apart stores like the other crazy people out there?"

I explained, "Not Black-owned stores like your mama's but Korean-owned stores. Stores that are owned by people like Missus Du. It's about time we showed them we're through with being terrorized and brutalized!"

Wanda said, "Girl, you crazy!"

I replied, "Maybe I am. You gonna join me or not?"

Wanda sighed and said, "I have to come with you to watch your back. If you end up in jail, you can kiss any chances of getting into the Naval Academy goodbye."

Wanda called Imani and asked if she could find a way to her house. Luckily, Imani was home alone; her mom hadn't come back from the Beverly Hilton, and her brother was busy protecting his store. Imani said she could convince someone to drive her to West Boulevard.

Soon, a Ford Pinto turned up on West Boulevard. Imani got out of the passenger's seat and a Black guy with a Caesar cut got out of the driver's seat.

Wanda opened the door for them and asked, "Who is this?"

Imani said, "This is Shawn Jenkins. He works at Mister Peterson's Barber Shop. Obviously, he can't go to work because of the rioting, but he said that burning down Korean stores makes sense to him. I *know* this is crazy but I'm mad as Hell too. The lawyers and Rodney King tried to do things the right way through the justice system, and that failed. It looks like we'll have to carry out a different approach to this for our voices to be heard. A picture speaks a thousand words, and I'm sure a photo of a robbed store will also speak a thousand words."

Wanda asked Imani, "Did your brother put a 'Black-Owned' sign on the door of his store?"

Imani replied, "I don't know. I'm guessing your mom did that to her restaurant?"

Wanda said, "Yep. The restaurant has 'Black-Owned' signs on the doors and windows. Of course, some people might ignore the signs; but if they do, Mama, the cooks, and waiters will be more than happy to put bullets in their asses."

I said, "Missus Brooks is a respected businesswoman in this community. Maybe her store will remain untouched." Then, I realized that Wanda said her mama and her employees would put bullets in anyone who tried to rob or burn down the store. I asked, "Since when does your mama approve of guns?"

Wanda said, "Since the riots started. Shoot, some folks are buying as many guns and bullets as they can, while others are straight-up stealing them."

I shook my head in disbelief at the world's craziness.

Shawn, who had remained quiet until now, said, "Can we please go out there and destroy some shit?"

We all left the house and got into Shawn's car. Wanda and I sat in the back while Imani rode shotgun.

I said, "Shawn, drive us to Vermont Vista, specifically, the intersection of Ninety-First Street and Figueroa Avenue."

Shawn said, "That's where Latasha Harlins was killed. I'm sure that store has been picked clean by rioters."

I asked, "But is the building still standing?"

Shawn said, "Maybe. Why?"

I said bluntly, "We're gonna burn that shit down."

Wanda and Imani looked at me like I was crazy. I know my idea sounded crazy, but I was dead serious.

Shawn said, "I got two gallons of gasoline in my trunk. It's not just for my car."

Imani said, "I'm okay with petty theft, but arson is a whole 'nother level."

I said, "Missus Du is the one woman whom my heart and soul despise with no mercy. She got off easy for murdering a Black girl who looks like me and you two. It's time to show her and all the other racist Koreans that they no longer have impunity."

Shawn revved up his car, drove down West Boulevard, and yelled, "Power to the people!"

The rioting looked different on television. When a person sees something bad on television, they usually say, "That's terrible." But they feel safe if the danger isn't happening to them personally.

As Shawn drove down Western Avenue, I saw that most of the stores, restaurants, and other businesses in South Central had been broken into. Windows had been shattered, and there was glass all over the sidewalk. Doors had been broken down and thrown into the streets, and people were coming out of stores with food, pharmaceuticals, electronics, hair care products, guns, bullets, and money! Some of the stores, such as the pharmacy, the dry cleaners, and the electronics store we drove by were owned by Koreans, but the take-out grill, the dessert shop, the hair care products store, and the pawnshop were all Black-owned! I didn't see why rioters would loot from Black stores! Marcus Garvey and Kwame Nkrumah would be heartbroken if they saw this. As Pan-Africanists, they understood the importance of Black people across the world sticking together.

I yelled out the window, "Black people need to stick together! Power to the people!"

Some people replied, "Power to the people!"

Some gave the Black Power salute.

The drive may not have taken so long if there weren't so many rioters blocking the road. Shawn honked his horn so the rioters would get outta the way.

When we arrived at Empire Liquor, we saw that it was in one piece. We got outta the car and stepped inside. The door had already been broken down so we could only be accused of trespassing, not breaking and entering; the shelves were almost completely empty, but we found some bottles of liquor that had been left behind. Shawn checked the cash register, but it was completely empty. The looters even took the change.

I asked, "Anyone have a lighter?"

Shawn took one outta his pocket and said, "Time to burn this bitch's store to the ground." Then, he took out the two gallons of gasoline from the trunk of his car.

We poured alcohol and gasoline on the floor, on the counter, and on the shelves. We also poured alcohol and gasoline outside the store and all around its perimeter. Then, Shawn took a rag out of the glove compartment of his car, put it inside a half-full liquor bottle, lit it up, threw the bottle into the store, and we all got back into Shawn's Pinto. The fire spread like crazy, and Shawn drove down the street so that his car would be away from the blaze, but we still had a good view of the store. Fire came out of the windows, spread along the walls, and soon made it to the roof. Flames shot out of the roof, and we heard a loud *CRASH* and *KATHUMP!* The roof completely collapsed, and Empire Liquor became a mountain of rubble! I looked at the smoke and was sure someone would figure out there was a blaze and call the LAFD. Shawn must have had the same thought because he drove us outta there.

While we drove back to Crenshaw, Shawn put a CD in his player and "Fuck tha Police" started blasting at max volume. Ice Cube laid down the truth.

HEAL THE HOOD

Fuck the police coming straight from the underground
A young nigga got it bad 'cause I'm brown
And not the other color so police think
they have the authority to kill a minority
Fuck that shit, 'cause I ain't the one
for a punk motherfucker with a badge and a gun
to be beating on, and thrown in jail
We can go toe to toe in the middle of a cell
Fucking with me 'cause I'm a teenager
with a little bit of gold and a pager
Searching my car, looking for the product
Thinking every nigga is selling narcotics
You'd rather see, me in the pen
than me and Lorenzo rolling in a Benz-o
Beat a police out of shape
and when I'm finished, bring the yellow tape
To tape off the scene of the slaughter
Still getting swoll off bread and water
I don't know if they fags or what
Search a nigga down, and grabbing his nuts
And on the other hand, without a gun they can't get none
But don't let it be a black and a white one
'Cause they'll slam ya down to the street top
Black police showing out for the white cop
Ice Cube will swarm
on any motherfucker in a blue uniform
Just 'cause I'm from, the CPT
Punk police are afraid of me!
HUH, a young nigga on the warpath
And when I'm finished, it's gonna be a bloodbath

of cops, dying in LA
Yo Dre, I got something to say

We all rapped with NWA. Then, Shawn put in Public Enemy's CD titled *Fear of a Black Planet*, and "Fight the Power" started playing. We also rapped along with Public Enemy.

1989 the number another summer (get down)
Sound of the funky drummer
Music hitting your heart 'cause I know you got soul
(Brothers and sisters, hey)
Listen if you're missing y'all
Swinging while I'm singing
Giving whatcha getting
Knowing what I know
While the Black bands sweatin'
And the rhythm rhymes rollin'
Got to give us what we want (uh)
Gotta give us what we need (hey)
Our freedom of speech is freedom or death
We got to fight the powers that be

Lemme hear you say
Fight the power (lemme hear you say)
Fight the power
Fight the power
Fight the power
Fight the power
Fight the power
Fight the power

HEAL THE HOOD

We've got to fight the powers that be

As the rhythm designed to bounce
What counts is that the rhymes
Designed to fill your mind
Now that you've realized the pride's arrived
We got to pump the stuff to make us tough
From the heart
It's a start, a work of art
To revolutionize make a change nothing's strange
People, people we are the same
No we're not the same
'Cause we don't know the game
What we need is awareness, we can't get careless
You say what is this?
My beloved let's get down to business
Mental self defensive fitness
(Yo) bum rush the show
You gotta go for what you know
To make everybody see, in order to fight the powers that be
Lemme hear you say
Fight the power (lemme hear you say)
Fight the power
Fight the power
Fight the power
Fight the power
Fight the power
Fight the power
We've got to fight the powers that be

Adaeze Nwosu

Fight the power (lemme hear you say)
Fight the power
Fight the power
Fight the power
Fight the power
Fight the power
We've got to fight the powers that be

Elvis was a hero to most
But he never meant shit to me you see
Straight-up racist that sucker was
Simple and plain
Motherfuck him and John Wayne
'Cause I'm Black and I'm proud
I'm ready and hyped plus I'm amped
Most of my heroes don't appear on no stamps
Sample a look back you look and find
Nothing but rednecks for four hundred years if you check
Don't worry be happy
Was a number one jam
Damn if I say it you can slap me right here
(Get it) let's get this party started right
Right on, c'mon
What we got to say (yeah)
Power to the people no delay
Make everybody see
In order to fight the powers that be

Fight the power
Fight the power

HEAL THE HOOD

Fight the power
Fight the power
We've got to fight the powers that be

Music was invented for the powerless. It allows powerless people to voice their concerns and allows the oppressed to tell their oppressor *exactly* how they feel about them.

Since there were roadblocks and crazy rioters, we went back to Crenshaw through a different route. We drove by the Baldwin Hills Crenshaw Plaza and saw people walking outta the mall with guns, clothes, watches, and even fast food. Even Cinemark Baldwin Hills wasn't safe. People were walking out of the movie theater with bags of popcorn and chips. Some people walked out chug-a-lugging soda. Cinemark wouldn't be showing any movies today, that's for damn sure.

I expected to see loads of cops driving around South Central as usual; but so far, I hadn't seen one. I figured that the cops must be hiding in their police stations or their homes like the sniveling cowards they really are!

I thought about Detective Crawford and Detective Hill. They had incarcerated the Crips who were responsible for Devin's death, which proved that some cops did use their brains; but this riot ain't about Detective Crawford, Detective Hill, or the other cops who use their brains to take down actual criminals. This riot is about cops like Officer Greene and Officer Wayne, who harassed Dr. Wilson, me, and Daddy. Shit, they tried to incarcerate Daddy for crimes he never committed! This riot is about cops like Officer Hawthorne and Officer Jones, who apprehend the first Black guy they find after a crime is committed even though the Black guy doesn't fit the description with the exception of his skin color.

Officer Jones is an Uncle Tom, just like that Black cop from *Boyz n the Hood* who told Furious that shooting a Black robber is cool 'cause "There'd be one less nigga in these streets we'd have to worry about."

Shit, that Black cop stuck a gun in Tre's throat and said he became a cop so that he could terrorize Blacks like Tre and his friends! People should become cops to protect and serve, not terrorize and kill. Detective Crawford said the LAPD needs to screen applicants more efficiently and I hope the riots will show Chief Gates, Mayor Uncle Tom Bradley, and other higher-ups how important it is to have good and decent people on the force.

Shawn drove through Crenshaw Boulevard instead of MLK Boulevard to make sure Hector wouldn't see his sister rioting and snitch to their mom.

When we drove by Mr. Yang's Laundromat, I said, "Stop right here!"

The door to the Laundromat had been broken down and all the windows shattered.

Shawn said, "I can't believe you care about your boyfriend's Yellow ass."

I got out and walked into the Laundromat. The lights had also been smashed, but there was enough light from outside to navigate through the place. Some of the machines had been bashed, but I was sure Mr. Yang could repair them or buy new ones. I saw a huge thing on the floor of the Laundromat, and I wondered what it was. Then, I realized that it was the machine where people exchange bills for tokens so they can work the machines. Well, it had been torn apart, which meant all the money in it was gone.

I got out and said, "The store's empty, some machines have been smashed, and the machine that's full of bills and tokens has been emptied of all its assets. Ronnie ain't in there; maybe he went home."

Wanda said, "It's Ronnie job to look after the store. He wouldn't leave unless Mister Yang told him to."

Imani said, "Maybe Mister Yang told him to, for his own safety."

Shawn said, "Maybe some looters beat him up so bad that he's either at the hospital or the morgue."

I exclaimed, "Shawn, don't be so negative!"

Shawn said, "That's what his Black ass gets for siding with our enemies!"

I explained, "Our enemies are racists, such as Missus Du and the four pigs who beat Rodney King. Koreans who haven't hurt us and cops who do their jobs right ain't our enemies!"

I visualized Joshua, his dad, and Detective Crawford. They had treated me with kindness and respect. Like I said before, I wasn't rioting because of them but because of the others who judge us based on stereotypes instead of merit.

I got into Shawn's Pinto and told him, "Take us home."

Soon we made it back to West Boulevard. We got outta Shawn's car and into Wanda's house.

Shawn said, "Wooow! I feel so free!"

I said, "Missus Du got what was coming to her, that heartless bitch!"

Imani said, "Okay, everyone, calm down. We should be glad the cops didn't arrest us for arson!"

Wanda rolled her eyes and said, "Yeah, we know, it would ruin your chances of being a doctor. Doctor King had a PhD, but he still had enough nerve to change the status quo."

Imani explained, "He didn't do anything too crazy until after he finished his schooling."

I asked, "Imani, do you think you can make it back to your apartment in one piece?"

Imani said, "Sure I can. Shawn can drive me."

Shawn said, "I hope they haven't destroyed the complex."

When I went back to my house, it was still empty. I turned on the news. There were roadblocks all over LA and neighboring cities. It looked like the riot had spread from South Central to the rest of the city. Even bougie neighborhoods were being torn up by looters and rioters! I wondered what position my parents were in.

I doubted Daddy would stay at the airport. He and some of his fellow baggage handlers probably ventured into Inglewood and were tearing Uncle Alonzo, Auntie Kalisha, and Malik's hood to pieces. Beverly Hills would soon feel the brunt of the riots, which meant Mama wasn't entirely safe either.

Another piece of news that made me worried was the state of Koreatown. The cops had mostly abandoned the Koreans and rioters were tearing their neighborhood to pieces. This was understandable; Koreans and Blacks have been at each other's throats since the 1960s. I wondered if Master Shin, Joshua, and Mr. Yang were alright.

First, I called the Yangs' apartment, but their phone went straight to voicemail. I figured they would be at the nightclub, protecting it from rioters. I called Mr. Yang's nightclub, but a female voice said the phone was out of service. Had their nightclub been looted and burned to the ground? I called their apartment again and left them a message, asking if they were alright and letting them know that I was alright.

I called Master Shin to find out if he was alright. Thank God he answered his office phone.

Master Shin asked, "The verdict made you angry, right?"

I said, "Of course!"

HEAL THE HOOD

Master Shin said, "It made me angry as well. Those four officers aren't worthy of their badges. They weren't trained in the way of the warrior. I'm sure you want to process your anger, just like every other Black person in LA."

I could sense that Master Shin knew that I had also participated in the rioting.

I told him, "Thank you for being so understanding. I'm guessing you're guarding the dojang."

Master Shin said, "Yes. Some of my students, people of all races, are helping me as well. Martial arts helps bring people from all walks of life together."

I smiled and said, "Okay. Stay safe."

I hung up and wondered if Master Shin thought I might do something *really* stupid. Did he think I would attack and kill cops to avenge Rodney King? Did he think I would attack and kill Korean shopkeepers to avenge Latasha Harlins? Master Shin had gifted me my *nunchaku*, wooden canes and staffs, knives, and *bonguk geoms*. I thought he sensed that things were gonna get crazier in the hood and that I needed all the protection I could get.

A really great surprise came on television. On KNBC, Bill Cosby, one of the funniest men on Earth, told everyone who was watching to stop what they were doing and watch *The Cosby Show* finale instead. I guess he was trying to calm down hostilities in South Central by having people watch the rich, successful, and well-educated Huxtables.

Theo graduated from New York University with a bachelor's degree in pediatric psychology. An earlier episode revealed that Theo got into NYU's grad school, so he would be studying for his master's degree in September. Who knows, maybe he'll get a PhD and become a Doctor of Psychology. Another Dr. Huxtable! Imagine that! Dr.

Heathcliff Huxtable remembered when Theo got Ds on his report card and told his dad that he wasn't planning on going to college. I also remembered the series premiere, and I laughed when they re-showed Theo planning on how to balance a budget on a "regular person's" salary. After the first episode, Wanda, Imani, and I thought the Huxtable kids were spoiled and didn't know how good they had it. My girls and I knew that if *our* parents were doctors and lawyers, college would be a guaranteed reality instead of a possible fantasy.

How much racism had the Huxtables endured? I'm sure Dr. Heathcliff Huxtable and Mrs. Clair Huxtable encountered and fought against racism in the past, but it hasn't been shown on the show. Did they face opposition from the other residents of Brooklyn Heights when they first moved in? Plus, there's no proof that their kids endured racism. Did Sondra face opposition against White students for getting into Princeton 'cause of affirmative action? Did Denise and Vanessa face prejudice from naïve Whites or Asians because they went to HBCUs? Did any of Theo's college professors treat him like he didn't belong at NYU? It really pisses me off that the Huxtables never encountered racism on the show 'cause it gives off the illusion – no, the lie – that once Blacks gain an education, climb up the socioeconomic ladder, and move to nice neighborhoods, that they won't have to face racist BS ever again. W. E. B. Du Bois was the first Black man to receive a PhD from Harvard, and he still drank from the "Coloreds Only" water fountain down South. Dr. King had a PhD, but he was shot while standing on a balcony. It doesn't matter what we accomplish 'cause some folks will only see us as niggers.

On the news, it was stated that nine people were killed and a hundred and fifty had been injured.

President Bush said, "I urge all Americans to approach this situation with calm, with tolerance, and with a respect for the rights of all individuals under the Constitution."

HEAL THE HOOD

I gave a harsh laugh 'cause that was the funniest shit I'd heard in a while. The pigs didn't approach Rodney King with calm, tolerance, or respect. Pigs never believe that Blacks are also American citizens under the Constitution. Shit, I remembered what Grandma said about the writing of the Constitution. That when it was written, Blacks were only considered *three-fifths of a person!* That doesn't sound very different from the way things are today! We're still not seen as completely human.

The news stated that the federal government would continue to investigate whether the racist cops violated federal civil rights laws when they beat Rodney King. Next, the governor declared a state of emergency and announced that the California National Guard had been put on high alert.

I'm sure every single Black person in America can agree that the Civil Rights Act was violated when Rodney King was beaten. According to the Civil Rights Act, it's illegal to discriminate against someone based on race, color, religion, sex, or national origin. Unfortunately, racism, sexism, and other isms are still an issue in our world today. The Civil Rights Act hasn't done shit for Rodney King, Latasha Harlins, Eula Mae Love, Bobby Hutton, et cetera.

The news said that Uncle Tom Bradley had declared a dawn-to-dusk curfew on South Central, had banned the sale of ammunitions, and had placed strict limits on the sale of gasoline. Since some gangsters do more damage at night, Uncle Tom Bradley figures forcing a curfew will calm things down. The coon is crazy as hell. Blacks can always get their guns, even if every gun store in South Central is closed and cleared out. Unfortunately, most Blacks rely on guns for self-defense 'cause they don't have hand-to-hand combat training. I got my hapkido weapons, so I'll be okay. Limited gasoline sales mean that cars won't be able to transport rioters across the city.

Plus, burning down stores and other buildings will be hard.

The news also said firefighters were attacked by rioters with stones, axes, and guns. Like I said before, the LAFD are no longer neutral in the race war.

After *The Cosby Show* finale aired, a reporter named Roger O'Neil said the curfew was somewhat effective but that there was still urban warfare throughout the city.

Shit was gonna get worse before it got better.

Chapter Twenty-One

The next day, Rodney King appeared on television. I was surprised by this 'cause the only other time he was on television was when they showed tapes of the beating; Mr. King rarely granted interviews over the past year; and a lotta folks didn't understand why Mr. King didn't appear on *The Oprah Winfrey Show*, *The Arsenio Hall Show*, or any other form of media to explain what happened to him. I figured that he didn't want to relive that awful night. I also remembered what Dr. Wilson said about defense attorneys asking prospective jurors their opinions about what they saw on the news. African Americans and some other non-Blacks, like Joshua and Master Shin, would feel sympathy for Mr. King because of the tape and any interviews Mr. King did. Therefore, they would be dismissed from jury duty.

Another reason Rodney King probably didn't do interviews might be because he doesn't want to be an icon or a symbol. His life story isn't as vivid as Dr. King's, Malcolm X's, Medgar Evers', Huey Newton's, or Nelson Mandela's. Those men were all leaders. Rodney King is the unlucky drunk driver who was picked out by the cops. I don't think that makes him qualified to be a leader in our Black Community, but I hope Rodney King finally sees that this riot isn't just about him. It's also about Latasha Harlins, Eula Mae Love, Gavin Cato, Yusuf Hawkins, Edmund Perry, James Powell, Matthew Johnson, Bobby Hutton, Fred Hampton, Mark Clark, the six kids from Birmingham, and Emmett Till. It's also about Dr. King, Malcolm X, and Medgar Evers. It's about Nelson Mandela and his bullshit twenty-seven-year prison sentence. It's about Kunta Kinte, Harriet Tubman, Frederick Douglass, Josiah Henson, and all the other Black people who were slaves. This riot is about the injustices all Blacks worldwide have faced and will continue to face in the future. Rodney King has the chance to be part of something bigger than himself, so he shouldn't stay quiet.

Rodney King wore a suit and tie on television. He is neither a pastor like Dr. Murray nor is he a lawyer like Thurgood Marshall; but his message is true.

Rodney King said, "People, I just want to say, can we all get along? Can we get along? Can we stop making it horrible for the older people and the kids? We've just got to, just got to. We're all stuck here for a while. Let's try to work it out. Let's try to work it out."

That is a very good question: Can we all get along?

My boyfriend is Korean, and my martial arts teacher is Korean. Joshua and I get along because of our many positive aspects. He admires my strong spirit, and I admire his humor, persistence, intelligence, and kind nature. Master Shin knows the way of the warrior doesn't belong to one race nor one nationality. Bruce Lee had no problem teaching non-Asians Jeet Kune Do. By showing different aspects of Asian culture, respect for Asians has risen over the decades.

Joshua has also become more open-minded about the trials and tribulations Blacks endure. He listened to me when I cried about Latasha Harlins' death, and he made great insights after he watched *Boyz n the Hood*.

The Wilsons live in a predominantly White neighborhood,

and they obviously get along with their neighbors, but I still dislike Stella's White friends. They refuse to accept that racism is still a problem in American and world society. I'm sure they cheered when the four pigs were acquitted by that predominantly White jury. I don't understand why Stella hangs out with them. They say racist stuff, and she rarely takes a stand. Is this what happens when you remove a Black person from an all-Black world and place them in an all-White world? You get brainwashed and turn your back on your people? The rich Blacks who live in South Central always take a stand when injustice is present. I'm seriously having second thoughts about moving out of South Central after I complete college.

I'm one hundred percent sure that Dr. King is up in Heaven watching the riots. I'm sure he's crying about all the violence people are inflicting on LA and on one another. Frederick Douglass and Medgar Evers are probably crying as well. Is Nelson Mandela watching the riots all the way in South Africa? Is he also crying? After twenty-seven years in prison, the world hasn't changed much.

I'm sure Malcolm X would have no problem with Blacks being violent, so long as they channeled their anger toward the cops and Koreans. But Malcolm X also believed that it was possible that all men could be brothers after taking the pilgrimage to Mecca. Maybe he's also sad about all the shit going down. According to the riots, humanity is far from sitting at the table of brotherhood. I'm sure the Black Panthers would also want Blacks to fight a proper war against the cops and our other oppressors. The problem with that is that a gun doesn't automatically make a person a soldier. People need extensive training in hand-to-hand combat and many other skills before they're ready for battle. Most folks in Crenshaw and other LA hoods don't have the time to be soldiers and, frankly, I'm pretty sure a lot of them ain't interested in going into a real war.

Out in LA, Shawn drove me, Wanda, and Imani to Gramercy Park and Manchester Square so we could burn down some more Korean businesses. We torched a Korean electronics square in Gramercy Park that had been looted and emptied out. Next, we torched a Korean restaurant in Manchester Square. It took us half an hour to drive to Gramercy Park and twenty minutes to drive to Manchester Square. Then, we heard on the radio that the 40th Infantry Division of the California Army National Guard was continuing to move into the city on Humvees. Shawn figured that it was best to drive back to Crenshaw and hide in our homes since it looked like we wouldn't be able to torch more Korean businesses with impunity.

We also managed to get food from McDonald's, KFC, Taco Bell, and supermarkets. Technically, we *stole* the food, but shit was outta control. We needed supplies to see us through these riots.

Wanda explained, "Everyone's acting the way New Orleans folks act during hurricane season. Folks are trying to get food, clothes, medicine, and other supplies, but since stores are boarded up, looted, or burned down, they gotta steal the shit. I don't think anyone is gonna be able to steal anything from the Creole 'n' Cajun Kitchen, not with my mama guarding it."

We had to deal with hostile rioters who were also stocking up on supplies. I didn't like to do it, but I took out my *bonguk geom* and used it to slice people's legs and arms, but I didn't chop off their limbs; I just gave them large cuts. I figured large cuts aren't as bad as severed limbs. One guy even pointed a Colt 45 at us, but I quickly disarmed him, and gave him a four-knuckle strike to the face and a side kick to his stomach! He looked like an out of breath marathoner, the way he was clutching his belly!

When we drove away from the supermarket, Shawn exclaimed,

"That was so cool! Lots of folks say you're like a Black female version of Bruce Lee, but I thought they were exaggerating!"

Even though I was still in shock at my first successful disarming outside of the dojang, I replied, "Women can become highly skilled martial artists. There are plenty in martial arts tournaments and the US Armed Forces."

At my house, Wanda and I ate McDonald's Chicken Nuggets with fries and soda.

Then, Wanda asked, "Any news from your parents?"

I said, "No."

Wanda said, "We have to keep thinking in the positive. Your dad's probably at the airport, unable to leave 'cause of the hell he would go through trying to drive back to Crenshaw. Your ma's in Bev Hills, and those rich folks at the hotel must have enough supplies to last for months."

I stated, "According to the news, there are electrical power outages all over the city, so it's a good thing West Boulevard still has power. Maybe my parents can't call because of the power outages. Plus, the buses have been canceled so using public transit to get back here is outta the question."

Wanda said, "Some businesses have sent their employees home. Ma sent her cooks and waiters home and told them to stay indoors. Some stayed behind to defend the restaurant, and I'm sure the rest are rioting. Do you think the airport and the Bev Hills Hotel sent your parents home?"

I said, "They ain't here so either they're still at work or they're holed up in somebody else's house."

Wanda said, "The US Postal Service ain't delivering no mail even though they always bragging about their reliability. The Lakers playoff game has been postponed until Sunday and moved to Las

Vegas. The Dodgers have also postponed their games. The Clippers moved a game to Anaheim. I wonder if Mickey and Minnie have box seats. Hollywood Park Racetrack and Los Alamitos Racecourse have also been shut down. I guess horseracing fans will have to sit tight."

I wasn't interested in going outside again because the city had transformed into Armageddon. It felt like Judgment Day was upon us. If that was true, then I was sure Jesus would sentence those four pigs to suffer eternal damnation in Hell. I hoped Jesus would provide a live feed for us so that we could feel satisfaction at the cops' just punishment.

I kept my windows closed, and Wanda kept me company. If anyone tried to break into the Brookses' house, we would be able to see and hear them from my house. Wanda and I watched the news, played cards, read books and magazines, and talked about college.

Wanda said, "I think I'll go to TSU."

I said, "You sure your bro wants you tagging along?"

Wanda explained, "He'll do his own thing, and I'll do mine. What about you? Where will you go if the Naval Academy doesn't accept you?"

I said, "My top choices are Freeman and Vanderbilt."

Wanda asked, "What about UC Davis? UC Davis and Freeman have both offered you full athletic scholarships based on your shortstop skills. With athletic *and* academic scholarships, most of your tuition and fees would be paid, which means less hassle for your parents."

I explained, "I'd like to travel outside the state of California 'cause I wanna see what else is out there. Besides, Atlanta is a cool city for Black folks; the Atlanta University Center, the MLK Historic Site, the Sweet Auburn Historic District, et cetera. If there's a city that will help me fully explore our heritage, it's Atlanta; but Vanderbilt is also a great school and Nashville is also a cool city. There are three HBCUs in Nashville, and the city played an important role in the Civil Rights Movement, so it's also a great place to learn about the Black experience."

Wanda said, "In my opinion, the Black Ivy League is as good as any White school, girl."

I said, "Wanda, just because a person decides not to go to an HBCU doesn't mean they're not Black enough. These riots are causing a lotta people to decide what is or is not Black. But no one is an expert on that because what it means to be Black keeps changing as the years go by."

Wanda looked up at the pictures of the famous Black people on the walls.

Then, she said, "A damn thing hasn't changed since the Civil War. We're still seen as African monkeys with no souls."

I said, "The more things change, the more they stay the same."

Wanda asked, "Do you think Malcolm X, the Black Panthers, and Toussaint Louverture would be happy about the riots?"

I said, "Nah, girl! Malcolm X only preached violence when it's used in self-defense, just like Master Shin and Mister Miyagi. The folks who attacked Reginald Denny and Field Lopez took their anger out on Whites, Latinos, and Asians that haven't done them any harm. Brother Malcolm wouldn't like that, especially inflicting pain on other people of color. If Huey Newton hadn't died three years ago, he'd say rioting and looting in our own communities is a thoughtless way to get our points across. But he probably wouldn't have a problem with burning and looting in other neighborhoods, such as Westwood and Beverly Hills. The BPP believed a war was the only way to get our civil rights. Too bad most of those rioters ain't trained in the art of war. Now, Toussaint Louverture was a real revolutionary.

He mobilized and unified the Blacks of Saint-Domingue to fight the French, the Spanish, and the British. As a result, Haiti, the world's oldest Black republic, was founded."

Wanda said, "Toussaint Louverture was the man! But the Haitian Revolution was the *only* successful slave revolt in the Americas. Remember Gabriel Prosser's, Denmark Vesey's, and Nat Turner's revolts? They were all stopped dead in their tracks."

I said, "Some people say you'll catch more flies with honey than with vinegar. Frederick Douglass, Doctor King, Medgar Evers, Harry Belafonte, Bob Marley, et cetera believed that peace, love, and understanding were better tools for activists than knives, guns, and cannons. In the end, President Lincoln's signature on the Emancipation Proclamation and the Thirteenth Amendment led to our people's liberation. President LBJ's signature on the Civil Rights Act, the Voting Rights Act, and the Fair Housing Act led to racism being seen as a sin."

Wanda said, "That hasn't done a lotta good! Missus Du, those four pigs, and other Koreans and cops get away with racist behavior with no consequences!"

I scrunched my face in thought and explained, "Since racism is seen as a great evil in the eyes of the law, bigots can get away with racist acts by claiming their actions weren't fueled by racism. They say that they were afraid for their lives, the person of color was commiting a vicious crime, stuff like that. Bigots won't reveal their true nature because it puts them on the same level as the Nazis and the KKK. The last place any person wants to see a monster is in their own mirror."

Wanda stayed silent, hung her head, and said, "What's the point of taking a stand when they beat us and shoot us down? What's the point of putting our faith in a justice system that just explains bigotry away? Doctor King, Malcolm X, Medgar Evers, Bobby Hutton, Fred Hampton, they all took a stand and they were all shot like dogs! Worse, their deaths weren't properly avenged!"

I stated, "Medgar Evers said, 'I'm looking to be shot any time I step out of my car … If I die, it will be in a good cause. I've been fighting for America just as much as the soldiers in Vietnam.' Abraham Lincoln and John F. Kennedy were Presidents of the United States, and they were shot for doing the right thing. Mahatma Gandhi was the most peaceful man on Earth after Doctor King and Jesus, and he was shot. Bob Marley wasn't shot, but his Rastafarian beliefs are considered the reason he died. He refused to amputate a toe when he had skin cancer since it was against his religious beliefs. Shoot, he died in Grandpa Gabriel's home state, Florida, in nineteen-eighty-one. I'm sure Bob Marley wouldn't have changed his mind if he knew that cutting off his toe would stop his own death. Medgar Evers also said, 'You can kill a man, but you can't kill an idea.' Bobby Seale said, 'You can jail a revolutionary, but you cannot jail the revolution.' Nelson Mandela said, 'A winner is a dreamer who never gives up.' As long as we keep these activists' revolutionary ideas alive, Doctor King's dream will never fade away."

The next day was Saturday. Saturday is every kid's favorite day of the week but, thanks to the riots, every kid in LA had been given a brief break from school. I wouldn't call this shit a holiday, no siree. When I opened the window, I could still smell smoke. LA is not a great city to live in if you have asthma. Smog is tough on asthmatics' lungs, but this smoke was no joke. It looked like the city was permanently burning, like the bowels of Hell. LA is often called Heaven on Earth, but it's become more like Hell Valley. Not just during the riots, but for all Blacks during all the years we've been here. LA is called a paradise, but for many people who are at the bottom of the barrel it's anything but that.

On the news, Army soldiers and Marines marched on the streets of LA with National Guards. My eyes were immediately glued to the screen when I saw the Marines. I knew shit must be extremely bad if the US Armed Forces are called to come and do their thing in a US city instead of a battlefield in a foreign country. I wondered if David was part of the Army team; but trying to find him among all those soldiers is like trying to find a needle in a haystack or a noodle in a macaroni factory.

Once again, I questioned whether becoming a Marine was the right thing to do. If there was another riot in another US city years from now, would I be asked to march there and restore order?

I watched news, ate the food Wanda brought me, and read books until my phone rang. I almost had a heart attack!

I ran to the phone and exclaimed desperately, "Hello, who is it?"

I was hoping Mama, Daddy, Grandma, or anyone else I loved and lost contact with would call me to explain that they were alright.

Joshua asked, "Hatima, are you alright?"

I immediately cried and exclaimed, "Joshua Yang, I am *sooooo* glad to hear your voice. Are you and your dad okay?"

Joshua said, "Yeah, I'm calling from the dojang. All these federal troops have helped get things under control in Koreatown. Unfortunately, Dad's nightclub was burned down. Some paramedics were able to get us to the hospital to make sure we didn't die of smoke inhalation, but Master Shin's dojang is in one piece. Some of his students used guns in addition to swords and knives and stuff and that kept the arsonists away from the dojang."

I said, "I'm sorry for your loss." People usually say that when a person's relative has died, not when a business has been destroyed. But Mister Yang's nightclub is an important part of his income so the Yangs might have to watch their budget carefully until the nightclub is rebuilt. Then I added, "The last time I saw your Laundromat, it had been broken into and vandalized, but it was still standing."

Joshua said, "Good. Dad's tried to call Mister Cho in Watts and Ronnie in Crenshaw but they're not answering the store phones or their home phones. Dad's worried something happened to them."

I said, "I'm not sure what happened to Ronnie. He wasn't at the Laundromat on Thursday when I checked. I hope he's alright."

Joshua asked, "What about your parents and grandmother? Are they alright?"

I explained, "I talked to Grandma on the phone on Thursday morning, but every other time I called her after that, her phone went straight to voicemail. Mama and Daddy haven't been in the house since Wednesday. I'm hoping Mama and Daddy are at the Beverly Hills Hotel and the airport and that Grandma is safe in her Watts apartment. But I'm afraid that's wishful thinking."

Joshua said, "'Cause of all the rioting they probably couldn't make it home. As soon as things quiet down, they'll come home."

I said, "Thanks for seeing the glass half-full."

Then Joshua asked, "Is it okay if I come to Crenshaw to pick you up?"

I asked incredulously, "For what, a date?"

Joshua explained, "No, for a peace rally in Koreatown."

I said, "Oh. I'd love to come, but I'm not sure if the streets are completely safe."

Joshua said, "Maybe I can ask the soldiers to escort me to Crenshaw. Sit tight, Hatima, I'll find my way to you."

He hung up.

Like I said, Joshua is persistent.

As the evening stretched into night, I heard a low, grumbling, gravely sound. I looked outside and saw two Humvees and a cream-colored Cadillac between them. Joshua honked his horn. I got my backpack, but the only weapons I took were my *nunchaku* and sticks. If I walk around with a sword, the Marines might turn me into the next Latasha Harlins.

I walked outside, closed the door, and locked it; and Joshua came outta his car, ran to me, gave me a big hug, and a *looooong* kiss. I wrapped my right arm around his neck and ran my left hand fingers through his hair. I couldn't believe how happy I was that Joshua was alive. He was also glad that I was alive. Some Marines wolf whistled and, just like that, the moment was over.

Joshua turned around and said, "Very funny, sirs. My girlfriend is planning to go to the Naval Academy so that she can join your crew someday. Y'all okay with that?"

I looked at the Marines in their uniforms. They weren't wearing fancy military jackets like Major Davis or Michael Jackson; they were wearing green camouflage outfits, just like in combat zones overseas.

The Marines replied, "She looks like a strong lady."

"The more, the merrier."

"Becoming a Marine is extremely hard work but, trust me, it's worth it."

Joshua drove us to Koreatown with help from his military escorts. Even though a lot of the streetlights weren't working I could see the damage done to La La Land; burned out buildings, wounded people, and smashed cars. I felt like I was part of some apocalypse movie. Even though LA is the Entertainment Capital of the World, I knew no director would yell, "Cut!" and then order a cleaning crew to come in and clear the set. It was going to take the biggest and toughest cleaning crews in the world to fix this mess.

The Koreatown Peace rally had just as good a turnout as the marches during the Civil Rights Movement. Joshua parked his car and we walked to the dojang. When Master Shin and Mr. Yang saw me, they had huge smiles on their faces.

Master Shin hugged me and said, "Hatima Parker, I am so glad you're here."

Mr. Yang said, "Leaving that message for us helped sooth our fears. I'm so glad you decided to come here."

I said, "You and Joshua marched with the FAME congregation when Daddy was unlawfully arrested. I owe you two."

Master Shin explained, "This rally is about peace and rebuilding. Many Korean stores were attacked, robbed, and burned down. But misfortune won't drive us back."

I asked, "Any chance y'all will show up to any peace rallies in South Central?"

Joshua, Mr. Yang, and Master Shin all smiled.

Joshua said, "We'll be there. I promise."

Thousands of people showed up at the Koreatown Peace Rally. Joshua and I carried broomsticks while Master Shin and Mr. Yang carried plastic garbage bags. Some Blacks and Latinos watched the Koreans march during the rally, and some old Korean men left the parade route to shake their hands. It was easy to spot me because I was one of the few Blacks participating in the rally. A Black kid on the sidewalk waved a South Korean flag and gave us the Black Power salute. I guess that means minorities should stick together.

We were led by the friends and relatives of Edward Lee, an eighteen-year-old Korean who was shot to death on Thursday while trying to fight off looters. Once again, there seemed to be more sympathy for the well-being of Koreans than the well-being of Blacks, but my heart still went out to Edward Lee and his friends and family. The Bible says you reap what you sow. Maybe the Koreans will finally see how their racist ways helped lead to the near-destruction of their community.

A Latino man taunted the crowd and made obscene gestures during the parade, but he was knocked to the ground by marchers and was arrested by the LAPD. I could relate to him. The Koreans haven't respected other minorities. Why should we respect them?

Because this cycle of hatred has to end somewhere.

The march lasted three hours; then, I helped the Yangs clean up the debris from their nightclub. I could make out the shapes of charred furniture, the turntables, the vinyl records, and alcohol bottles. We swept up all that mess and put it in the garbage bags. Radio Korea did a survey and said that there was an estimated three hundred and fifty million dollars' worth of damages to over a thousand buildings in LA.

The Koreans were mad that the cops didn't show up, and I said that the cops also abandoned the Blacks of LA. It turns out, some Koreans feel that the cops don't give a damn about their community. I was surprised by this, and I stated that I thought the cops cared about the Koreans and other Asians more than the Blacks. I explained that South Central is over policed and the cops often stop, harass, and arrest the wrong people. I stated that since Koreans and other Asians are believed to be smart, the cops don't expect any trouble from them, which is why the police presence in Koreatown isn't so high.

Mr. Yang told his fellow Koreans, "Many Blacks resent us, not because they're jealous of our businesses, but because we show a lack of concern for their communities. We don't hire Black workers and we treat *all* Blacks like gangsters. Some of you think Missus Du was

HEAL THE HOOD

justified in murdering Latasha Harlins, but others aren't. My son and his girlfriend convinced me to give the Blacks of South Central a chance. I hired a Black man named Ronnie McClure to help run the Laundromat I bought in Crenshaw a few months ago. Ronnie is a great worker and a good friend. Ronnie is not 'one of the good ones' nor is he a 'credit to his race.' There's so much goodness in this world, and it will only flourish if we learn to give everyone a chance, regardless of race, sex, religion, or nationality. We're all Americans and we all have a right to the American Dream."

Everyone applauded and cheered for Mr. Yang. Maybe Blacks and Koreans would finally start a rapprochement – I've been reading the dictionary during the riots.

Maybe Rodney King is right. Maybe we *can* all get along.

The next day, which is the Lord's Day, Mayor Bradley said on the news that the situation was, more or less, under control. That same night, troops killed a Salvadoran man named Marvin Rivas just because he drove his blue Datsun at a police barricade. That is when I figured out what my fate is: I *have* to become a Marine. I gotta show people there is a better way to bring about law and order, a better way to protect peace and freedom. I have to be the man in the mirror.

Chapter Twenty-Two

On Monday morning, I listened to the Jacksons' hit song, "Can You Feel It" and MJ's No. 1 hit, "Man in the Mirror." The Jackson brothers sang:

If you look around
The whole world is coming together now

Can you feel it, can you feel it, can you feel it
Feel it in the air, the wind is taking it everywhere
Can you feel it, can you feel it, can you feel it
All the colors of the world should be
Lovin' each other wholeheartedly
Yes, it's all right
Take my message to your brother and tell him twice
Spread the word and try to teach the man
Who's hating his brother, when hate won't do
When we're all the same, 'cause the blood inside me is inside you

Can you feel it, can you feel it, can you feel it
Can you feel it, can you feel it, can you feel it

MJ sang on his *Bad* album and at the 1988 Grammy Awards:

HEAL THE HOOD

I'm gonna make a change,
For once I'm my life
It's gonna feel real good,
Gonna make a difference
Gonna make it right

As I, turn up the collar on
My favorite winter coat
This wind is blowing my mind
I see the kids in the streets,
With not enough to eat
Who am I to be blind?
Pretending not to see their needs

A summer disregard, a broken bottle top
And a one man soul
They follow each other on the wind ya' know
'Cause they got nowhere to go
That's why I want you to know

I'm starting with the man in the mirror
I'm asking him to change his ways
And no message could have been any clearer
If you want to make the world a better place
(If you want to make the world a better place)
Take a look at yourself, and then make a change
(Take a look at yourself, and then make a change)
(Na na, na na na, na na, na nah)

I've been a victim of a selfish kind of love
It's time that I realize
That there are some with no home, not a nickel to loan
Could it be really me, pretending that they're not alone?

A willow deeply scarred, somebody's broken heart
And a washed-out dream
(Washed-out dream)
They follow the pattern of the wind ya' see
'Cause they got no place to be
That's why I'm starting with me
(Starting with me!)

I'm starting with the man in the mirror
(Ooh!)
I'm asking him to change his ways
(Ooh!)
And no message could have been any clearer
If you want to make the world a better place
(If you want to make the world a better place)
Take a look at yourself, and then make a change
(Take a look at yourself, and then make a change)

A lotta kids in South Central have been obsessed with making a difference since they learned about the Civil Rights Movement. Some kids claim that if they lived in the 1960s, they woulda been protesting and boycotting and whatnot. But Mama, Daddy, and Grandma said that not all Blacks participated in the Civil Rights Movement. Some Blacks thought Dr. King, Malcolm X, Rosa Parks, Fannie Lou Hamer, and other leaders were just stirring up trouble;

HEAL THE HOOD

some Blacks thought the system was too powerful to beat. Even in the present day, there are plenty of people who are too scared to make a difference or too stupid to realize that the isms still spread darkness over the planet. But Michael Jackson understands why it's important to take a stand. If you make a difference in the world, even if it is only once, then your life means something. If you don't try to stop the cycle of bigotry, then your life isn't worth a damn. I will *never* back down. I will *always* take a stand.

At a quarter past five on Monday evening, Mayor Tom Bradley lifted the dawn-to-dusk curfew. I guess that meant the riots were over. I walked out onto the streets and started walking toward MLK Boulevard. When I saw all the damage, I thought, *Damn!* Crenshaw's reputation was always bad in the eyes of the rest of the city, but we always got by. This time, I wasn't sure if the hood would be able to recover.

Mr. Peterson's Barber Shop had broken windows – thanks to some rioters throwing bricks and shit through them. But Mr. Peterson "shot those rioters in their legs and shoulders and they limped away, leaving a trail made of their own blood" – those are Mr. Peterson's exact words. The Pizza Hut was burned to the ground so now it was nothing more than rubble. It looks like Crenshaw folks would have to get their pizza pies elsewhere until it's rebuilt. The Fitzpatrick Gas Station and Convenience Store got siphoned of all its gas, but the store still had soda, chips, candy, and school supplies. That meant the Fitzpatricks would get by until Hector restocked the gas pumps. Since there were so many fires, I'm sure most of LA's gas was siphoned, and it might take a while to restock every gas station. Guess some folks will either have to get used to walking or riding bikes for a while.

On West Jefferson Boulevard, Mr. Hwang's Liquor Cabinet was completely burned down, another pile of rubble. But only one wall of Ms. Esther's Hair Salon had been burned down though the inside of the hair salon was a shampoo and conditioning nightmare with empty bottles and their contents spilled all over the floor. There was also blood on the floor so I knew I had to find out if Ms. Esther was still alive. The Creole & Cajun Kitchen and Oscar's Garage were both still standing and the structures and insides were intact. But the hood seemed to be permanently broken and so was my heart.

The presence of federal troops made things worse. Folks glared at them with hatred in their eyes, figuring they would do to us what the cops have been doing for decades, but among the Army soldiers was Captain David Igwe.

He stepped forward and said, "I am also a resident of South Central. My parents chose to live in this area above all others because of its rich history, culture, and community. Citizens of South Central Los Angeles, I apologize on behalf of the US Armed Forces for the circumstances that led to the riots. But we promise you that humanitarian aid will come to South Central and the rest of LA. We would appreciate your cooperation so that we can help the city of Los Angeles get back on its feet."

Some Crenshaw residents rolled their eyes while others listened intently to David's short speech.

I stepped forward and said, "People, we need to let go of our hatred for law enforcement. We have to cooperate by reporting crimes when they happen and testifying against *real* criminals in court. The 'no snitching' rule is absurd because it lets gangsters terrorize us with impunity. The cops can't tell the difference between real gangsters and innocent civilians, which has led to a high rise of racial profiling. In order to build a better LA, we need to develop new ways of thinking."

David said, "Thank you, Hatima Parker. Do you mind sticking around so my mom can write down what you said for the *Sentinel*?"

I said, "Sure, Captain Igwe. We all know the importance of the written word."

After Mrs. Igwe interviewed me and some other people, I decided to walk back home, so I could get my head together. I laid down on my couch and watched television. Someone started to open the door and I got my sword. I was ready to slice this motherfucker's hands off until the door opened completely, and I saw Daddy!

I exclaimed, "Daddy!"

I dropped my sword and ran into his arms. He hugged me, picked me up, and swung me around.

He exclaimed, "My baby girl is alive! My baby girl survived!"

I said, "Hey, I didn't take those hapkido lessons just for exercise!"

Daddy laughed and put me down. He asked, "Your mama?"

I stated, "Haven't heard from her since you two were here on Wednesday. I called Grandma on Thursday, and she answered. Unfortunately, I haven't heard from her since."

Daddy explained, "I was working a night shift at the airport, but the fellas heard how crazy people were acting the first night of the riots. I wanted to drive back home, but the fellas said driving home in the dark was a bad idea. Driving in the morning was just as bad since the riots spread to Inglewood. Folks were beating cops and burning down stores. I joined in since I was so angry over the verdict. Four pigs beat a Black man almost to death and it manages to be seen as a good thing. A damn thing hasn't changed since the sixties. The rioting got worse as the day progressed so the fellas and I stayed at the airport. There was plenty of food and space in the lounges. I tried calling your mama, but the line was busy and the voicemail was full. Soon, some of the phone lines weren't working at all. As soon as

Mayor Bradley lifted the curfew, I drove home. There are plenty of barricades and roadblocks, but I made it home."

I said, "I'm sure Mama will come home any minute. She's part of a carpool so it may take a while."

Daddy and I both smiled. I heated up some of the food Wanda brought me, and we munched on shrimp creole and mustard greens. There was a knock at the door, and I quickly ran to answer it.

It was Wanda, not Mama.

I said, "Oh, hi, Wanda."

Wanda said, "I thought I was your best friend. What, you ain't happy to see me?"

I said, "You are my best friend. But Daddy and I are just waiting for Mama."

Wanda squealed, "Your dad's here?"

She immediately rushed in, saw Daddy, and exclaimed, "Mister Parker, you're alright!"

Daddy got up, hugged her, and said, "It takes more than rioting to keep me down. Are you and your mama okay?"

Wanda replied, "We're fine and so is the restaurant. Some rioters ignored the 'Black-Owned' sign and tried to start some mess, but Mama and the staff sent them packing. The restaurant is in one piece, but it will be a while before Mama reopens. She needs to restock on supplies, and she also wants to help out the rest of the hood."

Wanda sat down with us and ate some of the shrimp creole. Then there was another knock at the door, and I ran to answer it.

When I opened it, my mama was standing right there with tears in her eyes.

I exclaimed, "Mama!"

We hugged, and she didn't let go of me for a while. Then, I heard Daddy clear his throat and Mama let me go. He had left the table and walked over to us.

He asked, "Aren't you gonna give your man a hug?"

Mama kissed Daddy passionately and cried into his shirt. Daddy told her it was okay, but I was able to get a good look at Mama. She had a white bandage wrapped around her head, like the headbands Prince and Jimi Hendrix wore.

I asked Mama, "What happened to you?"

Mama sniffled and explained, "My bosses decided to let us leave work early as soon as they sensed things were going to get very bad because of the verdict. The girls and I started to drive home, but some crazy rioters blocked our way home. They had formed a barricade on the road, stopping all cars. They only took out White, Asian, and Latino people from their cars. The girls and I got out to try and help the victims from the crazy rioters, but the rioters started beating us! One young man beat me with a hockey stick. He struck me across the head, and I lost consciousness.

I woke up in a hospital bed and a nurse told me that I was in the Cedars-Sinai Medical Center. She told me I had been unconscious for twelve hours. During that time, the riots had gotten worse and getting back to Crenshaw was impossible not just because of the lootings, burnings, and roadblocks. The nurses said I had to stay in the hospital until my wound healed. I said that I would most likely not be able to pay the bill, but the nurse told me not to worry about that. Thanks to the rioting, medicine was soon in short supply. I didn't need as much as the other patients so I got by. The hospital's phone lines were unfortunately damaged so I couldn't call home or Mama. By the time the troops came and the curfew was lifted, I felt much better. I got in a carpool, and they dropped me off at home."

Mama started crying again, so Daddy and I hugged her. Wanda joined our group hug as well. Since she's like my sister, so she's practically a member of the family, but one member of the family was missing from the group hug.

Daddy called Grandma's Watts apartment, her neighbors, and her friends.

Unfortunately, the news wasn't good.

Like Mama said, the rioting and roadblocks meant medical help was hard to get. Some of Grandma's friends stayed with her at the apartment so that she wouldn't be alone. When she was eating dinner on Friday, she started coughing and clutched her heart. Her friends figured out that she was having a heart attack! They knew that an ambulance wouldn't be able to make it to Watts so they tried to drive her to the Martin Luther King Jr. General Hospital, but the rioting and roadblocks made it impossible and Grandma died. They managed to make it to the morgue where the doctors confirmed that Grandma had had a heart attack. They asked her friends if she suffered from high blood pressure and her friends confirmed it. Grandma had had high blood pressure for years, but she never let it bother her. The doctors asked if Grandma drank alcohol, smoked, ate healthy hoods, and engaged in regular exercise. Grandma didn't drink nor smoke, but she did eat soul food and the only exercise she got was cleaning the brokerage firm.

Grandma's body was still at the city morgue, and I was sure there were a lot of other bodies there as well. When Daddy called the morgue, the people there said they kept the bodies in mortuary cold chambers to keep them from rotting until friends and relatives came to claim them. Daddy said he would be down there first thing in the morning.

Wanda said, "I'm so sorry for your loss, Hatima and Mister and Missus Parker."

Daddy told Wanda, "Maybe its best you head on home. You don't want your mom to worry about you."

Wanda nodded and left. I guess she sensed that we wanted to be alone while we grieved. Mama started crying hysterically, screaming for her mama. Daddy and I hugged her until she calmed down.

Daddy carried Mama bridal-style into their bedroom. I took a shower, put on my pajamas, and crawled under my sheets. I spent my time during the riots burning down Korean stores and stealing food. Why didn't I ask Shawn to drive us over to Watts to check on Grandma? We could have brought her to Crenshaw and made sure she was safe in the house. We might have been able to get her to the hospital in time, but my hotheaded decisions cost Grandma her life. I started crying, figuring I was a despicable human being. I figured *not doing* something can be just as destructive as actually doing something.

Mr. Grant was swamped with clients 'cause of the riots. He had several funerals to plan and oversee, so he told us to keep Grandma in the mortuary cold chamber until the scheduled funeral was just around the corner. According to the news, fifty-five people died during the riots and over two thousand were injured. Grandma's funeral was scheduled for the end of May.

I stopped by the Williamses' house to make sure they were okay. I didn't want any other Williamses buried six feet under. When I got to their house, Eric Grant was also there. He was holding Alicia tight – so my instincts about them were spot on. Eric, Alicia, Mrs. Williams, and little Jamal looked a little shaken up, but they were all alive.

Alicia told me, "Girl, USC canceled all the exams! I studied so hard, and now it seems all for naught."

Eric added, "USC actually hired a bunch of runners to go to the classrooms and tell everyone to get outta the school and go home while they still could. I drove Alicia home before I went home to my parents in Leimert Park. I remember thinking that if these riots were as bad as the ones in the sixties, then Dad and I would get *a lotta* new customers."

I also called the Wilsons to make sure they were okay.

Dr. Wilson exclaimed, "It's so good to hear your voice, Hatima! Are your parents okay?"

I said, "My parents are okay, but my grandmother died. She had a heart attack and her friends couldn't get her to the hospital in time."

Dr. Wilson said, "I'm so sorry for your loss. Everyone in my family is alive, thank God. My wife and kids stayed at home, while I was at the hospital, trying to help any injured folks who came through the doors."

I said, "Medical supplies are in short supply so that couldn't have been easy."

Dr. Wilson said, "No, it wasn't. But I took an oath to help every patient to the best of my ability. When the verdict was announced, Missus Wilson's bosses at AECOM let her and the rest of their employees leave work early because they sensed Armageddon would happen."

I said, "Alicia Williams and Eric Grant are students at USC. They were also told to go home because the staff sensed that things would get worse after the verdict was announced. Plus, all exams at USC have been canceled. I hope Dorsey High doesn't cancel exams 'cause I need those grades to get into college."

Dr. Wilson laughed and said, "Cal State has also canceled all exams. But the elementary, junior high, and high schools should reopen soon."

People did read what I told Mrs. Igwe in the *Sentinel*. Left and right, they had abandoned the "no snitch" rule; and plenty of folks in South Central were turning in neighbors who they knew stole shit during the riots; but they only turned in people who stole stuff for profit not necessity like Bloods, Crips, other gangbangers, and wannabe gangbangers who stole money and stuff they could turn into money, such as clothes, television sets, stereos, jewelry, et cetera. A lotta people stole food, clothes, diapers, flashlights, batteries, et cetera because they needed to keep their families alive. In a way, Black People were *finally* cooperating with the LAPD. Like Detective Crawford said, our problem is that we don't report crimes and we don't testify in court. In our own way, we are also at fault for the verdict. But we can't be silent, we gotta speak up.

The news showed that protests and acts of violence occurred in other US cities, including San Francisco, Denver, Buffalo, Providence, and Atlanta. I met Mr. Ngozi at the Creole & Cajun Kitchen, where he was taking a lunch break after helping the hair stylists clear the burned bricks outta Ms. Esther's Hair Salon. Ms. Esther is alright, but two of her stylists were killed during the riots.

I said, "Hi, Mister Ngozi!"

He exclaimed, "Hatima, so good to see you!"

He hugged me, and I said, "Okay, I can feel the love. You can let go."

Mr. Ngozi let me go and said, "My family called me during the course of the riots. My father told me I was crazy to stay in the ghetto when I could have gotten a better teaching job at another school. My brother, Emeka, who lives in London, told me what to do during a riot. He told me to stay indoors, make sure my fridge and cupboards are full, that I have a radio nearby, and to get a gun. The UK may have strict gun control laws, but we know the US is more lax about that. But I've never owned a gun and I'll never get one. If I got a gun, then my students would lose all respect for me. My brother, Amazu, who lives in Toronto, says the verdict and the LA Riots sparked a riot on Yonge Street."

I cut in and made a T with my hands, "Whoa, whoa, whoa! Time out! There was a riot in another country? There was a riot in Canada's crown jewel, Toronto?"

Mr. Ngozi nodded and said, "Yep. On May fourth, the day Mayor Bradley lifted our curfew, a few hundred Canadians marched on Yonge Street to show solidarity with Rodney King and to protest police brutality. Two days before, on May second, a twenty-two-year-old Black man named Raymond Lawrence was shot and killed by a plain-clothed police officer. Raymond Lawrence was the fourteenth Black man shot by the Toronto Police Service since nineteen-seventy-eight and was the fourth Black man to die as a result. When the protestors marched down Yonge Street to City Hall, a line of cops blocked their way. Rocks, cans, and even horse feces were thrown at the cops and the building. The protestors marched back up Yonge Street and the rioting started. Cars were vandalized, stores were broken into and looted, and people were beaten up. The same shit that happened here in La La Land happened at the Center of the Universe."

I was surprised to hear Mr. Ngozi swearing because he never swore in class. He must be really pissed off about how messed up the entire planet is.

Mr. Ngozi continued, "Some people have stated that burning and looting in your own communities shows a lack of intelligence; but people are angry, and the riots showed how angry they are. African Canadians feel that their concerns don't matter so they rioted. African Americans feel that their lives don't matter so they rioted. Stores and buildings can be replaced but Raymond Lawrence, Lester Donaldson, Latasha Harlins, and Lee Arthur Mitchell can't be."

I asked Mr. Ngozi, "Did your brother participate in the Yonge Street Riot?"

Mr. Ngozi explained, "He helped get injured folks to safety. Since he's a doctor, inflicting harm is against his principles. Since his wife is a lawyer, she'll try and get some of their arrested friends out of police custody."

I said, "I always thought your brother and your sister-in-law were Canadian versions of the Huxtable family!"

Mr. Ngozi laughed and said, "Doctor Martin Luther King Junior said, 'The limitation of riots, moral questions aside, is that they cannot win, and their participants know it. Hence, rioting is not revolutionary but reactionary because it invites defeat. It involves an emotional catharsis, but it must be followed by a sense of futility.'"

I said, "Yeah, I told Wanda that the LA Riots and the Haitian Revolution aren't the same. Toussaint Louverture organized the slaves and planned out the battles. During the riots, no one had a well-thought-out plan to take down the cops or the government. People were just reacting to the verdict, like wild animals react to hunters' attacks. The riots led to some people relieving their tense emotions, but others are still angry. In the end, people are led to a sense of ineffectiveness. We've torn down LA but the only positive outcome is that there's gonna be an investigation into whether or not Rodney King's civil rights were violated. But are things gonna change with the LAPD? Is the hood gonna be completely healed?"

Mr. Ngozi said, "Unanswered questions help us move forward, Hatima."

Joshua and his dad drove down to Crenshaw in Joshua's Cadillac. They looked at the Laundromat, but their faces were blank.

I was already at the Laundromat; I had walked there after Joshua phoned me to say that he and his dad were coming to Crenshaw to see how badly damaged the Laundromat was.

I asked the Yangs, "Will the insurance company cover the damages?"

Mr. Yang sighed and said, "There are over a billion dollars in damages across LA so insurance companies are going to be swamped with work. I doubt we'll get enough money from the insurance company to fix this place."

I said, "It's not as bad as other stores, such as the liquor store, the pharmacy, and the dry cleaners. They were all burned down but the Laundromat is still standing."

We went inside, but the Laundromat looked as bad as it did during the riots. The windows were smashed, the machines were broken, and the dollars-to-tokens machine was still knocked over.

Mr. Yang said, "I'm sure we can get new machines, but it's going to take a while. Crenshaw residents will have to wash and dry their clothes elsewhere until this place is fixed."

I asked, "Is Ronnie okay?"

Joshua said, "Yeah. He tried to defend the store during the riots, but some dude broke his arm with a baseball bat. He went to the hospital and got a cast. He was afraid Dad would fire him because he failed to defend the store."

Mr. Yang stated, "Stores can be replaced, but Ronnie can't be."

I nodded with respect and asked, "What about your Watts store? Is Mister Cho okay?"

Mr. Yang explained, "Mister Cho defended the Watts store with help from his shotgun. He said he shot some rioters and looters in their legs, but he didn't kill them. He doesn't want to end up like Missus Du. He told me that he's quitting working at the Watts store because he despises the hoodlums of Watts. All the other people in

Koreatown have turned down my job offer because they have their own businesses to run or because they're now scared to death of the ghetto."

I said, "Hiring a Black storekeeper is a small step in the right direction."

I thought of Uncle Alonzo and Malik, who helped turn the ghetto into a place most folks feared. They must have watched the riots on television; prisons have television sets to make sure the prisoners keep up with what's going on in the outside world. Were Uncle Alonzo and Malik upset that they couldn't join the Bloods in the looting and killings? Or do they feel guilty for allowing the Bloods' crime spree to lead to such a racially biased justice system?

I asked Mr. Yang a question that had been gnawing at me for months.

"How come there were no Asians at Missus Du's trial?"

Mr. Yang sighed and explained, "Californian juries are drawn from lists of registered voters and licensed drivers. Koreans and other Asians are underrepresented on both lists."

I asked, "Some Koreans don't register to vote?"

Mr. Yang said, "I do, but others aren't eligible to vote because they're not US citizens yet. Others choose simply not to register. I always say that every registered voter counts. Plus, most inner-city Asians, including some residents in Koreatown, don't bother to take driving lessons. Public transit gets us where we need to go. My son decided to learn how to drive because teenagers think it's part of being *cool*."

Joshua said, "A teenager without a car is like a lion without a mane."

I said, "Black people were bitten by dogs and arrested by cops for exercising the right to vote. When Blacks drive in cars, cops and other racists have stopped us over the years for DWB because driving is seen as a White privilege."

Mr. Yang asked, "What does DWB mean?"

I explained, "Driving While Black. If a Black person drives a car, they're usually stopped because cops believe the car is stolen or is hiding contraband. You're telling me some Asians don't give a damn about their basic rights?"

Mr. Yang didn't answer my question and instead said, "Charles Lloyd tried to do what the defense attorneys did for the trial against the four cops who beat Mister King. He used all his power to exclude Black jurors and Roxanne Carvajal pointed out that he was excluding jurors because of race, which is racist. Does that sound strange?"

I said, "A little. But there are plenty of Blacks in this world who are Uncle Toms. Uncle Toms have always been despised because they end up holding their people back."

Mr. Yang continued, "Judge Karlin knew that prosecutors usually want Asians on juries because they believe we respect authority and take police testimony at face value."

I asked, "Do you believe everything the LAPD says?"

Mr. Yang said, "I used to but not anymore. When Rodney King was beaten, I tried to justify what the cops did. I initially believed they were in the right for beating him. But as I restocked on alcohol in my nightclub, I remembered how many Koreans had left my club drunk and gotten into DUI accidents. They were often arrested and sometimes went to court, but they had never been beaten. Why was it okay to beat Rodney King? Because he was tall? Because he was an ex-con? No, because he was Black. I was just as bad. The first time Joshua brought you to my nightclub, I checked the cash register, the bar, and the turntable to make sure you hadn't stolen anything. Since the Bloods and the Crips are always causing trouble, I immediately had a good idea what the typical criminal looked like."

I said, "Me. You think all criminals look like me and the people who shop at your Watts store and use your Laundromat."

Mr. Yang sadly nodded and said, "When my nightclub burned down, I thought that maybe God was punishing me for my racist mindset. I thought He was punishing all of LA for the misery we've inflicted on every single Black, regardless of where they live or what they do for a living. I had an epiphany, and I knew that the prejudice had to end!"

I clapped for joy and hugged Mr. Yang. Then, Joshua hugged me and people walking through the hood stared at us. A Black woman and two Koreans hugging is a strange-looking group hug.

Point number one of the BPP's Ten-Point Platform states,

> "We want freedom. We want power to determine the destiny of our Black Community. ... We believe that Black People will not be free until we are able to determine our own destiny."

Dr. Murray and the FAME clergy are working with the humanitarians to raise money to help rebuild South Central. Dr. Wilson came to Crenshaw to help the clinic restock on medical supplies. Even Michael Jackson had started an initiative called "Heal LA" so that people could heal the hood. I'm so glad the King of Pop has the same vision for the hood as me. Detective Crawford and Detective Hill also came down to Crenshaw to talk with local residents on how to improve policing procedures in the hood.

Some people still viewed cops with mistrust, but Mrs. Williams said, "This fine detective brought my son's murderers to justice! She's proof of what can be accomplished when cops use their heads and folks in the hood cooperate with investigations! We can't let gangsters, drug dealers, thieves, pimps, and other criminals dictate the laws by which we live!"

Later I asked Detective Crawford, "Those four pigs who beat Rodney King still on the LAPD's payroll?"

We were sitting down on the sidewalk, drinking Sprite. Folks were cleaning up debris, laying down bricks and woodwork, and repainting buildings.

Detective Crawford sighed and said, "Officers Briseno, Koon, and Powell haven't shown up back at work but I'm not sure whether or not the department will rehire them or fire them. But Mister Wind's employment with the department remains terminated. Also remember that there is now an investigation to see whether or not Mister King's civil rights were violated."

I exclaimed, "Detective Crawford, almost every Black person in LA knows that Rodney King's civil rights were violated! Those four pigs broke the laws of the Civil Rights Act!"

Detective Crawford said, "I know they did, you know they did, and a lot of other people know they did. *But they don't think they did!* Officers Wind, Powell, Koon, and Briseno believe that they beat Mister King because he was a dangerous presence, *not* because he was Black. They believe that if he was White or Asian, they would have reacted the same way."

I asked Detective Crawford, "Would you have beaten Rodney King?"

Detective Crawford hung her head and stated, "You can't beat somebody almost to death for drunk driving and speeding. You can't beat somebody who has no weapons, drugs, or contraband in their car. You can't beat somebody who's unarmed. You can't beat somebody when it's a group against one person. If you do, you don't deserve to be a cop."

I stayed silent for a while and told Detective Crawford, "I don't hate all cops, and I don't hate all White people. I don't hate all Koreans, and I don't hate all rich people. But I do hate people who judge us based on the color of our skin instead of the content of our character. I've been wondering whether or not my fate is with the Marines, but I've realized it's not the uniform that defines who you are, it's the person inside. Whether or not I get accepted into the Naval Academy, I'll join the Marines. I'll change the public's perception of law enforcement by making sure I stay a good person."

Detective Crawford put her arms around me and hugged me. I never thought I would become so close to a cop but, miraculously, Detective Crawford had become a dear friend to me and my family.

Maybe we *can* all get along.

Chapter Twenty-Three

Principal Edwards was standing up onstage, speaking into the microphone on the podium. Some teachers, including Mr. Ngozi, were sitting behind him in chairs. My classmates and I were all sitting at the front, facing the stage, in our caps and gowns. Our family and friends were behind us, ready with cameras. We were all smiling because we did it. We made it through three years of high school. Some of us are gonna go to college, and others will stay here in the hood, but a diploma is nothing to scoff at.

Until the end of the Civil War, it was illegal to teach a slave to read and write. When the first schools for Blacks were built, they were little more than rundown shacks with inferior school supplies. Many Blacks dropped out of school to help their families sharecrop or to find better jobs in the cities. Parents have held onto the hope for generations that their kids will do better. Plenty of us sitting here in our caps and gowns are the first members of our families to get diplomas. Some of us are the first members of our families to go to college.

Our teachers helped us think intensively and critically about everything that is going on in our world. That way we'll make sure the mistakes of the past aren't repeated in the future so that we can change our world for the better. Our education and hard work will uplift our entire race, hopefully leading to a future with better opportunities.

Imani is the class valedictorian, so she is giving the commencement speech. But I'm the salutatorian, which means I get to introduce her and give a short, uplifting message to my classmates.

When Principal Edwards called us up, we walked together up onstage. I went to the podium first.

I said, "Martin Luther King said, 'The function of education is to teach one to think intensively and to think critically. Intelligence plus character – that is the goal of true education.' Malcolm X said, 'Education is our passport to the future, for tomorrow belongs to the people who prepare for it today.' Nelson Mandela said, 'Education is the most powerful weapon which you can use to change the world.' W. E. B. Du Bois said, 'Education and work are the levers to uplift a people.' Booker T. Washington said, 'Nothing ever comes to one that is worth having, except as a result of hard work.' Well, everybody, we did it! Despite the world's low opinions about Blacks in the ghetto, we are about to receive our high school diplomas!"

Everyone cheered and when they quieted down, I continued, "A good education is not going to make us immune to bigotry. No matter where we go, what we do, or where we live, there will be many people who will try to bring us down. But education is a powerful tool that can help us bring about a better future. Now, I'd like to introduce our class valedictorian, Imani Fitzpatrick!"

Everyone clapped and cheered! I sat down and let Imani take over the podium.

Imani said, "This has been one crazy year!"

People yelled, "That's right, my sister!"

Imani continued, "Last year, Rodney Glen King was beaten by the LAPD for drunk driving and speeding. Then, less than two weeks later, a Korean woman shot and killed a fifteen-year-old girl named Latasha Harlins. It was bad enough that Rodney King and

Latasha Harlins were targeted because of their skin color, something they have *no* control over, but Soon Ja Du was sentenced to probation and the four cops who beat Rodney King were acquitted by a predominantly White jury. Then, LA met its reckoning during one of the worst riots in US history. But, as we rebuild, we must learn to stop this cycle of bigotry, hatred, and violence that has taken the lives of countless people. Diplomas and degrees will not make us bullet-proof since our black skin causes most cops and certain other people to fear us. Diplomas and degrees won't guarantee us high positions in *Fortune* Five Hundred companies because some people resent having to answer to Blacks who are part of companies' C-suites. Diplomas and degrees won't guarantee us homes in the Hills because some people believe that decent housing is a White privilege. We can't change the views of all bigots, but we can change the views of some. Then, maybe, redemption will flourish in one city, then another, then across the USA, and finally the rest of the world. We are educated Black people, bigots' worst nightmare!"

Imani gave the Black Power salute and the audience clapped and cheered for her! Some people, including me, stood up.

I told Imani, "You go, girl!"

After Imani's speech, we sat back down with our class. Then, Principal Edwards called us up alphabetically.

"Wanda Brooks!"

Mrs. Brooks and Andre whooped and hollered, while everyone else clapped.

When Wanda accepted her diploma, Principal Edwards said into the mike, "Wanda Brooks will be attending Texas Southern University!"

When Imani accepted her diploma, Principal Edwards said, "Imani Fitzpatrick will be attending Howard University!"

When Marcus accepted his diploma, Principal Edwards said, "Marcus Miller will be attending UC Davis!"

When I accepted my diploma, Principal Edwards said, "Hatima Parker will be attending the United States Naval Academy!"

Mama and Daddy whooped and hollered, while I shook Principal Edwards' hand.

After the ceremony, Mama, Daddy, Mrs. Brooks, Andre, Ms. Fitzpatrick, and Hector all took pictures of me, Wanda, and Imani.

I exclaimed, "We did it! We did it!"

Imani added, "College, here we come!"

As great as it was, I couldn't help feeling that something was missing. Wait, not some*thing*, some*one*. Grandma should be here, reveling in our family's victory. She and her daddy never got high school diplomas because sharecroppers didn't need them. When Grandma told stories of her rough childhood, I could sense the pain and anger she still felt at Blacks' hopeless situation. Deep down, she hoped it was possible for a member of *her* family to do more than blue-collar work, but Grandma was now buried six feet under in Rosedale Cemetery in a magnolia casket. The magnolia is Mississippi's state flower, so it seemed fitting that Grandma be buried in a casket made from the wood of a Mississippi magnolia tree. She was dressed in her favorite muumuu and her hair was done up perfectly. Dr. Murray gave an uplifting sermon that brought us all to tears. He reminded us that Grandma was up in Heaven looking down at us and making sure we were alright.

So, I'm sure Grandma is also viewing my graduation and is proudly telling everyone in Heaven, "That's my grandbaby! She got the one thing me, my daddy, my mama, my daughter, and my son-in-law never got. Now, she's off to college so that she can become a Marine and an Africanist. The Naval Academy is tougher than the Ivy League with their military mindset, but my grandbaby can handle it."

Joshua drove to Crenshaw to wish me congratulations and join us at Denny's. Some people still gave us funny looks, but most smiled at us and gave us thumbs-up. Mr. Yang is still rebuilding his Laundromat, and a lot of folks have donated money and time to help. When Joshua and I went to the Senior Proms at our high schools, not as many people as we expected gave us funny looks. It's kinda cool how the worst riot in US history can bring an entire city together.

At Denny's, while we were waiting for our orders, Marcus asked Joshua, "Which college are you going to?"

Joshua replied, "UC Davis."

Marcus stated, "That's where I'm going too! I'm majoring in mathematics. What are you majoring in?"

Joshua replied, "Political Science."

Imani asked me and Joshua, "Are you two gonna try and maintain a long-distance relationship?"

I said, "We're pretty sure it wouldn't work. Besides, after I graduate from the Naval Academy, I'll be working my butt off to get my PhD, which will take five or six years. Then, I'll have to serve at least five years in the Marine Corps. I can't see how I'll be able to maintain a relationship in those fifteen years."

Wanda asked, "Are you planning on getting married or having kids?"

I said, "I don't know. I'll have to wait and see what the future has in store."

HEAL THE HOOD

At home I took out some of Grandma's old records. After she died, Mama, Daddy, and I cleaned out her apartment. We sold some of the furniture, donated the clothes to the Salvation Army, and added Grandma's records to our collection. The record I took out was "What A Wonderful World"; but this was a special edition of the song, with a spoken intro by Satchmo himself. I put the vinyl on the record player and listened to Pops' gravelly voice.

> *Some of you young folks been saying to me 'Hey Pops, what you mean 'What a wonderful world'?' How about all them wars all over the place? You call them wonderful? And how about hunger and pollution? That ain't so wonderful either. Well how about listening to old Pops for a minute. Seems to me, it ain't the world that's so bad but what we're doin' to it. And all I'm saying is see what a wonderful world it would be if only we'd give it a chance. Love, baby, love. That's the secret, yeah. If lots more of us loved each other we'd solve lots more problems. And then this world would be a gasser. That's wha' ol' Pops keeps saying.*

I smiled while the great Louis Armstrong sang "What A Wonderful World."

> *I see trees of green, red roses too*
> *I see them bloom for me and you*
> *And I think to myself what a wonderful world*
>
> *I see skies of blue and clouds of white*
> *The bright blessed day, the dark sacred night*
> *And I think to myself what a wonderful world*

The colors of the rainbow so pretty in the sky
Are also on the faces of people going by
I see friends shaking hands saying how do you do
They're really saying I love you

I hear babies crying, I watch them grow
They'll learn much more than I'll never know
And I think to myself what a wonderful world
Yes I think to myself what a wonderful world

Satchmo was the man, that's for sure. He also laid down the truth like MJ, Marvin Gaye, NWA, and Public Enemy. If humans stopped fighting, mocking the poor, and polluting the environment, then Earth would be a much better place to live in. Once again, I'm questioning whether or not humans should be in charge of the planet.

The rabbits in *Watership Down* and Shere Khan from *The Jungle Book* all despise humans because of the destruction they have wrought upon the Earth. But in The Chronicles of Narnia, Narnia isn't right unless a Son of Adam or a Daughter of Eve is sitting on the throne. Aslan Himself created that law way back in *The Magician's Nephew* when Narnia was created. I think Aslan senses something special in humanity that even I can't see. Maybe Aslan can sense all the love that dwells in humanity even if we don't show it most of the time.

Dr. King said, "Love is the only force capable of turning an enemy into a friend." He also said, "I have decided to stick with love. Hate is too great a burden to bear."

A lotta people think that since Joshua is Korean, he and I shoulda been enemies, but Joshua approached me with love in his heart and became my boyfriend instead of my enemy. When people participated in Koreatown's Peace Rally, they did it with love in their hearts. Mr. Yang and some other Koreans are being met with cooperation by some Blacks instead of resentment. When people expressed hatred, LA went up in flames, and when people expressed love, LA could start rebuilding. Love is an amazingly effective motivator.

Over the summer, I packed my clothes, books, Walkman, and everything else I needed. I also packed posters of Michael Jackson, Janet Jackson, Boyz II Men, Bobby Brown, and Whitney Houston. Mama and Daddy helped me. Victor also got accepted at Howard, even though he's smart enough for the University of California, Cal State, and the White Ivy League. The plan for Wanda, Imani, Victor, and I was a road trip with zero parent supervision! Yep, free at last! The plan was to drop Wanda off in Houston and help her move into her TSU dorm. Then, Victor would drive me and Imani to Maryland. According to Andre, the drive to Houston takes about two days. After Andre, Imani, Victor, and I help Wanda get situated, Imani, Victor, and I will drive straight to Maryland. First, we'll stop in DC, and I'll help Imani and Victor get situated in the Howard dorms. Then we'll drive to Annapolis, where they'll help me get situated in my dorm room at the Naval Academy.

Yep, it was just gonna be us, the open road, and college destinations. Would LA be a different and better place when we came back for the holidays? We would have to wait and see.

Author's Note

On March 3, 1991, a twenty-five-year-old African American man named Rodney King was speeding on the freeway. Two members of the California Highway Patrol noticed and tried to stop him. But Rodney King tried to out-drive them because getting arrested on a DUI charge would have violated his parole from his previous robbery conviction. Rodney King was pursued by several police cars and a police helicopter.

When he was pulled over, he was severely beaten and tasered by the LAPD. Unbeknownst to Rodney King and the LAPD, a man named George Holliday videotaped the beating. As soon as it made it onto the news, there was uproar across Los Angeles, the USA, and the entire world.

Less than two weeks after Rodney King was beaten, a fifteen-year-old African American girl named Latasha Harlins was shot and killed by a Korean storeowner named Soon Ja Du. Mrs. Du believed that Latasha Harlins was trying to shoplift and claimed to be intimidated by the five-foot-six teenage girl.

The history of African Americans in Los Angeles stretches back over a century. First African Methodist Episcopal Church was the first Black church built in LA and Second Baptist Church was, obviously, the second.

Large numbers of African Americans migrated from the

South to the West Coast during and after World War II in order to escape Jim Crow and to seek better economic opportunities. Most Southern migrants came from Louisiana, Mississippi, Arkansas, and Texas. Immigrants from Caribbean and African countries have also resettled in Los Angeles in search of better lives. But the Blacks of LA constantly face discrimination in the form of inadequate housing, high unemployment, exclusion from certain clubs and organizations, hostile Koreans, and over-policing.

In 1965, the South Central neighborhood of Watts erupted into a riot because of hostile policing. The Watts Riots lasted for five days and cost LA millions of dollars' worth of damages. Less than three years later, Rev. Dr. Martin Luther King Jr. was assassinated in Memphis, Tennessee. This sparked riots in over a hundred US cities. LA used a coalition of police and social leaders to convince people not to riot, but I believe some Blacks may have vented out their anger and frustration on the streets.

Koreans began to buy businesses in South Central LA after the Watts Riots because they were inexpensive and there was little competition. African Americans were at first welcoming to the Koreans, but the Koreans refused to hire Black workers and treated Black customers with disrespect. This is shown in the novel when Mr. Lee keeps a close eye on Hatima to make sure she doesn't steal from his convenience store and then orders her to leave immediately after she makes her purchases. Koreans, such as Mr. Lee, justified their racist attitudes on the high crime rate in South Central and their fear of being robbed and shot by gangsters. By 1990, Koreans owned sixty-five percent of South Central businesses.

Sadly, not much had been done to remedy racial tensions between the 1960s and the early 1990s. An African American woman named Eula Mae Love was killed by two LAPD officers– one White and one Black – in 1979. Her death was the first police killing that pushed officials to carry out thorough investigations into police brutality. African Americans continued to file many complaints about police misconduct over the next decade, but their cries weren't taken seriously until Rodney King was beaten.

Ten days after Rodney King was beaten, Officers Stacey Koon, Laurence Powell, Theodore Briseno, and Timothy Wind were indicted for felony assault. Timothy Wind was a rookie cop and got dismissed from the LAPD, but the other three officers only got suspensions without pay.

Soon Ja Du was also indicted for murdering Latasha Harlins, but the charge against her was manslaughter. In November 1991, a jury found Soon Ja Du guilty of voluntary manslaughter; but the judge who presided over the case, Joyce Karlin, gave her a light punishment – five years' probation, four hundred hours of community service, and a sixty-five percent fine. There was uproar in LA and across the US over this miscarriage of justice.

On April 29, 1992, a predominantly White jury found the four officers who beat Rodney King not guilty. It was stated that the verdict lit a fuse to a bomb and that bomb exploded into the worst riot in US history.

The 1992 Los Angeles Riots a.k.a. the Rodney King Race Riots resulted in mass looting and destruction. The riots started in South Central and soon spread to the rest of LA County. During the riots, Soon Ja Du's store was burned to the ground and was never rebuilt or reopened. The culprits were never discovered, so I made Hatima and her friends be the ones who burned it down.

Many Korean-owned businesses were looted and destroyed during the riots. Koreatown was also attacked by African Americans and Latino Americans who were angry at Korean Americans for their racist attitudes – and that Koreans were and continue to be viewed as "model minorities." The stereotypes of smart and hardworking Asians helped fuel the stereotypes of criminal Blacks and Latinos. As a result, most of Koreatown was looted and destroyed.

But many Black-owned, Latino-owned, White-owned, and other Asian-owned stores were also looted and destroyed during the riots. The police were unable to stop the riots because they were ill-equipped and ill-prepared. But other LA residents, such as Dr. Cecil Murray, had sensed darkness was about to fall on the City of Angels. The Blacks of Los Angeles collectively decided that they weren't going to sit back and accept the verdict.

Dr. King said, "A riot is the language of the unheard."

The LA Riots made the world to see how sick and tired Blacks were of being oppressed. Just because Dr. King said he had a dream and civil rights legislation has been signed in the USA, the UK, and Canada, it doesn't mean a racial caste system doesn't still rule the world.

The LA Riots ended when National Guardsmen, Army soldiers, and Marines came to back up the police and restore order to LA. Unfortunately, there were over fifty deaths and approximately one-billion-dollars' worth of damages. To this day, several LA residents continue to suffer hardship because the riots destroyed many of their livelihoods, and they have been unable to get money to rebuild.

Hatima Parker and most of her friends and family are fictional, but Dr. Cecil Murray is a real man who was the senior pastor of FAME between 1977 and 2004. When he became reverend, FAME only had about three hundred members; but thanks to his leadership, programs were set up to deal with health, homelessness, emergency food, employment, et cetera. Thanks to Dr. Murray, FAME's membership grew to over eighteen thousand!

In the real-life event, George Holliday never called Dr. Murray about the videotape in order to get it to the media; he took the tape straight to KTLA, and after KTLA aired the taping of Rodney King's beating, CNN and KNBC also aired it.

Lee Arthur Mitchell was also a real man who was killed by Mr. Park, a racist Korean. Unfortunately, Mr. Park was never arrested by the cops for murdering Mr. Mitchell. Even though Mr. Park's store, Chung's Liquor Market, was boycotted, Dr. Murray and the Blacks of South Central didn't organize a community-wide boycott of all Korean businesses. I decided to add this to the story to show how methods from the Civil Rights Movement are still effective in later decades and to show what happens when the oppressed decide to take the initiative to create a better future.

In the aftermath of the LA Riots, Michael Jackson launched Heal LA in 1993 – not in 1992. But in the novel, I had him launch this project much earlier so people can understand where I got the idea for my novel's title.

As people read this book, they will immediately think about the Black Lives Matter Movement, the biggest Black-led social campaign since the 1960s. When most people think about police brutality, the names that pop up include Aiyana Stanley-Jones, Rekia Boyd, Eric Garner, Michael Brown, Ezell Ford, Laquan McDonald, Tamir Rice, Freddie Gray, Oscar Grant, John Crawford III, Jordan Edwards, Sandra Bland, Philando Castile, Alton Sterling, Breonna Taylor, George Floyd, and Rayshard Brooks. There are also Black people who have been victims of racist attacks at the hands of ordinary people/civilians, such as Trayvon Martin, Jordan Davis, and Ahmaud Arbery. Hatima's story shows that the list of Black people brutalized or dead as a result of racist attacks was already high long before the BLM Movement was founded. On the list are Emmett Till, Addie

HEAL THE HOOD

Mae Collins, Denise McNair, Carole Robertson, Cynthia Wesley, Johnny Robinson, Virgil Ware, James Powell, Matthew "Peanut" Johnson, Bobby Hutton, Fred Hampton, Mark Clark, Andrew "Buddy" Evans, Albert Johnson, Eula Mae Love, Willie Turks, Edmund Perry, Dorothy "Cherry" Groce, Michael Griffith, Lester Donaldson, Michael Wade Lawson, Yusuf Hawkins, Marlon Neal, Rodney King, Latasha Harlins, Lee Arthur Mitchell, Gavin Cato, Raymond Lawrence, et cetera.

Rodney King is one of the few victims of police brutality to survive his ordeal. On June 17, 2012, he died of accidental drowning in his swimming pool, two months after his autobiography was published. Autopsy results reveal that he had alcohol, cocaine, and marijuana in his system, which must have been contributing factors to his death. After all those years, Rodney King still suffered from alcohol and drugs.

Rodney King is famous for asking, "Can we all just get along?"

After witnessing the rise of the BLM Movement and reading several fictional and non-fictional books that deal with the severe issues of racism and police brutality, I have found myself asking that as well. This is a question that we all need to ask ourselves, and we all need to come to a positive solution in order to ensure a better future.

Further Reading

The novels listed all deal with racism, police brutality, and other forms of bigotry. If you liked this work of fiction, then I believe you will love these novels:

- *Roll of Thunder, Hear My Cry* by Mildred D. Taylor
- *Let the Circle be Unbroken* by Mildred D. Taylor
- *The Road to Memphis* by Mildred D. Taylor
- *To Kill A Mockingbird* by Harper Lee
- *Mississippi Trial, 1955* by Chris Crowe
- *The Watsons Go To Birmingham – 1963* by Christopher Paul Curtis
- *The Rock and the River* by Kekla Magoon
- *Fire in the Streets* by Kekla Magoon
- *How It Went Down* by Kekla Magoon
- *All-American Boys* by Jason Reynolds and Brendan Kiely
- *The Hate U Give* by Angie Thomas
- *Dear Martin* by Nic Stone
- *Ghost Boys* by Jewell Parker Rhodes
- *I Am Alfonso Jones* Written by Tony Medina and Illustrated by Stacey Robinson & John Jennings

Acknowledgments

There are so many people who helped bring this novel to life.

First, I want to thank God Almighty because His power and grace makes all things possible!

I want to thank my parents, Zubbi and Chioma Nwosu, and my sister, Iku Nwosu, for their love and support of my dream to become a writer.

I also want to thank the rest of my family, who all reside in different countries across the world; and the Nigerian diaspora who reside in Nigeria, Canada, the US, the UK, et cetera. No matter where we go, we hold onto our heritage and form strong communities. Thank you all for being exceptional!

I want to thank the students and staff of Havenwood Public School, Whitehorn Public School, Fallingbrook Middle School, Rick Hansen Secondary School (the Mississauga location), and Carleton University for nurturing and cultivating my reading and writing skills.

I want to thank Lou Cannon for writing *Official Negligence: How Rodney King and the Riots Changed Los Angeles and the LAPD*, which gave me vivid details about this dark moment in American and world history.

I want to thank Anna Deavere Smith for all the interviews she collected in her book, *Twilight: Los Angeles, 1992*. Your interviews showed how Rodney King's beating and the subsequent riots affected so many people from several different backgrounds.

I want to thank Rodney King for telling his life story in his autobiography, *The Riot Within: My Journey from Rebellion to Redemption*. His autobiography also gave vivid details about his beating, the subsequent trials, and the riots. Mr. King, I understand that you never wanted to become a symbol or an icon but your beating still shows people today that racism and bigotry plague our world and that we have to take a stand against injustice. I hope one day that we all can get along.

I want to thank blackpast.org for its many articles on Black history, including its Black Lives Matter Movement page. The BLM page has a long list of African Americans who have died because of racist attacks, usually at the hands of law enforcement. Rodney King and Latasha Harlins are on the list, but it is still incomplete. Blackpast.org is aware that more names should be added and hopefully they will be.

Thank you to every single social movement that has taken a stand against racism, police brutality, and bigotry and continues to inspire activists today: The Abolitionist Movement, the Pan-African Movement, the Civil Rights Movement, the Black Power Movement, the Anti-Apartheid Movement, the Black Lives Matter Movement, et cetera.

Finally, thank you to every writer who has written about racism and police brutality. I know many chastise you for writing about serious issues and refusing to whitewash history and world culture. But if you don't know your history, you are doomed to repeat it. Obviously, the lack of enlightenment people gleaned from the 1992 LA Riots has led to so many other unarmed Black men, women, and children being murdered by racists. The people who don't learn about the sins that led to the 1992 LA Riots are setting up a repeat of history's darkest moments.

May God grant us peace throughout the world.

About the Author

Adaeze Nkechi Nwosu was born in New Jersey (USA) and spent her early years in Switzerland. The family moved to Canada where she actually grew up in Mississauga, Ontario.

She attended Rick Hansen Secondary School in Mississauga and thereafter studied English, History and African Studies at Carleton University - earning her Bachelor's degree in May 2019.

Heal the Hood is her first book.

Manufactured by Amazon.ca
Bolton, ON